LURKS
BENEATH

WHAT LURKS BENEATH

RYAN LOCKWOOD

PINNACLE BOOKS
Kensington Publishing Corp.
www.kensingtonbooks.com

PINNACLE BOOKS are published by

Kensington Publishing Corp.
119 West 40th Street
New York, NY 10018

All Kensington titles, imprints, and distributed lines are available at special quantity discounts for bulk purchases for sales promotions, premiums, fund-raising, educational, or institutional use. Special book excerpts or customized printings can also be created to fit specific needs. For details, write or phone the office of the Kensington sales manager: Kensington Publishing Corp., 119 West 40th Street, New York, NY 10018, attn: Sales Department; phone 1-800-221-2647.

This book is a work of fiction. Names, characters, businesses, organizations, places, events, and incidents either are the product of the author's imagination or are used fictitiously. Any resemblance to actual persons, living or dead, events, or locales is entirely coincidental.

PINNACLE BOOKS and the Pinnacle logo are Reg. U.S. Pat. & TM Off.

ISBN-13: 978-0-7860-3289-1
ISBN-10: 0-7860-3289-8

First printing: June 2015

10 9 8 7 6 5 4 3 2 1

Printed in the United States of America

First electronic edition: June 2015

ISBN-13: 978-0-7860-3290-7
ISBN-10: 0-7860-3290-1

To Matt, for the invaluable feedback, and for his love of fiction.
It's okay to bend the spine on this one.

PART I
THE SLEEPING GIANT

CHAPTER 1

It waited for them.

Concealed within the submarine cavern, its motionless body was loosely compressed against the wall of a large chamber. Here in the darkness, far from where it had entered in the open sea, it could sense but not see that the surface beneath it was smooth. Porous rock, worn down over thousands of years by others of its kind.

Every few minutes, it drew vast volumes of seawater into its massive body, causing the flesh to expand like an oversized bellows, before contracting to expel the spent fluid into the cavern.

It had spent the day resting, away from the sunlight and safe from any threat. Having attained its great size, it was no longer at risk of being attacked by virtually any marine predator, but its instincts had always ensured it remained safely tucked away from marauding hunters during the daytime. It was drawn to confined spaces. To shadows and darkness. Since its birth, it had spent most of its life on or near the ocean floor, concealed from predators and prey, and each dawn had pulled its soft body into a crack or crevice to protect itself and its exposed parts. In its lair now, deep under the landmass above and far from the open ocean, the water remained clean and saline, though low in oxygen. Here it would remain until dark. When it would emerge to hunt.

Half-asleep, the organism had first been roused when it felt something disturb the dark water near its eyes. With no light at all, it merely sensed the small, blind fish swimming past, oblivious to the presence of a being so large it was almost part of the cavern itself. Uninterested, it again began drifting into sleep.

It had not fed well on previous nights. An opportunistic feeder, it would consume virtually anything it could capture if, unlike the blind fish, the prey was large enough to be worth expending energy on. Yet it had been unsuccessful at ingesting the calories needed to fuel its tons of flesh. By resting in this environment, its metabolism reduced to a state of near hibernation, it could reserve its energy until it preyed again.

But then the still water in the chamber had moved.

The tide. The gentle flow of water had at first pushed lightly against the organism's skin, almost imperceptibly, slowly building into a light current as it passed through the cavern. Currents from above crept along its body and deeper down the passage, toward the distant opening from which it had entered hours ago. As the tidal fluctuation increased, more water began to push against it. And through the receptors in its flesh, it had tasted something. Something vaguely familiar.

Something *edible*.

Its eyes slowly opened in the blackness.

From the passage above drifted a dilute soup of organic matter, and within it trace amounts of something else. In its complex brain it quickly determined that mixed into the volume of water were molecules of some bodily fluid, recently emitted by a living thing. No, *things*. Things it had consumed before.

Something was coming toward it. Yet it did not react. It was a nocturnal being, and did not generally feed in the daytime. Nor did it ever seek prey while resting in a lair. It would retain its energy.

From far away, a weak pulse of sound bounced along the limestone walls of the underwater cavern and into its body. It drew in another massive quantity of seawater and spewed it back out into the broad cavern in a power-ful rush, causing a cloud of sediment to swirl in the darkness around it. Its mind processed the conflicting instincts that suddenly flashed through its multi-hubbed brain:

Retreat. Attack. Hide. Feed. Wait.

Wait.

It settled its bulk back against the cavern wall. There was no need to reveal itself. They were coming toward it. It would wait.

CHAPTER 2

He was still bleeding.

John Breck examined the small cut on the lighter skin of his palm. Although it was difficult to see the wound underwater, it didn't hurt badly, and wasn't very deep. But the nagging pain continued to distract him, and a small amount of bright red blood continued to seep out of the gash.

He clenched his fist. Perhaps he should have tried to address the wound before going under.

Breck had cut himself with his own knife just before the dive. It had slipped in his grasp as he had tried to pry open the stubborn latch on one of his equipment boxes, which they had stacked near the scrubby vegetation surrounding the entry hole. But he had quickly dismissed the cut as Pelletier stood by in full dive gear at the edge of the flooded cavern, ready to enter the water.

But now his hand was bothering him.

Breck unclenched his fist and refocused his attention on the void below him. He adjusted the strap on the expensive camera housing trailing behind his narrow frame as he loudly exhaled another lungful of bubbles, continuing a measured descent into the cylindrical shaft of warm water.

The midday brightness beaming down from above had gradually receded as he and the other diver sank down the middle of the great, water-filled maw. The dim water offered none of the familiar sounds common to the depths of the open ocean: no hum of distant motors, none of the clicks and crackles created by the activities of countless marine organisms. Only the intermittent clouds of bubbles he exhaled, the hiss of compressed air released through the regulator as he inhaled, made any noise. Otherwise, here in the essentially landlocked inland pool there was only an exhilarating silence.

When observed from above, many of these flooded holes appeared simply as deep freshwater ponds. But Breck, a professional cave diver and amateur marine geologist, knew from experience that there was much more to the big island's blue holes than the murkier layers at the top, where the waters were steeped in a tea of organic matter.

That layer of water was merely a disguise.

Deeper down, in passageways that sometimes ran for miles, a cavern like this often revealed spectacular geology and forms of life much stranger than those few concealed in the rock walls cradling the upper pool. The odd creatures dwelling much deeper, in more saline caverns, were remarkable—life-forms so alien that they existed nowhere else on earth.

Each time Breck entered one of these cavernous underwater holes, he felt as though he were entering the murky portal to another universe. Which wasn't really that far off the mark. In the few years that the water-filled blue holes on this island had been more thoroughly explored, already researchers had discovered that they contained a number of unusual new species, and geological formations normally found only in terrestrial cave systems.

He looked over at Arlo Pelletier, whose longish black

hair waved in the water around his dive mask as they descended. Breck would have preferred to have Mack with him for this job, but Mack didn't have the biological background Pelletier did. And Mack wasn't diving anymore.

At least the portly Pelletier knew his stuff. While Breck's role was to map and gather images of the geology of the underwater caverns, the French biologist had been assigned to document the undiscovered life-forms residing within them—life-forms that tended to be small, eyeless, and alien-looking. Because of the great depths to which many of the technical caverns extended, and the extended bottom time required to venture into them, few in the world were qualified to be here. Both men had been hired for their expertise at cave diving, using mixed gases that prevented unsafe levels of nitrogen in the blood. Even with all the proper equipment, their brief excursions offered merely a glimpse of the underwater caverns and the life within them, to give humanity a better idea of what existed beneath the holes dotting the island's surface. It would take decades and better technology to fully explore the geological wonders.

Almost a hundred feet down now, the men had already passed the toxic layer of water Pelletier referred to as *l'omelette*—because it had the discernible taste and smell of rotten eggs. Below that layer, they had then passed through a broader stratum of semi-saline water that mixed with freshwater above, and were now entering the dense, pure seawater that reached through dark tunnels out to the deep ocean.

Here, the visibility was much better than above—the clarity of bottled vodka. Breck could make out a large cone of rocky debris piled along the near vertical north wall of the hole. The rubble had accumulated below the mouth of the hole over thousands of years, the result of the cave roof collapsing gradually over time to form the hole. Nearing a ledge near the top of the rubble mound, Breck noticed several distinct objects littering the feature.

Bones.

He finned over to the wall of the hole and there, staring back at him from where it was perched on the rubble, was a human skull, half buried in silt. It was misshapen in such a way that the forehead clearly sloped backwards from the face. Breck reached for his camera, raised it to his mask and snapped several images. Each was accompanied by a bright flash.

He nodded at Pelletier, waiting beside him, and they continued their descent.

A hundred and twenty feet down, near the base of the hole, they finally located the dark opening to the third and final passage. It was the last of the three main tunnels, all branching off the central shaft of the hole, all previously undocumented. This one led off to the east. They probably wouldn't reach the end today, but would map it as far back as they could.

They swam toward the narrow opening and came to rest on a ledge of rock beside it. Breck finally clicked on one of his dive lights—they each carried three as one of many redundancy measures—and directed it into the darkness. He knew from experience that the tunnel's unassuming entry likely belied an extensive network of caverns linking to large chambers beyond. He carefully tied off a nylon line from his largest safety reel to a large rock on the cavern wall outside the passage. The line would likely be their only means of finding their way back to safety on their return. Pelletier nodded at him, and the men followed their dive lights into the jagged opening. Inside, Breck could make out about twenty feet of the passage before it turned abruptly downward.

As an unashamed Trekkie, not for the first time he thought of the *Star Trek* tagline. Here, in this cave, no man had gone before. He smiled. All the jock assholes who had picked on him as a skinny, awkward black kid in high school thirty years ago would never experience anything like this. They didn't have the balls.

Breck looked at his hand, which was throbbing some now. At least it looked like the bleeding had stopped. He lifted off the rock wall, Pelletier behind him. The safety line began to spool out as he kicked into the darkness.

CHAPTER 3

The disturbance was close now.

Alert, the enormous organism's brain processed the unfamiliar sounds of activity—muffled thumps and scrapes produced by the approach of something solid moving through the dark caverns, sending vibrations into a saclike organ in its body.

It had never before encountered any animals of significant size in this refuge; only the smaller creatures that perpetually dwelled within it. Nothing large enough to be of concern, as either predator or prey, ever entered these submarine caverns. Only the great beast itself was able to manipulate its nebulous bulk into almost any shape to allow passage through narrow tunnels.

But something was coming now.

It tested the water again. The taste was vaguely familiar. This was not its typical prey. But it was ravenous.

Its eyes began to detect movement. A dim light was moving erratically in an opening at the far end of the cavern. It again considered a retreat back toward the ocean, but its instincts stopped it. No potential threat existed in its refuge. In the daytime, it was safer here than in the open ocean. And now its innate curiosity overwhelmed it.

It would remain. But it would not be seen.

It slowly pressed its immense body against the wall of the cavern, drawing its branching limbs under it, flattening its bulk to shape itself into the cavern wall itself. Fully immersed into the contours of rock, it ceased moving.

Narrow rays of light appeared through the opening in the cavern and struck its flesh. Its skin quickly began to change color, to exactly match the drab hues of the cavern. Its eyes narrowed to slits.

It became the wall.

Sure of its invisibility, it calmly watched as the disturbance entered its lair.

In the beam of his dive light, Breck could see that several feet ahead the narrow shaft opened into some sort of larger room. A good thing, because the passage had narrowed enough in a few places that he'd been worried the heavier Pelletier might not pass. But the Frenchman had proven amazingly capable of squeezing his thick belly through tighter tunnels.

Breck released a breath of air to reduce his buoyancy, then pressed his body against the hard limestone beneath him and guided himself forward, kicking lightly to prevent stirring up ancient sediments. His scuba tank bumped against the convoluted rock above as he squeezed through the last few feet of the final restriction.

He felt a familiar sense of wonder as he entered the upper corner of a vast chamber. The artificial light revealed a considerable space spreading outward and downward, filled entirely with clear seawater, long enough that even in the powerful light the distance to the far wall was difficult to assess and distorted by lack of perspective. There was simply nothing to use for scale. He would need to be sure to get Pelletier into some of the shots.

He tied off their primary safety line, and then with his dive knife cut the line to free the spool. From a smaller spool clasped to his vest, he then affixed a new, secondary line to the primary line. He entered the chamber.

Breck raised his camera toward the ceiling and heard the faint click as its flash lit the silent cavern. Creeping along the rock above was an inverted reddish shrimp the size of his finger, with oversized antennae swaying in the current as it crept along the rough surface. As Breck gripped the camera, he noticed that his hand had stopped hurting. The mostly sterile seawater in here was probably cleansing the wound.

He snapped another image, this time directed into the open chamber. In the bright light he noticed that this cavern, which appeared to be at least seventy feet long and half as wide, was much broader than the others he and Pelletier had encountered in this network. This was by no means the largest chamber he had ever seen, but it was impressively large nonetheless. And there was something very unique about it. Nearly all the others this size had exhibited a beautiful natural architecture of stalactites, stalagmites, and other cave formations, but this one was different. *Barren.* Almost as though something had worn the sides smooth over the centuries—or cleared the space out. The lack of calcite formations made the chamber seem all the larger, giving it a lonely, empty feel.

Like a tomb.

He thought again of his friend Mack. He would love this place. But the last time he'd seen him, he'd thrown in the towel, finally fed up with the handicap he'd brought home from Iraq.

Breck glanced at his depth gauge as he attained neutral buoyancy near mid-water in the space. Two-hundred twenty-five feet down. Deep, indeed. And they were two or three times farther back than that laterally. He looked back to make sure his safety line—like Hansel's fabled trail of bread crumbs—was still affixed near the opening from which he had come, and saw Pelletier's (*Gretel's*, he thought, smiling) light appear in the dark cavity as he too arrived at the chamber. After Pelletier tied off and entered, Breck pointed out the shrimp suspended from the ceiling above, and the Frenchman nodded and moved toward it.

They had passed through a long, claustrophobic corridor in the cave system to get here. It hadn't been overly tight by cave standards—maybe five or six feet across for most of its distance—until the slightly narrower restriction here at the end. On the way, they'd encountered two other large grottos. The first one, three hundred feet in from the main entry shaft, had an enchanting ballroom feel, with a high ceiling and hundreds of conical stalagmites rising from the floor—graceful dancers frozen a thousand years ago as they twirled past one another. The other chamber was long and low and lined with hundreds of straws—calcite formations that spanned from floor to ceiling like prison bars, which had made passage difficult.

As Breck raised his camera again and continued to document this third chamber, he thought about his sister back in Philly. Deanna was going to love these pictures, and his nephew, Lucas, would like them even more. They already displayed several of his amateur shots, blown up and framed in her home office—all of images taken inside caverns from around the world. But none like this.

Deanna hated tight spaces. She would've freaked out

back in those tunnels, in knowing how far he was from the surface now. She'd always been a phenomenal athlete, especially before she'd had kids, but had never had the guts to do what he did. Not only because of the diving part, but also the squeezing-through-impossibly-tight-passages part. Few people did. But he had never been scared. And he didn't have kids. Never would. His independence was too important, and his profession too dangerous.

But this was the reward.

Pelletier tapped him on the shoulder. He turned to the Frenchman and saw that he was signaling a familiar message, as he did every three minutes. Time to assess their air supplies. Breck looked at his gauges and relayed the number via hand signals. They still had plenty of air. But to be safe, they would have to turn back in less than five minutes. Even on the low-nitrogen Trimix blend of gasses—which included helium in addition to oxygen—this far down they were already pushing the limits, and they knew it. When caving, it always paid to err on the side of caution.

Breck kicked into the center of the broad chamber and scanned its walls with his light. This chamber truly was different from all the others they had previously mapped—much more open. The surface rock here was much smoother than any other they had thus far encountered.

As he snapped another photo, he noticed something else. Something that bothered him.

A fine sprinkling of silt swirled in the open volume of the chamber, churning in the motion of Breck's fins. Too much silt for the men to have brought with them as they entered its expanse. Underwater suspended sediment was evidence of recent motion. And like in the other chambers, the water in this one should have been absolutely still before their arrival.

Unless something had stirred it.

Although they might be kicking up *some* sediment now, the particles spanned as far as his dive light could reach. Something had disrupted the still water in this chamber before they arrived. And recently.

Perhaps with the tidal shifts there was a stronger ocean current in here, which caused an eddy over the rubble at the bottom of the chamber. That might release a few finer particles into the room. On the far side of the chamber, he noticed several large, dark cavities that might lead to the depths of the ocean. They would have to be especially vigilant. If they were forced to fight a current on their return, that might cause serious complications.

Just then, Breck felt a slight movement of water against his face. He nodded to himself. *Yes.* There was some sort of current flowing through here. This passage must link directly to the open ocean, and probably was heavily influenced by moving water. That might also explain the smoother chamber walls, which could have eroded over time.

Pelletier, who looked ghostly pale in the artificial light, nodded at him, acknowledging the current. The Frenchman began to turn away. As his light struck the wall of the chamber, the rock suddenly appeared to move.

To *bulge.*

Breck shook his head to clear it and looked again at the cavern wall. It did bulge out toward the center, as though swollen, but no longer seemed to be moving. Had Pelletier noticed anything? If so, he wasn't reacting to it.

Breck realized he must be seeing things. That was a bad sign down here, but didn't make any sense since his air mixture was low in nitrogen. Narcosis was highly unlikely. But if it happened again, it would be wise to begin their exit immediately.

He glanced at his dive computer. *Better hurry, John.* Breck rapped on the Frenchman's tank with his knuckles to get his attention. When Pelletier looked back at him, Breck motioned for the biologist to move toward the bulging chamber wall. Having a person framed in some images would later provide them with crucial perspective to describe the geological formations and size of each cavern. And unlike Breck's drab blue wet suit, which hardly stood out underwater, the Frenchman's black-and-yellow neoprene made for sharp contrast to the muted background.

Once Pelletier had neared to within an arm's reach of the curving wall, he turned back to Breck. Breck raised the camera, and another flash silently lit the chamber. There. He saw it again.

The wall *had* moved—hadn't it? He took a deep breath.

He swam closer to Pelletier, shining his dive light past the Frenchman at the pale rock, which up close appeared to be textured by low, fist-size bumps. Almost directly behind Pelletier was a small crease on the wall. Was it his imagination, or was the rock there now taking on a shade of Pelletier's yellow wetsuit?

Breck moved closer and this time directed the camera past his partner, toward the odd crease, which was the length of his arm. He realized it was actually two small parallel ridges, forming a seam rising several inches off the wall. He depressed the shutter release and the flash went off. In the bright light, the seam momentarily looked more distinct. Almost like lips, or . . .

The seam parted.

Breck was looking into an eye.

He flinched backward and squeezed the camera reflexively, its bright flash illuminating the cavern. The huge catlike eye narrowed, and suddenly the walls of the cave itself seemed to be collapsing. Breck felt the rush of moving water all around him and watched in horror as the side of the chamber began to change shape. The entire wall was separating itself from the cavern.

Detaching itself.

Something as long as the cavern. Something *living*.

The camera flashed again. Breck dropped it and began to kick frantically away from the huge mass that continued to swell into the space. Pelletier, sensing the movement behind him, quickly followed. Other parts of the cavern face seemed to break free and squiggle into the water. Breck saw something dart up toward Pelletier. An instant later, the Frenchman was ripped backward so forcefully his regulator popped free of his mouth, releasing a cloud of bubbles.

He reached desperately for Breck, the whites of his eyes visible even in the dim light as twin snakes of rust-colored flesh coiled around his thighs. His face contorted in pain as the coils pulled in opposite directions, bending his legs sideways at impossible angles. A dark seam appeared at the groin of his splitting wetsuit. There was a muted pop as one leg came free in a dark cloud of blood.

Breck spun away. He spied the dark entrance hole near the cavern's ceiling and kicked with everything he had, then forced his way into the hole. His tank clanged against the rock as he struggled farther into the narrowing cave system.

Something touched his thigh and began to adhere to it, and he swung a fist at the taut, fleshy thing, beating at it. He felt a jerk as it pulled at him, at his equipment, and then he was free again as some of his gear fell away. He did not look back.

A minute passed. Two. *Keep going.*

He lost track of time as he fled the monstrosity, pushing away thoughts of despair as he again began to think about his air. He was a long way from the surface. There would be no turning back.

The tunnel branched, and he paused to scan his options. One tunnel appeared to end almost immediately, so he went the other way. Ten yards later, he ran into a restriction. He glanced back and saw that, at least for the moment, he was alone. And that his safety line no longer trailed behind him. He touched his belt and realized the spool was missing. It didn't matter. He wasn't going back anyway.

He began to wriggle into the oppressive opening that offered his only remaining hope. It was only a few feet across, and he was forced to slide along on his belly. He listened to his tank scrape along the rock above, but he was making progress. He thought he felt something touch his foot and then there was a surge of adrenaline and he was through the restriction. He started to kick again, then stopped.

A dead end.

Fifteen feet ahead, the tunnel tapered to a hole no larger than his fist. He moved to examine it, but was only able to confirm what he already knew. There was nowhere to go. He felt an overwhelming despair.

He turned around and came to rest in a sitting position, looking back into the shifting clouds of silt. Preparing himself. But after a few moments, nothing appeared. He glanced at his air. Maybe ten minutes left. Maybe less.

So this is it. He began to tremble.

He sat at the end of the tunnel, his light pointed into blackness, as he waited for the thing to reappear and claim him.

CHAPTER 4

He was dead.

Confined to the small space, the specimen simply had given up. The arrow-like male squid had settled to the bottom of the tank, where his arms had relaxed into a beautiful fanlike pattern below his mantle, but any appealing coloration he had once been capable of had faded from his body.

Dr. Valerie Martell sat on a stool beside the two-hundred-gallon tank, staring at the dead cephalopod. The latest batch of *Dosidicus gigas*—ten juvenile specimens in all, each about the size of a large lamp—had been relatively healthy. All were now gone. This little guy had been the last holdout.

She wasn't surprised. All along, she had disagreed with the aquarium director's insistence to continue trying to raise this species in captivity. They were animals that belonged in the open ocean. Still, she had hoped that maybe, just *maybe*, this one would survive. He had seemed tougher than the rest. But now he was gone too.

She sighed. This squid was just her latest failure.

Outside the lab, it was gray and raining in Moss Landing. January along the Central California coastline often brought slow-moving systems that yielded most of the year's precipitation, turning the hillsides a brilliant green. Despite the weather, Val knew that she should be doing something outside today. Getting some exercise. Going for a drive. Or even trying to catch a matinee. It was a Saturday, and she hadn't really taken a day off in a month. She glanced at her running shoes beside the door, where she kept them for when she needed to blow off steam, but didn't get up.

Looking back at the juvenile squid, she thought about Will. Her research on these squid had brought them together. So much had changed in the last year, though.

He probably had left home by now. When she'd departed early in the morning, he'd still been snoring on the couch, the blinds closed to the daylight. She had gotten him a job doing maintenance at the nearby shipyard, as he planned the next career move. It was only supposed to be a temporary job. But he wasn't moving forward. Just as she had done lately, he'd been immersing himself in his work. Avoiding her.

And then there was his drinking.

Val picked up a set of metal forceps and poked at the squid in the tank. Three days ago, Specimen Number Forty-four had been captured right here in Monterey Bay, where a resident population had established itself over the past decade. Hooked by an old fisherman who knew of the squid's value and thus brought the live specimens in.

Like this squid, her partner didn't seem to thrive in a sedentary life. After he'd almost died two years ago, he'd needed to undergo months of physical therapy. And his life had been in disarray. They'd been in love, though, and things had been wonderful. There had even been talk of marriage, which neither of them had expected. For the first time since junior high, Val had stopped fo-

cusing on her work. They had filled voids in each other's
lives, and she had released a remarkable passion in him.

But that was more than a year ago.

She'd waited patiently for him to get back on his feet.
He'd done quite well for the first year, although she
knew inside he'd never fully recover from some of the
losses he'd suffered.

And then, such a scary but wonderful thing had happened. Right before the bad thing happened.

Since that day, she had watched helplessly as he
slowly self-destructed over the past six months. As he
started drinking again, slowly at first. *Just a few beers.*
Then, not long after, more frequently. And then he bought
the first bottle of rum. He said it was to quell the nightmares, as it had in the past, and to deal with the constant
pain in his shoulder. Although she voiced her concern,
she put up with it, perhaps out of guilt. She knew that
his shoulder, and many of his scars, still represented
sacrifices made out of his love for her.

And then he had started to become dark. *Angry.* He
was never abusive, but frightening, his temper simmer-
ing beneath his cowboy hat like a pot about to boil over.

Val shook the thought away as she watched the rain-
drops spatter against the window. She wondered if she
too was dying from being in captivity. She had lost any
trace of the tan she had worn for years when doing fieldwork in Mexico. Her thick, dark hair had grown much
longer, since she no longer needed to keep it out of her
dive mask. But it had made sense to stop the field research. She had made significant progress in understand-
ing how these squid communicated, and the directors of
the Point Lobos Aquarium Research Group had decided
it would be too much of a liability for her to continue
her fieldwork.

Two of her papers on *Dosidicus gigas* had recently been published, which made PLARG's leadership very happy. But her last big project in Mexico had ended long ago. She'd considered applying for more funding to study the shoals of invasive squid emerging off the California coast, but as soon as the huge numbers had arrived, they'd suddenly disappeared. Since then, only a few smaller resident squid had appeared offshore here in the Bay. The creatures were very dependent on ocean patterns, and as climate shifts occurred and food sources rose and fell, so did their populations and migration patterns. They would be back, but for now they were gone.

The next obvious challenge had been to study live specimens here at PLARG. Val's employer was happy to fund her in the safety of a lab, studying the animals *ex situ*, but was no longer comfortable with the risks of funding her research of the animals in their deepwater environment. Besides the obvious dangers in working with *Dosidicus* in its natural environment, there was the opportunity of money to be made if her employers could display the alien creatures to the public, so Humboldt squid husbandry had become the focus at deep-sea-oriented PLARG.

The latest live squid had all been immediately separated, placed in their own tanks so they wouldn't attack and kill one another. Yet every one they had brought into captivity had become anxious, ramming at the walls of the large tanks. One had even managed to hurl itself out and splatter onto the floor one night, where it later died. None of the squid had eaten. And the bioluminescent communication the animals used in the wild, which had been the previous focus of her research, did not occur in the lab. Few natural behaviors did.

All had now died.

But Val admired their persistence. Unlike her, they hadn't been brought under the yoke. They had fought their captivity until they faded away.

She thought about the evening to come. Her presentation. The aquarium heads required all their researchers to prepare a quarterly PowerPoint presentation to the public on their latest research. To put on a smile and talk about how wonderful things were going. To make a passionate plea for their research, for the aquarium, to inspire its donors. But she wasn't feeling it today.

Eric Watson would also be presenting tonight. She would be opening, but he was getting the coveted final presentation. The precocious kid was getting all the funding now. He and his fancy unmanned underwater vehicles. But he'd been helpful with her own research. And she had to hand it to him: He knew how to follow the money.

Her lack of motivation wasn't just about playing second fiddle. Or even about her failures to keep captive squid alive, or make breakthroughs in her research. Setbacks were all part of science. But she had also felt self-conscious presenting lately. Although still quite lithe, she'd gained ten pounds over the last several months. And in the mirror she had started to really notice the tiny, sun-furrowed wrinkles near her eyes. She knew that she was just being hard on herself, and that she was still young and skinny, but it still bothered her.

She sighed again. She knew it was time for a change.

She felt like she might cry. Instead, she took a deep breath and turned away from the tank, searching for her black backpack. In it she had packed her workout clothes. She changed and laced up her still-damp running shoes, and then she pulled the hood of a waterproof jacket over her head, and stepped out into the rain.

CHAPTER 5

Like impatient children, its own limbs aroused it from its slumber as daylight faded far above. They were already stirring when it woke, busy snaking into dark cracks running off the low chamber around their master. But signals sent from the mindless appendages to the creature's brain reported no success in finding sustenance—only inedible bits of bone and other waste deposited from previous meals.

It needed to hunt.

The organism extended its limbs away from its body and, affixing them to the smooth walls of the underwater cavern, silently squeezed its bulk through the narrow cavity in a series of undulations. It soon arrived at the bottom of a funnel-shaped submarine pit, where it paused to peer outward from its concealed position. Then gradually, patiently, the beast slid its great form from within the deep recess in the carbonate platform and into the fading light at the mouth of the pit. There it stopped moving again.

Hidden by the darkness, it remained motionless for a short time, observing the darkening deep-ocean reef—a shallow, unfamiliar environment—for signs of prey. Over time, it had learned to ignore the smaller prey animals on which it had once fed—the benthic crabs and blind fish of the depths—and likewise it now ignored the smaller fishes that schooled past.

For years it had only focused on larger deepwater animals. Six-gill sharks, squids, giant isopods, oversized marine worms. And on the warm-bodied animals that in small pods plied the night waters of the open ocean above it. It saw none of these now.

Sensing nothing of interest, and comfortable that it was safe, it fully extended its appendages and jetted water downward from its soft body. It rose from the blackness of the hole to reveal its massive form to the open ocean. As its eyes cleared the rim of the pit, it spied a large, spotted ray above it in the gloom, just out of the range of its arms, but the ray saw its hulking mass as well and quickly spun away in a sweep of wings. The potential prey disappeared over the lip of the deep reef.

The organism moved out over the dark reef and relaxed its body, slowly settling toward the rough surface. Dozens of fish scattered as its flesh draped over a broad area.

Although the creature was unique in its size, like all of its much smaller relatives in the ocean, it was forced to leave the safety of its lairs to hunt for food. But usually these lairs, and its hunting grounds, were in much deeper waters than this. Now, it felt the powerful urge to descend. Larger prey might still be foraging the deep at this hour, but soon would cease for the night. And once its preferred quarry was back near the surface of the open ocean, the much slower beast would be unable to effectively pursue it.

Deep on the ocean floor, it had always sought most of its sustenance. Camouflaged on the abyssal plain near a rotting animal's remains, or some other attractant, it would ensnare larger animals that approached to investigate. Or it would hunt in the open waters above, only at night, its flesh replicating the patterns of schools of mid-size fish or squid to ambush even larger animals coming to feed on them. But the only predator of any real concern to it in its mature state sometimes plied the same depths of the open ocean. Thus, after consuming a meal, it always retreated to the safety found within caverns deep down the walls below the reef.

After watching the spotted ray depart, it turned its body sideways and gently pushed off the rock escarpment. It jetted sideways by expelling a few pulses of seawater, quickly moving away from the shallower water of the island shelf toward the blackness of much deeper water.

Toward the abyss.

It glided out past the edge of the shelf, where the sea floor dropped thousands of feet down a vertical rock face. Below it was a void of absolute darkness. It gathered in its limbs, forming itself into an enormous disc, and sank.

Occasionally, it extended a limb to rebalance and maintain an upright position, but otherwise it yielded to gravity. Its flesh was slightly denser than the seawater around it, so its foray into the abyss required little energy beyond an occasional pulse of horizontal propulsion. The water temperature plummeted, cooling the creature's bulbous body and blood.

It was not an efficient swimmer. Its biology was best suited to hunting along the ocean floor, within its recesses. Life was scarce in the depths of the ocean, but there it might have the best odds of locating a larger meal. A familiar meal. A meal of substance.

The light quickly faded as it made its long descent.

Soon it was black. The creature could not see here, even
with its large eyes. But it was not blind. It could still
feel. It could sense vibrations.

And it could *taste*.

After descending for some time, the sea floor eventually transformed from the sheer rock face to a more gently sloping bottom that curved toward the abyssal plain.
It reached a broad channel in the depths, cut by a north-
ward-flowing current of seawater. Here the quality of
the water changed almost imperceptibly, yet the organism sensed that this fluid was somehow denser, laden
with a fine silt of particles. The turbidity current sank
below and past the cleaner ocean water around it. Dropping into the current, the organism ceased propulsion
and reconfigured its body, such that its appendages were
splayed broadly beneath it, and after a moment its great
form impacted the ocean floor, releasing a cloud of fine
silt into the blackness.

It turned into the current. This required more effort
than moving with the flow of water, but it offered advan-
tages to the hunter. The organism retained the advantage
of receiving tastes and other stimuli that would alert it to
the presence of living things upstream. And by moving
toward the oncoming flow of water, the organism's prey
would have difficulty detecting its own presence.

Rolling its great body upstream on its many writhing
limbs, it began to hunt. Despite its massive bulk, it moved
with silent grace. Only slightly heavier than seawater, it
was not forced to exert significant effort to remain
above the ocean floor. Millions of receptors in each arm
continually tasted the currents, assessing chemicals and
feeling textures, seeking any sign of prey.

As each limb contacted the seafloor, it gathered information, sending signals back to the organism's brain.

The limbs worked in chaotic concert, managing to avoid one other while tumbling gently into the bottom and pushing off and forward, moving the creature into the oncoming stream of particle-laden water. In this fashion it could continue locomotion while constantly tasting for food.

It continued into the cold current, a long cloud of sediment billowing hundreds of feet into the black water behind it.

CHAPTER 6

Another cold, rainy day.

Val lay alone in her bed, looking out the window at the pale light filtering through the cheap vertical blinds. She'd hit snooze three times before shutting off her alarm and going back to sleep for an hour. Will had already left, which meant he had gone to his boxing gym before work.

It was Monday, and it felt like it.

She imagined that she felt the stare of Will's dog, Bud, boring into the back of her head. For more than a year, he'd sat a few feet from the bed each morning, his short, floppy ears perked up, waiting for her to rise and hoping for a morning run. The dun-colored mutt would wag his tail and push his muzzle into her face, his tongue lapping at her cheek. She would scratch behind his ears, and he'd groan in pleasure. For so long she had wanted a dog again, and they'd really developed a bond in the brief time he'd been in her life.

She finally rolled over, hoping in her half-asleep state that he'd somehow be there again. But he was still gone.

Val sat up and lowered her feet to the cold floor. She

threw a sweatshirt on over her tank top and found her slippers, then walked bare-legged down the dim hallway to the kitchen, the dog's ghost padding silently after her. She smelled coffee, and saw that Will had made a pot. He'd also left her a note on the beige Formica counter-top:

I'll be home late again—Have a good day
—W

She thought, *He used to write* Love, W.

She hadn't even seen him last night, since he had come home late from the bar and left again so early. She'd pretended to be asleep as he quietly dressed in the predawn darkness, not wanting to have a conversation with him. What was there to say? She knew he was prob-ably hung over again. Only Will Sturman would stay out late drinking and then rise to go to the gym, even though he wasn't training for anything. The man was nothing if not tough and headstrong.

At least he'd been honest with her when she'd asked him yesterday if he was headed to watch playoff football again. *It's a bye week,* he'd said. *Super Bowl's next week-end. I just need to get out of the apartment.*

Months ago, it had become a familiar late-night rou-tine. She'd wake to him bumping noisily about in their kitchen as he made himself an after-binge snack. Then his tall silhouette would fill the door frame as he stag-gered in, slid into the bed next to her. Never even realiz-ing she was awake in the darkness. When she'd called him on his growing problem, they'd argued. Then he started sleeping on the couch.

She told herself it was out of respect for her, so she

could sleep. But she knew he was just withdrawing. Again dwelling on the wife he'd lost, on the loss he now shared with Val, and feeling sorry for himself. As he became what she feared he might.

She had grown up loving a man like this. A man who wasn't capable of reciprocating her love. She wasn't going to do it again. Even if he had once saved her life.

She poured herself a mug of coffee, added cream and walked over to the sliding glass door that opened to their balcony. The rain had stopped for the moment, but it was gray outside. *Just need to get out of the apartment,* he'd said. What he meant was *I just need to be alone.*

Alone. Or with Maria. But not with her.

Over the green, rolling, chaparral-clad hills in the distance, a red light blinked on a water tower. It was a great view, but she'd planned to move out of this small apartment when Will had first moved up here to be with her. To buy a house. The one-bedroom unit on the outskirts of Marina had simply been a home base for her for four years, when she had always been away doing fieldwork. She'd never intended to spend a lot of time in it, especially if living with a man and a sixty-some pound dog.

She should probably have already gone into the office, but she'd worked on Saturday evening so her boss, Rob Carman, wouldn't care if she came in late. What could he say, anyway? They both knew she had paid her dues at PLARG over the years.

There had been a time when all she had wanted to do was work. When she had been so inspired. What had happened to her, anyway?

Will had happened. *They* had happened. And now they weren't happening anymore. She wasn't meant for relationships. She would never be able to carry a child, as she knew painfully well, and it looked like her best prospect for marriage was an alcoholic. Maybe she should just become single again, and remain that way forever.

Looking at the gray outside, she told herself that maybe the sun would come out, but she knew it probably wouldn't. She sighed and turned away from the window to look for her laptop. She would work from home until she felt enough motivation to shower and head into the lab. There wasn't much to do today, anyway. She'd just need to clean out the tanks to prepare them for another round of (doomed) squid. And if she didn't, it probably wouldn't matter anyway. They weren't likely to have more live specimens turn up for a few weeks or longer.

She brought her laptop to the couch and sat cross-legged on it, resting the computer on her knees. She fired it up and opened her Web browser. She accessed her Outlook e-mail account. A hundred and twenty-one unread messages. She sighed. She should at least get through her overflowing inbox today.

She began scrolling down the page to look for anything urgent. Mostly, the e-mails were just FYIs from colleagues, junk mail, and administrative notifications. She paused on an e-mail from rford@nes.org, received late last night: Richard Ford, from the National Exploration Society. NES had featured her work in a past issue of its monthly, photo-laden magazine, and had partially funded one of her earlier projects through a foundation grant. She opened the e-mail:

Hi Val—

How are you? Been a long time.

I don't know if you recall, but I've been working on a project in the Bahamas. Mapping blue holes on some of the islands, with a focus on Andros, where I just left a few days ago. But there was an accident. We just halted ops.

I don't recall you being a cave diver, so I'm hoping you don't know many in that close-knit community. You might have already heard, but we lost two of our best last week. They never surfaced, and are presumed dead. Operations are now postponed indefinitely.

Their names were John Breck and Arlo Pelletier, the latter a researcher from France. I'm sorry to be the bearer of bad news if you did know either man.

Pelletier's name sounded familiar—some biologist— but Val knew neither man personally. Her uncle, Mack, might know these men though. He used to be one of the best cave divers this side of the Atlantic. She continued reading the e-mail:

The main reason I'm e-mailing you is that we did find a camera John had been using. I thought you'd want to see one of the images that turned up on the device—the last one taken. We still can't figure out what it is, but it looks a hell of a lot like something you'd be familiar with.

See the attached, and let me know what you think. You can call me to discuss.

Thanks,
Rich

Val double-clicked the attachment icon to open a new window. On her screen popped up a blurry, dark image. She scanned the digital photo. Much of it was dim, al- most black. But not all of it. Val stopped breathing.

On the upper right quadrant was the obvious reason

why Ford had sent her an e-mail. Nearly obscured by the dim was a blurred, curved object covered in a field of small, white circles.

Suckers.

CHAPTER 7

"**V**al, you still there?"

Valerie Martell blinked, and pressed the cell phone against her ear. "Yeah. Sorry, Rich. I was just looking at your photo again. Are you sure you don't have any other shots of the object in the corner? Maybe from another angle?"

On the other end of the call, Richard Ford cleared his throat in obvious irritation. "No, we don't. I already told you that. Look, I'm really in a hurry here. So if you could just focus for a moment, and let me go over some background . . ."

"Sorry. I'm listening." She shut the cover of her laptop. Val had worked with the short, balding Ford before. As the executive vice president for research at the National Exploration Society, based in DC, he was intense, driven. Always in a tie. And never patient.

She said, "You were giving me background . . . saying you'd gathered mapping data on the holes, collected samples and multimedia. . . ."

"Right. But we've now postponed the operation. Indefinitely. To figure out what happened, and out of respect for the two divers' families."

"They'd probably want you to continue," she said.

"Probably. They were a lot like you and me. But you know the drill. Liability issues trump."

"Oh, I know."

Val sat at the small desk in her apartment, which faced the window. The afternoon had turned clear, sunny, and through the open blinds she had a distant view past the low hills to the flat, blue expanse of Monterey Bay. As Ford talked, her mind drifted again to the printout of the dark, blurry image he had sent her. The curved object in the corner, studded with white dots, possibly had a reddish tinge, or maybe that was just her imagination. Maybe she *wanted* it to be red. Wanted it to look more like a cephalopod arm, to give her an excuse to pack her bags and head for the Bahamas.

Ford finished his monologue: ". . . and we've been trying to describe a number of the blue holes in the area since."

"Uh-huh."

"This was their fifth foray into this particular hole. It's nicknamed 'The Staircase' by the locals, because the layers of limestone in its shallows look like giant steps leading to the rim of the main shaft. People swim and bathe in the freshwater on the surface, but until we came along, nobody had ever explored its depths."

"How did you retrieve the camera?"

"Another of our teams went in. Followed their safety lines to where one had somehow broken off in the tunnel they were mapping."

"But no sign of the men?"

"Just a few pieces of equipment," he said. "Let's see . . ."

She heard paper rustling before he continued.

"A swim fin . . . the metal spool for one of their safety lines, a couple other little things. Part of a flashlight." He paused to let it sink in. "But nothing else so far."

"How far did you get? On the larger project, I mean?"

"We were making relatively good progress before the accident, considering the logistical complications of diving these caverns. Know anything about the Bahamas's blue holes?"

"Not much. I know about the ones in Belize, though. The geology of the Bahamas must be similar to the Yucatán."

"Relatively speaking," Ford said. "The Bahama Bank is karst limestone, which over eons has eroded into impressive submarine cave systems. The more famous ones are perfectly rounded sinkholes, but there are also some fault-line holes offshore that look more like huge cracks."

"So some of these blue holes are landlocked?"

"Most of them, actually. Inland blue holes, like the one Breck and Pelletier were in. But few are really *landlocked*."

"What do you mean?" she said.

"Many of them link to the ocean through a network of caves. Like their marine counterparts, they formed over the last few million years, mainly during the Ice Ages."

"When sea level was much lower?"

"Exactly. Hundreds of feet lower. The Bahamian Plateau once towered four hundred feet over the sea. Back then, the limestone platform was exposed to the elements."

"And acid rain did all the work. Right?"

"You got it. Carbonic acid in rainwater pooled on the rock. Wore it down. Then, in periods where the holes were submerged in the ocean, tidal action helped scour out developing caverns. So now it's a pretty unique place, with a shitload of blue holes."

"You said those two divers were in an inland hole?"

"Yeah. We'd discovered three main arms off this one

hole alone. Side tunnels, extending more than three hundred feet beneath the surface, with two of the passages likely extending far offshore." There was a pause before Ford continued. "They got that shot I sent you on their last dive. I thought it looked like the arm of a squid or something."

"Well, it does. Some cephalopod, anyway. If this really is some sort of tentacle, it's very likely an undiscovered species."

"Just like everything else in those caves," Ford said. "You plan to look into this? Would PLARG send you down there?"

"Probably not. But I might go, on my own dime."

"Really? But you're not a caver."

"I have a few ideas."

"Well, if you do plan something, let me send you our data first, to get you up to speed. I have a lot of older papers on the area's geology. And since our teams had gotten to more than twenty new holes in just the past two months, we've got a boatload of images, maps, notes. You name it. We were hoping to map at least fifteen more holes before the money ran out, but then . . . well, you know the rest."

Val frowned. "What happened, Rich? I mean, you said those men were experts."

"The best," he said, and then paused. "I don't know, Val. Like most of the other inland holes, it appears that somewhere underground that hole reaches well out to sea. Maybe a strong tidal surge sucked them down. Maybe they got lost. We just don't know."

"Are you still working to find them?"

"Not anymore. But like I said, we already looked. It's too dangerous to keep sending men back in there."

Val heard muffled shouting as Ford barked at someone in his office.

He said, "Sorry, Val. I gotta go."

"What did you say was the name of the last hole they were in? The Stairway?"

"The Staircase. I'll send you an e-mail with more details. But I've really gotta run."

"Thanks, Rich. I appreciate it. One more question."

"Hurry."

"Was Mack on this project? Involved in any way?"

"Your uncle? No. He declined. Like always. I don't know why I ask him anymore."

"Thanks." It had been a long time since she'd seen Mack herself.

"Well, good luck," he said. "And Val?"

"Yes?"

"Be careful down there."

CHAPTER 8

Val stood alone on the deserted docks down in the Moss Landing shipyard. The early night was still, foggy. In the buzz of fluorescent lights, PLARG research vessels rested in their berths beside the main raised pier.

Sturman regularly worked into the night during the shorter days of winter, which worried her since he was often underwater alone. She'd had the connections to get him the general maintenance job with the Point Lobos Aquarium—a job that sometimes involved donning scuba gear to scrub boat hulls—thinking it would be short-term only. A paycheck. But he still hadn't looked for anything else.

She'd passed through the unlocked gate in the chain-link fence a full minute ago, then walked down the floating dock to Will's wet scuba gear piled in a fresh puddle by a larger yacht. He still hadn't surfaced.

"Will?" she called quietly to the vessels around her, but nobody answered. Maybe he was just finishing cleaning this one. But why didn't he have his gear on?

Suddenly, his stubbled head and square jaw burst above

the water fifteen feet away, to the left of the yacht. He exhaled loudly, then sucked in fresh air. He blinked the seawater out of his eyes and saw her standing on the dock.

He didn't smile. On his face was that same dull expression he'd worn for months now. He swam toward her.

"You were down there a long time," Val said.

Sturman spit into the water and nodded. "Yeah, I reckon I was."

"You must be cold."

He nodded and kicked toward her. She saw that he wore only a neoprene wet suit and weight belt, with no dive gear or even a mask on. She thought about asking what the hell he was doing down there, but didn't. He reached the dock and started to remove his weight belt.

"Can I help you with that?" she said.

He nodded and lifted the lead-laden belt out of the water. Her thick brown hair, which she'd grown out now for a year or longer, hung past her shoulders as she leaned down to him. She grunted as she hoisted the belt onto the cement next to his fins and scuba tank.

She said, "How's work going? Still good?"

"Yeah. I guess." He spit out cold seawater. "If you call cleaning boat hulls good."

"You really should think about buying another boat, Will. Maybe one you can fix up. To get out of all this . . ."

"I'm not ready."

She tugged at the ends of her hair. "I haven't seen you since lunch yesterday."

"Yeah. I was at the Pelican last night."

"Again?"

"I had a lot on my mind." He pulled himself out of the water and sat on the low dock, feet dangling in the water. She remained standing beside him.

"How much did you have to drink?"

He looked up at her. "You look really good, Doc," he said, the hint of a smile on his face. "I always liked that sweater on you."

She felt a girlish thrill at the rare compliment, and touched her tight yellow sweater self-consciously. Lately, she felt so insecure. As quickly as it had arrived, the thrill was gone.

"You're just trying to change the subject," she said. "I asked how much you had to drink."

His smile went away, and he rubbed the prematurely gray-tinged hair on his head. "More than I should've. But I meant it. You look nice."

"Thanks . . . Did you drive home? Or did—"

"I'm not having this talk now, Doc." He lunged to his feet and reached for his gear. "Let's head inside where it's warm."

She helped him carry his scuba gear and sponges back down the docks and into the large maintenance office. It was an older building, complete with a wood-burning stove. It was stuffy inside, and dimly lit by the single lamp on a desk on the far end of the room, but the warmth felt good, and it smelled pleasantly of burning oak. She moved to stand on the worn carpet by a couch against the side wall near the stove—another couch where he sometimes slept lately—while he dropped his gear in a pile near the door and turned away from her to add a log to the fire. When he opened the furnace door, orange light filled the dark half of the room.

Quietly, she said, "I got an e-mail from a colleague today. There may be a job for me in the Bahamas."

He looked at her for a moment, then stood and began to strip off his wet suit. "Through PLARG?" he asked.

"No. Freelance."

He nodded. He stepped closer to her, to study her face, the muscles on his bare chest, the large tattoos on his shoulders dripping with cool water. He still bore the scars on his chest from when he had saved her, and nearly died. She glanced down at the scratched gold wedding band on his hand, from his earlier marriage. She had grown to hate it, and what it still meant to him.

At almost a foot taller, he towered over her. For a man in his late thirties who'd been very hard on his body, he had a strong build, and was still ruggedly handsome. But Val had always thought he looked older than he was, from living a hard life. And spending too many summers in the sun. Now, in the harsh shadows of the firelight, his face looked even more tired, older. She wondered what he was thinking. Would he even care if she left?

She said, "He sent me an image of what looks like some sort of cephalopod. Something that doesn't belong where the picture was taken. It's a very interesting opportunity, Will. It might even be a new species." She glanced down at her feet, then back up at him. "I spent a lot of time thinking about it today. I've accrued a lot of leave at work, and—well . . ."

"You're leaving, aren't you?"

She bit her lip. "Well, I was thinking about it, but . . . I wanted to talk to you first."

"You planned to go without me?"

"Well, I figured . . . with your job, you couldn't—"

He snorted. "My *job*. Right. And where would that leave us?"

"I don't know, Will. Where are we now? It feels like you're always pushing me away."

"Hard to lead a horse that's already headed in the other direction."

He fell onto the couch and tore the wet suit off his legs, and then in only his swimsuit turned to hang the 7mm neoprene one-piece on a line suspended in the corner. He gathered up his weight belt and scuba tank and brought the equipment over to a tub of freshwater near the line and dumped it inside, wincing. When he got cold, she knew his shoulder always bothered him.

She remained quiet, letting his temper subside as he moved to gather the rest of his gear. She picked at a seam on the thigh of her jeans, unsure of what to say next. Her feelings for him were still there, but there was such a distance between them now. The walls he'd built around himself after losing his wife years ago, which had gradually come down as they grew to love each other, were back, built almost overnight.

As he grabbed his fins and mask off the cement by the door and tossed them into the tub next to the other gear, she noticed the one-inch stump of the middle finger on his right hand. Will had nearly drowned before. When he had saved her life. Before she had saved his. Or thought she had. She realized that despite his own courage, his incredible acts of selflessness, the women in his life had always been saving him.

But they weren't saving him now.

He and Bud had moved up here more than a year ago, to be with her. Her job was based in Monterey Bay, and so much in his life had suddenly changed that there was nothing left for him in Southern California. After a few weeks apart as he got his affairs in order, he had hurried up here. So excited to see her. Almost as excited as Bud.

There had been so much passion, so much romance. Their strong personalities added that much more excitement. Despite his lousy job, things had gone great.

Then Bud died. So unexpectedly. It had been much harder for Will than for her, but he had struggled through it.

As he was regaining his feet, the unexpected had happened. Just the thing they both needed, bringing wonder, joy, and a good measure of anxiety, distracting them from the loss of Will's dog. Six weeks of moving forward. Planning for the future. But then more bad news came, and Will, defeated, had sought familiar refuge in the bottle.

She pushed the thought away. None of this was her fault. Not Bud's rare heart condition. And not the grim fact she would never be able to bear children. Will had been through a lot, but so had she. She was tired of making excuses for him. For them. She finally took a deep breath and moved to the tank beside him.

"Will, I think maybe you need help."

He stopped dunking his gear, looked at her, then turned and leaned on the rim of the plastic tub, facing the firelight.

From beside him, she continued. "I don't know what to do for you anymore. Obviously, I'm not helping you."

"I don't know what you're talkin' about."

"Will. You know it's only because I care about you."

"Whatever."

"Don't you know how hard this is for me? To see you self-destruct?" Val fought the rare tears forming in her eyes. "I love you."

Sturman turned to her. His expression had softened, and she saw him fighting back his own emotions. He suddenly reached for her, his strong arms pulling her small figure into his huge frame. His wet skin smelled like the ocean, and his rough embrace brought back so many memories. It had been a long time since she had felt his touch. He was strong, but so weak.

She looked up into his eyes. He kissed her, and she returned the kiss fiercely. They had always been able to express themselves physically. Still kissing her, he reached down and began to unbutton her jeans.

Without thinking, she helped slide them off.

CHAPTER 9

On a stool in front of Val sat Eric Watson. He was cute despite the gold-rimmed glasses, with green eyes and sharp features, but shorter than Will, with a slimmer build. And younger than her. Cute, but not really her type.

She thought, *Maybe I just pick the wrong type*.

Thank God, nobody had walked in on her and Will last night. She already regretted her impulsiveness, her uncharacteristic weakness as she gave in to her desires on the worn couch in the dock's maintenance office. *No.* For once, she had given in to her feelings. But it had gotten them nowhere. As Sturman was getting into dry clothes afterward, pulling on his cowboy boots, she had again said they needed to talk about his problem. The smile had left his face. Like her father, he wouldn't admit he even had a problem. She'd suggested he attend a meeting, or seek counseling, and he'd laughed at her. Spoken the familiar words: *I don't need any help.*

And then somehow his dead wife had again joined the conversation, like she always seemed to. Will had compared Val to Maria, made some comment about how *she*'d never left him for her work. Val had finally felt defeated. She didn't know if they still had any chance, but she'd known then she had to go. To leave, and put distance between her and Will.

And if she was going to the Bahamas, she would need help.

When Val had walked into Eric's lab, he'd been hunched over a table soldering some part. It still smelled a little like melted plastic. At first, he'd seemed happy to see her. But he looked embarrassed now, having just apologized for having a near panic attack at his Saturday-night presentation the previous weekend.

She said, "So you had another episode. So what?"

He sighed and ran his hands through his unruly brown hair. He needed a haircut. "But it was during a presentation," he said, with a slightly nasal quality she remembered from past discussions. "Yeah, I managed to finish. But I was getting some funny looks when I was done."

"You maintained control. That's all that matters, Eric. Millions of people deal with claustrophobia. It's one of the most common phobias."

"I don't know. I hurried out of there afterward, to get some fresh air. I didn't even return for the meet and greet. I just couldn't go back in the building."

"Why not?"

"I don't know. I kept thinking about the earthquake again. Being trapped."

"For good reason." She had heard that in the earthquake last year, he'd found himself trapped in a small room until rescuers came, re-igniting a claustrophobia he'd had as a kid.

"I know it doesn't make sense," he said. "The meet-and-greet room at PLARG is a lot bigger than a broom closet."

She leaned forward and touched his hand. "Eric, what you went through last year was significant. Don't discount that. I'm sure others who were in that room with you still have nightmares, regardless of having any prior phobias."

"I don't know. Maybe. But what happened last weekend . . . That's never happened to me at a presentation before. It worries me. I even went to my therapist."

"And what did he say?"

"*She*. She said that it was just a setback. All the people in there, and the closed windows and doors probably triggered it."

He looked away, and rubbed his palm back and forth over the metal table in front of him.

"See? You're fine."

She thought again of how different Eric was from Will. So much accomplishment, but so little confidence.

He said, "You know we can't afford to botch our role at these fundraisers."

Eric Watson, like Val, worked at the Point Lobos Aquarium Research Group, or PLARG, pronounced by staff and local residents of Monterey Bay as if it rhymed with "large." At only twenty-seven, Eric already headed its Unmanned Underwater Vehicle Division because of his expertise in operating and maintaining the small, unmanned submarines—and in no small part because he had built his own prototype ROV, which had been the focus of his botched presentation last weekend. The ROV had proven so capable, despite the remotely operated vehicle's simplistic design and low production cost, that PLARG was now planning to build several identical models. But they needed funding first.

One of the most important parts of the Saturday fundraising event was having the scientists mill about with the crowd after the presentations, over wine and cheese. The casual conversations, fueled by a few alcoholic drinks, made the wealthy older couples feel comfortable talking science one-on-one with the young researchers—the men and women taking care of their oceans. The cocktail hour loosened their pocketbooks. That's when the money flowed.

Val said, "Next time, why not have someone simply man the doors? To make sure they stay open? I'd be happy to do it."

He nodded. "Yeah. I guess so. Say . . . why are you being so nice all of a sudden?"

"Because you're being too hard on yourself. But it's kind of cute."

He blushed, and she smiled.

The Saturday night PLARG presentations were especially important to Eric, whose position was funded entirely by grants. He'd done well at procuring funding on his own, upon completion of his master's degree here in Moss Landing a few years ago. The kid didn't even have a PhD, but he'd found the money right after graduating. As a freelancer. Oil companies in the Gulf needed inspections off a number of abandoned deepwater rigs, and Eric's self-designed ROVs offered a cheap and safe solution. Everyone at PLARG knew where that money came from, though, and some of the more left-leaning scientists still scoffed at Eric for profiting from the petroleum industry.

His ROVs offered advanced 3-D imaging sensors that allowed one to visualize underwater structures, like the rigs, and like the dams of deep reservoirs that he had next been paid to scan and measure in a larger project for a Swedish environmental firm. After that, PLARG had picked him up. The kid was clearly a cash cow for research. And now the rich philanthropists living around Monterey Bay were his bread and butter.

"Really, Val . . . why are you here?"

"I'm thinking of heading to the Bahamas, for a little private research. And I need another cave diver."

His smile disappeared. "You can't be serious."

She laughed. "I'm sorry. That wasn't funny. Really, though, I think you might be able to help me out."

He scratched his head. "You really can't think of another researcher? Maybe an actual *caver*? Or at least a certified scuba diver?"

"I'm not looking for a person to dive with me," Val said. "I'm looking for someone who is good with ROVs. You're the best sub operator out there, Eric. And your vehicle designs are perfect for caves—"

"Wait. Hang on. So you want to explore underwater caves, using an ROV?"

"Right."

"That simply isn't done, Val. It's too hard to remotely maneuver a machine through tunnels, when your camera only faces forward. Every time it's been tried, the machine gets stuck."

"Maybe. But what about your work on oil rigs? And in Mexico? You've had pretty good luck with that one ROV model . . . what's it called? Some girl's name."

He looked hurt. "Her name's DORA, Val. You know that. That's the same vehicle we used last year to film your school of squid."

Eric had lent other researchers at PLARG his assistance and vehicles for a few projects in the past few years, since he'd started work there. Although he specialized in 3-D and photographic imagery of underwater structures—oil rigs, sea mounts, cenotes—there were safety benefits to using an ROV to study more dangerous or remote undersea animals.

"Sorry, Eric. I wasn't very involved in that project, despite my name being on it. But I think you can do this. You *and* DORA." She smiled.

He frowned and took off his glasses. He was still clearly insecure around women. But she knew he found her attractive, and had purposefully worn a tight sweater and slacks, her citrus-smelling hair spilling onto her shoulders.

He said, "I've read about the blue holes there. In the Bahamas, I mean. Geochemical processes create these huge passages off each hole. Did you know they can sometimes extend *thousands* of feet into the substrate? To other blue holes, and even out to the ocean?"

"Yes. I just learned about them this week. And I'm impressed by how much you know."

He said, "I learned about them when looking for applications for my ROVs. There are like a thousand of them in the Bahamas alone, but only a quarter of them have ever been explored. Because it's too dangerous to dive them."

"But not for an ROV. You could be a pioneer on this, Eric. It could lead to more funding—"

"Well, I had already written them off as too difficult for my vehicles to operate in. But . . . I don't know." He thought for a moment. "I don't know. It would take time."

"I'm in no hurry," she said.

"I'd need to get to know the caves, and work on maneuverability. But if I get her stuck . . ."

"You won't."

"Can you pay to replace her if I do?" he asked.

"About that . . . this wouldn't be a salaried operation."

Eric laughed nervously. "This just keeps getting better."

"I'll provide the lodging, travel expenses, equipment, you name it. Except for the ROV, and your salary."

"All from your own pocket?"

She nodded. "It's like a free vacation. And a chance to test the limits of your ROVs."

"I'd only bring DORA. She's the best." He paused. "Does Rob even know about this?"

"No. Not yet." Val would have to talk to their boss later. "This isn't sanctioned by PLARG. Eric, let me back up. I told you I'm looking into what may be a new species of cephalopod. My hypothesis is based entirely on a single digital photo. Downloaded from the camera of two divers who went missing."

"Really? Are they dead?" He leaned toward her.

"Probably. Nobody knows."

"In a blue hole?"

"Yes."

He raised his eyebrows. "Like I said. Those holes are dangerous."

"They went missing in an inland hole on Andros Island. They were apparently exploring an arm off a main cavern, and never resurfaced."

"How does anyone know what happened, then?"

"Another dive team followed the safety lines in to where one had broken off six hundred feet into the tunnel they were in. . . . Look, Eric. I'm not an experienced cave diver. And I don't want to end up like them, or anyone else." She smiled at him. "But you and DORA can help keep me safe."

He blushed. "So you want my ROV to do the dangerous work. I get it. You also need samples? Oh-two? Salinity? Bottom composition?"

She shook her head. "Just footage. And 3-D images. I want to see if we can catch a critter on tape, and map the cavern contours. If you can get anything else, it's a bonus."

"So who else will be down there with us? No professional cavers, I guess. But at least someone to advise? Or help with logistics?"

She thought of her Uncle Mack, who last she heard

still lived somewhere near Tallahassee. The man who'd taught her to dive. They hadn't talked in years.

She said, "Nobody yet. But I'm working on it."

"Why not bring your boyfriend? He's a diver. You're still with him, right?"

"Sort of. I don't know. He's been dealing with some . . . issues. It's complicated. . . ." She felt herself redden, and ran her hands over her face, through her hair.

"Sorry. I didn't mean to pry."

"It's all right. So, are you in? It's a great opportunity. And you'd be in the *Baa-haaa-maaaaas*. Sun, warm water, girls. Better than the Central Coast in winter."

He smiled. "You should have gone into sales. *If* I agree to do this, when would you want me to start?"

"How fast can you pack your bags?"

CHAPTER 10

The massive submarine plain, divided by a broad trench, was unlike most abyssal depths. Tucked into the topography of an impossibly shallow, expansive bank on which ringing islands rested, the plain lacked a prominent presence of the creature's enemy—the larger, toothed leviathans that might seek even it as prey. Despite its formidable size, it sensed that, like all its living relatives, it was virtually defenseless against them in the open ocean.

As it blindly felt its way along the bottom, one of its snaking limbs made contact with a slow-moving, armored isopod lumbering along the bottom. It absent-mindedly snatched up the oversized, insect-like creature, passing it slowly up to its maw and tucking the morsel into its sharp beak.

The beak closed. The shell cracked.

But the proteins and fluids from the crustacean's body only made the creature hungrier. More impatient.

A curious and imaginative animal, it quickly became bored if not stimulated. Cruising through blackness but sensing nothing made it anxious. The pangs of hunger from its stomach increased.

A change in the current.

Chemicals, diluted in the flowing water, contacted its receptors. A cocktail of compounds. Wastes and secretions expelled by another animal. Not a dead one, although the organism sometimes scavenged on carrion littering the seafloor. No, this was living.

Prey.

It moved faster.

The scent was faint, and likely some distance away. In haste, the creature lifted off the bottom with a coordinated push of its limbs and contracted its balloon-like body, forcing a volume of seawater behind it as it jetted into the current. Prey was scarce. The animal it sensed ahead could not be overlooked once found. It felt its hearts momentarily cease to beat as its body contracted. It relaxed. It pulsed again, again stopping its hearts.

Swimming came at a cost. Its three hearts, working in concert to transport oxygen through its massive body, ceased to function with each expulsion of water. But it could move many times more quickly over short distances if it was free of the friction of the bottom.

In a rhythmic series of contractions, it hurtled forward into the light current, displacing tons of seawater with its huge form. Every few hundred feet, it ceased propulsion and drifted back toward the bottom, halting a temporary state of cardiac arrest and allowing its hearts to resume beating.

But it could not rest for long.

As soon as oxygen could replenish the cells in its brain and muscles, it pulsed forward again. The taste of prey continued to increase, driving it forward. It was shallower, up toward mid-water. The great organism angled upward.

A swirl of the current. In it, a much denser mingling

of fluids emitted by the animal ahead of it, and the organism again ceased propulsion.

It was close. *They* were close. Distracted, as they too hunted for much smaller quarry.

From the clicks emitted by the prey above, the creature sensed that there was more than one of them. Two, or more.

Its hearts quickened.

It infrequently encountered this, its prize prey. The animals were fairly large, though much smaller than itself. It had been weeks since it had come across them last. They were one of the only food sources that could now effectively sustain its great body.

It sensed the animals passing overhead, and gathering its muscular limbs beneath it, it thrust its body upward in the dark water. Jetting water to continue rising, it turned its expansive limbs above it and thrust them outward in all directions. Seeking . . . then finding.

Contact.

The tip of one arm struck something solid. The clicks in the water intensified.

The creature immediately twisted and thrust its body in that direction. It spun and plunged all of its limbs blindly toward where it had found the source of food.

But the prey had now become aware of its presence. Its arms swept the water desperately, and one of them again made contact with something. The limb reacted immediately, autonomously, coiling its tip around the undulating animal's smooth, tapered body. But the prey animal was powerful. It thrust its powerful tail flukes, and despite the deceptive strength of the organism's arm, the single limb could not maintain purchase on the thrashing body.

The prey escaped.

The organism lashed out its limbs, one final time, toward where it sensed the prey animals were rapidly departing. It swept the black water. *Nothing*.

The clicks faded. Then it was silent.

The prey was gone.

The creature relaxed its muscles, settling toward the bottom. Soon it again felt the cold current as it neared the unseen plain. It turned into the flowing water.

And continued to hunt.

CHAPTER 11

From inside a submerged metal room, Val watched pale shapes move past in the dark water. She was breathing through a regulator. The water was cold, dark.

Somebody was already gone. Someone she knew. *They* had taken him, his eyes bulging in terror.

And she would be next.

She exhaled through her regulator, the bubbles scrambling past her face as they hurried toward the surface far above. The ship around her groaned, its metal twisting as it struggled not to sink. She would never make it.

She realized she was holding something. Something small, wrapped in a blanket. An infant? But she was underwater—

A light. From above. It grew brighter. The shapes in the darkness retreated, and an urge to surface overwhelmed her. The light would keep her safe.

She lunged through the door. Kicked for the surface, holding tightly to the warm child in her arms. Exhaling as she ascended, she glanced down. Nothing was following her. She felt a pang of hope. She was going to make it.

The light winked out.

Inside her dive mask, Val's eyes widened. She was again surrounded by blackness, but now she was in open water. She kicked harder. The surface was just above her. In the dim, she could see the white line of froth where a wave was breaking against an object floating on the water—

Something touched her leg.

She recoiled, but her fin was torn away from her foot. She clawed at the water with her hands, reaching for the surface, desperate, and felt something close around her calf. She screamed into the regulator, pulling the child tightly to her chest. No, they would not take her baby. But then something wrenched at her midsection, and the child was gone.

Val's eyes popped open, her heart pounding in her chest.

She looked at the people around her, to see if anyone was staring, but they weren't. It was daytime, in the airport terminal. *Just a dream.*

She was at the Miami airport. Slouched in the row of blue vinyl seats at her gate, she'd fallen asleep. She looked up and saw that they just started boarding the flight.

She'd spent the last few days with her mom, who still lived in south Florida, in a retirement community now, with a man Val didn't like. She'd told her mom all about Will, and his problems, and asked for advice. *How did you deal with Dad?* she'd asked. Her mom, a gentle but weak woman, had simply said: *I just avoided him.* But Val wasn't an avoider.

It had been well over a year since she and Will had nearly died that night, in the deep ocean off Southern California, but Val still sometimes had nightmares. Who wouldn't, after what they'd been through? He'd helped her get through them. He'd been no stranger to many sleepless nights, and to years of nightmares, and he knew how to cope. There had been times when the man had actually known what to say to her.

She remembered how he had saved her. How they had saved each other.

But then, after the unexpected pregnancy, what even the doctor had called a miracle, and then the crushing blow of the miscarriage, things had changed. She couldn't keep using Will's past persona and actions, even if they were heroic, as an excuse to stay with him. Will Sturman was what he was. He was drinking again. He would always cope that way. And he would always dwell on the past. On Maria.

Outside the tidy new airport on Andros Island, a baggage handler helped Val's taxi driver maneuver a large box into the back of the van. They loaded the rest of Val's personal baggage, some of which spewed over into the backseat, and the handler nodded as Val handed him a few American dollars. He walked away, wiping sweat off his brow.

The subtropical summer heat hadn't arrived yet, but neither had the rain, and it was pleasantly warm in the Bahamas. Humid, but not damp. Just as it had been in Florida, with her mom. A sweet woman, but meek, she had never moved past the not so surprising early death of Val's father. Val had so little in common with her mom. But her mom's little brother, Val's Uncle Mack, was different.

"You ready?" the driver said.

Val blinked. "Yeah. Sure."

"How are ya today?"

"Good. How are you?"

"I have no complaints. Hop in." He smiled at Val, and she couldn't help but stare at the man's two upper canine teeth, jutting out past the others almost like blunt yellow fangs.

Inside the van, an ornate beaded cross hung from the rearview mirror, and a photograph of what appeared to be the driver's family was taped on the dash near his license. Otherwise, the van was quite clean.

"The Twin Palms, please," Val said.

His smile faded. "All right, den." He began to pull forward. "Welcome to Andros Island, my friend. First time?"

"Yes. First time in the Bahamas, actually."

"Well, you come to de best island. And de biggest."

Val had researched Andros before she left. Although politically recognized as one island, it was technically a hundred-mile archipelago with more overall land area than all the other Bahamas combined. Shaped like the conical part of some enormous, elongated conch shell, it was equally as hollow. Because of its limestone composition and the actions of water moving through it over eons, especially during the Ice Ages when sea levels were hundreds of feet lower, the island had as many holes running beneath its surface as a Swiss cheese. In fact, most of the Bahamas's blue holes were located on or near Andros.

Probably close to five hundred holes in all, between those offshore and the ones sunk into the island's surface. Those holes had made Andros an important stopover for privateers and slave ships, because rare sources of abundant freshwater accumulated almost daily in them, unmixed with the denser seawater below.

The snaggletoothed driver introduced himself as Mars.

"Like the planet?" she said.

"Yes. De big red one."

As he drove the van down a paved road fringed by dense, uniform greenery, he told her that despite Andros's size, its residents accounted for only about three percent of the population of the Bahamas. She wondered how much of their low-lying island might be lost in the coming decades, due to a rising sea level. Ford had explained that the urgency to explore the Bahamas's unique inland holes in particular—freshwater caves that led to saltwater deeper down, where they connected to the ocean through a network of tunnels—was not only because of limited funding, but because a rising ocean would greatly alter their water chemistry. Even a modest sea level rise would ultimately inundate these inland holes with pure seawater.

Mars said, "What you got in de big box?" He thumbed toward the back of the van, and then turned to look out the window as he merged into traffic.

"Scuba stuff."

"Ahhh. So you a diver, den. We still have alotta divers down here. Before Oceanus, dat about all we had for tourism. Dat and de bonefishin'. You diving our blue holes too?"

She wondered what he meant by "too." She said, "Yes. Some of them, anyway."

Mars reached cruising speed, driving on the left side of the road, despite the fact he also drove from the left side of the car, American style. Val figured it must be an American-made car, although these islands made up a former British colony. Cars headed the other way whizzed past her arm outside the window, just feet away on the narrow road.

"You will have much to see. Here on da island dere are tousands a dem holes. We call Andros 'The Sleeping Giant.'"

"Why?"

In the rearview mirror, Mars's eyes narrowed. "Because it lives. It breathes. It's alive."

Val smiled. "Is that supposed to scare me?"

He shrugged. "No. You look like a smart woman. Just don't do nuttin stupid, ya hear?"

"What do you mean?"

"You must know dem udda divers. Went missing a few weeks ago?"

"I know *of* them. Why?"

"I hope you not gonna dive where dey was."

Val didn't answer him.

The road turned south and ran parallel to the ocean. An ocean breeze through the open window played with Val's hair. The vibrant colors of the Bahamas were everywhere, with each low-lying cement or cinder-block house or building they passed—all designed to withstand hurricanes—painted a different color of the rainbow. Small churches dotted the route, nearly as numerous as the homes near the road. Nearly every business sign, whether a restaurant or auto shop, was hand-painted.

"Why are there so many broken-down cars?" Val asked, passing another pair of vehicles resting on cinder blocks outside a home.

"De roads. Dey bad, fulla sinkholes, and it's not easy to get parts here. But de roads getting better now dat Oceanus here."

The chatty taxi driver pointed out a good beach as they went by, brought up the best fishing guide (a relative), and named an inland hole he thought she should visit. Told her about how his daddy had worked in a lumber camp on the north side of the island. And he made a plug for Oceanus, the sprawling, world-famous resort built here several years ago. Val told him she'd be on the island for a month or so, probably until late February or early March.

Mars pointed out his window, toward the waterfront. "Dere's a good fish fry right down 'ere. Much cheaper dan de food at Oceanus. You gonna visit it?"

"Oceanus? Probably not. I'm here for work." Val already knew all about the resort. Built by some European tycoon, it had cost half his fortune to develop it.

One of her best friends from high school, whom she still kept in touch with, actually planned to take her family there this year. To Val, it had always seemed just an amusement park on a subtropical beach, except that it had casinos and other adult entertainment, and an impressive aquarium complex. But it was not the kind of place she would normally visit.

"I only been dare once, myself," Mars said. "Wit my kids. De resort gives us on de island a really good deal some a da time."

"Is that why Andros has the newer airport?"

Mars explained that a Greek named Sergio Barbas, the resort's owner, had largely paid for the airport himself, which now allowed many direct flights to Andros from Fort Lauderdale and Miami. Apparently, commercial travelers used to have to fly first to Nassau, then take a fifteen-minute flight to one of the airports on the island. Since the island was so broken up by water, and lacked the necessary bridges, it was important to fly into the right one. As the taxi neared an opening in the trees ahead, Val could see a trio of beige-colored towers rising from the edge of the island.

"Is that it? Oceanus?" she asked. "Those towers are huge." It looked to Val like they were rising right out of the ocean.

"Oceanus is built on a small cay just offshore," Mars said. "We use-ah call dat Chickcharney Cay, but dey renamed it 'White Sand Cay.' Tourists must like de sound of dat betta."

As they neared the towers, Val noticed that the hand-painted signs began to dwindle, replaced by newer businesses and some American franchises. It was starting to look more like Nassau. The taxi van slowed at a small traffic jam coming into a roundabout, and Mars honked the horn. A lot of traffic was headed down the road toward the bridges that led to Oceanus. Val looked out at a row of new shops and restaurants built near the roundabout. It was much cleaner here than some other island nations she had visited. A bougainvillea-like vine already clung to many of the new businesses' walls and fences.

Val said, "This is one of the problems with the new resort, right?"

"De traffic? Yeah, we never had no traffic here before. Now, all de time."

"I'll bet Andros used to be one of the quieter islands."

"Oh, yes. And one of de poorest," Mars said.

He honked again.

CHAPTER 12

A few miles south of Oceanus, the taxi turned off the paved two-lane road and onto a long, rutted drive raised on a bed of dirt and rock. They crossed a low, marshy area choked with stunted mangroves, most about the height of a man. Val was going to be the first to arrive at the place, since her uncle had called and said he'd been delayed. Something about airport security, and his prosthetic leg. Mack himself had recommended the lodgings, from many dive trips years ago, and had already set everything up. He knew the owners. She smiled. Having him here would be like having a free local guide. But she was still anxious about seeing him.

The taxi crossed a short bridge over the mangrove flat, interspersed by a patchwork of brackish water and one shallow channel of water where a culvert ran under the drive, and rounded a gentle bend in the dirt road before pulling up to the place. Val hadn't really known what to expect, but this wasn't any sort of hotel at all. More of a long, low, one-level house, which looked like it might have once been painted a bright yellow color higher on the pine walls. Hunks of coral were mortared together to form the lower half of the outer walls. Past the house she could glimpse the ocean.

"You sure this is the right place?" Val asked.

"Yeah, dis it. Twin Palms. Where de udda divers was staying."

"The other divers? The ones who died? They stayed here?"

"Lotsa divers stay here. When dey plan to be longer dan a week or two."

Val stepped out of the van and looked over the property. The house was shaded by a stand of tall, scraggly, Australian pines—non-native trees that could be seen growing everywhere in the overstory near the island's beaches. The wispy pines didn't actually look like pines at all, with clumps of limp, faded-green needles dangling from splayed branches. A small metal shed stood off to one side, and the front yard was composed of patchy, coarse-looking grass surrounded by sand. On the main building, a hand-painted sign suspended above the porch read Twin Palms Guesthouse. Val hadn't see any palm trees, besides a stunted clump of palmettos closer to the main road.

Val helped Mars unload her baggage at the edge of the drive.

He said, "You need anyting why you here, call me. I know everybody." He handed Val a card from his shirt pocket, then stepped into the van and slowly made his way out of the drive.

She stepped up onto the porch and tried the front door. It was locked. She sighed.

She rapped on it loudly, but nobody answered. She really wanted to change out of her jeans into some shorts. She glanced at her pile of luggage, and figured nobody could easily steal the heavier boxes. Besides, there didn't seem to be anyone around here anyway. She walked around the side of the house, toward the ocean, following a broad, sandy path lined with white hunks of coral, behind which grew native vegetation under sea grapes and other low trees.

She stepped up and over a waist-high wall composed of the same hunks of dead, white coral delineating the edge of the property and start of the beach. On a rocky outcrop behind the house, just before the beach itself, were two large coconut palms growing in a large V, both heavy with green fruit. The Twin Palms.

She smiled. Her home for the next month. A warm breeze touched her face, and she watched gentle waves lapping the white, sandy shore. She felt something in her awakening. Something she hadn't felt in a long time.

She looked back at the two trees, and her smile faded as she remembered Mars's words:

It's where the other divers were staying.

CHAPTER 13

Mack stepped off the blue-and-yellow mail boat and started down the dock. To Val he looked just as he always had, if a little older. The old Marine strode toward her, an air of self-assurance apparent in his posture, a heavy-looking duffle in each hand. If not for the narrow metal rod visible beneath the hem of his shorts, it would have been impossible to tell he had a handicap. But it was still odd to see him this way. Nearly all her memories of him were from when he had two good legs.

It was late in the afternoon in Fresh Creek, the sun hot on Val's back as she stood on shore, facing the water. Her uncle had just arrived with the mail coming over from Nassau. He had called her cell that morning, and had apparently reached New Providence last night, finding passage on some boat out of Florida.

Eric was already here with his ROV, DORA, and was back at the Twin Palms now. It wouldn't be long before they could actually get to work.

Mack smiled when he saw her waiting, and she waved. Alistair "Mack" McCaffery had once been her favorite uncle. He was the youngest of all her parents' siblings, always full of adventure and life. A wisecracking man, a blunt man, a soldier. To her, a hero.

But all that—the fun memories, the adventures he told her of, the cave diving, even his spirit itself, she thought—had been back before losing his leg in Iraq, more than a decade ago. Before losing a wife he'd been briefly married to. Before he'd become so bitter.

He'd taught Val to scuba dive when she was just a teen. He'd been an accomplished deep diver and cave diver, one of the rare few who even dared to explore many of the abundant springs and sinkholes in northern Florida. But he'd never taken his niece to any of them. Later, when she was in college, he had a few times mailed her pictures taken inside of caverns somewhere under the Bahamas. He'd be in the shots sometimes, with stalactites and stalagmites framed in the darkness behind him. Or he'd be diving off a colorful coral reef. Usually, the pictures were accompanied by a short letter, and Val had always been thrilled to receive them. She had saved every one.

She hadn't known until they talked last week that John Breck, one of the missing divers, had actually taken some of those shots. That he had been Mack's friend. When she got around to why she was calling, the already awkward call had become even more so, even though others in the dive community had already told Mack about the loss of the legendary Breck. But he hadn't hesitated when she'd asked for help. Just told her that he wouldn't be of much use.

Mack disappeared as he passed through a small building at the end of the dock, and then stepped out into the sunlight, squinting at her. Up close, she saw the familiar squashed nose. One of the toothpicks he liked to chew jutted from the corner of his mouth. His hair was no longer shaved short, and now bore a fair amount of gray. He smiled, and she saw some of the old spark in his eyes.

"How's my favorite niece?"

"It's good to see you, Uncle Mack." She hugged him tight.

He was only an inch or so taller than her, but at fifty was still built like a wrestler. He dropped his bags and embraced her, lifting her off the ground, as he used to. She felt a wave of emotion.

When he set her down again, she tried to take one of his bags, but he refused. "I'm not that old yet."

"Why did we wait so long for this?" she asked. "What's it been? Seven years?"

"Sounds about right." He grimaced, and looked down for a moment. "Listen, kid. I'm sorry about that. It's my fault—"

"Nonsense."

"No, hear me out. It is my fault. I'm your uncle. But you've always just been so busy. I figured you didn't need an old cripple around, bothering you."

"Don't say that."

"Well, hell . . . I don't know. I'm here now. It's good to see you, Valerie."

"Our cab's over here," she said, and started slowly toward Mars, Mack beside her. The snaggletoothed cab driver had become her go-to on the island.

She said, "Didn't you use to live here in the Bahamas?"

"Yeah," Mack said. "For a year or so, in the Abacos. The Out Islands."

"It must have been wonderful. Here on Andros anyway, the people are so friendly."

"Yeah. Wish I coulda stayed. It's one of the few places left you don't have to pay high taxes and the government doesn't screw with you. But by the time I actually moved here, I couldn't cave dive anymore." He tapped his leg. "My medical bullshit brought me back to the States. Enough about me. Any more word on Breck?"

"No."

"They've given up the search, haven't they?"

She nodded. "If this gets too hard for you to help me out, I'll completely understand."

"I wouldn't be here if I couldn't handle it. Breck was a good man. He and I dived in Florida together a couple times, maybe twenty years ago, and in some cenotes in the Yucatán. Also did a buncha blue holes in the Bahamas. In the Abacos, and here on Andros. He loved to dive. It was how he would've wanted to go."

Val had always thought her uncle would go in a similar way. She felt selfish for thinking it, but was sometimes relieved he'd lost his leg—because maybe it would keep him around longer.

"So how did you get held up in Miami?" she said.

"TSA wanted to take my leg off. Assholes could've just scanned it while it was still on me."

"I'm sure they were just doing their jobs—"

"It's not like I was wearing a fuckin' turban. Hell, they'd already swabbed me."

From what she remembered, his primary artificial limb was of a simple design, just a fake foot attached to a narrow titanium pylon and a molded socket that surrounded his knee-stump. She recalled that years ago he'd been asked to remove an earlier model so they could run it through the X-ray machine. He hadn't responded well then either. But that wasn't long after the war.

She said, "So, what happened this time?"

He scowled.

She shook her head and laughed. "Never mind. I won't even ask."

"Good. Let's just get to work, kid. Because we're gonna find out what happened if it's the last thing I do."

CHAPTER 14

"It's not gonna work," Mack said. "You're gonna get that fancy ROV stuck."

Eric tried to ignore the latest negative comment from Val's shirtless uncle. He'd only been there a day, but Eric could already tell that for some reason the guy didn't like him.

Alistair McCaffery was an angry-looking man who'd clearly broken his nose at some point in his life. He was older than Eric, and shorter, but thicker. He looked like a caricature of Popeye or Long John Silver, with his squinty face and missing leg, but he wore a white T-shirt and clamped a toothpick instead of a pipe in the corner of his mouth.

"ROVs don't work worth a damn in caves," Mack said. "Never have, never will."

Eric wanted to say something, but he couldn't find the right words. Instead, he took his glasses off and rubbed the lenses with the hem of his shirt.

"That's not true, Mack," Val said.

She stood near them at the water's edge, beside The Staircase. This was the "blue" hole (though Eric thought it was actually the color of green tea) where the divers had gone missing, and where somewhere deep inside, the image that led to this entire expedition had been captured. Some taxi driver named Mars had dropped them off on the side of the bumpy, unpaved road an hour ago. From the rutted roadside, they had navigated a rough trail about two hundred yards through brushy pine forest to the rock-rimmed mouth of the hole. It was circular in shape, maybe ninety feet across.

Val said, "Like I told you before, Eric has successfully operated this same ROV in a cave in the Yucatán. He used an umbilical there too, since he couldn't get a good signal to transmit."

"Two cenotes, actually," Eric said. "Last year. They were—"

"That's great, son." McCaffery glared at him from a sun-reddened face. "So your toy has been in a cenote before. A *cenote*. It's like a fucking underground swimming pool. Nothing like an inland Bahamian hole, full of restrictions."

Val moved closer to Eric. "Unbelievable," she muttered. "I come all the way down here, and I'm stuck with another Will Sturman."

Val's boyfriend had his own reputation, as a drinker and fighter. Eric smiled. But he also felt uncomfortable. Like he was stuck in some dysfunctional family's living room, being forced to watch them argue about domestic issues. Although Val seemed to share a bond with her uncle, they sure argued a lot.

"What did you say, Valerie?" Mack shouted over her shoulder.

"Nothing, Uncle Mack. Stop bullying us, will you? Why are you in such a foul mood, anyway?"

"Why? This plan ain't gonna work. That's why. You never told me when I signed on that we'd be using ROVs to explore caves. And Christ, there's only two of us, Val.

Heading into unexplored blue holes. No safety team. That's fuckin' crazy."

Val exhaled. "That's why we have the ROV, and Eric. So we don't need to go very far in. We've been over this, Mack. As long as we make sure to pull in the slack on the umbilical, the ROV shouldn't get hung up—"

"You realize one reason Breck and that other guy are dead is because there were only two of *them*? Because your friend, that cheap motherfucker Ford, didn't assemble full teams? With safety officers?"

Val's voice softened. "Is that what this is about? Breck?"

"What? No."

"Because he died here?" Val said.

Eric knew that her uncle and Breck had once been pretty close, and Mack had apparently even viewed the younger caving expert as a mentor of sorts. But Mack hadn't seen him in several years, since he'd given up on caving because of the awkward way he was now forced to swim. Val had said he now saw himself only as a liability to other cavers.

Mack said, "You know, that crazy son of a bitch could've remained calm standing on a rooftop, watching a tornado approach. He was the best I've ever known." He snorted. "But forget about him. He's gone now. I'm talking about our safety. *Your* safety."

He turned away from Val and stared at the surface of the pool his friend had entered, but never left. From above, it looked so tranquil beneath a pale blue sky. Eric suddenly felt sorry for Mack. He wondered if the guy was right. If this whole thing was a very bad idea. He walked over to Mack.

"Was he with you in Afghanistan?" Eric said.

Mack didn't turn to face him. "Iraq, not Afghanistan. And no. He wasn't even a Marine."

"You seem too old to have seen action in Iraq."

"Well, you seem pretty young to not be seeing action now." Mack spat into the water. He looked down at his prosthetic and cursed. "Fuckin' IEDs."

"I'm sorry about your leg," Eric said. It sounded so lame after he said it. Mack didn't respond.

After a few moments, the old Marine looked at him. "Dora. That's what you call your ROV, right?"

Eric nodded.

"Tell me, son, why does your machine have a girl's name?"

"Ever heard of 'Dora the Explorer?'"

"Huh?"

"She's a cartoon character. My niece loves her. That name just seemed to fit. But DORA actually stands for Deepwater Observation/Restricted Areas."

"You really think you can pull this off?"

Eric thought about his ROV, and all the hours he had logged on her. "I don't know. We'll see. Just make sure that you watch her umbilical. If it ever stops heading out for more than about a minute, start pulling back the slack. I'll do the rest."

Eric had always preferred to work alone, and tinker on mechanical devices. Growing up, his parents weren't around much. His father had travelled for business, and his mother always was heavily involved with the Church of Scientology. His siblings were all fairly older, so he was on his own. Took to reading lots of books, building models, and learning to fix things.

"There's no other way?" Mack asked.

Val said, "No. No other way. Not in the time we have."

Val and Eric had already visited the few local dive operations, asking about whether they'd ever seen anything with tentacles in an inland blue hole. None had. Their only lead was still a single dark, blurry image.

Mack turned back toward the water. "Well, for the record, I still say she's gonna get stuck."

CHAPTER 15

Will Sturman sat on a bench in the dim light of the public aquarium, on the visitor's side. He was hunched into the black wool peacoat he'd again started wearing since moving north up the coast. In front of him was one of the aquarium's mid-size tanks, maybe a few thousand gallons, its volume about that of a bathroom. It was dark inside the tank, and it appeared empty except for the rocky structure built into it, and a few shells on the bottom.

But this was his favorite tank.

And it wasn't empty.

Over speakers built into the walls, he heard the final announcement that the aquarium was now closed, asking anyone still in the building to leave. A moment later, two young boys ran past him, laughing, chased by their mom. Sturman grinned. Close behind them was Chuck, the security guard. He was a big guy, about Sturman's height, but thicker in the middle.

"Hi, Sturman."

"Evenin', Chuck."

"Back here again, huh? You must really like this one."

"Yeah. I do."

"You stickin' around for a while?"

"That okay?"

"Sure. Just let yourself out through the back. I gotta catch these people—"

"I know. Night, Chuck."

Chuck hurried around the corner, and Sturman was again alone. He removed his dark blue beanie and rubbed his stubbly head. In Monterey, in winter, the beanie suited him better than his cowboy hat. And fewer people looked at him funny. He never used to care, but lately he didn't want people looking at him.

He moved his hand down to gingerly touch his face. To remind himself why he needed to be here, and not at the bar. He still had a shiner under his left eye, but he'd had worse. A couple of fishermen had roughed him up a few nights ago. He'd probably deserved it. He couldn't really remember.

Val hadn't even asked where he had gotten the bruise. She had just glanced at him, as she was packing clothes into a suitcase, smiled sadly, and said, *Again?* Then she had gone back to her packing.

And now she was gone. There was a part of him that felt relief. If she wasn't in his life, he wouldn't ever feel the pain of losing her.

He knew he probably needed some sort of help. But asking for it? Accepting it? That was another thing. He could sort this out on his own.

Off work now and showered, he'd decided to linger at the aquarium. It was raining outside, and he didn't have the energy to go to the boxing gym he used to frequent. He hadn't for a while. With Bud dead now, the animal in the tank in front of him was the closest thing he had to a friend. His dog had died so unexpectedly. He'd been getting a little older, and had a little white under his chin, but was still so spry and muscular. He'd loved running with Val and their trips to the dog beach. He'd been Sturman's best friend for years, and had never once judged him. And now he was gone, leaving a huge void.

Sturman stared into the tank, imagining himself floating inside. This was the best time of day to see this one, even if his keepers weren't feeding him yet. As if on cue, Sturman thought he saw something move in the darkness of the tank.

"Hi there, Oscar."

He stood and walked over to the aquarium, bent down to look into the tank. He tapped the tank lightly. It looked empty again, except for the rocks on which clung a few colorful anemones, and a section of pipe.

"You awake yet, amigo?" Sturman said quietly.

He waited. He wasn't positive he had seen the animal move before, but he was sure he was hiding somewhere in the tank. Not likely he'd escaped again. After the last time, they'd made adjustments to the lid of the tank. Sturman looked around to make sure he was still alone.

"I got into a fight again. I knocked one of those fellas down, but there were two of 'em. Got my ass kicked this time. But nowhere near as bad as that number your cousins did on me a few years ago." He rolled his shoulder around, checking its stiffness. He still had chronic pain from those injuries.

He leaned his head forward, against the cold glass. "Hopefully, I didn't hurt that other guy too bad. The one I took out. I think I mighta started the whole thing."

He remembered, as kid, how it felt to tell his dad about when he'd gotten in a scrap. How his dad would be upset, but he could tell he was also a little bit proud. Especially if Will had stood up to a bully. Maybe he'd gotten some respect for the family. He'd been a fighter his whole life. Except for when he was with Maria. She had calmed him.

Sturman tapped the tank again, searching for Oscar. He usually only became active at night. And when they fed him.

He remembered the *Superfriends* poster on the wall over a fish tank he'd had in his room as a kid. His mom had given it to him for Christmas, before she'd died, since it was the only one she could find with Aquaman on it. He had known the other kids didn't much like Aquaman, and his orange and green costume *was* kind of goofy. But Sturman had thought he had the coolest powers of all. He could breathe underwater, and he could control all the animals in the ocean without even talking. That suited the quiet country boy, whose favorite book was *Twenty Thousand Leagues Under the Sea*, just fine.

"What do you think, Oscar? If I was a superhero, would you wanna be my sidekick? 'Cept then I'd need to call you Tonto—"

"Who you talking to, Sturman?"

Sturman started. Chuck was standing behind him.

"Nobody." Sturman put his beanie back on and moved over to the bench.

Chuck looked at him a moment, then walked off.

Sturman spied movement at the top of the tank. Feeding time. He smiled.

He heard a quiet *tap-tap-tap* as the keeper on the other side rapped the tank three times, as he always did before feeding Oscar. He watched as a thawed shrimp plunged into the water, waved around on the end of a skewer near the end of the narrow pipe. After a minute,

Sturman saw Oscar start to appear. He made sure nobody was around before speaking toward the tank again.

"You get to eat early today, huh?"

Something wriggled out of the end of the pipe, and Sturman smiled.

This animal was *always* hungry.

CHAPTER 16

Cicadas chorused in the warm night as the four teenagers hurried through the bush. The narrow, rough
path wended over the crumbled rock surface through the
scrubby brush, cutting the shadows of tall pines, before it
finally opened as they reached the last few yards of trail.

Moonlight gleamed off the elevated, rocky rim cir-
cling the dark pool of water, and illuminated the sentry-
like pine trees ringing the broad hole. But there were no
artificial lights on this part of the island, no dwellings.

There were other blue holes frequented by tourists,
closer to the road and with wooden walkways running
out to them, ladders built into the rock to make it easier
to get out of them. Why couldn't they just go there?

But Selena already knew why the boys had wanted to
come here, to this remote spot. For the same reason that
motivated everything boys did.

She watched as Timothy tossed a blanket down near a
clump of brush. He grabbed her friend Reghan's hand
and pulled her down next to him, and she giggled as he
rolled on top of her.

"Ouch!" she protested. "Dem rocks is pokin' me."

"Ain't da rocks pokin' ya, girl."

Selena rolled her eyes and looked at her own boyfriend, Daniel. He was smiling at her.

"Wanna go in the water?" he asked. He was tall and lean, his hair long and coiled into matted dreadlocks.

"I don't know, Daniel. Is it cold?" she said. She suddenly felt scared. Maybe they shouldn't have come here.

Daniel looked down at her, his dark eyes shining in the pale light. "No. It'll feel good."

But she wasn't hot, even after the short hike and despite it being an unusually warm February night. Like almost every night had been since New Year's.

"Haven't you ever swam here?" he said.

"No."

He reached his hand out. "C'mon, girl. We should at least give my homeboy some privacy."

She crossed her arms over her chest. "My nana always said not to swim here. That it's dangerous."

When she was growing up, Story Time legends often were about creatures living on the island. Ground-dwelling owls three feet tall that ran through the forest, other animals that stole things from careless children or reported bad deeds to parents. And of things much worse than that, dwelling in its blue holes.

But they all were ridiculous. Just tales to scare children. Still . . .

"Your nana says *I'm* dangerous." His white teeth flashed as he smiled. "You're not really scared, are you? C'mon."

She hesitated. She didn't want to disappoint him. "Maybe for just a minute," she said.

They stripped down to their underwear, dropping their clothes in two piles on the porous stone that formed a ledge rising several feet over the water. She hesitated as she watched Daniel tiptoe over the jagged rock and leap eagerly out over the pool, making a loud splash as he en-

tered. He must have already known it was deep enough
here. Or else he was just taking stupid risks to impress
her.

He was treading water, waiting.

"How will we get back out?" she said. She didn't
think she could pull herself up the steep, sharp-edged
rock. The water level looked to be almost ten feet below.

"There's a spot right over here where it's easy to climb
out," he shouted. "I promise, Selena. It feels good."

She glanced back toward their friends, but quickly
looked away. They were already very busy. Shameless.
Reghan would be big up soon if she wasn't careful, and
then she'd have to marry the boy. She wondered if
Daniel expected the same of her tonight.

She looked back at the water and realized he had
kicked farther away from her.

"Wait, Daniel!"

She winced as she crossed the sharp rocks in bare
feet, then found a notch in the rocky ledge and eased
herself down closer to the water. Beneath her feet the
rock dropped straight down another few feet before disappearing into water.

"Are you sure it's safe?" she whispered.

"Except for the sharks," he laughed.

"Shut up, Daniel!" She looked down into the blackness. "There aren't really sharks in here, right?"

"It's mostly freshwater. No sharks here."

She jumped into the water. It was cool enough to give
her goose bumps. She swam toward Daniel.

He moved toward her and kissed her lightly. "I'll keep
you safe. C'mon, let's swim to the other side."

"But it's so far away . . ."

"It's not as far as it looks. There's a nice beach on the
other side."

She doubted there was any beach by this remote inland pool, where the landscape was composed of only exposed rock and clumped vegetation.

He said, "Follow me."

She swam after him, toward the middle of the pool.

It had not eaten for days.

It slid its great bulk through the narrow submarine tunnels, the water around it acting as a lubricant for its tons of flesh to pass. Methodically, patiently, like an earthworm tunneling through soft soil, it forced the front end of its body into the tunnel ahead, then anchored itself in the rock to drag the trailing end of its body and remaining limbs forward before repeating the process.

The quality of the water was different here, becoming slightly more toxic. This was no longer ocean water. It was becoming something else: the water that burned.

The huge organism would not be able to proceed much farther, as its gills and organs would begin to absorb too much of this strange water, bloating it and diluting its own internal chemistry, eventually killing it. But its ravenous need and innate curiosity drove it to examine the branching tunnel until it was forced to turn back.

For many hours, it had moved deeper into the caverns, away from the sea. Exploring. Resting. Exploring again.

And now, hunting.

It relied on taste, on touch. Its eyesight was functional but often ineffective when and where it was most active—in the darkness of the deep ocean—and in the lairs where it slept during the daylight hours. Rarely was it able to find food within these caverns, but the open sea had not provided. So it had entered the caverns. At times, they had led to unexpectedly productive nooks elsewhere on the reef. And it had been successful when prey had entered its own lair recently. Possibly there was more of this prey in the tunnels under the island.

Something moved past its eye.

The organism realized it had only noticed its own slithering arm. But it had *seen* it. Its eyes were beginning to detect dim light trickling into the tunnel from some-where ahead.

The passageway soon began to expand, faint light fil-tering down from above to reveal the vertical contours of a broad pool. The organism spread its extensive ap-pendages into the chamber, each wriggling in the dark-ness along the rough rock surfaces in a mindless search for prey.

There.

Something in the water above. A taste, a vibration, a *signal*. This was the same unusual prey it recently had fed upon. Reaching silently upward, it slowly guided its appendages into the pool, toward the surface, seeking. Feeling.

Tasting.

"We're almost there," Daniel said.

Selena felt uneasy so far from shore. The hole was much bigger than she had thought, and despite Daniel's encouragement, the other shore was still a short distance away. She knew the blue holes of Andros could also be very deep, and nobody really knew what was down in them. And she was starting to feel cold.

"I don't like this, Daniel." She was breathing hard, but not from exertion.

"Look. The beach is right there."

"I'm gonna head back."

She stopped swimming, began treading water, unsure

of what to do. They were close to the other side of the pool now, but she wasn't feeling very romantic anymore. Daniel *was* really sweet. He had been good to her. But, like the other boys, she knew he would have only one thing on his mind once they were alone on shore. She wasn't sure if she was ready.

Daniel turned and started swimming back toward her. She looked away from him, gauging the distance back toward where her clothes were.

"Selena, if you're worried about—" His last word was cut off by a small splash.

She turned around. He was gone.

"Daniel, stop it." She looked around, waiting for him to surface. She bit her lip. "I mean it. This isn't funny."

Daniel was a prankster. She looked down, wondering if he was planning to swim toward her and grab her. She could make out her legs in the light of the waxing moon, scissoring underneath her. But otherwise it was dark, too deep to see anything. She waited, but Daniel didn't grab her legs. Didn't surface. Could he have swum to the near shore? Maybe he was hiding by the rock ledge there.

"I'm going back," she shouted.

She knew he wouldn't be able to hear her underwater, but he had been under for thirty seconds now. Maybe longer.

"I mean it! Daniel? Daniel!"

After a minute, he still didn't surface. She began to feel sick. He couldn't hold his breath this long, could he? And something bothered her, almost as much as not being able to see Daniel anywhere. A feeling.

She felt panic rising in her, and tried to calm herself. To fight the suddenly overwhelming urge to swim to shore. Any shore. To get out of the water. But was he stuck underwater? Trapped? She took a deep breath and swam tentatively toward where she had last seen him, looked down again. *There.* She could finally see the bottom rising up. It was still quite deep.

She scanned the bottom beneath her. Had it been this shallow all along? The moonlight glowed off the textured surface. It looked sort of like—

Selena felt a sense of vertigo, her mind trying to process how she was somehow moving. *No.* It was the bottom that had moved.

The entire surface beneath her shifted sideways. Glided. Something was again moving under the water. Rising. Something impossibly big.

There was a great churning in the pool beside her, and in it a dark mass floated to the surface and swirled toward her. Dreadlocks. Several of them, seemingly still attached to a piece of scalp, but nothing more.

She gasped and kicked wildly away, then turned facedown and swam for shore, not coming up for air, fighting harder than she ever had in her life. Because she knew. Knew what had done this to Daniel and what was coming for her now. It was the demon of her childhood nightmares.

It was the *lusca*.

PART II
THE TONGUE
OF THE OCEAN

CHAPTER 17

They'd lost another hydrophone.

Several of the seafloor devices in the grid had failed lately. One had even been destroyed by something. This was practically becoming routine.

Lieutenant Commander Tom Rabinowitz sat in a darkened room, in a row alongside several other naval personnel. All wore matching service khakis and audio headsets. A few of his colleagues spoke quietly into their mouthpieces, but otherwise the room was silent.

In front of them was a wall covered in monitors, with images ranging from cloud-swept satellite views of the Bahamas to black-and-white feeds from undersea cameras to updating screens of radar sweeping the ocean surface. He glanced at one black-and-white monitor—a feed from an ROV-mounted camera. The vehicle had been deployed to gather data on the most recently failed seafloor hydrophone. One located near an old naval shipwreck, more than 3,000 feet down.

Rabinowitz's duties at the Navy's Atlantic Undersea Test and Evaluation Center, located on Andros Island's east coast, were relatively benign—and usually very boring. He was charged with tracking all in-water observational data and writing up daily summary reports for the higher brass. Vessels of interest, deepwater weapons testing, research-oriented video feeds, weather anomalies. He tracked it all. And if anything ever merited an immediate inquiry, which was rare, he had to run it up the flagpole. That was it.

When he joined the Navy, he'd briefly travelled the world on a ship, trying to tag along with crewmates like Will Sturman and Joe Montoya as they raised hell. But he'd quickly been placed on a techy path. For more than a decade now, he was usually cooped up in a windowless room staring at computers. Now that he had a family, it was kind of nice to work something more like a nine-to-five. But it was usually dull—except for rare events.

Like finding your hydrophones, thousands of feet underwater, destroyed by an unknown culprit.

It used to be the cookiecutter sharks. The little bastards would latch on to anything soft on the devices— neoprene covers, rubber cable sheathings— and gouge out hunks with their serrated teeth. But after the Navy figured out the culprit, they'd added fiberglass or other protective covers to vulnerable areas. He thought of the last failed hydrophone in the grid. That damage wasn't from any small cookiecutter shark.

He was part of an important project involving the use of a massive hydrophone array in TOTO—naval slang for the Tongue of the Ocean. The Navy had been doing very interesting things in TOTO for decades.

He thought about the beaked whales that had most recently washed ashore, a few weeks back. Within days of their last test run. But even the biologists who were supposed to be kept apprised of all sonar testing, ever since the Navy had admitted involvement in the first whale strandings many years ago, were not aware of this latest research.

The government would deny involvement, like it usually did, if anything bad happened. It would continue to do so, until there was too much evidence to dodge the bullet.

But he knew there was no coincidence here. He knew the whales were dead because of whatever the Navy was now testing here. And he wondered what other effects the novel sonar frequencies were having on ocean life in the Bahamas.

He again looked at the black-and-white ROV feed. Lieutenant Menendez sat next to him, focused intently on the screen. She usually piloted the unmanned crafts, which involved mostly looking at nothing, and guiding them more from GPS coordinates than video feed. Rarely did they see any life on the cameras when the vehicles went down to make repairs, because so little could survive in the cold, crushing pressure at the bottom of the trench. They usually just saw water, and a largely featureless ocean floor.

But some things did live down there.

Just before the last hydrophone failed, it had captured an unidentified sound, thought to be natural in origin, before something made contact with the device itself and disabled it. When an unmanned submersible had been sent down to assess the hydrophone—one of many in the network that formed a grid on the bottom of the mile-deep trench—its camera had again captured something unusual. On its way in, just before it arrived at the hydrophone. Not a juvenile-delinquent whale, or a Chinese spy submarine, but in the soft sediments thousands of feet down, there had been what appeared to be some sort of broad, faint trail on the bottom. He'd seen one in their footage before. Thick skid lines, with small dots on either side. As though some sort of lightweight, incredibly broad sled had been dragged through the soft snow of sediment by a pair of giant children. But they didn't know what it was.

And the hydrophone had been pulverized. As if *crushed*.

When the ROV had gone back several days later to install a replacement hydrophone, the wide trail had already faded significantly in the turbidity current of the trench. The current had deposited fine sediments in the depressions, covering most of the track. If the obvious skid line filled in that quickly, it meant something had made it very recently—most likely when the hydrophone had been disabled. And if it was something the Navy owned, nobody was telling him.

Based on GPS data, the ROV would be arriving at the failed hydrophone at any moment.

"Check this out, Wits," Menendez said. "There's that track again."

She was right. It was less discernable than the last time, but on the screen was a recently dredged, broad trench in the soft sediments. With similar depressions dotting the bottom on either side. The trench dropped off the screen as the ROV nosed up and headed for the hydrophone.

"How big is it?" he asked.

"Pretty big. Those marks on the sides? They range in size, but some are maybe a meter or more across."

"What the hell do you think made that?"

She shook her head. "I don't know. But I'm sure it was whatever did this."

Something came into view on the screen. The motionless object looked like a small car that had been in a very bad accident—the sort that no longer even looks like a car after a horrific collision—before sinking to the ocean floor.

Like the last one, the hydrophone housing on the screen was demolished.

CHAPTER 18

Gentle waves lapped the sugary-white beach beneath the coconut palms. Offshore, above the distant horizon, the orange rays of the morning sun backlit a long cloud bearing a flat bottom and jagged top, a heavenly, upside-down saw blade cleaving sea from sky. Even the air smelled clean.

It would have been a beautiful scene, if not for the dying whales.

Over the past week, Val had been diving under her uncle's tutelage, mainly in a single, well-explored, shallower blue hole. While Eric tinkered with his ROV and practiced piloting it out of their way, Mack was showing her the ins and outs of cave diving—how to dive with a lot of extra equipment and multiple tanks, how to maneuver without stirring up sediment in caverns, how to feel your route, how to manage lines.

Safety lines were critical in cave diving. She had learned to lay and follow a spooled nylon line, to use secondary lines whenever leaving the main line, and to retrace those lines back to the thicker main if needing to turn around. And they worked on proper line laying, to avoid entanglement, and what to do if you did snag one. Even for Val, a highly experienced scuba diver by anyone's standards, it was all very new, very different, and even very intimidating. The added gear alone, from tanks to spools to lights, highlighted the risk.

Mack had blindfolded her yesterday, and made her find her way to a main line using a series of short excursions in different directions, until she found the main line and followed it out safely by feel alone, using plastic arrows affixed to it that pointed in the right direction. The drill was designed to mimic the conditions in a cave if all lights were lost or so much sediment was stirred up that visibility became nil. After that drill, she decided to take a day off. She'd risen early and gone running, and after just the first mile ran into the commotion on the beach.

Still trying to catch her breath, Val knelt by one of the smallest ones in the pod, likely a calf. Next to Val were several others who had joined in to help, including a young woman who, like her, appeared to be out for an early morning run.

The group had gravitated to this particular whale for its small size—and the fact that it was still visibly alive. Each time a wave had climbed up the beach to meet it, they had tried to roll it back into the water. Without success. And the tide was going out.

Time was running out.

Four larger whales, small by whale standards but each probably fifteen feet long and weighing a ton or more, dotted the beach nearby, where they had apparently stranded themselves overnight. Groups were gathered around a few of those animals as well. They appeared to be having no better luck moving them back into the sea.

"Heads-up, everyone!" the other runner shouted. She was an attractive Bahamian, tall with an athletic build. She seemed to know what she was doing, and Val had allowed her to take charge. She seemed to know some of the others in the water with them. Even an older man with gray-speckled hair who looked like he might be a banker followed her lead, as did a plump woman who panted beside him.

"Ready, everyone . . ." the runner said.

A long wave rolled up the beach, washing around the ten-foot whale and splashing Val's bare legs below her running shorts.

"Now!" the woman shouted. They heaved against the animal's smooth body.

It moved.

The calf inched down the beach, following the wave back toward the sea, before settling into the sand.

As the next wave hit, Val leaned her shoulder against the whale, soaking her tank top and shorts, hoping the momentum they generated wouldn't stop this time. These were the biggest waves they'd seen in ten minutes, but she knew how hard it was to try to free even a beached dolphin. With the others pushing beside her, the semi-buoyant, thousand-pound animal began to lift off the sand in the slightly deeper water. The group splashed behind it as they managed to float it out past the shore break. Cheers began to erupt from other people on the beach.

Val was up to her waist in the water now, her drenched white top flattened against her chest. She whipped the wet tip of her long ponytail out of her face and helped the others turn the whale's body, directing its head out toward the sea. And then they stepped back and waited.

The whale began to roll over onto its back.

The Bahamian runner lunged forward, Val behind her, and they tried to grip its smooth skin, to prevent its body from rotating.

"We can't let this girl roll over," the woman said. "Her breathing hole needs to stay above the water."

"I know," Val said.

Near her face the whale's small, cow-like eye met hers. It hardly appeared to be seeing her. Only she and the other runner were still struggling with the whale. She glanced behind her. The others simply stood back, resigned to the whale's fate as the two women struggled against the slow turn of the calf's body. They didn't understand the situation, or didn't care enough.

"Help us, Jeffrey! Please!" the runner shouted at the older man and a woman who might have been his wife.

The others slowly stepped in again beside them, starting with the older couple. Together, they all managed to keep the small whale's blowhole above water for a few minutes. But it didn't respond. The animal simply refused to move. To fight for its life.

One by one, the people began to step away.

They stood in the shallow water, panting, too exhausted to continue. The calf remained rolled onto its back. The waves were pushing it back toward the beach. Only the tall Bahamian woman remained by its side, trying to roll it upright with each wave.

Val finally placed a hand on the woman's shoulder. "It's too late for this one," she said.

The runner shrugged off Val's hand, then glared at the others. "Don't you all understand? If we don't help her, she's going to die!"

Val squatted beside her. "Look. What you're doing is admirable. But I know what I'm talking about. There's nothing we can do now."

The runner turned away, moved her hand soothingly

over the whale. After a few moments, she stood, and Val followed. They stepped back, watching as a wave carried the animal gently back toward the beach.

Val knew what was going to happen. She had seen this before. But she didn't want to watch it die on the sand. It, and its family.

She looked out past the whales, over the ocean. Under the saw-blade cloud, dark splotches of sea grass growing on the shallow bottom broke up the shimmering expanse of aquamarine water, which farther out yielded to the deep ocean beneath. There, visible from shore where the water turned a profound blue, the Great Bahama Bank abruptly ended and deep water began.

"The Tongue of the Ocean," the runner said, as if reading her thoughts. "That's where a lot of these whales live."

"Yes. I've read about it," Val said.

The undersea feature—a mile-deep trench off the east coast of Andros Island and wedged between the shallow banks of the Bahamas islands—was like nothing else on earth. Its beautiful, protected waters offered unique and magnificent sea life, like these beaked whales, and drew the scuba divers and other tourists here that fueled the economy.

"It's their undoing," the runner said.

"What do you mean?"

"The trench. These whales wouldn't be here without it. But it serves other interests, you know. Interests that are bad for the whales."

"You mean the Navy? Its sonar research?"

The woman nodded.

"I thought they had stopped all that, though," Val said. "After all the bad publicity. You think it may have affected these whales?"

"I know it did." The runner looked down at her. "How do you know about the naval research here?"

Val smiled. "I read a lot."

For decades, US Navy warships and research vessels had apparently plied the waters over the Tongue of the Ocean, stationed out of the base at Fresh Creek, farther up the coast. It wasn't those ships themselves that were of concern, although Val knew all about shipping vessels ramming into and killing full-grown whales in other parts of the world. It wasn't the Navy's weaponry either. It was something else. Something you couldn't see.

Sonar.

The Tongue of the Ocean concealed a broad, U-shaped undersea depression 150 miles long and almost completely protected from the open ocean. Hundreds of islands and reefs, and the banks that provided a platform for them, apparently sheltered it from background noises carried across the Atlantic that could complicate undersea testing. And the submarines and listening devices of other governments would not be able to easily detect the sound waves generated by the Navy's own research activities.

The woman said, "The first time the whales washed up dead was the fall of 2000. I was just a young girl." Her accent had faded now, and she spoke in very American English.

"Beaked whales, right?"

"A lotta people speculated about the cause, but it was years before the Navy finally admitted its testing probably disrupted the whales' behavior. But we too thought they'd stopped."

"Don't they have to disclose any testing now?"

The runner shook her head. "When I was a teenager, they started allowing researchers to come to the base in

Fresh Creek. They said the goal was to learn more about the effects of sonar on Blainville's whales, like these. The Navy still says they let them offer input, to prevent more accidents. And they've promised to stop using whatever caused the other strandings. But there have been more dead whales."

"Maybe it's something else," Val said.

"Maybe." The woman smiled at Val. "I'm sorry I was rude before. It's just that—"

"No need to apologize."

"No, really. I just get passionate about this. It's happened before." She reached out her hand. "I'm Ashley. Ashley Campbell."

"Valerie Martell."

"You here on vacation?"

"Not really. I'm here for work."

"How do you know so much about Andros? About these whales?"

"It's related to my own work. I'm a marine scientist. Do you want to grab a cup of coffee? I'll fill you in, and maybe you can help me out too."

Ashley glanced at her watch. "Maybe if we hurry. I have to be at Oceanus by nine. I work there. Are you staying with us?"

"No. A guesthouse called the Twin Palms."

Ashley nodded. "You're a diver, then."

"Yes. I do research."

The cloud offshore, which now resembled a long battleship, hovered indifferently over the ocean. Ashley turned away from the water and the whales, and smiled at Valerie.

"Let's go get that coffee," Ashley said "So we can get warm. And you can tell me about what you're doing here."

The women turned and walked back toward the road. They didn't look back at the whales.

CHAPTER 19

Mack knelt in the shallow, tea-colored water at the edge of the pool, in full scuba gear. In the hole that had swallowed Breck.

He and his niece were rigged for caving, with European-style DIN first-stages that allowed them to tightly secure their regulators instead of loosely mounting them to their tanks. A bump to a more standard A-clamp inside a cave might knock it loose. They also were laden with extra everything—extra lights, two tanks, extra masks—all redundancies in case something failed in a cavern far from the surface. They would be breathing lower-nitrogen Trimix gas instead of regular compressed air. From the rutted roadside, they had lugged all the gear a few hundred yards down a rough forested trail, over jagged, lumpy ground, to the rock-rimmed hole.

He had grown irritable waiting for Eric to fire up his yellow ROV, kneeling awkwardly in the water at the mouth of the hole, his prosthetic leg removed. Valerie had already gone under, and he was struggling to keep the weight off his stump, which was planted on the rocky shelf at the edge of The Staircase.

Resting in the water next to Mack, like a dog on heel,

was DORA. At just over four feet long, she was the smallest ROV he had ever seen. On her side was a rubberized rectangular keyboard, the keys touch-sensitive and flush with the exterior. Otherwise, the housing was smooth and nondescript. She lacked the external arms and other apparatus that most ROVs possessed, but on her stern low-profile thrusters and an umbilical—which provided power and data transfer capabilities—still jutted from the sleek body. They were the potential snag concerns.

DORA's simple design and small size apparently allowed for maneuverability in tight spots, but whether she would work here would largely depend on the skill of the operator.

"I just want to make sure you fully understand how DORA operates, and our protocols, before you go under," Eric said. "Once you and Val are down there—"

"Valerie's already down there."

"I know. Once you're both under, we won't have any way to communicate, other than texts on the keyboard."

Wading knee-deep in the water, Eric bent down and carefully lifted the ROV off the bottom, her weight now supported by the water and a built-in buoyancy. He pointed inside the clear acrylic nose cone.

"DORA only has two ways of gathering information: the camera, which allows me to see where she's headed and gathers high-res video footage, and the sonar mapping device. Both are located in her nose, along with low-wattage LED lighting."

"We've already gone over this."

Eric ignored him. "The sonar device can create high-res imagery of every underwater feature, regardless of light levels, using multidirectional scanning to create 3-D point clouds. Which results in me later being able to re-create an underwater scene—"

"Blah blah blah."

". . . but we don't need much light, because the camera is designed to film in darker environments. The rest of the housing contains batteries for power and the motor to drive the prop. Any physical samples Val wants—water, biological specimens, sediments—will need to come from you two, and it will help if you can also note the actual depths of specific features—"

"Got it."

Eric said, "Come on, man. It'll really help if you can record depth markers, like the entrance to any main tunnels. To help me calibrate the 3-D imagery."

Mack looked at his watch. "Look, son, I got it. Time to shit or get off the pot." He grabbed the top of the ROV and roughly spun it in the water.

Eric shouted, "Hey! What are you doing? That's a very sensitive piece of equipment!"

"It was pointed the wrong way."

"Well, at least you're patient."

"I don't need your sarcasm," Mack said. "Is she ready or isn't she?"

"She's ready."

Mack raised his hands toward the sky. "Halle-fucking-lujah!" He turned, pushed his regulator into his mouth, and started to dip underwater. He stopped and spit out his regulator, and looked at Eric one last time.

"Twenty bucks says you get DORA stuck," he said.

"You're on. But not if it's because you forget to retract the cord—"

Mack didn't hear the rest as he ducked under.

As Mack submerged, the sound changed immediately, his breathing punctuated by the loud hiss of air coming in or bubbles going out.

He kicked past the shallow shelf of rock, and could

see his niece through the slightly green murk, hovering in open water twenty feet below, looking up at him. Valerie had become one hell of a good scuba diver, after all her research in Mexico. Unlike him in only a three-mil neoprene shorty, she'd worn a full wet suit again, since she cooled faster than her uncle. Mack dumped the air from his BC and kicked down toward her. Halfway there, he looked back. Eric's legs were no longer visible, where he stood at the edge of the shelf above and fumbled with the ROV.

Mack and Val continued their descent toward the bottom of the hole. A few moments later, the yellow ROV followed. Eric had remained in place to operate her, like a child playing with an RC car. The kid was able to operate the ROV's propulsion and steering system using a waterproof remote control wired into the umbilical.

It was a relief to have only Valerie with him down here. She knew what the hell she was doing underwater, and she had wonderful buoyancy control. A must for cave diving. Eric clearly wasn't a cave diver, but his ROV had the lead role. The divers had been relegated to mere chaperones, charged with making sure DORA was directed to the right place.

As they sank farther from the surface into the pool, the water began to change. Around forty feet down, they encountered a cloudy, motionless layer of water. Hazy and whitish, tinged with yellow, it looked like the thin mats of cotton fibers Mack's mom had strung into Halloween spider webs around the house when he was a boy. But these webs indicated a poisonous cocktail of toxic hydrogen sulfide gas excreted by bacteria and decaying organic matter, trapped between the freshwater above and seawater below. It was impossible to see past the layer, but unlike the cotton webs he passed right through, not feeling them at all.

The motionless water in this hole, like in other inland blue holes in the Bahamas, was density-stratified into what Mack had earlier described to them as a layer cake, with little mixing due to the lack of a strong tidal influence. At the top of the cake, he had explained, nearest the surface, floated the least-dense layer of freshwater, fed by tropical rains and acting as a lens, at times allowing one to peer well into the depths of the hole. Somewhere around five to ten fathoms down, divers encountered the thin, cloudy layer of hydrogen sulfide-infused water with the smell of rotten eggs. This layer could be white in color, or take on hues of yellow or red or green, depending on the vegetation surrounding it. Below it was a broader stratum of semi-saline water that mixed with freshwater above, and finally, beneath that, only dense seawater of exceptional clarity that reached through dark tunnels out to the deep ocean.

As they hastened through the still, poisonous layer of water, Mack felt his skin begin to itch. He kicked through the haze into the clear water below, but the itching intensified on his exposed face and hands that his thin wet suit did not protect. He felt dizzy momentarily, similar to the sensation of standing up too fast and getting a head rush, but then the feeling passed.

He had expected this. The dizziness, caused by the effects of the toxin hitting his bloodstream, could cause nausea. He would not puke into his regulator, as he had on one of his first blue hole dives with Breck. He shook off the memory of his friend and looked over at Valerie, who was shaking her head and wincing. Mack tapped her on the shoulder and they made eye contact through their dive masks.

Mack made an *okay* symbol with his thumb and forefinger. *Are you okay?*

She nodded, and then intentionally crossed her eyes.

Mack laughed, sending a burst of bubbles into the layer of toxic water above them as they sank into deeper water. She had her asshole dad's sense of humor. But thank God she hadn't picked up his addiction.

The water quickly cleared, and eighty feet down the shaft, they came across the first tunnel, a black opening in the porous rock, marking a side passage. He could see the start of a nylon safety line tied off just inside the opening, but this wasn't the right passage.

They descended another twenty feet, and Mack saw a pile of bones on a ledge. Resting on them was part of a human skull. It was misshapen, with the forehead sloped steeply back above the eye sockets.

Like other skeletal remains he had seen but left untouched in Bahamas blue holes, these were probably the remains of ancient island natives. The Lucayans, who had inhabited these islands for many centuries before disappearing six hundred years ago, had tied boards to their children's foreheads to force the skull to change in shape during development.

He sank a few more body lengths and found another side passage. This was it. Valerie looked past his shoulder and squinted at the panel of LED lights on the ROV. A red light blinked steadily in the nose, indicating that the camera was running. They could type something into the keyboard to communicate with Eric, but apparently she didn't see the need. Not yet. Instead, facing the camera in DORA's nose, she made a grand gesture with her arm.

After you.

The ROV's propeller churned the water as it whirred past them, kicking up puffs of sediment into the mouth of the tunnel. Mack again worried about the reduced visibility they would face if the ROV stirred up too much sediment. They couldn't follow it very far in. Behind it trailed the sturdy transmission cable, sheathed in thick rubber. After a moment, the cable settled onto the rocks, but continued to slither forward.

Unlike the motionless, white safety line drawn tight beside it, leading into the darkness. Left by two divers who would never come back.

CHAPTER 20

The sun was low in the sky as Ashley Campbell walked down the beach, away from the main grounds of the resort. It wouldn't allow any of the local vendors onto the property, but they tolerated their presence here. She could see her old friend on the sand, at the far end of the resort, near a woman packing up her own wares for the day. Ashley had met the woman before, a vendor who sold jewelry and handmade sarongs, but she wasn't very friendly.

She approached the pair, carrying a Styrofoam restaurant container. The woman nodded at her and turned to leave, but Clive was focused on his work—some huge piece of driftwood.

"Good evening, love," Ashley said.

The old sculptor stopped working and smiled up at her. Clive was dressed in jeans and a well-worn T-shirt, his feet bare. On a handmade green blanket beside him were smaller finished pieces, most of them painted, depicting mainly tropical fauna—reef fish, parrots, lizards.

"My Lady Ashley. I am wonderful. How was your day?"

"Lucky to be alive."

"As are we all."

"Here. I brought you something to eat." She handed Clive the Styrofoam box containing leftovers provided from a poolside restaurant. She knew the cook well.

He shook his head. "You don't have to do this, child. I'm fine."

"Nonsense. You have a family. And so much food gets thrown away here."

He opened the box. "Ahh . . . pizza. And even some vegetables. Bless you."

She handed him a fork.

Out of the brush, from near a pile of rubble, a stray mutt emerged and trotted down the chain-link fence that encircled most of the property. The old girl, white and spotted, scarred up, was jumpy around everyone. Except Clive. The dog looked at Ashley warily, then approached him, tail wagging. He patted her head, then opened the box and handed her half the pizza. As she wolfed it down, Ashley shook her head.

"The food's supposed to be for you, Clive."

He waved his hand. "I know. I know. I'll save da rest. But she got a family too."

The bitch, with obvious rows of nipples on her belly, probably had a litter somewhere out of sight. Sometimes Clive was surrounded by a family of tabby cats that lived outside the resort, through the fence. One of them had a limp from a broken front leg. A mean-hearted guest had probably kicked that one.

The resort where she worked was supposed to be an eco-friendly paradise, merged with nature, which would draw in families who wanted to get up close with sea life and enjoy the island's beaches. But it also drew gamblers, wealthy high rollers who came here to take risks and indulge in selfish pleasures. Selfish people. But it was what it was. It was where she worked.

It was Oceanus.

CHAPTER 21

"You owe me twenty bucks, son," Mack said.

"You already said that," Eric mumbled to the old curmudgeon, who stood in the setting sun by the water's edge, stripping out of his wet suit. It was the first thing Mack had said when he surfaced.

Eric sat beneath a large Bahamian pine, looking over DORA for damage. He knew this might happen. It had happened before. But Eric had prayed it wouldn't happen today, in front of this asshole.

DORA had gotten stuck.

After the ROV had gone back a couple hundred feet, and Eric was guiding her out on the return trip, he had somehow wrapped her umbilical around a stalagmite or some other cave feature—he wasn't sure, since DORA had kicked up so much silt that in no time he'd been unable to see anything on the monitor. After a while, as Eric sat alone on the surface wondering what to do, helplessly watching clouds of pale silt shifting across his laptop monitor, Val and Mack, still underwater, apparently had realized the ROV was stuck—probably because the umbilical had ceased to move. Mack had followed the cable back and freed DORA in the tunnel.

Eric knew when he arrived at the trapped submersible, because of the motion on the camera. The wave of a hand in front of the lens. Plus, he'd finally used the ROV's external keyboard at that point to type Eric a message. Two words:

YOURE WELCOME

At least DORA hadn't been *too* far back, or Eric wouldn't even have her now.

Val, her hair still wet, shivered in the cooling air as Eric watched her slide out of her tight neoprene wet suit. He realized he was staring at the faint line of cleavage between her breasts, where a gold chain dangled. He quickly looked up and met her eyes. She smiled faintly, then opened a cooler and brought out some sandwiches and a large Tupperware of fresh fruit.

"Take a break from that, Eric," she said. "Let's eat some dinner."

"That's all right. I don't have an appetite."

"But I do. Being right makes a man hungry," Mack said, grabbing a sandwich. He sat down, a towel draped over his thick shoulders, and bit into the food as he reattached his prosthesis. Eric grinned when he swore and swatted at a sand fly on his neck.

Val said, "I just texted a woman I met a few days ago. She works at Oceanus. I'm going to have her over for dinner so we can get a little more background on this area."

Mack said, "Is she a diver?"

"No. But she might know more about the holes here. Maybe she can get us in touch with more of the locals. She said she's free on Saturday night. Valentine's Day."

Mack finished tightening a strap above his knee.

"Talking to her won't help Watson here pilot his toy any better."

Eric said, "Really? Will you let up already? I've never actually piloted her in a cave like that. It's like a video game. I only have so much control."

"Well, I'd think a guy like you would be better at video games. All you fuckin' Gen-Y-ers, all you do is play on your Ataris."

"On our whats? What the hell are you talking about? My ROV would work fine if you'd just do your job and mind the damn cable." Eric felt himself getting angry.

Mack glared at him. "What are you saying?"

"I'm saying if you had kept the slack pulled in on her return, like I told you to, I wouldn't have had a problem."

"You listen to me, son—"

Val waved her hands in the air. "Enough! Mack, you can't expect him to master this in the first try," she said. "DORA's never been in this environment."

"Excuses are like assholes," Mack said.

"What?"

"Everybody's got one." Mack grabbed another sandwich off the cooler.

Eric said, "It will go faster once I get a little more experience. You've got to be patient."

Val said, "Eric's right. Besides, this wasn't a total failure. DORA operated smoothly, and made it two hundred feet into the side passage."

"And the video and sonar captures were good," Eric said. He had gotten good visual, even recorded a blind fish with a translucent tail flitting through the darkness, and the sonar device would be able to produce a three-dimensional map of the tunnel on his laptop.

Still, DORA had gotten stuck.

Eric connected a cable to the ROV's output port, then to his laptop. Val sat down cross-legged in front of him, now wearing only a swimsuit, a towel draped over her shoulders. He tried not to stare. He removed his glasses and cleaned them with his shirt.

He cleared his throat and said, "Val, this morning you said something about a kid going missing. What do you think happened?"

Munching on fruit, she said, "I don't know. Mars said a teenager disappeared in another hole on the island. Last week."

Mack said, "Was he diving?"

"No. He and his friends were swimming, at night. I guess a reporter from Nassau has been on the island asking questions."

"Mars sounds like a better source of local information than any newspaper," Eric said.

"He is."

Val said, "You've been down in a lot of these holes, Uncle Mack. What do you think happened?"

Mack sat down against a pine. He rubbed his right forearm with a calloused hand. "When I was fifteen, diving for lobster down here with your grandpa—the locals call them 'crawfish'—I got ahold a this big fella." He paused, his eyes far away as he brought back the memory. "That bug was inside a sunken boat. Didn't wanna come out. And I was runnin' outta breath. Wouldn't let go, you know."

"You?" Val smiled at her uncle. He grinned.

"See this?" He ran a finger down a long scar on his forearm. "My arm got stuck. Some piece of metal. Cut it real nice when I finally jerked it free. Lost the lobster."

"You think that teen was diving for lobsters?" Eric asked.

"No. Lobsters don't live in these inland holes. Maybe he was after something else, got stuck. I don't know. There's also the tides, they create suction. He coulda gotten pulled down. It happens sometimes. Blue holes are dangerous."

Eric pictured a boy's corpse floating in the darkness, wedged into some submarine passage. Limbs swaying in the current. He shuddered and looked down at his laptop. The download was nearly complete.

"But they didn't find his body either?" he asked.

Val shook her head.

"Check this out," Eric said. The download was complete. He turned the laptop toward them.

On the screen was a colorful three-dimensional image of what looked like a tunnel.

"Is that where we just were?" Val asked.

"Yep. The different colors depict surface hardness, or density. Things like algae and silt appear lighter than solid rock." The image changed as he zoomed out, re-orienting the view so that they were looking at the entire image from the side. The tunnel now appeared as a long, jagged yellow line, running out of a much thicker yellowish column—a vertical stack of pancakes that had to be the main shaft of the hole—all on a field of black.

Mack said, "Huh. Pretty cool, actually. But you still really believe we can rely on that thing to do this job?"

Val said, "We have to, Mack. None of this is worth anyone else dying."

CHAPTER 22

An urge.

It felt compelled to move. To seek. But this was an unfamiliar impulse.

A current of water pressed against its skin. *There.* Again, it sensed something in the water. *She* sensed something. A taste, or a smell.

A faint cocktail of some chemical. Perhaps from another of her kind. Perhaps a male. And the urge increased. The organism slowly uncoiled her thick arms and began to slither out of the structure on the seafloor.

At dawn, she had not retreated under the island, into the labyrinthine caverns, as she so often now did. Instead, she had spent the day resting in this great mass partially buried in the ocean floor. This object that did not belong here.

She had returned to the decomposing structure from the deep ocean plain, having fed little. The only meal she'd found was the rotting flesh still clinging to whale bones resting on the bottom, and the hapless shark scavenging there.

Here, where the object rested, the water was much shallower than the abyss, but still too deep for her eyes to make out much more than its curved outline rising from the sediments, the right angles defining its other side. But she could form a mental picture of the object through touch. The massive structure was even larger than she herself, and on one end opened in a jagged, rusting maw that had been more than large enough to allow her entry. It had provided her shelter before.

In her advanced age, she required a steady intake of vast quantities of food. Her size had doubled in a relatively short time, and now, fully mature, she possessed a hunger which she had been unsuccessful at satisfying. This had made her sluggish, as she sought to preserve energy. Seeking refuge here had allowed her to rest. To expend less energy for locomotion—

Whump.

She felt the deep, familiar pulses, vibrating in her beak, between her eyes.

Whump. Whump. Whump.

The silent pulses hurt. Similar sounds, emitted from the seafloor and objects above it, had almost always been a part of her life. But these were emitted from very close by. Much more powerful here than elsewhere in her range. The pulses continued for several minutes, and then they were gone.

She emerged from the skeletal remains. Sensing she was alone, she raised her arms into the water column, tasting.

She moved a short distance across the soft bottom, sending billowing clouds of sediment into the water as she pushed off with each writhing appendage. She came across a protrusion on the ocean floor, and ran the suckers of one arm over it. It was hard, inedible. Frustrated, she coiled the powerful arm around the hard object and crushed it.

She extended her arms and tasted again.

But the faint chemical in the water had dissipated. The urge to mate slowly faded, replaced by the urge to—

Click-click.

She tensed at the sudden sound, a new sound very different than the others. A sound her instincts insisted she fear. It had come from very close by. Her arms splayed themselves instantly, prepared to defend.

Click-click-click-cliiiiccckkk. CLICK.

The sounds boomed into her. Sounds emitted from the enemy. Why had she not sensed its presence before?

She drew her arms together and darted back toward the structure on the bottom, and, finding a hole in its side, desperately forced her soft body back into it.

The clicks continued in the darkness outside the makeshift lair, seeming to come from all directions, and although she knew she should be safe here, her arms remained reared toward the opening in defensive posture.

But the enemy never drew any closer, never appeared.

And then, as quickly as they had begun, the clicking sounds ceased.

CHAPTER 23

Sturman sat in his truck in the parking lot at the aquarium, the engine running, staring at his cell phone. On the screen was Val's name. All he had to do was hit send.

He remembered a time back in high school, when he tried getting into rodeo with his best friend, and got bucked into the dirt by a bronco. Had the wind knocked out of him. Ached all over. He knew he was lying in the dirt now.

But this time, he didn't know how to get up. Or even if he wanted to get up.

He sighed and put the phone down on the seat next to him. What the hell would he say to her? Happy Valentine's Day? He probably owed her an apology for his verbal attack the other night, when she'd called to ask how he was, and tell him what she was up to, then scolded him for being at a bar.

Funny thing was he missed her anyway.

He pulled out of the parking lot and headed for home. He rubbed his temples. His head hurt from all the thinking he'd been doing. He'd pretty much been thinking all day at work. Or maybe his head still hurt from last night. Either way, he had a headache. He neared the turn to the

Pelican and thought about heading in, for a little hair of the dog, but decided against it.

Instead, he pulled into a McDonald's drive-through and ordered a chicken sandwich, then got back on the road. At a stoplight, as he was reaching in the bag for a handful of French fries, he saw a promotional billboard for the armed forces, and suddenly thought of an old friend. One of the few he had left. He picked up the phone again and found the number. Tom "Wits" Rabinowitz had always been a good listener, back when Sturman had first joined the Navy and was always getting into trouble. The phone rang, and there was a click as someone answered.

"Rabinowitz."

"Hey, amigo."

"Sturman? You sorry son of a bitch! What's going on?"

"I was just thinking about how cute you are, it being Valentine's Day and all."

"That's funny. I was just jerkin' off to an old picture of you . . . hang on."

Someone in the background started yelling at Rabinowitz, and Sturman laughed. Same old Wits. Dumbass was a lifer in the Navy, but he would be done with his twenty in a few more years. A horn honked and Sturman realized the light was green. He pulled forward and got into the merge lane for northbound Highway 1.

Rabinowitz got back on the line. "My wife just heard my jerkoff comment. She's sending me outta the room, so the kids can't hear. . . . All right, I'm going, Barb!"

"How's the family?" Sturman said.

"They're good. Kids are getting old fast. You ever marry that chick? The marine biologist?"

"Val? No. We're kinda on the rocks."

"No shit? You stickin' your dick where it doesn't be-long?"

"No. We're just . . . well, you know. She's out of town now. Went down to the Bahamas to do some research."

"Down here, huh? Have her stop by the base," Rabinowitz said. "I'll set her straight."

Sturman sat up. "What do you mean? I thought you were in Norfolk."

"No, man. I'm stationed in the Bahamas now. Uncle Sam moved us down here a year ago. I thought you knew that."

"I guess it's been a while. What are you doing down there?"

"More tech stuff. Has to do with sonar research we've been doing down here for decades. Ever hear about the Atlantic Undersea Test and Evaluation Center? The Tongue of the Ocean?"

"Wasn't that the name of a whore you met back in Thailand?" Sturman said, smiling.

"Funny, asshole."

"Really. So what are you doing there?" Sturman said.

"You know I can't talk about that, man."

"I'm not asking for classified information. Are you blowing shit up, or seeing how deep people can dive, or what? What's this tongue thing you're talking about?"

"It's a deepwater trench, in the middle of the Bahama Bank. All surrounded by shallow water. Navy's tested here since the sixties, because the Commies couldn't listen in from across the Atlantic."

"So you're testing sonar? Weapons?"

"I'm not telling you anything. I mean it. What's your woman doing down here?"

"Looking into some sort of unknown squid or something. You know anything about something like that?"

Wits was silent.

Sturman frowned. "Wits? You still there?"

"Sturman, I gotta run. My wife's yelling at me, and my daughter's screaming. Can I call you back?"

"Sure. Take it easy, man."

"You too. But seriously, let me know if you want me to meet up with your lady friend. I could always use another wife."

Sturman heard Rabinowitz's wife hollering at him as he ended the call. He pulled into the parking lot of his apartment complex, shut the truck off. Opened the paper bag containing his Valentine's Day dinner.

Then ate in the cab, alone.

CHAPTER 24

Across from Eric at the splintered wooden table, on the back patio at the Twin Palms, sat Ashley Campbell. In the candlelight, she looked to him like a young Halle Berry, but taller and less delicate. Her long, straight hair was pulled tightly back in a ponytail. Her smile had a gap in the middle, but her teeth were a brilliant white. She wore a small gold cross around her neck.

On either side of them sat Val and Mack. They were eating a Valentine's Day meal Val had put together, of steamed grouper with a tomato-caper sauce and canned yams. In the middle of the table, beside a mostly empty wine bottle, a candle burned inside a cracked glass jar. The stars were out, and the night was pleasant. Tiki torches burned along the coral-rock wall ringing the patio, to ward off biting insects

Eric found himself staring at Ashley. He couldn't help it.

Between bites, she said, "It's hard to believe this guest-house is still here. You know this area was hit hard by Hurricane Sandy."

"In 2012?" Eric said.

"Yes. You have a good memory. That one came late in the season. Damaged the reefs, flooded all these coastal buildings. This one was filled with sand until the owner got back to cleaning it."

"That must have been hard for everyone here," Val said.

Ashley said, "Yes. But this is Andros. Here in the Bahamas we take it as it comes."

"About Andros," Val said. "I wanted to ask you about that boy who went missing in the blue hole. You didn't know him, did you?"

"Only of him."

"Apparently there was a witness, right? A girl, who claimed she saw a monster under the island kill her boyfriend. . . ."

Mack grunted and shook his head, then took another bite of fish.

Ashley told them what she knew about the teenager, who had vanished the previous week. Apparently, the whole story had been relayed by his girlfriend, who had been found half-naked on a roadside miles away the next morning, still in shock, her bare feet raw and bloody from running through the jungle. Two other teenagers there had only heard her scream. Nobody had seen anything. No body had been found.

Ashley traced the top of her glass with her finger. Her neatly painted fingernails were lime green, a few shades lighter than her eyes.

She said, "In some ways, this island is very different from other islands in the Bahamas. There are legends here. But I don't believe most of them."

"What sort of legends?" Eric said.

"Stories about monsters, sometimes related to accidents in the blue holes. About Obeah witchcraft." She smiled at Eric. "About naked Arawaks who still hide in the bush, stealing from the unwary. There's more mythology here than where I grew up."

"And where's that?" Eric felt emboldened by the wine.

"On a small island in the Abacos. North of here."

"Mack lived there for a time, you know," Val said.

Ashley leaned forward. "Really? Where?"

"Great Abaco." Mack leaned back in his chair. "Moved there after my wife left me. Guess I wasn't any good without a leg."

Ashley regarded Mack. "She didn't really leave you for that, did she?"

Mack shrugged. "Never figured her out, or why she left. I still had my dick, didn't I?"

Eric thought of saying something, but Ashley only laughed.

"Mack . . ." Val said.

He said, "Anyway, we never had kids. Probably a good thing. So I decided to go where I used to love diving so much. The Bahamas are unbelievable."

Ashley said, "Why did you leave, then?"

He lifted his prosthetic leg up off the floor and dropped it onto the edge of the table. He rapped the titanium rod with his knuckles. "Because of this goddammed thing. Couldn't dive where I wanted to anymore, inside the holes, and I had too many medical issues."

"But you are a hero, Mack. You should be proud."

"Whatever." He looked away from her.

Ashley said, "I had to leave the Abacos too. For work. I started taking seasonal jobs in Nassau when I was sixteen, then I moved there a few years later for full-time work. When they built Oceanus, I came here. But I try to visit my family whenever I can."

"Are they still where you grew up?" Eric said.

She nodded. "On Two Finger Cay. My dad's a fisherman. A good man. Mom still stays home with the youngest. I'm the oldest, ya know. I send them a little money to help them get by."

Val said, "You said something about monsters, Ashley. Why are there more monster stories here, on Andros?" Val raised the wine bottle to refill Ashley's glass, but she covered it politely with her hand. Mack gestured at his own, and Val poured him the rest.

"This is a very big island," Ashley said. "A hundred miles long. With very few people. And with the number of blue holes, the swash on the west side, the Tongue of the Ocean, there are lots of legends."

Val said, "And when people go missing on a place like Andros, like that boy . . ."

"Yes," Ashley said. "It leads to more stories."

"What was that thing you mentioned? That creature the girl said she saw?"

Ashley laughed, her brilliant teeth lit momentarily by a distant flash of lightning offshore. It was going to rain soon.

She said, "Something some locals call the *lusca*. It's a mythical creature. Half octopus, half shark, half as big as Oceanus."

"Sounds like bullshit," Mack said, then downed his wine. Eric figured he'd drunk more than a bottle by himself by now.

"Mack, there's a lady here," Eric said.

"Oh, for Christ's sake—" Mack started, but Ashley touched his hand and he stopped.

"Mack's right," Ashley said. "Of course it isn't real."

"Maybe," Val said. "But it intrigues me. We're looking for some sort of undiscovered animal. Something that might live in the blue holes. We're not sure how big it would be."

They had run DORA through an easier oceanic blue hole for a few days, one that was broader and more accessible than The Staircase. They had returned to The Staircase today. Eric was getting much better at guiding the ROV through its tunnels. But not good enough. DORA still couldn't even go as far in as Breck and Pelletier had, let alone the rescue divers who had gone in after them, due to a restriction too narrow for Eric to risk running DORA through. For now, they would have to look for Val's new cephalopod species somewhere else.

Ashley said, "From what I hear, nothing much lives in those holes. They're dangerous, and the water's sometimes poisonous, right?"

"Hang on," Val said. "Let me show you something." She went inside and came back with the printout of the blurry image taken in The Staircase. She handed it to Ashley. "This is why we're here."

"What is it?"

"We think it might be a tentacle, or the arm of some cephalopod."

"A what?"

"A cephalopod. A squid or octopus," Val said. "What you say about the island's holes is right. Many of them are toxic, and dangerous. That's why it would be such a find to observe a new species of megafauna living in them. Do you know anyone that is very familiar with this island? The waters offshore?"

"One man. You should come and meet Clive. He might be able to help."

"Clive?" Eric said.

"He's a sculptor. He sells his work at the resort, at the end of the beach. He used to be a fisherman like my dad. He worked these waters for years. A lot of people say he's crazy, for the stories he tells. But I think he's an honest man."

"We'd love to visit," Eric said. He heard Mack snort. Looking at Ashley, he found himself struggling for something else to say. He realized he was leaning toward her and sat up as a rumble of thunder passed by.

"We'll certainly come by," Val said. "We need a lead. So far we haven't had much luck."

After dinner, Val thanked Ashley for coming by to talk to them.

"Thank *you* for the dinner," Ashley said. "You grill a mean grouper. And it was lovely meeting you both." She smiled at Eric and Mack.

"Can we give you a ride back?" Eric asked. "It looks like it might rain."

"You don't even have a car, Romeo," Mack said. "What you gonna do? Carry her?"

"I thought maybe we could call her a taxi—"

Ashley said, "That's sweet, Eric. But I think the rain won't come for a while."

"Ehhh." Mack waved a hand at them. "Fuckin' Valentine's Day." He said good-bye to Ashley and walked away, grumbling.

Val said, "Don't mind my uncle, Ashley. He has a sailor's mouth."

"It's okay. Where I work, I see all types. And hear all sorts of language." She turned to Eric. "I appreciate your offer, love, but I will take the bus. I insist."

"Can I walk you to the bus stop?" Eric said.

"I'm fine." Ashley smiled. "Really. Good night." She pecked Eric on the cheek, and he felt himself blush.

Eric watched the easy sway of her hips as she walked down the dimly lit path toward the road, another flash of lightning coursing across the sky. He finally shut the door when she was out of sight.

He looked over at Val. "What?"

"Nothing. Told you she was cute," Val said. She smiled at him, but looked sad.

"Yeah. She's amazing. Are you all right, Val?"

"Yeah. I'm fine."

"You just seem . . . I don't know."

"Maybe it's because it's Valentine's Day. I'm not really a romantic, but it's weird to not even talk to Will today."

"Why don't you call him?"

She shook her head. "He's still mad at me for coming here. But every time I try to talk him about his . . . problems, he gets upset. I don't want to bother you with our issues, though."

"It's okay. I'm a good listener."

She looked at him, differently than she ever had before. His heart skipped a beat. Maybe he had a chance, right now. But they worked together, and she was with another guy. . . .

Then the look was gone. "Goodnight, Eric," she said, and turned and went to her bedroom.

CHAPTER 25

Tom Rabinowitz looked at a unicolor monitor on the wall of the dim room—a greenish radar image that depicted crafts on the ocean surface. Directly above the midline of the ocean trench, where they were now picking up the large, unknown vessel. Not one of Uncle Sam's.

"Stand by," he said to Lt. Menendez.

Their sonar had detected no submarine activity, but he was interested in one large vessel moving directly over the grid. He'd need to verify its identity before they could proceed with the test. It was time to run Moby Dick again.

Usually, they ran the more innovative trials at night, to help avoid detection from the public. But this month they were ramping things up, because Russia was again showing renewed aggression toward its neighbors and acting dismissively toward threats from NATO and the President. The Navy had been running round-the-clock sonar testing, even running exercises with older techniques—like the antipersonnel sonar—as well as the novel ones he was using now. It seemed appropriate, since this testing center had been devised during the Cold War.

"Zoom to target bearing two-three-seven, lieutenant."

"Aye, sir." Menendez began to zoom in on the craft using the most recent satellite image, taken minutes ago.

Zoomed in on the sat image now, Rabinowitz could see the white craft on the rippled blue surface of the ocean. It was hard to tell from directly above, but it didn't appear to be any sort of warship; probably a private yacht.

"Zoom another three hundred, lieutenant."

Menendez zoomed in farther. Rabinowitz nodded. Definitely a private vessel, or a clever ploy at one. Because on the upper deck, there was a nude, or mostly nude, woman reclining in the sun.

"Jackpot," he said, grinning.

Menendez, beside him, gave him an elbow.

"Not of concern?" she said, ready to designate the vessel.

"To you, maybe," he said. "You see more action than this married sailor. Designate."

"Aye, sir." The flashing blip on the radar screen went away, replaced by a solid dot.

"All systems ready?"

"Affirmative."

He felt a twinge of butterflies in his gut. "Single ping on my mark."

"Aye, sir." Menendez leaned forward and held her hand over a panel of buttons.

"Mark."

In the dark room, an audible click came back to them over the speakers, but the sound was faint, just enough to give them an indication of a successful ping. Underwater, they'd just sent out a 230-decibel boom that would have sounded like a hunting rifle being fired next to your ear. Louder than all but one sound produced in the animal kingdom. A sound designed to disable a number of marine organisms.

Also a sound that could travel miles underwater, and bounce back to convey information, but likely would go unnoticed by the enemy.

"Proceed with Series One," he said.

They were underway.

CHAPTER 26

On the upper deck of the yacht, Tony D'Amico paused from repairing the speaker to watch as his boss's girlfriend rose from her recliner. She was naked except for a white bikini thong and a set of large hoop earrings. A mane of blond hair hung past her shoulders. She caught him looking and smiled coyly, pressing her breasts together playfully with her arms, nipples hard in the cool breeze, as she gripped her elbows in her hands. She shivered.

"I'm cold, honey."

"You look fine to me," he said. He wasn't a refined man, but in the late-day sun, with her bronzed skin, she was, he thought, truly a work of art. He replaced the plastic console over the wiring next to the all-weather speaker and rose to his feet.

Jenna wrapped her towel around her shoulders and hurried over to him, dancing on her toes, and pressed her lithe body against him. She nibbled his ear.

"Not here." He pushed her away gently, feeling his excitement rising. "I mean it."

"I thought maybe you could warm me up." She reached down between his legs. "Wanna take a shower with me?"

He smiled. "We can't, Jenna. We need to wait. Once we're on shore . . ."

"I can go down there first. Just meet me in my quarters." She licked her lips. "Just a quickie. Dan will never know."

"No. I mean it. We've gotta be more discreet, or I'll be out of a job, and you'll lose your sugar daddy."

Tony worked for Phillip Marks, Jr., owner of two NASCAR racing teams—and the sixty-five-foot yacht they were on now. Tony was the chef and maintenance specialist on *Checkered Flag*, and was everything Mr. Marks wasn't—tall, young, handsome. Virile. And he wasn't wealthy. Working for the past two years on the man's yacht was the closest he had come to living like the rich. He didn't want to lose this job, even for this girl.

He stepped away from her and shouted down to the captain, "Dan, can you fire up the music?"

A moment later, a song erupted over the speaker: Lou Reed's "Walk on the Wild Side." It was fixed. He knelt to replace the screws in the panel.

"Stop ignoring me, Tony." Jenna was putting her bikini top on, and beginning to pout.

"We'll be in port in a few hours," he said, looking up at her. "I promise, we'll find some time together there."

They were in the middle of the ocean, somewhere between a few larger islands of the Bahamas. They had left Nassau two hours ago, bound for Oceanus, the newer resort off Andros Island. Mr. Marks was flying down to board the yacht there, to see his girlfriend, and to try his luck in the resort's casinos.

But not until tomorrow.

Jenna said, "Whatever. I guess you'll just miss your chance." She turned and headed for the stairs near the stern, and he watched her walk away, hips swaying.

Marks had paid for her to fly down to Nassau to meet some friends last week, while he was held up on business. It had been a good week. Best Valentine's Day ever. Even if she wasn't his girlfriend.

She tossed her hair, gave him one last playful look, and disappeared down the stairs. He stood and took a deep breath, watching the sun dip toward the horizon. Beneath it, in the distance, he could make out the dark, flat line of Andros. He tried to push Jenna out of his head, but couldn't.

"You're an idiot, Tony," he muttered, and then rushed down the stairs after her.

The vibrations were growing louder.

Hundreds of feet beneath the surface, she knew that the massive object above was not prey. Nor was it a known threat. But the drone emanating from its belly, which hummed through her flesh, had piqued her curiosity. She was very hungry, and she had been successful at reaching an advanced age only because of her opportunistic nature.

She forced a volume of seawater out of her mantle and rose toward the approaching object.

The light from above had faded in the past hour, triggering her active state, and the sounds of her enemy had again driven her from the depths. She had not encountered one of them for a very long time, and was unsure what would happen if she did. But she could not risk it.

As she neared the surface, her eyes began to make out the pale underbelly of the passing object. There was still some light from above, but it was very faint. Night had fallen. The colossal shape was moving smoothly, steadily, trailed by churning seawater. Despite its size, it was nothing like the leviathans she still feared. Lacking a protective external skeleton or shell, the organism was vulnerable here, near the surface in the open ocean. She had always relied on camouflage and intelligence to avoid her few natural predators, but fully grown now, she felt much less threatened.

Alert to any other possible threats, she began following the huge object, tasting the water. She sensed nothing edible, and after a short time, she started to turn away, toward the reefs. Where she might find nourishment.

But then she tasted something else in the water through the chemical receptors in her flesh.

A hint of food.

She turned back toward the object, and with a few pulses of seawater moved directly beneath it. She pivoted her body slightly, directing her arms upward. She reached.

And touched the smooth surface.

Tony cursed to himself as he replayed the scene in his mind. He wondered if he would still have a job tomorrow. What had Dan really seen?

After he and Jenna had finished, he had peeked out of her cabin door, and then, thinking the coast was clear, had hurried into the galley to find Dan staring at him.

Dan hadn't said anything, and Tony had been fully clothed. But his hair was still wet. And he could tell from the captain's expression that he was suspicious. Why the hell had Dan been there, below deck? He was supposed to be driving the goddamn boat.

All Tony had been able to blurt out was, "What are you doing down here?"

To which Dan had replied, "Getting coffee. What are *you* doing?"

He'd tried to come up with an excuse. "Dumping the

tanks," he'd said, then moved toward the console that controlled the pumps for the yacht's gray water and sewage. Offshore dumping was illegal in many places, but easier than doing it in port.

Tony now sat hunched on a bench in the stern of the yacht, in the dark, his head in his hands. He'd been there for a half hour. They'd agreed to meet here, where the loud rumble of the engines would mask their conversation. They would be arriving at their next port soon.

He heard the door behind him open and glanced over his shoulder. It was Jenna.

She walked hesitantly toward him, and then stopped a few feet away. She had put on a skirt and sweater. She handed him a tumbler with a few fingers of whiskey, and he downed it.

"Where's Dan?" he said.

"Back at the helm. Do you think he knows?"

"I don't know."

"Has he asked you any more questions?"

"No. But I'm worried, Jenna. He's really loyal to—"

Suddenly the boat lurched. Shifted. Then it slowed, settled in the water, as if it had somehow taken on a heavy load of cargo.

"What was that?" Jenna said.

"I don't know. Shhhh!"

The loud drone of the engines died off as the captain put the motors in neutral. Tony jumped to his feet just as Dan, calm in virtually any situation, came running down toward the stern. He turned on the overhead light. He looked rattled.

"Did we run aground?" Tony said.

Dan, in his captain's whites, scowled at him. "Aground? It's more than a thousand feet deep here." He leaned over one side, then the other. "Have you seen anything come out from under the stern?"

"Like what? There's nothing out here."

"I don't know. Maybe part of another boat."

Tony frowned. "Another boat? You think we—"

"Oh, my God, Dan," Jenna said, covering her mouth with one hand. "We didn't hurt anyone, did we?"

"I'm not sure yet. You two. Watch either side of the boat. See if you can see anything under it. And shout if you do. I'm headed to the bow." Dan ran around the side of the boat, his thigh striking the chrome railing.

Tony moved to the port side and looked down into the water. They hadn't been travelling fast in the dark, but the boat was still drifting forward at about five knots. In the dark, he couldn't see past the surface. Nothing appeared to be floating.

Behind him, he heard Jenna moan. "I'm scared, Tony," she said. "We're not gonna sink, are we?"

"I'm sure we're fine. And we have a dinghy onboard."

"But we're in the middle of nowhere. What if—"

"Dammit, Jenna!" Tony turned to face her. "Will you just look over the other—"

He stopped, his mouth open. Behind Jenna, on the well-lit gunwale, something had moved. Something fleshy and orange.

For a moment, Tony thought maybe it was a person's hand, from the smaller boat they indeed had just demolished. A wounded survivor, trying to climb onboard.

But the slithering, meaty thing continued over the side, stretching. *Growing.* Like some enormous, slender tongue, longer than a person. But it wasn't a tongue.

It was covered in suckers.

"Tony?" Jenna was staring at him, but he couldn't respond. "Tony, are you okay?"

"Jenna. Come here. Right now." He reached out a hand.

The tentacle slithered down to the deck, toward Jenna's feet. Another one slid quietly over the gunwale to join it.

"What?"

"NOW!"

She started to step toward him, but stopped. And looked down, to see what was touching her calf.

CHAPTER 27

Val's lungs were beginning to burn, but she held tightly to the two long, spiny antennae in her fists and braced her feet on the coral bottom. She tugged again, but the big lobster wouldn't come out of his hole.

She and Mack had been hunting in twenty feet of water, free diving with only their scuba masks on. The legal way to catch some dinner. He'd taught her how to do this as a teenager, in the Florida Keys. Back then, she'd cut her hands more than once on the sharp antennae, learning not to let her grip slip. The injuries hadn't stopped her from going back to do it again and again. It was fun to catch spiny lobsters, and even more fun to eat them.

When Mack had come around, he'd given her and her mom the attention they lacked from Val's father, who was often absent. Drunk somewhere. And when Mack came to town, he left intentionally, since the two men couldn't stand one another.

Mack had once been Val's idol. He wasn't a drunk, and he was nothing like his sister—Val's mom—who had always been so meek. He was a scuba diver, a fisherman, a traveler. A hero to her. He'd already been a career soldier then, visiting them whenever he had leave time, but that was before he went to war. To Iraq.

Back then, he'd been so young, still so optimistic and confident, when he still had both of his legs. He wasn't bitter or angry. But in the war, he hadn't just lost his leg.

After that last tour, he'd never taken her in the water again.

She pulled at the antennae. She was making progress—she could see the front end of the crustacean appear in the mouth of the hole. He was an impressive specimen. As his carapace cleared the opening, but before he could try to swim away, she let go of the antennae with one hand and reached for his tail. Just as her hand neared the hole, something big slithered out of it, making her start.

A tentacle.

She flinched as the squirming thing rushed toward her hand. She jerked at the lobster and felt its antennae break off in her hand, and smiled despite herself, her heart now thudding in her chest, her lungs burning even more.

It wasn't a tentacle. Only an eel.

Val watched her lobster dinner flap its muscular tail and dart away across the bottom, escaping her and the pesky five-foot moray eel that remained in the hole, jaws agape. Val was out of breath. She pushed off the bottom.

At the surface, she looked back toward the boat a hundred feet away and saw that Mack had remained aboard this time, having already caught two or three lobsters. Even with just one leg, he was still better at this than her. She'd only gotten one so far. She gulped in air for a few moments before putting her face back in the water. Searching.

She was thankful for the traits she had gotten from Mack, whether inherited from their lineage or simply learned—her tenacity, her courage, her need to explore. He'd expect her to keep trying until she caught this damn crawfish. She wondered if she also shared his cynicism, his anger. If she would be the same as him if she too saw war, and lost a leg.

Floating facedown, she continued looking for the runaway lobster. Below her in the shallow garden erupted an abundance of bright corals, such as she had hardly seen anywhere. Brain corals. Purple, branching Gorgonians. Pillar corals in all hues. And bright yellow sponges standing out on the less colorful reef like highlighted text on a legal document. Just above the Andros Wall, this fully intact barrier reef was the third largest in the world, yet had remained pristine. But would that change in the coming decades, with Oceanus now here? Hopefully they wouldn't ever blast a hole through the reef to create a deepwater port for the cruise ships, like she heard they had in Cozumel.

Near the edge of her field of vision, a long shark appeared, swimming close to the bottom. A hammerhead, maybe eight or nine feet long. Just passing through.

She thought about the tattoo on Will Sturman's shoulder. His own hammerhead. Like Mack, anything related to a hammer suited him. A blunt instrument, with a thick head, that operated on sheer force, with no tact or precision. She liked to think she, on the other hand, was more like the blue octopus tattooed on her own hip—intelligent, patient, always inquisitive. How had they ever gotten together in the first place? They were so different. Still . . . he'd been so wonderful for that first year, becoming the man she'd seen inside all along, until—

There.

The lobster was almost directly below her, fifteen or so feet down, the remaining six-inch stubs of his antennae poking out from a recess under one of the numerous human-sized knobs of coral standing on the bottom. She took in a lungful of air, dipped down and thrust her legs above her. She kicked for the bottom, scattering a school of young snappers.

As she neared the lobster, he shrank back into his new hiding place. Val slowed, eyeing the situation. As long as the critter couldn't fit out the back end of the hole he was in now, he was trapped. She darted a hand out, her hand pressing into his carapace, pinning him to the bottom. She gripped the shell tightly and then picked him up carefully, anticipating the strong tail flapping that followed. Quickly, she folded his segmented tail up under his body. She held it in place with a tight grip.

Now the lobster couldn't swim. She turned him on his back and he ceased moving altogether. Like sharks, the animals always seemed immobilized in this flipped position, and she almost felt sorry for them as she brought them back to the boat. But she had tonight's dinner.

She turned her head toward the surface and was just starting for the top when she first felt it.

Whump. Whump. Whump.

She didn't hear anything, but some sort of throbbing pulsed through her chest, her abdomen. She winced, shook her head, and kicked for the surface. Suddenly, the feeling pulsed through her again, and she dropped the lobster. She felt a powerful wave of nausea overcome her. Something was wrong. She felt disoriented, her stomach churning, the muscles in her diaphragm quivering now. She was going to throw up.

Desperately, she kicked for the surface.

CHAPTER 28

On break, Sturman stood against the back wall in duck overalls stained with grease from working on one of the facility's boilers. He sipped his Pepsi. Waiting.

Across the room, the aquarium's youngest guest interpreter, Courtney, had just arrived to wait by a clear tank used to temporarily house animals needing inspection or care. After a minute, a door opened and a chorus of voices filled the room as a group of sixth-graders piled in, followed by their teacher. Courtney waited until the children gathered around her, then clapped her hands together.

"In here we have a real treat. A giant Pacific octopus. One of the most amazing animals at the aquarium."

"Where is it?" A long-haired boy asked.

"He's hiding. Normally, he'd be sleeping in the daytime." From a stainless-steel bowl, she picked out a piece of frozen fish and dropped it into the tank. A sucker-lined arm appeared from inside one of the plastic shelters provided in the tank. The arm snaked toward the hunk of pale flesh, snatching it up before it again withdrew into the shadows. The kids crowded around the tank, oohing and aahing as Courtney plunged her own arm into the water, another piece of fish in her hand. When another tentacle appeared, she cradled it, lifting it out of the water. The pink, fleshy appendage, laced with what looked like veins, quickly coiled around her hand, causing a few of the children to squeal.

"Guys, this is Oscar. He's a mature male. And this is just one of his arms. Who knows how many arms an octopus has?"

A few children shouted, "Eight!"

"Good. Now a harder question. Does anyone want to guess where an octopus's nose is?" she asked. This time, a long pause. Sturman raised his hand behind the kids, and Courtney smiled at him.

An enthusiastic, twenty-something employee who usually showed younger kids around the aquarium, Courtney was leading the class on a special behind-the-scenes tour of the aquarium. Oscar was on the agenda, as he had been temporarily moved into a tank in the working area of the aquarium, for a routine checkup earlier in the morning. Although roused by the treats, most of the shy animal's body was still concealed inside the plastic cube. But he was obviously interested in contact. Being touched.

"Nobody has a guess?" Courtney asked. "I promise, you'll get the answer right."

One little girl finally raised her hand.

"Yes?" Courtney said. "Where do you think Oscar's nose is?"

"Under his eyes?" she said.

"Good guess. And you're right. But actually, an octopus's *entire body* is like a giant nose. They have taste receptors all over. And that's not all their skin does. Do you guys know what a chameleon is?"

The same little girl shouted, "A lizard that changes colors!"

Courtney said, "That's right. And did you know that an octopus can do the same thing, but even better?" She gently placed the six-foot octopus's tentacle back in the water, and he reluctantly released his grip. Sturman wondered for a moment if he was lonely, and actually enjoyed this interaction.

"Octopuses not only change colors, to take on different background patterns," she said. "They also can change the texture of their skin, to match a smooth, sandy ocean bottom or a rocky reef. This helps them to hunt, and to hide from predators. They're nature's masters of camouflage."

One Hispanic boy raised his hand. "How big do they get?"

"Good question. These are one of the largest species of octopus. Some biologists believe they can weigh as much as four people, and be as wide as a school bus is long, from the tip of one tentacle to another. But not long ago scientists discovered another species of octopus in the Atlantic Ocean that may grow just as large, or even larger."

"Will Oscar ever weigh as much as four people?" The boy leaned toward the glass, trying to figure out where the rest of the animal was hidden.

Courtney smiled. "Probably not. Very few get that big. They stop growing when their bodies tell them it's time to reproduce. Once that happens, they stop eating, and stop growing."

"If they stop eating, don't they die?"

"Unfortunately, they do. These octopuses don't live very long. Only about four years in the wild. For *this* species. Which is actually very long for an octopus."

"How old's Oscar?"

"He's four now. Okay, guys, time to move on to the tide pools. Who wants to touch a starfish?"

The teacher herded her students out of the room, with Courtney following. Sturman nodded at her, and she smiled back at him. After the door shut behind the group, the room became very quiet. Without the kids here, it felt very sterile, the walls and floor a plain white, the fixtures all metal and glass.

He walked up to the tank and touched the lid, which Courtney had been careful to close. And latch.

"You miss your own tank, don't you, old man?" he said.

One thing Courtney hadn't talked about was the main trait that impressed Sturman: an octopus's intelligence. He knelt and looked at the animal, which had again compressed most of its body into the impossibly small plastic cube resting in the tank. He again wondered if Oscar ever got lonely.

The lead aquarist once told him that they used to keep mature Pacific octopi—no, *octopuses,* the correct plural form, he reminded himself—in the larger tanks, with other animals, despite the possible concern that they might be eaten by sharks and wolf eels. But they discovered, to their surprise, that the larger fish and small sharks started to turn up dead and mostly eaten. They soon realized it was the octopus who had become the tank's top predator. Since then, Oscar and other giant Pacific octopuses were kept in separate tanks.

Sturman wished he could get a look at Oscar before he went back to work. He glanced around to make sure nobody had re-entered the room, then grabbed a half-frozen shrimp out of the metal bowl, accidentally left near the tank. He unlatched the lid of the enclosure.

Pinching the morsel between his fingers, he dipped his right hand into the water. He wouldn't use his left, as he'd been warned that Oscar might steal the wedding ring he still wore. He waved the food around as he'd often seen Bill do at feeding time. He'd heard that some octopus species were venomous to people, but not this one.

After a moment, there was movement. The octopus's arms reappeared from the dark cube, seeking the new stimulus in the water. The animal had now taken on a reddish hue. One arm rolled out toward Sturman's hand, wrapping around his fingers. He felt the smooth suckers pulling at his skin, then the tentacle retracted, taking the shrimp with it.

But Sturman could now see one of Oscar's catlike eyes. It appeared to be looking back at him.

Sturman held the steel bowl of food up to the glass, to show the octopus what was inside, and then set the bowl on the table next to the tank. He stepped away from the table. Dimmed the lights. And waited.

He heard a thump behind him, and again glanced at the doors to the room, wondering if he could lose his job over this.

Oscar's body suddenly boiled out of the small opening in the plastic cube, swirling, as if oil poured into the water. The octopus's football-sized mantle inflated in anticipation, and then the animal was sliding its bulk up the side of the tank. The first of its arms rose from the water, tentatively.

Once, shortly after Sturman had started working at the aquarium, Bill had allowed him to observe one of Oscar's checkups. Afterward, the aquarist had placed a clear, five-gallon plastic bottle in the tank. The kind used for office water coolers. Oscar had been smaller then, but still weighed in at maybe forty-five pounds, yet he had somehow crammed nearly his entire, boneless body inside, through the tiny opening. Sturman had been hooked. Another time, Bill had placed a closed glass bottle into the tank. The octopus had immediately located the lid, and worked to open the bottle. Sturman had asked if this was an octopus's idea of play. Like a person doing a puzzle.

You might call it that, Bill had said. *But it really comes down to something else.*

What's that? Sturman had asked.

He's trying to figure out if he can eat it.

A moment later, the octopus had removed the lid.

CHAPTER 29

"Antipersonnel sonar," Mack said.

"How can you be sure?" Val said. "You weren't even in the water when I felt it."

"Because of how you described it. What else could it be? I'm telling you, kid, it was the Navy's goddam antipersonnel sonar."

Val looked down at the dinner of minced lobster that her uncle had made for her and Eric. They sat around the cheap Formica table in the kitchen of the guesthouse, eating inside for a change. The rain had finally come, and outside was a downpour, hammering on the tin roof of the shed outside. The last few days had all been quite rainy for the normally drier winter season in the Bahamas.

The meal would have appeared outstanding to almost any diner—the large pieces of succulent shelled meat mixed with tomatoes, onions, and peppers and served over sticky rice in large bowls. But Val still felt ill, and it looked awful.

"How come I've never heard of something like that before?" she said.

Mack laughed. "The Tongue of the Ocean is a goddam testing ground. They don't tell anyone in the outside world what they're doing here. It's all top-secret shit. But I'm tellin' you, those fuckers here are playing with their sonar frequencies again."

Eric said, "And you think Val felt one designed to make divers, or people inside submarines, feel like shit?"

"Damn right. Breck and I have both felt it."

"Seriously?" Val said.

Mack nodded, sipping his beer. "Breck was ex-Navy. Had some strong connections at the testing facility here on Andros. Even did contract work for 'em, because he was one of the only guys brave enough to dive on some of their deeper deployments. Anyway, we spent some time diving some blue holes here when I still had two legs, holes that Breck was training others to dive. One time we both got really sick on an offshore dive."

"What happened?" Eric said.

"We felt what Val felt today. And Breck told me about the top-secret testing the Navy did here, which included using antipersonnel sonar."

Eric shook his head. "It's amazing what our own government is getting away with here."

Mack shrugged. "I guess. But somebody's gotta keep Americans safe from their enemies. If a few whales die in the process, or a few divers get sick, so be it, I guess." He looked at Val. "Did I ever tell you that Breck found one of their ROVs? Right off Andros? The Navy actually lost it." He chuckled. "It carried some sort of advanced weapon. He lied when they asked him about it, said he'd never seen it. Showed it to me one time, though. I wonder if it's still there."

"Where?" Val said.

He smiled at her.

"So you're an accomplice to stealing from the US Navy?" Eric said.

"I never said I took it," Mack said. "Just saw it once."

"Well, let's see. Maybe the next time you find a Navy torpedo on the bottom, or an unexploded mortar in the forest, you should say something to somebody. Unless you don't mind someone else losing their leg—"

Mack got to his feet and lunged toward Eric, but Val grabbed his wrist. "Enough!" she said. "Please, you two, stop. You're making me feel sicker."

Mack gave Eric a cold look and sat back down. "Fine. But just for you, Val. You're getting lucky today, pretty boy."

"Whatever," Eric muttered.

"Anything I can do for you?" Mack asked Val.

"No. I'll be fine if you two stop arguing."

Val watched her uncle and Eric eat, poking at her own plate with her fork. No one said a word.

CHAPTER 30

When Val woke early the next morning, she no longer felt sick. She convinced Eric to join her for a run. The sky was clear, but the air still smelled wet from the night's rain.

As they turned off the main road and jogged toward the beach on White Sand Cay, Val could see the turquoise ocean waters start to appear between the trees that enclosed the narrow side road. The uneven path ran from the paved road toward the water, and appeared to be the last turn toward the beach before arriving at the gates of Oceanus. Although the path was strewn with trash, there was a fragrant, floral smell coming from the vegetation alongside it. The greenery was striking in the early morning light.

Val looked behind her and saw that Eric was falling farther behind. She shouted at him to catch up. They'd just run almost three miles from their guesthouse, mostly along the narrow shoulder of the Queen's Highway—the island's main thoroughfare—within feet of horn-beeping taxis and other morning traffic. Ever since they had started up a towering bridge that ran from the main island over to the small cay where Oceanus had been built, Eric had struggled to keep up.

He and Mack needed a break from each other. And they all had wanted a break from the blue holes for a few days, as Val tried to figure out what to do next. They were finished at The Staircase. Eric had guided DORA along the taut safety line left by Breck and Pelletier, a huge spider's silken strand coursing through the curves of the dark passageway, all the way back to a restriction hundreds of feet back. But there, their underground expedition had stopped. Eric said he couldn't risk piloting the ROV through, as it would likely get stuck.

That was it. Val was frustrated, but there was nothing else they could do. She wasn't about to ask Mack to go back there, because she knew he would.

The night before, after the uneaten lobster dinner, Val had tried to contact the teenage girl who'd lost her boyfriend at the remote inland hole. The girl's mother wouldn't let her talk, but the woman relayed what her daughter had told her. How she had described something under the water. Something big.

The mother wasn't sure about any tentacles, but she believed that her daughter was telling the truth. It didn't seem possible, that some huge living thing was hidden inside an inland hole. There wasn't even enough life there to sustain the caloric needs of a large animal. But they would need to explore it—soon.

Val had decided that since she was going to get some exercise, she would take a look at Oceanus and try to find the sculptor Ashley had told them about. The ex-fisherman. Maybe he would know something about a rare cephalopod in the area.

She stopped in some shade and turned, jogging in place, as she waited for Eric. She was starting to feel a little hot, despite the cool air.

Eric arrived, hobbling now.

"You gonna make it back, Eric?" she said.

"My knees . . ." he huffed. "Damn rocky road shoulder. Hang on." He stopped and bent over, hands on knees, breathing hard.

"Just your knees, huh?" She poked at his leg with her toe. "You're young. You need to get in better shape."

He sucked in a few deep breaths. "I knew the whole surface of Andros was just a bunch of weathered rock. Now I know it sucks for running." He spit onto the ground, then stood upright and managed a smile. Sweat streaked his glasses. "And I know that I shouldn't run with you."

Val suppressed a smile. Eric was cute. And he was everything Will Sturman wasn't—sweet, cerebral, sensitive. And a light drinker.

Eric caught her gazing at him. "What?" he said.

"Nothing. C'mon. We can walk the rest of the way."

A handful of local vendors loitered on the beach near a small guardhouse marking the edge of Oceanus. They were settled on the sand above a high-tide line strewn with bits of trash and vegetation.

An older couple was looking over one heavyset woman's wares, as she displayed a series of cheap sarongs. The other vendors merely chatted in pairs. Another woman approached Val and Eric, but didn't press when they politely declined. This early she probably expected business to be slow.

Just past the cluster of vendors was one other man, alone on the beach. An older man carving a piece of wood.

Val walked ahead of Eric, and stopped several feet from the sculptor. He didn't look up as they approached.

He was sitting cross-legged on a green blanket, beneath a palm tree, carving what looked like a parrot. His skin was as dark and weathered as the raw wood in his hands. Beside him were other, finished carvings, all brightly painted and gleaming in the morning sun.

She said, "Excuse me, sir."

"One moment, please." The sculptor spoke slowly. His full head of dark hair contained no gray, but his face bore deep lines that betrayed his age.

Val waited, squinting out over the ocean toward the sun. The waves lapped gently against the white sand shore. She looked away from the glare on the water, to where a quarter mile farther down the beach, and several hundred feet inland, the hotel towers of Oceanus jutted into the sky. She looked down at the man, still focused on his work. He had some nice wares, but obviously needed to work on his sales tactics. She cleared her throat.

"I'm sorry to bother you, sir, but by chance is your name Clive?"

The man paused and finally looked up at them, then again went back to his work. "Why ya lookin' for old Clive?"

"Someone told us we should talk to him. That maybe he could help us."

"You all right? You look like ya been workin' real hard."

"We were just running. Do you think you might be able to help us?"

"Help you with what, dear?" He cut into the soft wood with a pen knife, slowly revealing the parrot's beak. His hands were thick. Scarred, like those of any old fisherman.

"We came to Andros for research. We're looking into the possibility of an unknown species of squid, or octopus, living in the blue holes here." Val noticed that his hands had stopped moving, just for a moment.

He lowered the pen knife, regarding first her, then Eric. "I'm just a poor sculptor," he finally said. "I can't help you with dat." He swept a hand over his finished works. "See anything ya like here?"

"They're all very nice," Val said. "But first, can you tell us if you know Clive? Ashley said he worked here. That he was a sculptor. I thought maybe you were him."

He set the parrot down and smiled. "Ashley sent you, eh? Please, sit."

Val and Eric looked at each other and shrugged, then squatted in the sand next to the old man. He reached into a leather pouch and withdrew some papers, then began rolling a cigarette.

"I'm the man you lookin' for," he said. "I'm Mista Clive."

Val said, "Ashley said you used to be a fisherman. That you were familiar with the sea life here, maybe even in the blue holes."

"How ya know Miss Ashley?"

"We met recently." She smiled. "I was running that day too."

"Yes. She a runner. Not me." He lit the cigarette and offered it to them, but they declined. He took a drag and held in the smoke. "I don't fish no mores. Too many udda fishermen. And fishin' no good now anyway." He raised the half-finished carving of an angelfish off his blanket. "I make more money sellin' dees fish dan da real ting." He chuckled.

"Did you ever catch anything unusual? Any squid, or octopus? Maybe something big?"

"Ashley told me 'bout you," he said. "You didn't bring the quarmin' man with you?" He gestured at her outfit. "Because you was running?"

"Didn't bring who?"

"The man that walks funny. Missin' parta his leg. I heard about him."

"You mean Mack. He's my uncle. He's back at our hotel." She wished he would just answer her questions. "So you don't fish anymore?"

"Only for my dinner. Da increased tourism here changed things. Allowed me to make more money carving."

Eric pointed at a very large hunk of raw wood behind Clive, perhaps an uprooted stump, draped under a paint-smeared white sheet. "What are you making there? It's huge."

"Not big enough." Clive turned and pulled the sheet down to hide what looked like roots. "But it'll do. That de stump of an Australian pine. It too don' belong here. Wouldn't be here if people didn't make such bad choices."

"The Australian pines, you mean?" Val said.

"I suppose."

She frowned and said, "Do you know any other fishermen who might have encountered something unusual in the blue holes here? Some larger animal? We'd appreciate any help at all you can provide."

Clive leaned forward, looked into her eyes, unsmiling. "What's in dem holes, you say? It ain't nothin' you wanna find, dear. Let it alone."

"I can't. It's my job. I study octopus and squid."

"Then you wastin' your time. None'a that here." He smiled, sat back. "You sure ya don' wanna buy something?"

CHAPTER 31

Ashley couldn't believe he was actually flirting with her. Telling her she had gorgeous eyes. His wife and kids were right behind him.

Standing behind the marble-topped check-in counter, she touched the small gold cross she wore around her neck. She politely flashed her biggest smile back at the balding, Russian-American tourist.

"I mean zis in a good way. You are very beautiful," the man continued. He was a big man, with large sweat marks staining an expensive pink shirt. He leaned forward on the counter. She could smell alcohol on his breath.

She forced herself to keep smiling. "Oh, thank you, love."

"*Love.* I like how you say zis. I wish my wife would call me that." He shook his head, regarding her like some sort of exotic animal.

The big man stood at the front of a long line of tourists that snaked into the enormous lobby, natural light filtering down between sculpted marble columns from windows near the vaulted, seventy-foot ceiling. Oceanus was the finest resort in the Bahamas. Ashley looked down at her computer monitor. She tapped at her keyboard, not inputting anything as it processed an earlier request, but eager to break the awkward moment.

Her green eyes, which nearly matched the turquoise polo shirt she and other resort staff wore above black slacks, drew a lot of comments. Ashley also had coffee-and-cream-colored skin, and her black hair was naturally wavy. Rumor had it that her great-great-grandfather, a charming, handsome white man, had frequently bedded his slaves. Whether or not that was true, Ashley was fairly sure that her promiscuous mammy on her mom's side had been involved with a Caucasian, because her own mother was even lighter-skinned than she was.

She knew she had a unique look, but most compliments she drew were less blunt. Comparisons to American actresses or singers, usually. And usually not made by a man whose wife was within earshot.

Working the front desk at a tropical resort invited the stares of a lot of wealthy, foreign men. Usually Americans. The white tourists in particular seemed to be drawn to her more than the other women working at the resort—even the ones more attractive than Ashley. She hated to think it was true, but wondered if it was because she looked less black. The one and only time she had stated as much out loud, though, when she was new to her front desk job at the hotel, she had been pulled aside and told in no uncertain terms that if it happened again she would be fired.

She'd heeded the warning. This was a good job, with wonderful benefits, and there were plenty of other young Bahamians happy to take her place. The resort had employed her for a year. She had been working at hotels for six years, since before she turned nineteen, and this was the best job she'd ever had.

She risked looking back at the Russian-American, who was now leering at another woman in line. She'd just been told by her manager, Rick, to treat this guest well. Mr. Melnikov apparently had a lot of money, and was staying in an expensive suite. Planned to drop a lot at the casino. She figured him for Russian mafia. The man's college-age son, a kid with curly brown hair and stud earrings, was still leering at her. Just like his dad.

"I need to grab your keys. I'll be right back," she said. She turned away from the counter, relieved. At a row of polished mahogany cabinets on the back wall, she bent down to look for a box of hotel keycard blanks and felt a light slap on her rear end. She glanced over her shoulder, and saw that it was just her best friend, Georgina.

"Better not bend over, baby girl. Dat one likely to have a heart attack," Georgina whispered. Her plump figure filled out her own resort-issued slacks.

"Maybe I should shake it for him, then."

"Oh, my, my, Ash. You a wicked thing. Poor man just wanna get some lovin'. Probably hasn't wet his little doggy in a month."

"Not in his wife, anyway. He's more your type, Gussy G."

"All men are my type, Ash." Georgina ran both hands over her hips. "So much woman here to go around, and so little time."

The women giggled, and Ashley covered her mouth with her hand. She glanced at Rick to make sure he wasn't looking. He didn't have a sense of humor.

Georgina frowned at her. "Really, Ash. You need a piece a leg. Time to forget about Mr. New Jersey."

"I already forgot about him."

"Maybe. Maybe not. But you hasn't moved on. Wouldn't kill ya to give in for once."

She hadn't thought about Shawn in a week. She was finally over him, after almost a year. The college boy from Newark had seemed so sweet, and she'd finally broken her own rule about getting involved with a guest. At least he'd e-mailed her several times after he left, before dropping out of her life. In the end, just a player like all the others, whose charm was only intended to get her pants off.

Her work made it easier to forget about Shawn. Six days a week didn't leave much time to think about a man, especially since she usually volunteered on her one day off. She didn't need a man anyway.

Moving through the resort, Eric identified a distant water park by the eight-story waterslide that rose above it, and marveled at the abundant sea life in small saltwater pools that lined the cobbled pathways. In them were stingrays, turtles, reef sharks.

The sculptor on the beach, Clive, had proven very evasive. Eric wondered if maybe they had bought something he would have opened up, but neither had brought cash on the run. Or maybe the guy was just superstitious—didn't want to upset the island spirits or something.

Val had left to jog home, but Eric wanted to check out the aquariums. He had drip-dried after an ocean dip, then been allowed onto the property by a guard at the edge of the resort's beach after mentioning Ashley's name. It seemed to carry some weight, and made everyone smile. She wasn't kidding when she said she knew everyone.

He continued down a long, winding path, past planted palm trees and lush greenery onto the impeccably groomed resort grounds. The place smelled of funnel cakes and other fried foods, and was already alive with activity— mainly children dashing about near the pools, their parents trying to catch them to apply sunscreen before they jumped in.

He paused and looked over a discarded resort map he'd found. Even compared to the world-class Point Lobos Aquarium, the exhibits at Oceanus seemed pretty impressive. The resort apparently offered a total of six named tanks, plus dozens of other smaller aquariums. Each named tank had a theme: Shark Alley, The Reef, Pirate's Cove. Oceanus also boasted a massive, enclosed saltwater lagoon, just off the ocean, where visitors could pay extra to swim with a pair of captive dolphins.

Besides the aquariums, the sprawling resort, which looked like it might cover half a square mile and dominated most of the small cay, included five swimming pools, two casinos, a shopping center, twelve restaurants, nightclubs, and a water park for children. An ambitious endeavor, indeed, with some merit in that the aquariums educated the visiting public. But Eric wondered about the environmental consequences of constructing the resort on this previously pristine cay.

He turned left, toward a ramp that ran underground to one of the larger tanks. He paused and took a deep breath. If it was too confined, he would simply turn back.

Out of the sunlight and surrounded by stone walls, it was much cooler at the bottom of the ramp. He headed farther into a curving tunnel. Just as he was beginning to become very uncomfortable with the shrinking space, he came across a clear acrylic wall that separated him from a massive saltwater tank on the other side. He stopped, stunned. The tank rose some three stories above him. Inside were sharks, huge rays, suitcase-sized grouper. A gaggle of tourists, led by a young woman in a resort uniform, came around a bend in the tunnel, and he listened in when she stopped near him and turned to address the group.

"As you can see, the aquariums at Oceanus are engineering marvels," she said, her voice echoing in the manmade tunnel. "They are among the largest in the world, because we have utilized a natural underwater cavern in the limestone to build the tanks *below* sea level. The tank you see here is up to nine meters deep and holds six million gallons of water. The huge volume is possible because it can flow in passively, from the ocean, but we aid the turnover of water with pumps and large pipes that expel spent seawater offshore, near the reef edge.

"This is what we call an 'open system,' and the water quality remains as good as that of the ocean. Although this tank links directly to the reef, screens and filters prevent all but the smallest sea life from entering or leaving."

"How did you build it?" an older man on the tour asked.

"The acrylic viewing panels were put in place by cranes and dive teams, and then the water on this side was pumped out before the tunnels were built."

"Could those glass walls ever break?" asked another tourist.

"No." She laughed. "And it's not actually glass." She rapped on the clear tank. "This is six inches thick, and made of a shatterproof material. Apparently even bullets wouldn't break it. Mr. Barbas, the owner, is truly a visionary."

As Eric half-listened to the rest of the woman's description, he turned away from the tank and looked across the tunnel, up a towering stone wall opposite the tank. He could see the edge of a railing a few stories above, and some tables up there, in what looked like a fancy restaurant. He suddenly realized how far he was below ground level.

As he hurried out of the underground aquarium, Eric passed a sign that indicated he was headed toward the lobby and one of the casinos. He headed up a winding ramp.

At the top, he found himself in an enormous, echoing room, frigid from overuse of the air-conditioning. The hotel lobby. Two rows of ornate marble columns rose to lofty heights, capped by a curved, fresco-adorned ceiling lined with circular windows on all four sides. Most of the people walking past were dressed up: button-down shirts, slacks, fancy dresses, their loafers and high heels clicking on the marble floor. There was money here. He looked down at his damp T-shirt, red swim trunks, and running shoes and suddenly felt self-conscious.

On a long, dark table against the wall was a copy of the daily paper out of Nassau. The resort must have arranged to receive copies each morning. He walked over and picked it up, staring in shock at the headline on the front page:

AMERICAN YACHT LOST AT SEA

Captain Reported Seeing "Tentacles"

Below the headline was a photo of an old man—apparently the owner, who had been lucky enough to be elsewhere when the vessel vanished—taken some time in the past beside the expensive-looking boat. The caption indicated that the boat's captain claimed to have seen "tentacles over the side" in a final transmission picked up by a Bahamian cargo vessel.

He scanned the article. Apparently, a search had thus far yielded no evidence of the boat's whereabouts. Normally, he would laugh at such a story. But now . . .

He thought about the missing divers. The teenager who had disappeared in the blue hole. Val's blurry image—

"Eric?"

He stopped, and turned. Saw Ashley waving at him from the other side of the lobby, near the check-in counters. He smiled and waved back, feeling his face flush, and tucked the paper under his arm as he reluctantly started toward her.

She met him under the middle of the domed lobby. She wore a turquoise short-sleeve shirt and tight black slacks that flattered her athletic figure. She was even taller than he remembered, eye-to-eye with him in the heels she wore.

"What are you doing here?" she said. "Did you come to see me?"

"No. I mean, yeah, sort of. Val and I were running this morning. I thought I might check out the resort while I was here."

She looked over his shoulder. "Where is she?"

"She headed back already." He nodded past her shoulder. "Were you helping those people?"

"It's okay. I was just about to go to one of the private suites, at the top of a tower. I need to do a final inspection before a VIP arrives. Want to join me?"

"I don't want to get in the way. I know you're working. . . ."

"Nonsense. You Americans worry too much." She smiled.

"All right. If you're sure it's okay."

She asked what he thought about Oceanus as they crossed the lobby and entered a hallway. It suddenly hit him. *The top of a tower. The top. No stairs.* They turned into a dead end flanked by a bank of . . .

Elevators.

". . . and the resort has been great for the economy. Since Barbas opened the doors, he has employed almost . . . Eric, are you okay?"

He removed his glasses and rubbed the lenses with his shirt. "I'm fine. Look, I really should be going."

"This won't take long. There. One has just arrived."

The light over one elevator came on, and she tugged gently at his arm, leading him toward the opening doors. He swallowed as he put his glasses back on.

A family entered the car ahead of them, buying him a moment. He pictured himself inside, the doors shutting. There would be at least six people inside. What if something happened? If he had a panic attack? He stopped at the doors.

"Eric?"

"I really need to go, Ashley," he said.

She regarded him with a puzzled expression. "Are you sure?"

A young father was holding the elevator doors open, looking at them.

"Yes. I'm sorry. Thanks for the offer."

She looked disappointed. "No problem. Will I see you again soon?"

"I'll come back." He smiled weakly.

She stepped into the elevator and turned to face him, smiling at him as the doors began to shut between them. Then she was gone. He took a deep breath, at once relieved and ashamed.

He hurried back toward the lobby and headed outside to hail a taxi.

CHAPTER 32

Val exhaled and sank farther into the massive fresh-water hole. Now past a gently sloping, silty bottom that started thirty feet down, she neared a distinct halo-cline between freshwater and saltwater above a dark shaft that plummeted into the center of the hole. The red-tinged layer was quite thin in this particular hole, perhaps due to its great width. But the shimmering bar-rier and its refraction of light made her feel like she was on shore, standing next to a swimming pool and looking down at its mirrored surface.

Beneath her, Mack had already descended through the cloudy layer of hydrogen sulfide at the juncture, and down into the darker shaft. She looked past his blurred visage toward the unseen bottom. A few small sunfish, which looked to her like bluegills, moved lazily across the edge of the hole.

They were finally exploring the inland blue hole where the kid had disappeared two weeks ago. It was no wonder nobody ever dove this hole. The access was terrible. It had been a terrific pain in the butt to get DORA and the gear all the way out here on an overgrown, narrow path through what the locals called "the bush." The deceptively flat ground, hidden under waist-high ferns and other brush, was an ankle-twisting mess of jagged rock outcrops. She and Eric had together hauled the heavy ROV short distances, stopping for breaks, as Mack lugged the hundreds of feet of coiled umbilical cable. But they didn't stop long, because back here, without an ocean breeze, the minuscule biting midges locals referred to as "no-see-ums" would swarm their exposed skin.

When they crossed a marshy spot that sucked at their sandals, it had nearly pulled Mack's leg off. Eric offered to help him, and Val knew it was a good thing her uncle's leg had still been stuck. The man wouldn't accept what he thought was pity.

Rain was in the forecast yet again, so they didn't have the luxury of time. If they got stuck back here in a downpour, it would be a miserable return trip.

Her biggest anxiety today was that that they would find the boy's body down below, well-rotted from resting in the microbe-rich water for weeks, its flesh calving off in hunks. But she knew they probably wouldn't. Rescue divers had already been in here, and found no corpse. No evidence at all. Like the other missing divers, the teenage boy had simply vanished.

She looked over her shoulder, squinting at the bright lights on the nose of the ROV. Eric was on the surface, piloting her.

Val wondered what the hell they were doing here anyway. She had come to the Bahamas to try to find a new species of cephalopod. Not to chase down monster sightings. What the girl had described here was impossible. Nothing that large could live in here, and there was no evidence of the physical passage of anything sizeable around the hole, either. But she knew there *was* one other possibility.

Something could have come from below.

As she descended through the toxic, red-tinged sulfide layer into clear salt water, she thought about the newspaper article Eric had shown her. Many of the inland holes here had extensive tunnels that ran all the way out to the Tongue of the Ocean, where in the article the reporter claimed a missing yacht had supposedly encountered some sort of kraken. Val had initially been as stunned by the article as Eric—and excited. While they scoffed publicly, every cephalopod biologist secretly drooled at the mention of the legendary sea monster, and every sighting was investigated to determine if there was any authenticity. Could the yacht have encountered a giant squid? As implausible as the story sounded, the animals had been theorized to have been responsible for mariners' legends.

Yet there was no physical evidence at all to support their claim. No boat, and no pictures. It was intriguing, but highly implausible.

She checked her air, and then looked back down at Mack. The walls of the hole continued to close in on them as it narrowed even more, farther from the surface. Mack stopped descending where the bottom of the hole became a narrow, black maw. A sweep of her dive light revealed no other obvious side passages. Mack pointed at the opening, nodded at her. She couldn't see the start of a previously laid safety line. Either nobody had been in there before, or the line started farther in, away from where amateur divers might find it and foolishly follow.

The black tunnel appeared sufficiently large for a diver to enter, but would surely narrow. She kicked over to DORA and found the keypad on its side. And began to type Eric a message.

* * *

YOURE ON

Eric nodded as Val's message came through. He typed back:

OK. BACK IN 20. WATCH CABLE.

He waited, watching the text box. Wind whispered through the third-growth overstory of Bahamian pines overhead, and a lone bird sang.

ONE TUNNEL ONLY. DONT GET LOST

Eric smiled. On the laptop monitor, he could see Val as she appeared in front of the camera, and gave the okay signal.

"All right then. Showtime."

Eric nosed DORA around Val, toward the black opening beneath her swim fins. The darkness immediately swallowed the light emitted from the vehicle's panel of LEDs. He eased DORA forward, and as her propeller engaged, she entered the opening.

They had a simple plan. Mack and Val would explore the main shaft of the blue hole while DORA checked out any tunnels below. This blue hole, which the locals simply called the "Big Hole," was large and broad, and beneath the surface apparently shaped like a funnel. More than a football field across on the surface, its sides closed in quickly farther down, to where it was much narrower at the bottom and ended in this opening. There didn't appear to be any other side tunnels.

On the monitor, Eric watched as the smooth walls of the passage slid past. He glanced at a level indicator on the corner of the screen. Merely looking at the image before him, it was impossible to tell which way was up, so he had built in the indicator. DORA was headed almost straight down now.

Ideally, they would have sent DORA into the inland cave as far as the tunnel went, to see if she could reach the open ocean, but there were too many limitations: the cord length, her power supply, the increasing risk of snag and impossible retrieval. So they would just get what they could.

He glanced at another readout, where a green light confirmed that in addition to the video he was using to steer her now, DORA was also gathering three-dimensional sonar imagery so he could map the hole later.

Suddenly, the passageway appeared to end, and Eric reversed DORA's thrusters. He pivoted the ROV upward, back toward a horizontal plane, and saw that the passage continued. He nudged her forward, and she entered a chamber studded with ancient mineral speleothems, like the teeth of some prehistoric beast. There were stalactites, stalagmites, soda straws. Several spanned from floor to ceiling, long, slender columns attempting to support the tons of rock above them. They had formed on the limestone here a long time ago, when this cavern had been above sea level, over a very long period of time.

Eric had read that the fragile-looking mineral formations grew at a steady rate of no more than five centimeters every thousand years. Thus they could hold records of the past, of climate change. He sighed, wishing DORA could take a sample.

As the ROV proceeded, he noticed that, curiously, none of the speleothems on the monitor grew in the middle of the tunnel to obstruct DORA's passage. He paused to take a long video shot of debris from broken-off speleothems on the bottom of the tunnel. At some point, something, perhaps before the sea had flooded the cavern, had broken these off. But there was something odd about the rubble. It appeared not where it had fallen, but in small piles, gathered in depressions. Drifts. And the floor almost looked scoured, as though a massive piece of mining equipment had bored through here, grinding down the rubble and shoving it aside.

He guided the ROV farther into the shaft, which again began to narrow. The compass indicator on his monitor showed that DORA was now headed east. Toward the ocean.

She had sensed the foreign presence some time ago, the light it cast bouncing down the tunnel alongside the quiet, steady vibration it emitted. Now the source of the stimulation had almost arrived.

After crushing part of the large, pale object floating on the ocean surface three nights ago, causing it to fill with water, she had left, frustrated. She had found a few edible things within it, but not enough to sustain her. When it finally sank, she had not followed it into the depths, but had moved on. Just before dawn, as she returned to the island, she had managed to ensnare an adult member of her favorite prey species. The animal had been unusually easy to capture, seemingly disoriented, swimming in slow circles near the surface. Her bite hadn't even been necessary to subdue it, although it had struggled. Its flesh had helped to fill her stomach.

But that was three nights ago. So she had returned to this familiar passage, where she had recently found a meal. Not just to feed, or because of a familiar impulse to retreat to the sluggish environment under the island to rest. There had also been another urge.

The urge to build a den.

She had spent much of the day clearing out a large

chamber, piling rubble in a crude wall along the opening of the chamber, but there wasn't enough material to sufficiently close off the space. Despite the safe distance from the predators of the open ocean, it was too exposed. She had finally ceased her effort. She would need to build her nest elsewhere. But she had remained, to rest. And digest.

A bright light appeared now, a powerful beam striking the ceiling. The whirring vibration intensified in her skin.

She calmly flattened her body against the bottom, her flesh smoothing out to match the rock, the pattern on her thick skin becoming that of the drab limestone. Her eyes became slits. Moments later, a bright yellow entity appeared. The colorful object moved steadily over her head, crossing the chamber, then stopped, hovering. It spun in a slow circle. Then it continued on its course.

As it turned away from her, she slowly released the grip of the suckers lining one arm and lifted it quietly toward the object, dwarfing it. The tip of the tentacle paused behind the object, tasting. But it shed few organic chemicals, no real evidence of life. It was not food.

Slowly, she retracted her appendage.

She watched the yellow entity disappear through a large opening in the cavern. As its sound faded, she filled her body with seawater, expanding to her full size, and released her grip on the cavern floor. Turning in the darkness, she felt for the small opening through which she had entered.

CHAPTER 33

Val stumbled into the kitchen to find Eric already sitting at the chipped Formica table, shirtless and in running shorts. In front of him was his laptop. On the screen appeared to be a news article with the word "Iraq" in the headline. She frowned.

"What are you doing up?" she asked.

He quickly closed the window on his screen, and glanced toward her. "Nothing. I just couldn't sleep."

"That damn clunking AC?"

He nodded. "It keeps waking me up too. What time is it, anyway?"

"Almost three o'clock."

"No shit. Why are you up?"

"I couldn't sleep either. Too much on my mind, and it's too easy for me to get restless. I spent years staying up all night studying squid in Mexico." She filled a glass with water and sat down at the table beside him. Still half-asleep, she tried to figure out what he might have actually been doing. "What were you looking at when I came in?"

"Just some other research I'm working on."

"Oh?" When he didn't reply, she decided to drop it. "You're not up e-mailing Ashley?"

"Ha-ha."

"Seriously. If you're still thinking about what happened at Oceanus, let it go. There'll be other chances."

"I know. You're probably right."

After dinner, he'd told her about his fear of entering the elevator at the resort. About how it had triggered the recent earthquake episode.

On the computer, he expanded another window and turned the monitor toward her. "Since I was up anyway, I thought I'd create a visual file of the 3-D imagery we got today. I found something very interesting."

Val studied the image on the screen. Eric had shown her images like this before, most recently after they explored The Staircase. A cross section of the tunnels under an inland hole, gathered by DORA's sonar device. Lighter shading within the yellow coloration gave the appearance of depth. This time, they were clearly looking at the tunnels under the funnel-like hole where the boy had gone missing.

Rendered on a flat screen, the yellow silhouette of the hole and caverns below reminded her of looking at an MRI image of the anatomy of a gigantic eyeball: widest just below the surface lens of freshwater, then tapering as depth increased. At the bottom, a narrow squiggle of tunnel angled downward, the optical nerve sending signals back to the island's brain.

"I love these things," she said. "But to me, this one looks like all the others."

"Right. But hang on. Let me explain. When I piloted DORA back out of the tunnels today, I came across a larger, more open cavern. One I didn't remember passing on the way in." He pointed at the image. "Take a good look. At this spot, right here. That's the scan from the way in"—he clicked a button, and another window appeared—"and here's the scan from the way out."

In the second window appeared a similar yellow shape.

"It looks about the same to me," she said.

"But not *exactly* the same. Granted, they never are. For an out-and-back like this, when DORA passes the same points twice, it's like proofreading my work. I use the second dataset, taken from different angles, to validate the first dataset. I usually blend the two images for the best representation, since they don't ever match exactly."

"Yeah. You've explained this to me before. The blue-colored areas on the second image are the variations. The spaces that don't match up between the two scans."

He nodded. "There are always anomalies. But not like this. And they're never this big. Here, let me zoom in." He enlarged a portion of the second image, the one scanned on DORA's return trip. On the screen was a large, blue bulge on the bottom of the winding yellow ribbon, just past where it curved toward the horizontal—a tumor growing on the optical nerve.

"That's significant?"

"It's more than significant. I can't explain it. Do you know how large that area is?"

"I'm sure you're going to tell me," she said.

"Well, I don't know the *exact* volume of that one particular variation. I can calculate a rough one. But I do know the overall volume difference between DORA's first and second pass."

"And . . . ?"

"Well, according to the program's calculations, on the second pass the volume of the chamber grew by about 120 cubic meters."

"And that's significant?"

"Very," he said. "For reference, in a cavern like this, I'd expect the overall 'blue area,' as you call it, to depict a difference of no more than about *ten* cubic meters."

She frowned.

"It means that this one blue area alone" —he rotated the image so it could be viewed from another angle—"is the volume of, say, one entire level of a three-bedroom house."

Val leaned in to look at the blue, three-dimensional volume swelling out from the bottom of the tunnel. It was oddly shaped, curved on the bottom, a thick blob pressed against the bottom of the cavern, filling in a side chamber like some piece of chewing gum smoothing over the uneven tread of a shoe. But along a few of its upper edges, there was an oddly symmetrical quality. Val thought she could make out circular masses curving out and back into the blob in several locations.

"What the hell is this, Eric?"

"I don't know. I thought maybe DORA's sensor malfunctioned, but it appears to be working fine. So I wondered if the bottom of the chamber somehow collapsed right after DORA passed, as unlikely as that may seem. But there's very little rubble apparent in that blue area. If there had been a cave-in, I'd expect to see a very jagged bottom to that shape, where detritus accumulated. And we would have seen huge clouds of sediment when DORA returned through here."

"But what else could account for this?" Val fought to remain rational, but in her mind raced thoughts about the missing yacht; the local girl's claim that she had seen something dwelling in this hole. Something that had pulled a boy under.

Eric shrugged. "The only other rational explanation is that DORA's 3-D scanners aren't working properly, and that I'm not able to recognize it. We should probably go back for a third and fourth scan to see what we find."

Val continued to stare at the image. "All right," she finally said.

"There's one more thing, Val."

She squinted at him. "Uh-huh . . ."

Eric zoomed in even farther on the blue blob's upper edge. Zoomed in so far, Val could now see that the top of the image was broken up by a series of uneven horizontal lines, both blue and yellow, where the blob met the main tunnel.

"What are those lines?" she said.

"They indicate a poor reading. DORA was unable to clearly scan the bottom of the cavern here on her first pass."

"What would cause that?"

Eric took his glasses off and leaned back in his chair.

"Eric?"

"Usually, it's because whatever is being scanned is *moving*."

CHAPTER 34

The side cavern narrowed further, and she paused. She extended the tip of a long, serpentine arm deeper into the crack, into the increasing flow of water. Here, the particles in the current were dense, overwhelming. Tasting of waste, of life, of food. Elongating further directly into the flow, the arm tip made contact. Something was blocking the source of the outflow, but allowing water to pass through it.

Lightly, the tip of the complex appendage explored the obstruction. It was hard, encrusted in barnacles. But there were uniform openings in the heavy steel lattice, through which the water flowed.

She was intrigued by this concentrated scent of food, which drifted steadily toward her now in the light current. But the impulse that had driven her through life—hunger—had faded some, and was weak at the moment.

She moved farther into the deep crack, into total darkness. She had been here before. Into this side cavern. From the remains outside its opening, far below at the dark bottom of the main fissure, she knew this was a den frequently used in the past by her own kind. Others had dispelled waste material from this space many times over thousands of years, to sink to the bottom of the pit.

This place was not unlike the one she had been raised in, in which she had remained, devouring most of her siblings until she was strong enough to venture out and hunt the deep ocean. The current was ideal here, its steady flow bringing oxygen and freshwater. And the space was just adequate. It narrowed quickly, was compressed laterally, and the lack of extra space would make it easier to protect.

But for now, there was still nothing to protect. For now, she needed to satisfy her other, constant urge.

She manipulated her body, slowly turning it, and squeezed back out the mouth of the broad crack, into the main shaft of the fissure.

Her immense form nearly spanned the entire shaft as she rose toward the light above, snakelike arms trailing many yards behind her, toward the gaping mouth of the submarine pit. Then she emerged quietly from the gloom.

CHAPTER 35

Mack floated facedown in the water. Watching. Waiting.

Eighty feet below him, a few stories below the shallower coral shelf clearly visible through the lens of his dive mask, the dark, crescent-shaped mouth of a crevasse gaped up at him. A marine fault-line hole. The great fissure opened liked a torn seam in the expanse of rough fabric that was the sea floor, not far from where the edge of the shelf dropped into the abyss. The water above the hole had remained gin-clear for some time, an indication that warm seawater had been draining from the open ocean back into the cavity.

Mack breathed in through his snorkel. Exhaled. Concentrated.

A large spotted eagle ray came into view as it winged languidly past the edge of the hole, keeping its distance. He watched until it disappeared into the blue. Not much farther in that direction was the edge of the island shelf, where long, curly whip-wire corals poked out of the top edge of the vertical wall, like the sparse hairs on the back of some beast, its skin pocked with numerous caverns and recesses. The steep drop-off there ended 6,000 feet below, in a submarine trench.

This marine hole, nicknamed the Bottomless Hole by local dive shops because of its great depths and poor entry access, was located just off the coast from White Sand Cay, and the beach at Oceanus. But guides only brought the most experienced divers here. It was simply too dangerous. The last time he'd been here was years ago, also with John Breck.

Ocean blue holes, unlike the inland holes, underwent massive exchanges of water each time the tides changed. For smaller ocean holes, with larger mouths, the cycling of water wasn't a major concern. But this was a massive feature, reportedly extending into a fissure more than four hundred feet below the ocean floor, and its opening was comparatively small.

The fissure had been formed during the Ice Ages, when water levels had receded. A dome of rock above a huge cavern had collapsed, in the absence of hydrostatic pressure that had been supporting the rock overhead. This collapse had revealed the deep fissure, and created the resulting rubble piled along one side, narrowing the width of its mouth. Mack knew from experience that the exchange of tidal water in a narrow-mouthed feature like this could create deadly rip currents. Even a whirlpool.

A diver caught above the mouth of the hole when it was sucking in seawater would be as helpless as a tiny piece of food swirling into the garbage disposal of a draining kitchen sink.

Mack had heard this hole had claimed a lot of divers. Somewhere down there, stuffed into cracks leading back under the island, Mack knew there were probably a bunch of corpses. A real-life Davy Jones's Locker.

The trick to diving a hole like this was simple timing.

The best time—the only time, really—to enter was after the hole had just sucked in warm seawater, but before it began to expel cold, cloudy subterranean water regurgitated from the underbelly of the island. Timing dives properly could mean the difference between life and death.

Dive too soon, and you got swallowed up. Too late, and you wouldn't be able to see a damn thing, which also was very dangerous if you were hundreds of feet underwater and inside a narrow fissure.

Peering into the dark crescent, Mack decided it was time. He swam over to the boat, unable to kick without a prosthesis, instead pulling with his arms.

He struggled up the slippery, rounded steps of the aluminum swim ladder. The rented pontoon boat, a twenty-five-foot outboard with a blue-painted double hull, was anchored to the reef. The vessel had come cheap, owned by a diver he knew. Mack nodded at his niece.

"Is it time?" Val said.

"Now or never. Besides, wind's picking up."

The red-and-white dive flag flapping in the breeze over the stern had begun to stiffen. Along the reef crest stretching in both directions on their landward side, just offshore of numerous smaller cays poking above the barrier wall, the waves had begun to break more violently.

Next to Val, Eric was tinkering with DORA on the deck. The kid was obsessed with the thing. Like some stupid pet. But Mack had to admit, the submersible's 3-D renderings of the inland holes were pretty amazing. He was looking forward to seeing what this hole really looked like inside, after DORA got a good look, and finding out how deep it really was.

"Your girlfriend ready?" he asked Eric.

Eric glared at him. "Yes. Val, let's get her in."

She helped Eric lower DORA into the water.

"This the same umbilical we've been using?" Mack said. "Same length?"

Eric nodded. "Stop questioning me. It's four hundred feet. And it should be easier to prevent snags in this hole."

Val sat next to Mack, and he helped her strap on a scuba tank, and then pushed his shoulders into the vest affixed to his own tank. Finally, he strapped on the special prosthesis he'd created for diving, which was connected to a fin, and slid the other fin onto his remaining foot.

Nodding at Val, he rolled back into the water. She followed.

They sank toward the hole like deadweight, not kicking. They needed to relax to conserve air.

Mack felt good about their timing. He couldn't detect any suction of water into the hole. They dropped like stones, quickly passing by large coral heads growing like giant sores on the mouth of the depression, on a ledge forty feet above the dark crescent of the hole.

Near the coral heads, large schools of grunts and sergeant majors gathered. He also spied a trio of lionfish, one much larger than the others. The damn things were everywhere now. Native to the Indo-Pacific, the invasive fish had established themselves in the Bahamas and Caribbean after the release from some aquarium in Florida. They were good to eat, but their spines were deadly and they killed off a lot of native marine life.

Mack had to admit, he was as puzzled as the others by DORA's data from within the big inland hole. They had gone back the next day to confirm the ROV's earlier findings. The readings had been the same. But there was no way to know if something about the cavern had indeed been different when DORA had first entered the hole, or why she had somehow not detected what was obviously a large recess off one side of the cavern.

Mack listened to the loud hiss of compressed air passing through his regulator as they sank past the three-story vertical wall and passed into the maw of the hole. Although there were fish all over the reef, nothing was moving in the blackness below them.

As his eyes adjusted, he could see the crack begin to widen. In the powerful beam of his dive light, the curved, pale walls sank under the island and into blackness. Something moved within it. Four ghostly jacks, each a yard long, emerged and swam in formation beneath the curved wall, barely discernible in the gloom before disappearing back into it.

He looked up. The fissure's opening, brightly lit from above, shrank into a slit as they sank deeper. He glanced at his gauges. The water temperature remained constant, about seventy-five degrees. No thermocline here.

He thought he felt a light current flutter past, from a dark opening in the side of the cavern. He'd heard that the main outflow pipe for the resort aquariums was concealed somewhere back in there. The builders had ingeniously utilized the natural caverns below the island to minimize the length of pipe necessary to extend the facility's outflow away from the beaches. He continued to sink, and after a moment the current was gone.

Val's plan now was to simply get 3-D scans of as many holes as possible, including those in the ocean. They would start with this one. A week later, they would go back to each for a second scan, to see if they could once again detect a significant change in shape or volume. It seemed like a good idea. And if they detected the same thing again . . .

He gazed down into the blackness, suddenly feeling like something might be down there. He looked over at his niece, and she gave him the okay signal with thumb and forefinger. She not only had guts. She had a big heart.

He couldn't let anything happen to her.

A hundred and thirty feet down, about fifty feet into the gaping maw, Mack and Val had finally stopped and watched the ROV whir past, nose down, dwarfed by the rough, curved walls of the hole as it disappeared into blackness. That had been ten minutes ago, and still its transmission cable continued to sink past Mack. But he was growing restless.

He tapped Val on the shoulder and pointed to where he was headed, and then turned and swam toward the side of the expansive cavity. She remained behind, hovering and watching the cable.

He neared the rough wall, but it lacked anything interesting. There was virtually no coral living inside here, and there were few fish. Despite the tidal fluxes, water circulation in the holes was usually poor. The water often became anoxic deeper down, and deadly to most sea life other than bacteria. He wondered what on earth the jacks had been doing in the darkness, or if he had merely imagined them.

On the vertical wall of the fissure, twenty feet to one side, he spied an odd-looking object resting on a ledge. A length of something, encrusted in barnacles. A pipe? He kicked over to it, and it became apparent what he was looking at. Some sort of bone.

He picked it up. Was it human? He couldn't be sure, as it was badly decomposed and encrusted in barnacles. It looked like it had been here a very long time. But it looked like it could be a femur. Mack thought about Breck. His body was rotting in that other, godforsaken inland hole. It wasn't right. He'd been a good man, and a hell of a diver. A friend.

He needed to know what the hell had happened to him.

Maybe Valerie would know what kind of bone this was. He turned away from the cavern wall. And stopped.

In front of him in the dark, semicircular shaft of water, running vertically down from the opening in the hole above, was the cable, which had now ceased moving. But his niece wasn't there.

He kicked forward, searching. His field of view was limited by the dive mask, and he had to twist his head in all directions. But he saw nothing. She was gone.

He began to feel a hint of panic. He looked down the length of the cable, to where it faded into the gloom maybe seventy feet below him. She wouldn't have gone down there. They hadn't planned on going that deep, and she wouldn't go alone. She wasn't that stupid.

His eyes caught movement on the wall directly below him. Bubbles. He exhaled in relief.

She was directly beneath him, maybe thirty feet deeper, against the cavern wall. In the dim light, without any color at this depth besides drab blues and grays, he had simply been unable to see her. He swore into his regulator. She was too far down, using different mixed gasses than they had in the inland holes. She'd take on a lot of nitrogen. And she was too far from him, her dive buddy, if anything went wrong.

Detecting movement, he looked back at the cable. It had twisted. Mack watched as it continued to turn. It was moving, but it wasn't headed down. Was the ROV already coming back up?

Below him, Valerie began her ascent. She was through with whatever had lured her down there, or else she too figured DORA was headed back up. Viewed from above, her face and shoulders stood out in bright contrast to the black void below her. As she gradually rose, just as he began to make out her eyes in the mask, something moved in the darkness behind her. It wasn't the jacks.

Mack's heart jumped. He squinted into the void. *Nonsense.* He had to be just seeing things, letting his imagination—

The bone dropped out of his hand, and sank toward Valerie.

Beneath her, the entire curve of blackness was changing, beginning to take shape, rising rapidly upward from the depths and toward her. He shouted into his regulator, even though he knew she couldn't hear him. Still twenty feet below him, she was focused on the bone sinking slowly past her. She had no idea what was beneath her.

The shape began to take on form as it caught the light from above. It was something pale, sinuous.

Something huge.

CHAPTER 36

Sturman heard his cell phone ring behind him, but ignored it the way he ignored the ache in his bad left shoulder. He lunged toward the heavy bag and released a series of hard punches, grunting each time a wrapped fist made contact. Sweat beaded in his close-cropped hair and ran down his face. He could smell the alcohol being expelled through his pores.

He hadn't formally boxed much before, although in the Navy he'd used his fists a few times. He mainly came to the cheap gym in Seaside for the workout, and didn't really compete. He was too old, anyway, surrounded by young bloods in their early twenties. Guys hungry for competition. But he did spar with the other cruiserweights and even the bigger heavyweights, and he'd earned their respect. He didn't mind taking the punishment. He deserved it.

Hitting the heavy bag also helped with his aggression and frustration. He was mad at himself. For last night. He'd promised himself he wouldn't drink, even though it was a Friday. But all it took was one offer: *C'mon, Sturman. Just come have one with us. . . .*

No wonder she didn't love him anymore.

He launched into another harsh combination, and

heard the phone ring again. Goddammit, what the hell could be so important? If it was Val, he didn't want to talk to her. They'd talked a few nights ago, and it had gone relatively well. He'd told her he was back on the wagon. But that was before last night. He continued to ignore the ringing.

Then a thought hit him: What if something bad had happened? To his aging father . . . or to her?

He stopped, panting, and jogged past the few other guys there, who were practicing their footwork, to his duffel in the corner. He dug out the phone just as it rang the final time. On the screen it indicated he had two missed calls, both from Rabinowitz. He picked up the phone and called his friend back, stepping into the cooler air outside the gym as he heard the phone ring on the other end. Late-morning fog obscured the chaparral hills sometimes visible past a dirt parking lot to the east.

"Sturman?"

"Hey, Wits. I just missed you. Everything all right?"

"I'm near a pay phone. Let me call you back from there. When I do, don't use my name."

"What? All right . . ."

"Hang on."

Rabinowitz hung up and Sturman stood staring into the fog, wondering what the hell his old friend was up to. The phone rang again, this time displaying an unknown number. He answered.

"What's going on?"

"I need to tell you something," Rabinowitz said.

"What's up with all this spy shit?"

"Just listen. Last time we talked, you mentioned that your woman was down here looking into giant squid, or something like that."

"Yeah . . ." Sturman had called Rabinowitz a few days ago, after environmental groups had publicly blamed the

Navy's sonar testing for dead whales washing up in the Bahamas. Sturman had badgered him, since he worked on naval research projects in the Bahamas. Maybe he'd know something about what Val was looking for, perhaps something about giant squid living in the area. Something that could help her. But on that call, Wits had insisted that he couldn't talk about his work, or anything he'd learned.

"Well, look, I might have . . . something," Rabinowitz said. "But I could get court-martialed for this."

"If you know something, Wits, you need to tell me."

"Dammit, I said don't use my name."

"What's the problem? It's not like we're talking about the weapons you're testing . . . are we?"

"No."

"Well, spit it out."

"Hang on," Rabinowitz said. A pause. "Look," he said, speaking more quietly. "We lost another submersible recently. The brass stated there was no accident, and no details were revealed publicly. But there were two men onboard."

"What happened?"

"I don't know. But I talked to a friend here, who managed to see some of the footage the sub gathered before it was lost. She thought she saw something on the camera. Some sort of big . . . tentacles."

"What the fuck? Why didn't you tell me—"

"I'm not even supposed to be talking to you now. That's all I can tell you. I gotta go."

"That's it? That's all you're gonna tell me, you prick? What was it? What did she see?"

"That's all I know. One other thing. Do a Google search about a sea monster attacking a yacht in the Bahamas. Something happened last week."

There was a click, and Wits was gone.

CHAPTER 37

Val toweled off her hair in the bow of the boat. She felt relaxed, relieved, her wet suit stripped to her waist and the sun warming her back while the craft bobbed gently on small waves. She now understood why nobody entered the hole below them. There had been a few long moments where she'd been worried they wouldn't make it back.

She'd left Mack when she spied something shiny beneath her—what looked like something artificial. She decided to hurry down to it, only to find it was an old beer can carelessly dropped from the surface by some tourist. As she'd begun her ascent, and was almost to her uncle, a billowing cloud of cold, sediment-laden water had overtaken them, washed up from below as it was expelled from the caverns woven under Andros Island.

With the visibility suddenly at zero, and a swirling, turbid current forcing them up too fast, she and Mack had held on to one another and tried to control their ascent without slamming their heads into the rock wall that curved in over the shaft's opening. After several hair-raising minutes, they'd cleared the mouth of the hole and calmed down as they hovered in the warmer, clear waters beneath the boat. Needing to clear the excess nitrogen from their bodies, they remained for some time there, watching the sediment cloud haze the waters around them.

"I guess all that rain last week musta gotten under the island," Mack said. He hadn't bothered drying off, and was leaning back in the captain's chair.

Val thought again of the dark cloud of cold water rising toward her and shuddered. "Yeah, I guess so."

She sat down on a padded bench seat to put on dry clothes. Eric was in the stern, in the filtered shade under the black mesh strung over the top rails, setting his laptop up to play back the ROV's video footage. Mack stood, a wooden toothpick dangling from the corner of his mouth, and moved over to Eric. Val buttoned shorts over her swim bottoms and got up to join them.

"You were right, Val," Eric said, the hint of a smile on his face. "These holes not only suck. Now we're seeing them blow."

"Like you," Mack said.

Val shook her head. Was he hard on Eric just because he'd never served in the military? Her Uncle Mack had always been confrontational, but now he'd become a bully. She wished this fieldwork could be more lighthearted. Suddenly she had a flashback:

Almost two years ago. Will Sturman. With his friend, Mike Phan, arguing and telling lewd jokes. Off Southern California, on Maria, *named after the wife he'd lost. Him looking at her, the way he used to.*

Will had been a drunk then, before he'd gone clean with her. He was trying to get clean again now, and maybe he would. But he'd never move on from Maria. She looked at Eric.

"Got anything yet?"

He looked down at the computer. "Almost . . . Okay,

there. The raw download's ready. Might be hard to see, out here in the sun. Someone hold up a towel."

As they'd boarded the boat, he'd informed them that the hole indeed dropped to more than 350 feet below the seabed, but how far he wasn't sure. DORA had never reached a discernible bottom, so they would need to view the 3-D scan to determine actual depth. And he'd excitedly described some interesting features DORA had encountered. Some sort of what he considered man-made debris piles outside a few side tunnels, and larger, club-like objects just inside one passage. All now captured on video.

She and Mack crowded in on either side of him on the seat, squinting to see even under the towel they held over them.

"There isn't much worth watching in the beginning," Eric said. "I'm going to fast forward until DORA is farther down . . . here . . . no, hang on, I passed it." He messed with the display. "I'm bringing us to where the hole first narrowed to a series of ledges."

He played with the feed some more, and then on the screen was a lighter-colored shape, surrounded by a darker background. "Here. This is where I recorded that first weird pile of rocks or something, by the mouth of a side tunnel."

Val leaned toward the monitor. "Can you turn up the brightness?"

"This is the best we're gonna get. Mack, move that towel over the screen."

He did, and suddenly the playback was a little more discernible. In the paused video, DORA's lights were fixed on a pile of rubble. It was located on a relatively flat surface, with the black opening of another branching fissure behind it.

"Where is that?" Mack asked.

"About three-hundred-twenty feet down. This is where the shaft clearly narrowed, starting with a wide ledge on one side. It looked like a bulldozer had excavated the tunnel here, so I took DORA just past this pile, into it."

He played the video feed again, and bits of marine snow moved *upward* on the camera, and Val realized she was seeing the first hint that the upward flow of cold water was about to begin.

"There." Eric again paused the image and pointed. "There's one of the clubs."

"Looks like a big tooth or something," Mack said.

"I doubt it," Val said. On the screen was an elongated object with a heavier mass on one end, more pointed on the other. Something about it was familiar. "It's hard to tell with it half-buried in the sediment like that. But I'd guess it's probably some sort of bone. Maybe from a whale."

"How the hell would a whale bone get back into that narrow cavern?"

"Good question. I don't know." Val thought for a moment. "Maybe the same currents that pushed the rubble out brought the bone back in. Let's send some stills of this footage to Karen."

"Back at PLARG?" Mack asked.

She nodded. "She studies marine mammals. Maybe she'll be able to ID this."

"I found a bone too," Mack said. "Smaller than that one. I dropped the damn thing when that sediment kicked up. You saw it, Val."

"I couldn't tell what was sinking toward me. But I'm not surprised we're finding bones. With the lower oxygen levels in these holes, bones and other matter might preserve longer than they would elsewhere in the ocean."

Eric fast-forwarded. "There." He paused the video.

"Here's the other pile. The bigger one. Maybe forty feet deeper."

It was indeed another mound of debris, perhaps five or ten feet high, also located just below an opening in the rock wall. She scanned the image. There appeared to be the skeletal remains of sizeable arthropods, and maybe a few large bones jutting from the pile.

"What do you think these are, Val?" Eric asked.

"Well, they could be debris cones, from the collapse of the rock above."

"Like the pile of snow that forms when you shovel off a deck?"

She nodded.

"DORA found something like this in Mexico's cenotes," he said. "But here they're at the mouths of tunnels."

She said, "What do you think, Mack?"

He shrugged. "Debris cones seem plausible. Or maybe like you said, the currents piled that stuff there over time."

"Maybe." She frowned.

"What?" Mack said.

"Well, with the bones, the shells . . . they sort of remind me of something else." She watched as the dense cloud of sediment finally overtook the ROV and obscured the camera, effectively ending the video. Eric stopped it.

He looked at her. "What? What do those remind you of?"

"Well, it really isn't possible. They're far too large. But they look like middens."

"Middens?"

"Yes. Middens."

"What the hell are those?" Mack asked.

"Basically they're trash heaps, usually composed of bits of rock or coral, and shells . . . or bones."

"Made by what?"

Val got up and moved to the edge of the boat: She leaned over the side, gazed down into the water. The dark hole beneath the surface remained obscured by the cloudy water.

"Nothing that gets big enough to do that," she said.

CHAPTER 38

Passing by the last vacant lifeguard tower was like passing some invisible line drawn in the white sand of the beach. The bright lights of the resort were quickly replaced by dim starlight and the faint glow of a crescent moon. The loud music behind them soon faded into the quiet, rhythmic sound of waves lapping the shore, and a gentle breeze coming off the dark ocean brought the smell of salt. Gloria finally began to relax.

With the back of one hand, she wiped a drying tear from her check. As they continued down the beach, she looked at Beth. She could barely see her partner's short-haired silhouette in the dim light, but her hand was warm in her own. *No, not my partner*, Gloria reminded herself. *She's now my wife.*

She smiled for a moment at the realization, which still hadn't fully sunk in, but then the smile faded, and she felt the lump rise in her throat again. Even if they were legally married now, much would never change.

Four days ago, back in Delaware, Gloria had married her partner of eight years at a small ceremony attended by close friends and a few accepting family members.

Until a few years ago, gay marriage hadn't even been legal in the state. But it hadn't mattered anyway. Beth had been deployed overseas until just last year.

She was everything Gloria wasn't. While Gloria was loud, outgoing, all bulging breasts and bright-red lipstick, bangled in beaded jewelry, her longtime partner was ever the soldier: tough, stoic, and determined, with short hair and angular features. They were so different. But they worked.

Back at the resort, when the young men had made the first "lesbo" comments as the late-night party had started to break up, even Beth had at first shrugged it off. They were used to not being accepted. But then the one really drunk asshole, who'd continued to needle them in a heavy Boston accent, had made a lewd comment about Gloria (*I don't blame you,* he'd said to Beth. *I'd totally bang her.*). Gloria had thought for a few tense moments Beth was actually going to get into a fight.

Gloria stopped walking. Looked back again.

"Don't worry," Beth said. "They didn't follow us."

"Are you sure?"

"I'm sure. We're alone." She squeezed Gloria's hand.

They continued down the ribbon of smooth, densely packed sand. A woman working at the hotel had told her that the beach was made up of tiny shell fragments and bits of the island's limestone. In the weak moonlight, Gloria could see where just offshore the sandy bottom yielded to darker sea grass beds on the bottom.

The beach and the water were warmer than she'd hoped for, having read that it could be cool here in February. But the night was pleasant, and the clean water that washed over her feet was cool and soothing. She let go of Beth's hand and touched the ring on her left hand. It was so real. She felt a surge of emotion, and stopped to wrap her arms around Beth's neck and kiss her.

"What was that for?" Beth asked.

But Gloria didn't answer. Instead, she kissed her again, this time with her tongue. Beth began to kiss her back, and slid one hand down to her crotch.

"Not here," Gloria whispered.

"Why not?" Beth smiled. "That's what honeymoons are for, right?" Her hands ran over Gloria's body.

Beth started to lead her up the beach, toward a low rock outcrop. They dropped their sandals in the sand, and Gloria took a final look back down the strand toward the resort. Nobody in sight. She felt Beth's strong hands sliding up her thighs. She looked down the beach, in the other direction—

"Wait, honey."

"What," Beth asked breathlessly. "Is everything okay?"

"What's that smell? It's awful."

"What are you talking about?"

"I think I see something. Farther up the beach." Gloria pointed.

There, in the surf a short distance away, a wave washed against a long, dark blob. It wasn't moving.

"What *is* that?" Gloria clung to Beth's arm.

"Only one way to find out."

CHAPTER 39

Moving silently through the dark water, she sensed a change in the water. A taste. She slowed, testing the currents.

Prey.

She had been unwilling to venture into the abyss. The terrifying vibrations were constant, the sounds of her one enemy pulsing from points everywhere, and if she descended the vibrations brought pain. So she had hunted higher up, just below the reef crest, for the early part of the night. Prowling the offshore depths near her new den, moving in a large circle.

But she had been unsuccessful. Returning to the den now, from a different direction, she pulsed through the water in slow, powerful bursts. As she had moved along the rim of the mile-high escarpment soaring above the undersea canyon, still seeking food, her impulse to hunt had been overcome. By an urge to return to her nearby lair, to continue clearing it, arranging it. The urge to feed had faded.

Until now.

She pulled herself over the top of the steep wall, dislodging a hunk of coral that sank past her into the darkness. Moving over the deep reef, she passed through a groove in the reef crest, feeling the waves crashing into the shallow ridge above, and paused. These shallows were not her usual habitat. But the taste of flesh was strong. She entered the lagoon.

In the shallow water, her eyes began to make out a pale, sandy bottom broken by dark coral and, closer to shore, beds of sea grass. The taste grew stronger.

Rarely had she ever ventured into shallow lagoons such as these. And never recently. But there was something here, now, closer to the shore.

A surge of water ran past her and the sensation became more distinct. She slowed. In the water, the scent was suddenly very strong. *Sour.* The smell only emitted by carrion.

She was not always a scavenger. Like her smaller cousins, she was designed to capture living prey, subdue it. Her organs were not best suited to digesting decomposing flesh, or deal with microorganisms amassing within it. But to accommodate such a large size at maturity, her kind had evolved to become highly opportunistic.

She continued forward into the sandy flats.

The bottom sloped steadily upward, and soon it was no longer deep enough for her to move freely. Small schools of fish in her path darted away from her shadow. But they were of no interest to her. Flattening her body, she slid her great form along the bottom, her mantle only feet below the surface now, the motion of the waves above caressing her skin. As one long arm groped along the bottom, she suddenly sensed something else.

Vibrations. Slow, rhythmic. Faint. But they were there.

Then, in the water, she began to taste something else. Something alive.

It was not something on which she often fed, but it

was familiar. She had fed on this prey recently. Further flattening her immense, muscular body against the sandy bottom, until her entire body was no thicker than one of her arms, she slithered forward. The vibrations grew louder. Off to one side.

She turned, and dragged herself into the surf. Toward the vibrations.

To intercept whatever was making them.

The dark spot in the surf was a dead whale. At least, Gloria thought it was dead. In the water near her, it wasn't moving, and the *stench* . . . just awful. It was definitely too big, too dark to be a dolphin. Even if it was the smallest whale she had ever seen. She looked down the beach, toward the three other dark shapes they had now spotted.

"Do you think they're all dead?" she whispered.

"I don't know about the others," Beth said. "But the smell . . . I doubt they stink like this when they're alive."

"What do you think killed them?"

"I have no idea."

Gloria suddenly felt an overwhelming urge to leave the whale. To get out of the water. "We should go back. Maybe somebody at the resort will know what to do."

"What's the point, babe? Even if a few of them aren't dead yet, there's nothing we can do."

"How do you know? Maybe we can help them."

Beth looked back toward the lit towers of the hotel, which rose defiantly into the night sky. They were a good ten-minute walk away. She looked back at Gloria.

"Please?" Gloria said.

Beth sighed. "All right. But hang on."

She waded farther into the water, now up to her thighs. She leaned down toward the front end of the motionless animal. Poked it with her hand. "It's cold," she said.

"Be careful," Gloria said. She moved deeper, next to Beth. She thought she felt something lightly brush her calf.

"I *am* being careful. There's nothing a dead—"

Gloria suddenly felt herself plunging downward, into the water. Her face went under. She instinctively struggled to stand, to raise her head above the water. She pushed off the bottom, feeling soft sand against her hands and knees. And she felt something else, and she knew.

Something was holding on to her. Wrapping itself tightly around her ankle.

Desperately, she forced her face out of the water. Looked at Beth, who was splashing toward her, wide-eyed in horror.

The thing encasing her ankle squeezed. *Hard.*

"Beth," she gasped.

The last thing she saw was her lover reaching for her. Then she was jerked violently under.

Her chemical receptors tested the writhing creature. Tasted it.

Food.

The desperate prey writhed in the organism's grasp as she dragged it along the bottom, methodically coiling more of her arm around the flailing appendages. She was dimly aware that one of her other arms was trailing the other small creature now clumsily splashing away, toward the beach, but her focus quickly returned to the prize already wriggling in her clutches. She rolled another arm out to further ensnare the creature to ensure that it would not escape. Two other arms snaked hungrily into the surf line and wrapped themselves around the dead whale, and began to drag it into the lagoon.

Clutching her two prizes, she quickly began to move away from the beach.

As she neared the cleft in the reef and the drop-off to the abyss, the still-living prey began to flail wildly in her grasp. She brought it to her beak and pierced its soft flesh, injecting toxins from her salivary glands. A tactic she used on larger prey. With a final tremble, the prey ceased moving.

She pushed through the gap where the coral-encrusted bottom fell away and began to slowly turn her body in the deeper water. Once it was deep enough, she again maneuvered the meal toward her mouth. Her own bulk blocked her view of the prey, her eyes being on the other side of her body. But she did not need to see in order to feed.

She felt the prey enter her maw. As her beak began to close on the creature, it suddenly tensed a final time. Somehow, it was still alive.

Her jaw clenched, and there was a muffled crack as the creature's hard, round head split between her jaws, like the thick shells that protected many of her other prey. She continued to force the food farther into her beak, quickly consuming the small animal. Then she turned her focus to the dead whale, still clasped in her other arms. Methodically, she began to scrape the ribbon of her hundreds of teeth against the carcass, each time removing large, ragged hunks of flesh.

She moved out past the vertical wall, continuing to feed as she slowly sank into the depths. Back into the darkness.

CHAPTER 40

When they reached the beachfront, Val leaned on a heavy rope railing to remove her tennis shoes and zipped them into her daypack. A morning breeze off the ocean brought a clean salt smell and the sound of rustling palms. Over a delectable lunch of blackened grouper, which Ashley had gotten them free from the kitchen, they had talked quite a lot about Val's struggles with Will, and about Eric. Val could tell Ashley was interested in him.

They had just walked from the Oceanus lobby all the way through the resort, a walk that had taken nearly ten minutes. The place was huge, and it appeared to be still growing. A yellow crane towered over the far side of the resort, where they were apparently constructing another hotel wing.

Ashley, removing her own shoes, said, "If Clive didn't have any information last time you met, what makes you think he will now?"

"Maybe he was hiding something."

"I don't think he would lie to you. He's a decent man."

"It's not that I think he was *lying*," Val said. "I just

think he didn't trust us. With you there, maybe he'll open up a little more."

Val had come today by taxi, ostensibly only to have lunch with her new friend. But upon arrival she had felt compelled to speak again with the old sculptor. This time, with Ashley beside her. And this time, with the last image taken by John Breck.

"Like I said, he may not be there," Ashley said, as they started onto the beach. "Sundays are holy days, and many Bahamians don't work."

Last night, back at the house, Val had repeatedly watched the video of the Bottomless Hole. She'd become more convinced that the piles of rubble bore the right characteristics to be enormous middens—of some sort or another. Octopuses usually made them when cleaning out their dens. Mack had scoffed at the notion, saying that no octopus was that big. Even Eric had admitted that he too was surprised Val was considering such a theory. They were both justified, based on what she knew. No cephalopod, no *animal* was that big, except for a whale. Still . . .

She was supposed to be a scientist. Yet she was actually considering some enormous new species, unknown to humanity, living within underwater caves right off a crowded tourist area. Was that even possible?

It certainly didn't seem very likely. But being a scientist, she needed to follow the evidence. And right now, the only evidence she had was a dim photograph, reports of attacking krakens, and what appeared to be oversized middens.

"What if Clive does help you find something?" Ashley said. "What do you think it will be?"

Val thought for a moment. "I don't know. But new species of cephalopods are actually discovered all the time. Sometimes even really big ones, ones that have been here all along, but spend most of their time in the deep. The colossal squid, off Antarctica. More recently, the seven-arm octopus, first in the Atlantic and then off New Zealand."

"But nothing as large as what you're looking for here?"

"No."

"How could something even get so big?"

"Squid and octopus grow very fast. Did you know that in just three or four months, a newborn Caribbean reef octopus grows from just a centimeter to a foot-and-a-half long?"

"Really? That fast?"

"The speed is one thing, but the relative change in size is another. As long as there's enough food, their mass increases by thousands of times, like an acorn becoming an oak. But reef octopuses stay small because they live in warm, shallow water."

"What do you mean?" Ashley said.

"Usually animals living in low-oxygen, deep-ocean zones, under higher pressure, are the ones that reach impressive sizes."

Val figured the best chance she had of getting information from Clive was if she brought Ashley. And not the men. Especially not Mack, as confrontational as he was. She thought again of his request last night. To get DORA back in The Staircase, to go even deeper. He needed to know what had happened to Breck, and seemed even more bothered now that they had found the midden-like piles deep in the offshore blue hole. She couldn't blame him. The two men had been friends, of the sort only soldiers and adventure-sports partners might understand. He wanted answers.

So she'd finally agreed to go back, but not until the day after tomorrow, because Eric wanted a little more practice and a chance to tinker with DORA if he was to somehow pilot her even farther into the cavern. Val had conceded mostly to prevent her uncle from doing anything stupid. Still, they could justify the excursion as the second sweep of that cavern, to see if anything had changed.

As they approached Clive, Val could see that the weathered old man was sitting in the same place as before, on the same handmade green blanket. A rolled cigarette dangled from his mouth as he carved into a huge piece of wood. It appeared to be the stump that had been under the sheet last time. As they got closer, the sculpture started to look like something. Some sort of inverted tree, or . . .

Val felt her arm hairs stand up.

Ashley said, "Hello, love. How are you this fine day?"

He looked up from his carving. "I have no complaints, my Lady Ashley. Good day to ya." He squinted at Val. "I see ya brought your friend. Hello, dear."

"Good to see you again," Val said. She pointed at the mass of wood. "Can I ask what you're carving there?"

He regarded her for a moment, taking a puff of his cigarette. "Miss Ashley here says you still goin' into dem holes."

"Yes, we are."

"Not a good idea."

"Why?"

His eyes narrowed. "You already know why, don't ya?"

Val swallowed. "I'm not sure what you mean."

He stubbed the cigarette out in the sand, and dropped the butt inside his leather pouch. "It's called a *lusca*."

"Go on." Val couldn't believe her ears.

Clive grasped the sculpture, hefting it with surprising strength. "Dis here. What I'm carvin'. You ever hear of it?"

Val sighed. "Ashley said something about it. Some myth. Is that what it looks like?"

"Dey hide in da blue holes"—he spread his arms high and gathered the air, pulling it back down toward him with his hands—"and suck down passin' ships." He laughed.

Ashley said, "It's just a sailors' legend. A Story Time tale, told to scare bad children." She looked at Val. "Right?"

The carving, for which Clive had used the tree stump, was far from finished. But the overall form was clear. It was a frightening thing, a monstrosity with a shark's head—carved into the remaining foot or so of trunk—that merged into a squid-like body with long tentacles, which the sculptor had cleverly fashioned from the roots. She could see that the tip of one mostly finished tentacle ended in a barbed point, like a spear.

Val said, "Yes. That definitely would give children nightmares."

Clive said, "Dis how tourists think it should look, so I make it dat way."

"But maybe you know what it *really* looks like?"

Clive smiled. "How would I know, dear? It don't exist."

Val reached into her day pack, pulled out the printout of Breck's image taken in The Staircase. "Please, Clive, tell me . . . what do you make of this?"

He took the image, looked at it. "What we got here?"

"A picture taken in an inland hole. Look in the upper right corner." She pointed. "We think that may be a tentacle."

Clive shook his head. "I'm sorry. It don't look like anything to these ol' eyes."

"Are you sure? Look closer."

He brought the image to his face. "I just see some circles. Could be anything."

Val took the picture back. "Maybe you're right." What was she doing? She'd come down here looking for a legitimate new species, or perhaps just to get away from a messy love life. Instead, she was following the trail of a mythical monster.

She said, "Well, thank you for your time, Mr. . . ."

"Just Clive, dear." He was smiling, but behind his eyes was what looked like concern.

"Thank you, Clive." Val stood to leave.

Ashley hugged the old sculptor and he hunched over and went back to carving. Val and Ashley turned away and started back down the beach.

"I'm sorry this didn't help you," Ashley said. "But I'm worried that he's—"

Behind them, Clive was shouting. They turned back to him.

"Wait, wait," he said. He gestured for them to return.

As they neared, Val saw that Clive's face looked pained, as if having some internal struggle. When their eyes met, he looked down at his feet.

He said, "I can't let another woman disappear. Like da one last night." He looked back at Val. "Not you, dear."

Ashley said, "How do you know about that?"

"I know."

"What are you two talking about?" Val said.

Ashley said, "A tourist has been missing since last night. She may have drowned at the beach."

"Why didn't you tell me?"

"We're keeping it quiet, so we don't upset the guests. I didn't see how it could relate to what you're doing."

Clive put his hand on Val's shoulder, his grip strong. "Nevamind dat. You need to talk to the Obeah woman."

"What? Who's that?"

"She live back in da bush. She know things."

"How can we find this woman?"

"I take you to her tomorrow."

Back in the hotel lobby, Val said good-bye to Ashley and headed for the wall of glass doors that led to taxis waiting at the curb. Ashley had explained that all she knew was that a newlywed woman had gone missing last night, at the beach. The hotel's security staff and police were speaking with the missing woman's spouse today, and looking into possible foul play.

As she reached the doors, to her right Val saw a young man get up from a bank of computers on the far wall. She stopped. Only one of the other four computers was being used by a guest. Like most hotels, she guessed, Oceanus probably provided free computer access to guests with a passcode. She walked over to the computer the young tourist had just left. He'd forgotten to log out.

She sat on the stool in front of the computer and opened an Internet browser, brought up Google. She typed in five letters: L-U-S-C-A. Clicked the search key.

A moment later, on the screen appeared a list of websites about the mythical sea monster, and sample images gathered from the web, some of which looked very similar to Clive's sculpture. She knew what he meant now, about carving what the tourists expected to see.

She opened a second site and read about the creature, then browsed another. She stumbled across information for a 2010 B-movie called *Sharktopus* and shook her head. Ridiculous.

She went back to the first site and read:

Lusca
The **lusca** is one name attributed to a legendary
Caribbean <u>sea monster</u>, usually associated with the
<u>Bahama Islands</u>. Anecdotal evidence suggests the
gigantic, octopus-like creature grows to 100 feet or
larger, and may have the head of a shark or other
features borrowed from a variety of sea life. Legend
has it that the lusca pulls boats under and attacks
scuba divers who enter its lairs—or even those
walking too close to them at night.

Walking. At night. She continued reading:

The <u>St. Augustine Monster</u>, which washed ashore on
Florida's Atlantic coast in 1896, has been deemed a
possible candidate for a specimen of the creature.
Also, in January 2011, the head-and-beak remains of
what appeared to many witnesses to be a <u>colossal
octopus</u> washed ashore on Grand Bahama Island.
Local fishermen estimated that had the specimen
been intact, the octopus would have been up to 30
feet long. Unfortunately, the remains could not be
verified by scientists because . . .

She stopped. They couldn't be verified because it was
all nonsense. There were no valid references here to sub-
stantiate any of these claims. But the Saint Augustine
Monster mention intrigued her. She remembered hear-
ing about it as a kid in Florida, and then later having her
professors dismiss the myth in college as the remains of
a whale. She scrolled down and read about reported attacks, with a few artist renderings of the beast appearing

on the page. She clicked on some of the links, scanned them. It was all unsubstantiated garbage. At the bottom, it read:

> The majority of reported lusca sightings are from the blue holes off <u>Andros Island</u>—the largest island in the Bahamas. Blue holes are inland island caves and underwater sinkholes in the ocean that formed during the last <u>Ice Age</u>, and as such are connected to one another via vast cave systems. The features are only recently being thoroughly explored, and were described in a 2010 *National Geographic* article focusing on the geological wonders.

References were listed, but none were valid except those for the blue holes. Clearly, this mythical beast was some sort of joke. Half-fish, half-mollusk: a biological impossibility. She closed the browser, but remained on the stool. She stared at the desktop image on the monitor: a photograph of a sailboat cutting through turquoise waters at sunset.

The *lusca* couldn't possibly exist. It defied the laws of nature. But a colossal octopus . . .

The Tongue of the Ocean, just offshore, offered a true deep-sea environment, largely cut off from the rest of the world's deep oceans and near what had been until recently a sparsely populated island. The sort of place where abyssal gigantism, and a species going unnoticed, were both certainly possible.

She pulled Breck's final image from her purse, looked at the pale circles curving across the corner of the image. To remind herself why she was here in the first place. *Those certainly could be suckers.*

She thought of Clive's sculpture. Despite its fantastical appearance, it had made her think of the old-time drawings of the fabled kraken, dragging sailing ships under. Val and her ceph-head colleagues had more than once started spirited debates over multiple bottles of wine, about the merits of legendary sea monsters. Most fascinating was the idea of a colossal octopus. Even a zoology professor at Berkeley, who had helped her through her PhD years ago, had made a good point one time, at a pub near campus, about the animal's possible existence: If you looked at almost any old oil painting of a kraken attacking a schooner, its deck scrambling with terrified sailors, the beast rising from the sea rarely looked anything like a giant squid.

It always looked like an octopus.

CHAPTER 41

From the couch, Val stared through the doorway at Eric. He sat alone at the kitchen table, his back to her and Mack, tapping away at his laptop. He was already on his fourth glass of rum punch.

The night had started out nice. Val had made them a round of drinks, and for once they'd all gotten along and enjoyed a sunset as red as their cocktails. Val told them about what Clive had said, and her plans to join him in the morning. But when the sky darkened, so did Mack's mood, and he'd again started in on Eric, criticizing his ROV for their lack of success. Now, as Eric bent over his computer, Mack was not letting up.

"Looking for girls online again?" Mack shouted at Eric. Val's uncle sat in a chair across from her in the living room, fiddling with one of his prosthetic limbs.

Eric ignored him.

"You should try meeting one in person for once. Head into town. You might actually get laid."

"What are you doing, Eric?" Val said.

"Nothing." He continued to work.

Val considered saying something to Mack, but decided not to. She knew that at some point Eric would have to stand up for himself if her uncle was ever going to respect him.

Mack looked at her. "When I was his age, I didn't let my libido go to waste."

"Well, you're not him. Listen, I want to talk more about what Clive said."

"About his shark-headed monster?"

"Yes."

"That's horseshit, Val, and you know it."

"Maybe that legend is grounded in reality. What if I can get Clive to help us?"

Mack said, "Why not? Clearly Watson's ROV isn't gonna find anything for us. That reminds me. Hey, Watson! You still owe me twenty bucks."

Eric slammed his cup down on the table, causing Val to jump. "Double or nothing," he said quietly.

"Oh?" Mack said, grinning. He'd clearly had too much to drink himself. "You have a bet, huh?"

Eric turned to face her uncle. "I've got another twenty bucks that says if we ever see any hint of a *lusca*, Mack will cut and run."

Mack laughed. "Right. *I* would be the one running. You're too scared to even go underwater."

"Maybe. But at least I don't parade around pretending to be a war hero."

Mack's eyes narrowed. He set down his prosthetic and looked at Eric. "Watch it, you little shit."

"I know what really happened in Iraq, Mack." Eric held out his laptop, looking defiant and frightened at the same time. "It's all right here."

Val said, "What are you talking about, Eric?"

"I started looking into his record. I wanted to learn more about his brave deeds, so it would be easier to stomach his insults. But I didn't find what I'd expected.

Your uncle here isn't a hero at all. Tell her how you really lost that leg, *Mack*."

"She already knows. I stepped on a goddam IED."

"Yeah, but does she know the whole story?" Eric said.

Val said, "What are you doing, Eric? Mack's been through enough already. Leave him alone."

"I'm tired of his shit, and you always defending him because you think he's so much better than he really is. He isn't the guy you think, Val. He's nothing but a coward." He paused. "And he got American soldiers killed in Iraq."

Val tensed, expecting her uncle to lunge at Eric then, but he just reached for his drink and took a long swallow.

She said, "I don't understand—"

"It's all online, if you know where to look," Eric said. "There are unprotected blogs, a few public records. I even found a news article about it." He thrust out the laptop, screen toward her. "Come take a look. It says Mack here was a deserter. Lost his leg when he went AWOL, and stepped on a mine in the dark. When his buddies came to find him, they ran into Taliban. Three American soldiers died."

Mack clenched his jaw.

"Unless, of course, there was another Alistair McCaffery who lost a leg in Iraq."

Val regarded Eric. "I don't believe you."

"Of course, you don't. It's right here, but you're not even willing to come see the truth for yourself. He barely avoided a court-martial, but men from his own unit went online and publicly called him out after they got home."

"But I thought . . ." Val stood and started toward Eric.

She stopped. The computer screen glared back at her with a harsh whiteness. She turned back to her uncle. "It isn't true. Right, Mack?"

He set down his empty glass. "Val, I can explain."

"Explain what?" She stood frozen, part of her wanting to go look at Eric's laptop, another part terrified of what it might have on it. "Uncle Mack?"

"Oh, fuck this. And fuck you, Watson. You goddam weasel." He began to hastily reattach his prosthetic leg.

Val looked at Eric. "Stop smiling. Whatever you're doing here, it isn't funny."

Mack stood unsteadily and started for the back door. As he hurried away, he stumbled and his artificial leg bent sideways under his weight and came free. Mack cried out as he collapsed to the hard floor.

Val knelt to help him. She glanced back at Eric. At that moment, she hated him.

CHAPTER 42

Midday heat penetrated the dense pine forest, its reach greater than that of the light that filtered down from the same sun. Val followed Clive through the bush, on a narrow footpath that ran through dense underbrush concealing holes in the rock underfoot. He was carrying some sort of package for the woman they were seeking, and she hadn't asked what it contained.

"Are you sure this is the right way, Clive?"

At the sound of her voice, a solitary mourning dove took flight from the trees above, its wings whistling in the still air.

"Don' worry," he said over his shoulder. "We almost dere, dear."

Only she had been allowed to join him today. He'd said the old woman they were visiting didn't like outsiders—especially men. *But she puts up with old Clive.*

There was absolutely nothing, nobody, out here. Val was glad to be away from Eric, and from her uncle. She needed time to think.

Before starting down the footpath fifteen minutes ago, she and Clive had rode in Mars's van for an hour. He'd brought them a distance down the Queen's Highway before turning onto dirt roads, and had finally driven them for miles down what might have been an old logging road. It wound westward over low, rocky ridges tangled with underbrush, deep into the island, until the ruts became impassible.

From there, they had waded through a lower, wetter area Clive referred to as "swash," at the head of one of the island's many brackish tidal creeks. She'd seen nothing but water birds—herons, red-winged blackbirds, kingbirds—and had to swat almost constantly at small, biting insects on her legs that swarmed her where mangroves dug their roots into the murky bottom. They had crossed through a disused fruit-tree farm, and passed by a small, unattended brush fire creeping in the grass on one side, the smoke smelling of vanilla. The fire worried Val, but Clive assured her they happened all the time. Just past the popping flames, they had left an overgrown road in the abandoned farm and he led them down the unmarked trail into the pine forest.

"This trail doesn't look like it ever gets used," she said.

"Obeah woman don't get out much."

Val thought she could still smell the smoke from the creeping forest fire, but then she spied another low rise through the trees in front of them. Smoke rose in lazy tendrils through a shaft of sunlight. She was wondering if they were walking toward another wildfire when Clive spoke.

"Dere it is."

She peered past his shoulder, through the underbrush and narrow columns of third-growth pines. A few hundred meters ahead, squatting on top of the low rise, was what appeared to be a small shack.

"After all this, I hope she's home," Val said.

As they approached, she could see a small fire burning inside a ring of rocks in a clearing beside the shack. The fire was putting out a tremendous amount of smoke, but flies still buzzed noisily around a wooden lattice over it, trying to get at what looked like raw meat hanging in pink strips. At the far end of the clearing, a small vegetable garden was somehow growing in the rocky soil beside the tin-roofed shack. The structure was very different from all the solid structures she'd seen elsewhere on the island. Even this far from the coast, if there was a hurricane—

There was a cackle behind Val, and she jumped.

She turned to see a heavyset old woman wrapped in a filthy, colorful sarong moving toward them out of the forest. She carried an armload of sticks. Her head was wrapped tightly in a bright red strip of colorful Androsia, the local batik fabric. The sarong's dominant color was also red, with vertical stripes that might have once been white, and as she moved the waving folds of fabric looked to Val like the sinuous movements of a fish. The woman dropped the sticks on the ground beside the fire and smiled at Clive.

"Mithta Clive. I knew you was coming," she said in a lisp through missing front teeth. Her broad face was mapped with wrinkles.

"Good day, my old friend. I hope you well," he said.

"I's well. What you bring me dere?" She nodded at his hand.

Clive stepped toward her and handed her the small plastic bag, rolled up tightly. She opened it and smiled, then stuffed it into a fold in her sarong.

"How kind a ya," she said. "But nothin' come for free, do it?"

"We need your wisdom today."

She nodded, and then finally looked over at Val, as if seeing her for the first time. "An' who might you be, sista?"

"My name's Valerie Martell. I'm here on the island doing research."

"What kinda research?"

"I'm a marine biologist. I'm studying life in the blue holes."

"Ahh." She nodded. "You are welcome here. Both of ya."

"Clive still hasn't told me your name. . . ."

Clive shot her a warning glance, but the old woman waved her hand at him. "It's okay, Mithta Clive. I like this one. Come. Let's talk inside, where da forest can't hear nobody."

She turned toward her shack, not waiting for them. She pulled aside a heavy blanket that served as a door and disappeared into the dilapidated wooden structure.

Val wondered, not for the first time, what the hell she was doing out here.

Clive took her arm gently as she started forward, stopping her. "Please, dear, don't ask her name again. And don' make her mad. When some folks here want someone dead, dey come to her."

She followed Clive past the blanket, into the dim shack. As a thick cloud of marijuana smoke assaulted them, an orange cat dashed out, past her legs and into the underbrush. As her eyes adjusted, she saw that the old woman was sitting on a crude pine chair, puffing on a pipe, the bag Clive had brought her beside another cat on her lap. The stuffy shack was crammed with boxes and hand-woven baskets full of personal items, with a narrow bed raised off the ground in one corner and a crude table built against one wall. Brightly painted crafts

fashioned from wood, shells, and other natural materials
hung from the walls and ceiling.

"Come in, come in," she said. "Sit down. You want
any a dis?" She extended the pipe.

Val shook her head. "No. Thank you."

"It help me with my visions."

Val thought, *I'll bet it does*, but said nothing.

Clive sat down on the floor in front of the woman,
cross-legged. Val remained standing. The heat in here
was even more oppressive than outside, with no breeze
at all. She waited in silence as the old woman puffed on
the pipe, then carefully set it on a wooden crate beside
her chair. Finally, she looked at Val. Her large, dark eyes
practically bulged from their sockets, like those of a
fish.

"Come here, sista."

Val looked at Clive, and he nodded. She stepped over
to the Obeah woman, who reached a hand out and rested
it gently on Val's abdomen.

"Ah, yes. As I thought. You big up, ain't ya?"

"Excuse me?"

Clive said, "She asked if you're with child."

"No. What?" Val's neck and arm hairs stood up, even
though she was sweating. She stepped back. "What are
you talking about?"

"Oh? You didn't know?" The Obeah woman cackled,
a squawk like that of an angry parrot. "Well, no matter.
Please, sit."

"I'm not pregnant."

"As ya please," the woman said. "But ya wanna talk
tah me, you gonna sit down."

Val finally sat, stunned and irritated by the woman's
statement. Maybe she was grasping for some bit of truth,
like any good charlatan. They'd watch your expressions as

they tried different approaches, then continue to peddle falsehoods once they'd struck on something real in your life. Obviously, in this case, Clive's sage didn't know what she was talking about. She was already looking very much the fraud.

"What can I help ya wit today, Mithta Clive?"

He leaned forward and said quietly, "We need you to tell us about the *lusca*."

"Shhsssstttthhh!" Her eyes darted toward the door. She held her hand to her chest, as though about to swoon. "No more mention of her name! Not in here."

"I fear she's back," Clive said. "That she's been killin' again."

She nodded. "Yes. Perhaps."

"What exactly is this *lus*—I mean, what is this creature? This legend?" Val looked at Clive. "And what do you mean 'She's back'?"

The Obeah woman said, "She da wrath of nature. She come back now and again, to restore balance. To protect Andros."

Ah, yes. Andros Island's Godzilla. Ridiculous. But Val kept her mouth shut, not wanting to offend Clive . . . or the Obeah woman. She wiped her brow.

"Is it an octopus?" Val said.

The old woman unwrapped the soiled red rag on her head, revealing bald skin marked with scars. She looked at Val and said, "Yes. But she not natural. Ya hear?"

"What do you mean?"

"She a child of man. When we put out bad things, we end up wit bad things. If we was all good people, doing only good things, she nevah come back."

"Why do you keep saying 'she'?"

"Because she probly big up too. Da mamas da most hungry. Late in life, when dey build da nest. Dey stop eating later, before death come, but before dat . . ." She leaned toward Val. "Dey have da *hunga*."

The old woman stood and shuffled past Val. She dug through a basket, muttering, then moved to another. "Ah-hah! Here it is."

She turned and produced a small object, dangled it in front of Val's face. A necklace. From a leather thong hung some sort of small pouch, shaped like a whale and crafted from what looked like dried animal innards. Val took it and sniffed warily, but it smelled earthy, almost sweet. Familiar somehow.

"What is this?"

"It's for you. For luck. It keep ya safe, sista."

"Safe? How will this keep me safe?"

"Wear it aroun' ya neck. Here . . ." She leaned forward and with wrinkled hands helped fasten it around Val's neck. She smelled like sour sweat and an odd mix of kitchen spices.

"Thank you," Val said. "But what we really need is information. How do we find this animal?"

"Dat easy. Where do mamas spend dere time?"

Val thought. "I don't know. In a safe place. At home."

"Right. She a mama, like you be soon. So she find a place to build a nest, and she stay near dere. Dat where you find her."

A nest. Did she mean a *den*? Val thought again of the mounds of rubble DORA had filmed in the blue hole off Oceanus. *Middens*. But they'd already been there. If something aggressive was living there—

"You could learn from her, sista," the Obeah woman said.

Val blinked. "What do you mean?"

"From da beast. To be a betta mama yourself."

"I already told you. I'm not pregnant. And I don't have kids. I *can't* have them."

The woman squinted at her. "Soon. You need a change. Not 'bout you anymore."

Val was sweating profusely now, and she'd had enough. She hurried to her feet. "Thank you for your time . . . ma'am. Clive, I'll be outside." She pushed out through the door, back into the sunlight, and took a deep breath. Even in the stagnant smoke and smell of rotting fruit, it was better to be outside.

The woman was a fraud. Clearly. *Lusca* or no *lusca*, she'd proven her ineptitude right after Val had walked in.

You big up, ain't ya?

It was all nonsense. She couldn't get pregnant. The last time was a fluke, and it had failed. Besides, she'd only slept with Will a few times in the past several weeks, the last time almost a month ago, when she'd given in to her emotions. But it occurred to her that it had been much longer than usual since she'd had her period. . . .

No. She wasn't pregnant.

She glanced back toward the shack, to make sure she was still alone, and felt a surge of emotion as she placed a hand on her navel.

Over her womb.

PART III
OCEANUS

CHAPTER 43

The date had gone well. Really well, for Eric.

Ashley actually seemed interested in him, in his work. She wasn't looking at her cell phone now, or making some lame excuse to get up and leave, like many of the women he'd gone out with in California.

They'd just had a few drinks and finished an early dinner, on an outdoor patio at Oceanus, overlooking a saltwater lagoon embedded in man-made rock terraces. The towers of the hotel rose off to his left, silhouetted by the early twilight. Eric had wanted to take her someplace else on the main island, but she'd insisted that the food here was the best.

He'd just told her how he'd grown up on the West Coast, how his parents weren't around much when he'd been a kid and so he'd taken to reading lots of books, building models, taking apart handheld radios and old television sets and putting them back together.

"So you're the baby?" she said.

"I am. And you?"

"I'm the oldest. I have three siblings too."

He smiled. "Tell me again where you grew up."

"In the Bahamas. But not here." She leaned back in her chair and looked past him, out past the resort and toward the ocean. "A place called Two Finger Cay."

She touched the gold cross around her neck. "When I was young, I spent a lot of time at a small church on the island. It's a little one-room building, made from old shipwreck wood. I always prayed that my daddy would make more money, or that I could get off the island and do it myself."

The waiter moved up beside the table and asked them how everything was.

"This conch salad is amazing. I could eat it every day," Eric said. The savory crunch of the cold salad, the fresh citrus and spice, perfectly complemented his bottle of Kalik.

The waiter grinned at Ashley. "You betta watch out for dis one, girl."

"Hush, Lionel."

The waiter walked off with a tub of dirty dishes, laughing to himself.

"What was that all about?" Eric said.

She blushed. "In the Bahamas, conch is thought to be an aphrodisiac. He thinks you're trying to get us in the mood."

Eric scooped a large spoonful of the salad and offered it to her. She smiled and took a small bite. She studied his face. "You never came back to see me again, until now. And you're leaving soon. I don't understand."

That morning, Eric and the others had gathered data on what was supposed to be one of their final blue holes. It had been awkward, with nobody getting along. But they were wrapping up this week, after almost a month, and had visited almost every accessible marine blue hole or submarine cave in the vicinity. They'd decided to visit The Staircase a final time, tomorrow.

They still had nothing, even though it was almost time to pack it up.

He said, "I was going to come back sooner. It's just that . . . it's about the elevator." He took a deep breath. "I have a hard time with elevators."

She raised her hand. "No need to explain."

"It's more than that. I'm claustrophobic. But I don't usually tell anyone." He took a sip of beer. "One time, when I was seven, my older brothers made me crawl into the bottom of a sleeping bag. Curl up in a ball. They promised they would give me a piece of candy. Before I knew it, they rolled up the bag and sat on top of me. I couldn't breathe. After a few minutes, I passed out."

Ashley leaned toward him. "That's terrible. What happened next?"

"I woke up with my dad shaking me. Ever since then, I've struggled with tight spaces. That's why I operate ROVs, instead of diving."

She placed her hand over his. "You should be proud of yourself, for doing something good with your life."

"Yeah, I guess so."

"Can I ask you a question?"

"Sure," he said.

"You're scientists, right? So why are you looking for some sea monster, when there are other important problems here? Problems we already know about. Like lionfish? Or whale strandings?"

He said, "I know what we're doing may seem odd, but cephalopods are Val's specialty. Not fish, or marine mammals. She hired me to help her look for some new species of octopus or squid. And the crazy thing is I'm starting to think that it's possible. That maybe, somehow, there *is* some undiscovered species living in the holes. Something . . . really big."

"It just seems like there are more important things for you to investigate than local legends."

"Look, I know how concerned you are about the whales here. Maybe we can talk to some colleagues when we get back. I'm friends with one professor who researches whales, and Val's been in this business a lot longer than me."

He thought of Karen, the marine mammal expert at PLARG. She'd gotten back to Eric about the object DORA filmed in the offshore hole. She said it was probably a jawbone, from a beaked whale. Of the sort Val and Ashley had seen dying on the beach. He decided not to mention it to Ashley.

"So when are you going back to California?" she asked.

"I had planned to leave this week."

"Maybe you can stay a little longer?"

"Maybe. If we don't have to go in an elevator."

She smiled. "No elevators. I promise. But I do want to take you somewhere you might find a little uncomfortable."

After college, Eric had travelled through Europe for a few months with a high school friend. They'd spent several days in London, and had to get around mostly using the city's underground metro system—what Londoners called "the Tube." Back then, he'd had pretty good control over his phobia. Looking down the deep underground stairwell now was like looking down the impossibly long escalators leading to the London Underground.

"Mind the gap," he whispered.

"What?" Ashley said.

"Nothing. Let's do this before I chicken out."

He took a deep breath and followed her down what had to be sixty stairs, to the viewing tunnel for the largest aquarium at the resort. She put her hand in his halfway down, and he resolved not to panic as the walls seemed to draw in closer and their footsteps echoed back at them. They reached the bottom. Another couple passed them, laughing as they headed for the stairs. It was darker down here, lit only by recessed lights in the ceiling, which like the walls was fashioned from the uneven rock.

She led him a short distance through the underground tunnel to the beginning of the tank. When they arrived, Eric forgot for a moment about where he was.

The tank, even larger than the other one he'd seen, rose an incredible four stories above the floor of the tunnel to the surface above, with a fake shipwreck that looked like an old galleon resting in the center. Swimming in slow circles around the wreck were two huge manta rays, the larger having a wingspan of perhaps fifteen feet, as well as several two-hundred-pound groupers, mature nurse sharks, and countless smaller fish.

"You okay?" Ashley said.

"Yeah. It helps that I can see the surface through the aquarium."

"You like it?"

"I'm impressed. Those mantas are enormous."

"We're releasing the bigger one this weekend," she said.

"How?"

"With a helicopter. You should come watch."

She led him slowly through a horseshoe-shaped tunnel encircling most of the exhibit, and he realized the fake shipwreck had been strategically located to keep the animals near the aquarium glass. And the tank lacked any real hiding places for the sea life. Otherwise, the sharks and other fish would likely spend most of their time hidden within it, out of sight of paying guests. On the tunnel walls opposite the tank they had also passed a few recessed doors. From behind one came the sounds of ongoing construction.

"What's going on back there?" he said. "It seems late for anyone to be working."

"They're working to finish another tunnel. They have to work from below, so guests don't have to see a construction zone above."

"What's it for?"

"Another access tunnel to this exhibit. When it's nearly done, they'll come from above to open it up."

They had run into Oceanus's owner before dinner, a charismatic tycoon who apparently spent a lot of time at his resort. Some Greek guy named Sergio Barbas. His well-trimmed beard and worldly charm made Eric think of a refined older actor he'd seen in popular Mexican beer commercials.

Barbas had seemed to be in a good mood, saying something about a clogged aquarium outflow pipe finally clearing itself. But his expression had changed when he'd pulled Ashley aside to talk about something serious. Eric had caught parts of the conversation.

They reached a fork in the tunnel, and Ashley asked if he wanted to see the adjacent tank. He told her he already had, and was ready to head above ground. They started up the tunnel that sloped up toward another stairwell leading to the surface. It was almost dark out now.

He said, "I overheard Barbas talking to you earlier. About that woman who's been held here by the police, ever since her wife went missing."

"You heard about that too?"

"I read an online article about it. It's all over the

news, you know. And the missing yacht that was headed here. Oceanus seems to have a pretty bad safety record."

She stopped, at the top of the stairway, and let go of his hand. "That's not true. It's just been a bad week."

"It can't be good for business to have so many guests go missing."

"*One* guest is missing. The yacht was far offshore. We're not at all responsible for that."

"The article said some other people also disappeared here last year."

She put her hands on her hips. "Do you know how many people visit Oceanus? We've had a few accidents, but we have a good safety record. Mr. Barbas does everything he can."

He reached for her hand. "Please don't get upset. I'm not saying this has anything to do with you. It's just too bad you have to work for him. And work here."

She narrowed her eyes. "What's that supposed to mean?"

A part of him knew he was digging himself a hole, but then his mouth just kept going.

"This place is beautiful, it really is, but it's just so *fake*. Even the aquariums. They're supposed to look like the natural features Barbas built the hotel around. But we both know they've not natural at all."

"This resort is the best thing that ever happened to Andros," she said.

"I understand that a mega-resort like this brings a lot of jobs to the country. To the island. But think about it? Where does all the *real* money flow? Back to investors in the US and China. To Barbas's bank account."

"Maybe. But that's so easy for you to say. This is the best job I ever had. Whether or not it gets someone else rich isn't important to me."

"I just don't understand. You seem to care so much about the ocean. Look at the environmental impact here.

I've heard there's already talk of blasting part of the barrier reef apart, to make way for a deepwater port. So the cruise ships can come in."

"That's just a rumor."

"For now. But do you want to be part of destroying this reef? It's one of the most pristine in the world."

"You listen to me, Big Man Eric. There is fairy-tale land and there is real life. It's easy for you to live in the former. You have everything you need back in sunny California. But guess what? I don't. My family don't. A lot of people down here don't. And this resort pays our bills. Lets us buy better food, better homes. Lets us all pay for cell phones and televisions. Things you Americans all take for granted."

"I hear you, but I'm just saying—"

She raised a finger, her eyes menacing. "I would like to keep the Bahamas exactly the way they are. The reefs, the oceans, the culture. That's a *want*. But I *need* a job. Mr. Barbas gives me, and a thousand others, good jobs. That's the difference between fairy-tale land and real life. Want, and *need*."

"You're right. I'm sorry, Ashley. I wasn't trying to upset you."

"Well, you did. Good evening, Eric." She climbed the last few stairs and started down the path. He hurried after her.

"Wait. You're *leaving*?"

"Don't even think of followin' me." She strode off in the deepening darkness.

Eric stood there mutely as she walked away.

CHAPTER 44

In the sunlight, listening to the wind whisper through the Bahamian pines ringing the blue hole, Eric thought again that it looked so peaceful here. Safe, even. But they had returned to this bottomless pool of water because it *wasn't* safe. Because somewhere in its depths there were two dead bodies.

And now Eric had to find them.

He took a deep breath, trying to forget about his date with Ashley. He hunched back over his ROV, sealing an exterior panel. He hoped that his modification would allow DORA to make it past the restriction, because if it didn't, at best they would be wasting their time here. At worst, he would get his ROV trapped.

They were back at The Staircase because this was the one place where hard evidence—a possible tentacle captured in a digital image—had been gathered, and because Mack wanted to know what happened to his friend. *Needed* to know.

When they'd been unable to continue here before, it had been in part because DORA wouldn't fit through a restriction in the hole's cave system. *Probably* wouldn't fit, anyway. Eric hadn't been willing to risk it. To address that problem, he'd ordered in a part from Florida. When it had finally arrived yesterday, he'd replaced the rear propeller with a smaller one and tested the device in a shallow offshore lagoon. DORA ran about the same as before, but a bit slower. With the modification, the opening would probably be large enough to allow DORA to pass. By a hair or two, anyway.

He was anxious anyway. DORA's girth hadn't been the only reason he'd turned her back at the restriction last time. Eric hadn't been confident enough to try his luck. Submarine cave navigation using an ROV was simply too difficult. Now, after a lot of practice, he knew he was getting better at operating the little ROV in tight spaces.

He could do this. Well, DORA could, anyway.

"Are you ready?" Val stepped up beside him, zipping the back of her wet suit with a pull cord.

She was still mad at him. He felt bad about what he'd said about Mack, and that he'd done it in front of her, but couldn't understand why she hadn't taken his side.

He said, "Almost. Where's Mack?"

"He went to take a break."

"Can I ask you a question?"

"What?"

"That *lusca* thing Clive told you about. That you looked up?"

"Yeah? What about it?"

"Could it be possible? Some half-shark, half-octopus thing? "

Val laughed at him. "Obviously you're not a biologist."

"What's that supposed to mean?"

"It means you wouldn't realize that that idea is ridiculous. Have you taken much biology?"

He shook his head. "Just 101, a long time ago. I was always more interested in physics, engineering."

"Well, even in 101 they should have taught you something about evolution. Unless we have a mad scientist working in the Bahamas, we aren't going to have blended phyla in the animal kingdom."

"No, I guess not," he said.

"But our whole idea of an undiscovered marine species has some backing. And not just from Breck's picture here, or the stories we've heard lately."

"How so?"

"There isn't any real credibility to the *lusca* legends. But there have been globsters that have washed ashore in Florida and the Bahamas. Those lend some potential credibility to there being a large, undiscovered cephalopod here."

"Globsters?"

"Whenever you hear about some unidentified organic mass washing up on shore, which later turns out to be part of a dead shark, or maybe a jellyfish? That's what they call a globster. The most famous one, attributed to a sea monster in Florida, was *probably* from a whale, but after a few separate analyses, the tissue samples are still inconclusive."

"Listen, Val, about the other night—"

Eric stopped as Mack appeared from behind the bushes. He limped toward them, adjusting the sleeve of his wet suit and grumbling. Eric knew it was even harder for him to walk on the rough ground back there, in his prosthesis, than it was for him and Val. He wondered if he really was the bigger asshole.

"What are you two talking about?" Mack said.

"Nothing," Val said.

Mack spit into the tea-colored pool. "Let's get this show on the road."

Eric saw Val rubbing her stomach as she looked into the hole, a concerned look on her face. "Are you all right?" he said.

"I'm fine." She reached for her tank.

Eric swore as DORA thudded into the cave wall again. He knew she had made contact because the on-screen image had shuddered. He needed to do better than this, or he was sure to get her stuck again. And this time, she was too far back to allow anyone but the most experienced cave diver to go back to retrieve her.

He had guided DORA as she descended behind Val and Mack, who were now probably 120 feet down in the main shaft, helping feed out the ROV's cable as she progressed forward. She was hundreds of feet beyond them now, in the side tunnel.

Eric had again followed the dead men's primary safety line. He was careful not to snag it, or to sever it. If the line was cut and then disappeared in the sediments of the cavern, Eric could always follow DORA's own cable back out, but without an intact safety line, they would have no way to ever find out where the divers had disappeared. These caverns were a labyrinth in every sense.

DORA was making great progress. She had followed the line through a large chamber with a number of stalagmites rising from the floor, and past another long, low cavern lined with hundreds of fragile calcite formations running from floor to ceiling. Eric had winced when he was fairly certain he'd run DORA into one of them, hoping he hadn't broken it off. Now the ROV was nearly to where she'd made it last time. But besides bumping the ancient formation, Eric had already run the ROV into the sides of the tunnel several other times.

He was struggling to concentrate. His mind was on something else. Someone.

He knew it was so petty to still be thinking about Ashley now, when they were here, looking for the body of Mack's dead friend, but he couldn't help himself. He took a deep breath.

Focus.

DORA entered a long, cylindrical passage Eric remembered well, and he piloted her forward smoothly. After fifty feet or so, he slowed her to a stop. She was there. He leaned back from the controls.

When he had navigated this tunnel previously, on his computer monitor he'd thought it looked like he was watching the view of one of those scopes going down someone's esophagus. Now he'd reached the sphincter.

"What do you think, DORA?"

He sat upright on the rocky ground, and swatted another midge biting into his neck. The little bastards were no bigger than tiny splinters, but they were leaving red bumps all over his body. On the screen, a puff of sediment rose past the camera. Without any commands from Eric, DORA had settled to the bottom.

Eric leaned forward again and touched the control stick. Hundreds of feet below, through layers of porous rock and water, DORA rose slowly off the bottom, and then pivoted upward until her nose was directed at the restriction. He stared at the dark slit where the tunnel curved upward, as more clouds of dust stirred past the camera. This was where he had stopped the ROV last time. The safety line from the other divers continued, though. From where it had been tied off to a small nub of rock, it angled upward and disappeared into what appeared to be some sort of natural chimney.

"Here goes nothing," he muttered, and eased DORA forward.

Smooth curves of rock inched past on the screen. Although to Eric it appeared as though the ROV was still moving forward on the level, parallel to the ground he sat on now, he could tell from a digital bubble on the screen that she was slowly making the upward turn. He tapped the stick, and she lurched forward. The screen shook as some part of her struck the cavern wall.

"Shit."

He pulled gently back on the stick, as a pilot does to make an aircraft climb, and then tapped the thruster again. Suddenly, he could see farther down the shaft. Up, actually. He reminded himself that he was now looking straight up. He could see maybe ten feet forward, maybe more, but it was hard to tell. The motionless safety line left by the divers led the way to the next bend. This was farther than he had dared last time. He nudged her forward again.

DORA bumped once. Twice. But she was still moving. Making progress.

"No turning back now, girl. . . ."

He accelerated, and a cloud of sediment filled the screen. He put the prop in neutral and waited for the dust to settle. When it did, he smiled. She was through.

The cave began to gradually widen and he shouted, even now wishing Val and Mack were here to share in the good news. DORA continued along the line, moving forward in the broad tunnel. He slowed her as the tunnel gradually narrowed, but was still easily passable, then she passed through a minor restriction, and the shaft opened into a huge grotto.

DORA was at the upper part of the chamber. Her lights revealed a great cavity below, filled with gin-clear seawater. Unlike the other grottos, this one lacked many calcite formations, with walls that were mostly smooth.

He shook his head. People had actually swum back this far. Cave divers were some crazy bastards.

The chamber had to be fifty or so feet across, and nearly as high—the largest one yet. Here the safety line ended, tied off to a nub of rock, but two other lines began. Each ran into the chamber. The men must have separated here. And based on what Val had told him, this was where the camera had been found.

He piloted DORA into the space and followed one of the lines. It quickly began to slack, dropping far down to the bottom, where it lay in coils. He frowned. He followed it for another thirty feet or so, where it entered another dark recess lit only by DORA's LEDs.

He pivoted the ROV and steered her back toward the top of the chamber, back to the main line, then followed the other of the two secondary lines. It remained taut, and ran across the top of the chamber to an opening in the ceiling not far from where DORA had first entered. He paused, considering the options. He decided to follow this line first.

The line ran into another tunnel, and he navigated past a few curves. Then, perhaps twenty yards from the chamber, he caught a glint in the ROV's lights. A reflection, off some sort of small, man-made object. His heart thudded in his chest. He pushed her forward and zoomed on the object. It was round, made of metal. . . .

A spool. A diver's spool, containing the safety line.

There, the line ended.

"Now what?" he said. He allowed DORA to settle again, and stood to stretch his legs. Overhead, a vulture soared in the breeze coming off the distant ocean. He'd seen the ugly, red-headed birds many times on the island, often picking at the remains of land crabs crushed by the tires of cars bumping along the roads. He walked back to the laptop and sat again, looking at the screen. He'd come this far. He could go a little farther. As long as the tunnel didn't branch again.

But it did.

After a short distance, there were two options. He pivoted DORA at the juncture. Thankfully, one branch appeared to end almost immediately. He moved DORA down the other one. Ahead was a restriction, probably only two feet across. *This may be it.*

He eased the ROV to the opening. She probably wouldn't fit, but . . .

A shape. Something dark was in the ROV's lights, just past the restriction. He turned her nose to face it, and then he saw him.

A few yards away, sitting down at what looked like a dead end. Facing him. A man.

A diver, in blue neoprene.

He would almost have looked as though he was resting, if the flesh hadn't been coming away from his lips. His regulator had fallen from his mouth, and in the ROV's lights Eric stared at the gaping mouth, where white teeth parted in a final scream. No bubbles rose from his lungs. Or ever would again. Eric swallowed. He'd never seen a dead body before.

He couldn't make out much of the diver's face, the glare off his mask obscuring his eyes and nose. But dark, curly hair was coming free from the scalp, settling on neoprene-clad shoulders. And the flesh around the lips, now beginning to rot away, appeared to be that of a gaunt, middle-aged black man.

He'd found John Breck.

CHAPTER 45

The big octopus had stopped eating.

He hadn't fed since he'd left his tank for the bowl of shrimp—when he'd actually made it out of the other tank, across the table, and then returned to the water with a few armloads of the crustaceans. That was more than a week ago.

Now Oscar looked funny—slightly emaciated, and his color had begun to fade. Sturman had first noticed the change in appearance a couple days ago. And he was starting to act strange, even for an octopus. He never hid anymore. He was always right out there, pressed against the glass as he was now, moving around in plain sight, his tentacles groping the corners of the tank. Even in the daytime. Livelier than ever.

Then this morning Sturman had run into Bill, who took care of the aquarium's octopuses, and asked him why. Even though he'd had a bad feeling he already knew the answer.

Senescence, Bill had said. That's what the scientists called it. It sounded so nice. *Unfortunately*, Bill said, *Oscar is quite old, and he's starting to exhibit signs of octopus senescence.*

What he meant was that Oscar was dying. Yes. He, too, would be dead soon.

Oscar was starting to act like an old man in the early stages of dementia. Wandering. Starting to not think straight. In the wild, he would start leaving his den more and more in the coming weeks, in broad daylight, wandering carelessly around the ocean floor. Until some shark or orca came by and snatched him up. But in here, he had a month or more to relish the end, the pleasure of slowly developing skin lesions, losing most of his coordination, and wasting away before he died. While everyone watched it happen.

No way to go, even for a mollusk.

A family walked in front of the tank, blocking Sturman's view, and he took his wool beanie off, rubbed the gray-tinged stubble on his head. The hat had started to stink, like sweat, cigarette smoke, old beer. Like who'd he'd become again. Just a goddam drunken sailor.

And his headache was coming back. Maybe some sort of withdrawal. He hadn't had a drink in three days. He was proud of himself, and thinking more clearly, but he was getting headaches. He thought about his regular bar, the Pelican. It was Tuesday afternoon. Two-dollar happy hour drafts, and everyone at the bar would be in high spirits. Good company. He took a deep breath, closed his eyes. Suppressed the urge. He knew he never went there for the company.

One day at a time.

He waited until the family walked off, then went up to the glass. Put his hand against it, where the dying octopus was pressed up against it, right where its tentacles came together in the center. Sturman tapped his gold wedding band against the glass.

"Hey, amigo," he whispered. "You're not afraid, are ya? And you don't even have a backbone."

After a moment, Oscar moved away from Sturman, pressing his soft pink body into the upper right corner of the tank. Sturman pulled his hand away, brought it down with his other to hold the beanie. He held the hat in front of him, below the waist, as if paying his respects, and re-alized it was an absurd notion. The octopus was alive, and wouldn't die for a few more weeks. Still, Sturman knew all too well that simply having a heartbeat wasn't actually living.

Apparently, mating was what triggered senescence in male octopuses in the wild. But Oscar had never even gotten to mate. He'd lived in isolation his whole life, though not of his own accord, except for interaction with the staff. He'd spent his existence confined within a few small aquariums. And now he was going to die. At just four years old.

But that's old for an octopus, Bill had said.

Sturman was thirty-seven. Not that old, for a person. And he'd mated. Married. Loved. Then, even after meet-ing another great woman, had gone into his own senes-cence. Somehow, he'd been able to squeeze himself down into a bottle, just like an octopus. But he wasn't going to die in one.

"I'd break you out if I could, pal. But I reckon you wouldn't enjoy being out in the open ocean now. After you grew up here . . . right?" Sturman rubbed his un-shaven jaw. *No, bad idea.* Oscar extended a tentacle to-ward him, and he grinned.

A couple walked up, holding hands, and marveled at the big octopus for a few minutes. Sturman nodded at them.

"Amazing, isn't he?" the man said.

"Yes. He is that," Sturman said.

"But he hardly fits in that tank."

Sturman nodded. The idea that had been forming started to snowball.

He waited for a few minutes, until the couple walked off to the next exhibit. He tapped the tank lightly, watching Oscar search the sides of the enclosure. Like always, he seemed to be looking for a way out.

"I'll be back," he said, and walked away.

"I can't believe I'm doing this sober."

Sturman looked into his rearview mirror, trying to glimpse the ten-gallon water cooler in the bed of his truck. He couldn't see it in the dark.

Before he'd left the aquarium parking lot a few minutes ago, Oscar had still been in the plastic water cooler, the one he'd placed in the octopus's tank, waited for him to enter, and then used to smuggle him out—lid on. It hadn't been all that difficult (other than stuffing all the arms inside to get the lid on in the first place) since nobody was working and Sturman had the alarm code. But he'd have to hurry so Oscar wouldn't suffocate.

Sturman had used a dolly to roll the container out, carefully placed the orange jug into the truck bed, then placed a cinder block on the lid, just in case. He'd seen Oscar do some amazing things in the past year. If he didn't hurry, he'd have a seventy-pound octopus loose in the bed.

He hadn't thought that far ahead. How the hell was he going to get that big bastard down to the water if he got out of the plastic jug? He pressed down on the accelerator.

He arrived at Point Pinos a few minutes later and pulled up to the curb. He killed the engine. He was alone. He'd expected as much, it being midnight. He stepped out of the truck into a fine drizzle. He could hear the waves crashing into the rocks a few hundred feet away.

He walked back to the bed. The lid was still screwed on the cooler, the cinder block resting on top, but seawater had sloshed into the bed. Oscar had been busy. Sturman dropped open the tailgate and jumped in. He removed the cinder block and slid the heavy jug to the edge. The lid spun slightly and rose as Oscar reached the tip of an arm out.

"Sorry to stuff you in there, pal, but this will be the last time either of us will be inside a bottle."

He didn't bother trying to screw the white plastic lid back on. He jumped down and hefted the jug full of octopus, then hurried toward the water. As he waded into the surf, realizing how crazy this was, he laughed. He saw the headlights of a car approaching on the road, but it didn't matter. He was committed now.

"We're not gonna see each other again," he said. "You enjoy a little freedom now, you hear?"

After a small wave passed, he stumbled into a calmer tide pool, his arms and back burning from the heavy load. Wet up to his crotch, he leaned down into the water and sunk the jug in a protected spot in the rocks. It began to float, but he held it down. He watched as the dark form of his curious friend slid into the pool, then halted.

Oscar reached an arm back to Sturman and stroked his left hand. Then the octopus settled onto the bottom.

Sturman watched him for a moment, a barely discernible dark blob on lighter-colored sand, and then looked out to sea. He shivered as the white spray of waves crashed into an exposed point of rock some distance away. A cold onshore breeze blew into his face, smelling of salt and kelp. Of life.

He was not a religious man, but he believed in God. He wasn't sure what that meant exactly. But when he was outside, in the elements, he felt closer to Him. Or Her. He smiled. Val would surely say God was a Her. Just like Maria had.

He saw Maria's smiling face in his mind's eye. They'd had a good run. But they'd never gotten to have kids. You didn't get to choose your fate. But you got to pick your path. She'd love what he was doing now, even if she scolded him for it.

She was gone now. Just like so many others. He wasn't, though. And neither was Val.

He'd probably already blown it with her. But there was still a chance. As long as he was alive, there was still a chance. He wasn't quitting on her that easy. On them. He was getting back on his horse.

He glanced down at his ring, the one he'd gotten from Maria. He wasn't able to see it in the weak starlight, so he felt for it with his thumb. It was gone. His gold wedding band was gone. He felt a rush of anxiety. Where had he—

He grinned. "That son of a bitch."

He looked back down into the tide pool. But Oscar was no longer there.

"You sneaky little bastard." He exhaled deeply and nodded. "Okay, then. So that's it." He looked past the dark pool, into the deeper water where the dying octopus was moving to freedom. Where he belonged.

"Thanks, Oscar. When those sharks come, you give 'em a fight."

Sturman headed back toward the truck, taking the un-washed beanie off his head and tossing it into a public trash can. If anyone had seen him here, it was now evidence, he knew, but part of him hoped they'd figure out he was responsible. Justice had been served.

Still, it was time to leave town for a few days. Maybe he'd known that all along, and was trying to light a fire under his own ass.

When he reached his truck, he tossed the plastic cooler in the bed and dumped the water out of his boots. He jumped inside the cab, jeans sopping wet, and turned the key still in the ignition. He cranked up the heater and picked up his cell phone, dialing as he pulled away from the curb.

As the line started ringing, he looked over at his old cowboy hat. It sat on the bench seat, where it had been for months. He picked it up and slid it on his head. It still fit.

He'd need a good shade hat where he was going.

CHAPTER 46

"Is that you, Mack?"

Val's uncle was bent over in the darkness outside the guesthouse, and appeared to be wiping vomit off his lips with the back of his hand. He stood up straight, weaving slightly, and squinted at his niece where she stood below the front porch light. After Eric had confronted him, he'd admitted he'd lied to her, and promised he would explain. But he never had.

She said, "We've been worried about you. It's after two in the morning."

"I needed to get out."

All afternoon, Mack had been unable to stop thinking about his friend, and how he'd looked on the monitor, sitting at the end of the dark tunnel. Val too had tried to imagine Breck's last moments. Something had sent him scrambling through the cave system, without even spooling out safety line, to a dead end. And then he had simply turned around and come to rest in a sitting position, looking back. Perhaps waiting for something, or perhaps preparing himself as he watched his air run out. His remains, like those of a perished climber on Everest, would have to be left where they lay. There was simply no safe way to retrieve them.

"I understand. Did you just get sick?" she said.

"A platter of cracked conch tastes a helluva lot better going down than it does coming up."

"I'm sure it does." Val stepped off the porch and walked over to him, but he turned away.

"Are you okay?" she said.

"Yeah. I just need some water. Why are you up?"

"I couldn't sleep again."

They headed inside and Val filled a glass with filtered water from a five-gallon jug in the kitchen. He told her that Mars had brought him home. Apparently, the snaggletoothed cab driver, whom they'd gotten to know fairly well, had pulled his van over and picked up Mack as he stumbled home from some local tavern. Mars hadn't charged him anything.

They walked out back where TIKI torches still burned in the darkness, their flames bent by the breeze coming off the ocean. She and Eric had waited up here for hours, before he had finally gone to bed a half hour ago.

Mack kicked at an unlucky land crab that happened to be on the cobblestone patio. It landed with a crack on the hard ground a few feet away. He fell into a chair and found a toothpick in his pocket, which he put in his mouth and began to grind between his molars. Val sat quietly, watching him. He stared off into the night, over the ocean, listening to the waves hit the shore. Without looking at his niece, he finally spoke.

"After I came home from war, that last time, I looked up one of my buddies from my first tour. Ernie." He took a gulp of water. "He was a skinny black fella. Looked a little bit like John Breck used to. But prettier."

Val nodded.

"I guess he'd really struggled to get over the war. We all did, but he did more than the rest of us."

"How so?"

He shifted in his chair. "You know, I keep thinking not of our good times, but of this one fuckin' hot day. Our troop carrier was rolling over dead bodies in the street as we moved in on a town held by the enemy. The bumps seemed so small, so insignificant." He paused. "That was the day that haunted Ernie."

Val said, "How's he doing? Have you talked to him since the war?"

Mack ground down on the toothpick. "His wife answered when I finally called. It was the only time I ever talked to her." He looked through his niece, and she began fidgeting with her fine gold necklace. "Three months before I got back home, I guess he'd wrote his blood type and the words *donate organs please* on a cardboard sign, using a Magic Marker. Hung it around his neck, and then walked into an ER in South Carolina." Mack bit his lip, closed his eyes. "Then he shot himself in the head."

Val shook her head, trying to imagine what her uncle had been through. "I'm so sorry, Mack."

"I still haven't told you the whole story. About what happened in Iraq."

"It's okay. Some other time."

He held up his hand. "No. Let me finish. Watson was right. I was technically AWOL. But I wasn't deserting. I was gonna come back."

"What were you doing?"

"Going to meet a woman. An aid worker, from Britain."

"You were married."

"Yeah. But you know how things were with Clarice. I just felt so alone. All the death over there . . ." He spit out his toothpick. "I was ashamed to tell you. I fuckin' hate myself for what happened. Marines died because of me. . . ." He began to choke up.

Val didn't know what to say.

"I don't know anymore. Maybe I *was* deserting. Because I was so tired of the killing." He sniffed. "I understand if you don't respect me anymore."

"Nonsense. You're still a hero to me, Mack." She wiped her eyes.

They sat quietly in the darkness. Waves lapped against the beach, and a cool breeze rustled the palm leaves.

"Do you want to talk about Breck?" she said.

He stared into space for a moment, and then smiled.

"What? What are you thinking about?"

"One time, I tried to wriggle headfirst into a restriction. When he and I were younger. It was right at the mouth of a little inland hole in the Abacos, buried in some coppice." He smiled. "Pushed my tank through first, then tried to wriggle in, with one arm in front, one in back." He pantomimed the action. "Got stuck in there. *Really* stuck. Couldn't even move. I was wondering what the hell I was gonna do."

"What happened?"

"Well, lucky for me, Breck couldn't fit through his own hole nearby and came to find me. The fucker tickled my feet before he helped me out. Can you believe that?" He laughed. "The bastard actually tickled the feet of a friend who might already be out of air. He was one crazy fucker." Then the smile vanished. "Why didn't he try to get out? I just don't get it."

"I don't know."

"He should've easily found his way out of that passage. But he just sat there, the dumb fuck, as his air ran out."

"Maybe he was narced," Val said. Sometimes, at depths

beyond one hundred feet or so, divers would start to experience nitrogen narcosis, an anesthetic, drunken effect as too much of the gas built up in their bodies.

"No," Mack shook his head. "Not Breck. He'd done this too many times. He could keep his head."

"Maybe some of the toxins in the water of those holes made him unable to think clearly, or maybe—"

"No, Valerie."

"Well, maybe he just lost his way. I know it's hard to believe, but even an experienced diver like him . . . It's a dangerous profession."

"If you lost your way diving in a cave, what would be the last thing you'd do? Before your air ran out?"

Val shook her head slowly. "I don't know. I guess I'd keep heading down a main tunnel. Try to find a way out."

"You wouldn't sit down at a dead end."

"No. But maybe he was already out of air. Maybe he'd accepted his fate, and decided to reflect in his final moments."

"Or maybe he was afraid to leave that tunnel. Even if it meant he would die."

CHAPTER 47

It was almost time.

Throughout her life, she had sought refuge in dens. They offered safety, for daytime rest and nighttime feeding. But this was a special den. It was one with the perfect currents to clear away sediments, and sweep away her own wastes, while providing an influx of fresh oxygen. A cavity that wasn't much more than twice her volume, and safe from threats. Here she had found comfort, but she hadn't been content with the opening to the space she had chosen. It needed to be smaller.

She had labored for several nights, cleaning out the lair, using the coral rocks and sand cluttering a side cavity to build protective piles in front of it. To close off most of the opening. She had even left the den several times to find the right materials, returning to add to the growing mound in front of it.

The location she had chosen, a narrow recess in the wall of the deep shaft, was ideal in most senses. It was of the perfect size, offered a steady flow of water, and was ideally situated for protection from threats. It was also much shallower than it should have been, but it had to be here, because she was no longer willing to return to the deep. She had been feeling the pain again, from the low vibrations that sometimes spread through the water, unescapable, hammering through her body. It was worse in the deep.

She slid her bulk free of the snug confines of the den, into the void above the dark shaft, and sank down toward her middens. She had located them on a ledge deep within the underwater hole, ensuring that waste and rubble she ejected could be neatly piled well below her lair. Some of the material in the middens had been added recently, the leftovers of her meals, or excavated from within the lair in shallower water.

Reaching the deep ledge, she felt for one of the mounds in the darkness and pulled herself on top of the pile of bones and shells. She released a thick string of feces into the water. It coiled like a serpent as it came to rest on the refuse pile. Small fish, too tiny to bother with, rushed in to feed on the fatty excrement and the cloud of particles around it, picking at a grinning skull poking out of the fresh coil.

She still had not found a viable mate. But that urge was now gone.

Her hunger was driven by the ache of unfertilized eggs now fully matured in her slab-like ovaries—two masses of granular flesh that occupied much of the space within her great body. She had not mated months ago, when the timing was ideal; not stored a male's spermatophores inside her body, separate from the eggs, until the time was right to impregnate herself. But she was not aware of this. Only that she needed to maintain a den, and that she was still hungry.

Her hunger had been a fleeting thing, sometimes there, sometimes not. She had left the den only one of the past two nights, just before morning, to unsuccessfully pursue a shark and then, at dawn, to hunt down a wounded dolphin. She had managed to ensnare the weak animal and feed on it, her energy surging from its calorie-rich flesh.

She rose in the vertical shaft, the dim light from the night sky above revealing pale, muted walls as she passed. She returned to her den, locating it by the steady current of water emitted from the dark opening in the rock. She squeezed her huge body past the rubble at the entrance and stopped moving.

Soon restless, two of her arms extended from her curled body and began to work again on the pile of rubble, arranging the rocks, tucking a discarded steel drum in a gap in the barrier. Everything had to be perfect.

It was almost time.

CHAPTER 48

The truck slowed, and Sturman hopped out of the bed, landing on the roadside beside the recently paved two-lane highway. He thanked the driver, tipping his hat, then shouldered his big duffle, and stepped into the shade of a stand of tall, scraggly trees on the corner. The driver drove off, between low walls of thick green vegetation on either side.

The midday subtropical sun pressed down on Sturman's head and shoulders, his damp T-shirt clinging to his back and chest. He still wore the jeans and shit-kickers he'd had on since departing California on a red-eye last night. The rutted drive running away from the highway looked to be a few hundred yards long, raised over swampy flats on either side. He wiped his brow and started down it toward the guesthouse.

He hadn't even met with Rabinowitz yet. He had come for her. But would she even be here? He figured it would be harder to turn him away in person than over the phone.

Sturman's boot heels scuffed worn wood as he crossed a low, flat bridge where a culvert connected the waters of the marsh. As he neared the end of the drive, he glimpsed the ocean through the vegetation close to shore, and felt its cooling breeze. The clean smell of salt replaced the fetid odor wafting up from the swamp beside the road.

He rounded a single curve in the drive, around some more of the strange-looking scraggly trees, and finally had a clear view of the rocky beach, the aquamarine waters, and the yellow one-level house. A crude sign hanging over the front porch said TWIN PALMS GUEST-HOUSE.

He stepped onto the porch, took a deep breath, and knocked loudly on the front door.

He heard movement inside, and a short, shirtless older man swung open the door. He was tough looking, with a powerful build and close-cropped, graying hair. He had only one leg.

"Yeah? Whataya need?" the man said, squinting at him from a sunburned face.

"You must be Val's uncle."

The man stepped through the door. He eyed Sturman's boots, his cowboy hat. He was more than a head shorter, but clearly not intimidated.

"Will Sturman," the man said.

"Yes, sir. Are you Mack?"

Mack shoved a toothpick into his mouth. "What in the hell are you doing here?"

"I came to see her."

"She know you're here?"

"No, sir. I reckon she doesn't."

Mack scowled. "Came all the way down here, huh? But you didn't even tell her. You must be dumber than Valerie says."

Sturman took his hat off. "Is she here?"

"No. She'll be back. Guess I'm supposed to invite you inside now. But let me tell you something first, son." He stepped closer. "You hurt my niece, you're gonna answer to me. You hear?"

"Yes, sir."

After a moment, Mack stepped back, still measuring Sturman with his eyes. He thrust out his right hand. "Alistair McCaffery."

They shook hands. Sturman fought off a grin as Mack subtly tried to pull him off balance and continued to size him up. The man's grip was powerful, and he had incredible stability for a man with just one leg.

"You don't need to call me sir. I just go by Mack."

"Yes, sir. I mean, Mack."

"You hungry?"

"Yes, sir. Starving."

"Mack. Not 'sir,' goddammit. Fuckin' Navy brainwashed you."

"Sorry, Mack."

"Well, come on in, will ya? You're letting the bugs in."

"You can't just show up unannounced, Will."

"Already have."

"I can see that," Val said.

Sturman walked beside her on the remote, deserted beach ringing the bay north of the guesthouse. The evening was comfortably cool, the sun now settled low into clouds over the island.

He'd apparently arrived a few hours ago, when she and Eric were in Fresh Creek getting lunch and buying a final load of groceries after their morning dives, and had now changed into shorts and a fresh shirt. He still wore his old Western hat, his shirt unbuttoned and flapping in the breeze. Dressed the way he used to, on his boat back in San Diego.

"You know I was planning to come home early next week," she said.

"I know. But I couldn't wait. You look good, Doc."

She self-consciously rubbed her thighs. "Thanks. I've been running. And diving a lot. I've lost a few pounds."

"You know I never cared about that. I just meant your hair, your tan. You got it back. You look good."

She stopped walking. He took another step, and then turned back to her. "What's the matter?" he said.

"Why are you really here, Will?"

"I been worried about you," he said.

She crossed her arms. "You? Worried about me? You can't keep trying to save me."

"Why not?"

"You haven't even learned to save yourself."

"I know." He swung his sandals in the breeze, looking uncomfortable. "I guess I been worried about *us*." He met her eyes.

She stared back at him, but said nothing. What could she say?

"I been clean," he said.

"How long?"

"Six days."

"Almost an entire week. Good for you." She had to admit, he did look good. His strong jawline was peppered with a little stubble. And his gray-blue eyes were clear, bright. For the first time in months, she was seeing him without eyelids puffy from boozing late the night before.

She said, "What about your job at the aquarium? How long can you be off?"

"I told Harold I had some family business to take care of. But I may not have a job if I go back."

"'If'? What are you talking about?"

"I'll tell you some other time. Val, I'm not good with words. You know that. But I guess . . . I guess I came down here because I wanna give us another try. I mean I know I do."

She felt an unexpected surge of emotion. "I don't know, Will. I don't know."

"I'll stay clean. I mean it."

She smiled, sadly. "I know you'll *try*. And I know how you feel about me, Will. But it's more than that. I'll never be good enough for you. There will always be Maria."

She looked down at his left hand, where he still wore the gold band that served as a constant reminder of a woman she might never stack up to.

Her heart jumped. The ring wasn't there.

"Where's your ring?" she said.

"I won't be wearing it anymore. A friend finally convinced me to move on." He took his hat off. "I don't know what to say, Val. I'm sorry. Just give me a chance."

Looking at him, such a strong man, and yet so fragile, she suddenly felt like one of the merchant vessels Mack had told her about. Hundreds of years ago, privateers used to light fires along the island's shore, to lure unwary Spanish vessels onto the shallow reef, so they could plunder them the next day. The merchants were drawn to what looked like protective harbors. To safe haven. They ended up running aground, battering their vessels apart on hidden dangers.

She turned away from him, and felt tears welling up. She hated to cry in front of anyone.

He stepped up behind her, wrapped his arms around her shoulders. As he embraced her, she realized how much she'd missed him. She turned toward him and saw the fire in his eyes. And that familiar pain.

She knew it wasn't a good idea, but she kissed him anyway.

CHAPTER 49

It was time.

Deep inside the cavern, her body began to tense, to bulge outward. To contract. A part of her knew it was not right, that they weren't ready, but they would not wait. They were coming. Now.

Another contraction, and she felt the first of them arrive.

She coiled an arm back, under her, reaching down to welcome it. Gently cradling the pale, teardrop-shaped egg, she brought it to her dominant eye in the near darkness, feeling a sort of elation. The feeling was quickly overtaken by another, more painful surge as the muscles in her mantle contracted again.

After the next few came, the others began to arrive very quickly, spurting into the water in rapid succession, bursting forth in twos and threes in the swirling darkness beneath her.

When she had entered the den the previous night, she had completed construction of the mound of rubble at its entrance, topping it off with the twisted metal remains of a small boat hull, and then settled herself inside. She knew she would not be leaving again, ever. So she had positioned herself comfortably, her eyes facing toward the den's opening, and waited for many hours.

Now, as her body tensed and bulged, contracting again and again, her young finally came forth into the cavern. Thousands of them. Whitish secretions swirled around the cavern, clouding the water.

Even before the contractions first began to subside, her doting arms began to pluck each group of eggs from where they drifted near the bottom or spun through the dark water beside her, and carefully began to braid them together. Using the stringy, sticky tissue trailing off the end of each, the slender arm tips deftly twisted them into neat clusters, then in turn wove these into long bunches, organizing them so that none of her young would be lost, none would be neglected. So all would be safe.

She lined them up in neat rows on the ceiling of the cavern, affixing them to the rough surface using their own sticky secretions.

As the final cluster emerged, she closed her eyes in the darkness, the last of her energy slipping away from her, and placed it by the others clinging to the cavern above and behind her. She caressed the unhatched young, knowing she must protect them. Guard them vigilantly from predation, groom them of parasites, keep them clean and oxygenated until they hatched many months from now. Only then would she allow herself to die.

And so here, until the end, she knew she must remain.

And yet, still nagging at her beneath the fatigue and the urge to watch over her brood, remained another compulsion, a craving that even now would not go away.

CHAPTER 50

"I keep asking myself, if there's some sort of giant octopus down there, why's it here now? All of a sudden, when we've never heard of this before? And why suddenly attacking people?"

Sturman shrugged. "You're the biologist. You tell me."

"I don't know," Val said. "There are lots of unusual clues, but the solid evidence just isn't there. I think I need to head back home before my imagination runs completely wild."

In the dancing torchlight, with the sound of surf behind them, they leaned against the rock wall on the patio of the guesthouse. They'd eaten dinner with the others, but like usual there hadn't been much talk.

Yesterday, Val had finally apologized to Eric for getting upset at him. She realized that he'd simply been sticking up for himself. And she'd also forgiven Mack. But her uncle was still mad at Eric, and Eric was still glum from his date ending badly the other night. Apparently, Ashley still hadn't returned his calls.

Sturman said, "When I was a kid, we lived in the same ranch house for more than ten years. One year, right before we moved, we had a few weeks of really wet weather. Then these weird mushrooms appeared. They were everywhere, and I mean everywhere. Growin' in thick clumps that sprung up all over in the pasture by the house.

"We'd had plenty of wet seasons before that, plenty of rain. But in a decade there I'd never seen those mushrooms in my life."

"So what are you saying?" she said.

"Maybe, in nature, sometimes it just takes the perfect set of conditions to trigger something. With the mushrooms, maybe it was all the rain, or some cyclical sorta thing. Here, in this case, maybe the final bit of rain your octopus needed was the naval testing."

The perfect set of conditions.

She touched her belly. She considered telling him, but stopped. No. Not now. Not until she knew for sure, one way or another. Maybe this was all in her imagination too.

The market they'd been to today didn't carry any home pregnancy kits, so she'd have to wait. But she'd talked to more than one doctor in the past. She was damaged inside. Permanently. From a poor decision she had made so many years ago, as a foolish young woman. Back when she made decisions only with her heart, and her loins, and not with her head.

She was always making bad decisions in her personal life. She was still mad at herself for kissing Sturman. But she hadn't been able to send him away. He'd come all the way here just to see her.

Will Sturman was like an overgrown teenager, or a perpetually failing college student. Who else flew almost 4,000 miles after a woman, hoping he might find a place to crash? Maybe that was what happened to a man after he spent years in the Navy, then became self-employed, lived on a boat, and never raised a family. But a part of her liked the hopeless romantic in him.

He said, "Did you know that thousands of years ago, Egyptians hunted octopuses for food? They lowered clay pots into the water, and when the octopuses went inside they just brought the pots back up. Just like that, they had dinner."

Val smiled. "No, Will, I did not know that."

"Thing is, I can't figure out why such smart animals can be trapped and killed so easy."

"An octopus is like a cat, I guess."

"Curiosity kills them?" he said.

"Exactly. You're really getting into them, aren't you? Working at the aquarium?"

He shrugged. "Well, I thought it was a safer interest than squid. Now I'm starting to wonder. With what Eric told me about that woman missing at that resort, and the kid in the swimming hole . . ."

"It's got you wondering too. About the *lusca.*"

"Yeah. Why not?"

"Well, right away, we write off the shark-head part. We focus on the large size, and the image of what might be a tentacle—"

"Don't forget bone piles," Eric said, walking out onto the patio.

Val turned to him. "Right, and the features in the marine hole resembling middens." She thought for a moment. "I keep coming to the same conclusion. I guess it's possible to have an undiscovered species of giant octopus, or maybe a novel type of giant squid, but it's very unlikely. And we're not going to find out on this expedition unless it decides to come out and meet us."

Sturman snorted. "Same old Doc. Never believes in anything she can't bring back to the lab."

"That's because I question things, instead of just believing everything I hear. It's called science, Will."

"But he's got a point," Eric said. "You are pretty skeptical, even for a scientist."

"Ganging up on me now, huh?" she said.

Eric turned to Sturman. "I still think it's possible. Did you know we know more about the surface of the moon than about our own deep oceans?"

Sturman nodded. "I've heard that before."

"It's true. You can look it up. NASA's annual research budget for space exploration is four *billion* dollars. But you know how much the US government spends on ocean research?"

"I suppose you're gonna tell us," Sturman said.

"Less than twenty-five million bucks. That's it. Less than *one percent* of what we waste to explore lifeless planets and distant stars every year. So we really don't know what's living deep down in the ocean. Nobody does."

Val said, "Eric's right about that. But it doesn't mean there's a bunch of giant octopuses living here, undiscovered for hundreds of years. There's virtually no legitimate documentation. No real evidence for an undiscovered species. Besides, what on earth would it eat to sustain itself? This part of the ocean isn't nearly as productive as, say, the North Pacific. Or Monterey Bay."

"Maybe they eat those little whales down here," Sturman said.

Eric laughed. "How would an octopus eat a whale, even if it was big enough? Do they even have teeth?"

Sturman regarded him for a moment. "You really don't know? They have a beak."

"I know. But it's just a beak."

Sturman smiled, extending his right hand toward

Eric, palm up, as if to flip him the bird. Where his middle finger should have been there was a stump. "Bad drivers all over Southern California have a beak to thank for this."

"*That*'s from an octopus beak?"

"No. But close enough."

"What are you talking about?"

Val said, "I'll tell you some other time. But back to the whales. If our hypothetical giant octopuses feed on them, then why don't we ever see sucker marks on the ones that got away?"

Eric said, "You said yourself that scientists know very little about the whales here. And there are other animals to eat. Sharks, rays, groupers. Other big fish."

"But octopuses prefer to eat shellfish. Smaller animals that move slower."

Sturman shook his head. "Maybe. But even a pretty small octopus can kill and eat a shark. Seen it myself, in an aquarium video."

Val sighed. The ridiculousness of it all hit her again. Even though Andros Island historically had a small human population, reducing the chance of sightings; even though they had a picture of a suckered arm from inside a blue hole; even though people were going missing, with witnesses claiming they'd seen a sea monster—

"Why *are* you here, then, Val?" Sturman said. "If you don't think what we're talking about is even possible, why did you come down here in the first place?"

She looked away from him. At first, she thought maybe it was mainly just to get away from him. To give herself room to think. As she tried to figure out what to say, Eric spoke up.

"Sturman, you work back at the aquarium. You'd really appreciate the exhibits they have here at Oceanus.

The place is a monstrosity, full of rich assholes, but the aquariums are first-class."

Sturman stared at Val a few moments longer, as if reading her thoughts, then looked over at Eric. "Yeah. I think I'd like to see those while I'm here."

Val said, "You should bring him with you tomorrow, Eric."

He said, "Sure. You want to join me tomorrow? They're releasing a manta ray, first thing in the morning."

"Aren't you going, Val?" Sturman said.

"I still have more work to do."

"Well, hell, I'm in. I gotta see this."

After the men went inside to get ready for bed, she remained. She watched as the clouds began to blot out the stars. Moisture was on its way.

She mostly thought about Will. He had such determination. But would he ever have the ambition to do any of the things he was so capable of? She thought maybe she'd go after all.

CHAPTER 51

On the shallow bottom, she ceased moving, tasting the water in the lagoon. Tonight, there was nothing.

On another recent night, near here, she had found the dead whale. And the other, living prey on which she had also fed. The unusual prey that had now become a regular part of her diet.

She could not stray far from her den. Not now. But she could not suppress the nagging urge.

She moved along the familiar sandy bottom, again pressing herself low beneath the gentle waves, and maneuvered her great body toward the beach, over coral heads and sea grass beds until the waves started to break over her leading arms. There, she stopped. Felt. Tasted.

She slid back into the deeper water of the dark lagoon and moved down the beach, remaining in the shallows. This place was not safe, not comfortable. But perhaps it would again yield sustenance.

She felt the first vibrations.

Click. Click-click.

She stopped moving. She turned back toward shore. The clicks rose in intensity as she neared, arousing her, but again she was confronted by the impassable shallows.

Click-click. Click-click-click-click.

This was food. And it was very close.

She moved quickly toward the source of the vibrations, compressed between the waves and the jagged coral bottom, now past the sandy beach. As she slid into a rough channel of deeper water toward the sounds, her writhing arms slid fluidly around most of the obstructions, but in her haste she broke off many fragile coral fans and pillars, scattering the terrified sea life.

Mild waves now crested over the small island of her protruding flesh. She paused in the shallows at the very edge of the ocean, at the very edge of her own world, and extended the first of her arms.

Immediately, the long, exploring appendages crossed the surf line. They felt impossibly heavy as they left the water and entered the space above it, and then met with the firm shore. The friction between her own flesh and the rigid surface of the land was incredible, but the arms found it even harder to raise themselves into the thin, unsupportive air above.

Testing the unfamiliar world, moving in various ways, some of her arms soon began to move most effectively in hydrostatic fashion, by inching themselves along the hard ground in short, regular sequences. Extensions, followed by contractions. This collective information was shared, passed through her brain and to each of the other limbs.

Still, no food was encountered. And the clicking sounds were gone. From where had they come?

The arms explored, on land and in the sea. One of the arms still submerged beside her found a break in the land; a narrow hole, where the seawater extended farther into the hard, unyielding landscape.

Click.

The single pulse of sound reverberated from within the narrow hole and again passed into her soft body. Whatever was emitting the clicks was close. Very close. Somewhere within the hole, or just past it. But even the tip of her tentacle could not pass into the tiny opening.

There was food here. She was certain. But she could not reach it. She expelled an enormous measure of spent seawater, clouding the darkness around her with sand.

Ingesting more water, she calmed. More patiently now, she carefully felt at the opening. Water flowed slowly past the exploring arm, steadily, into the hole. There had to be water beyond.

She remained in the surf line for some time, testing the shore for a route. But there was no deep water. No submerged tunnel besides the tiny hole. No passage. Her hunger nagged at her, a wrenching thing inside her. Commanding her to action.

She focused on the four arms still extended out of the water, and pulled her huge body several more inches from the water.

In coordination, the arms heaved her forward, this time assisted by the push of the arms gathered behind her. The oppressive weight of the outer world increased, and for the first time she found it difficult to take seawater in to oxygenate her gills.

She contracted her arms again.

Dragging her immense, saclike body out of the water and onto the dark rocks, she felt impossibly heavy. The rough edges cut into her skin as she crept forward, as tons of flesh pressed down on itself, unable to rise off the surface without the necessary hydrostatic support of water. But the jagged surface was narrow, quickly re-placed by an equally hard, but mercifully flat, surface. As she moved farther from the water, the weight of her boneless body crushed down on itself, flattening painfully, the oxygen in her blood quickly dwindling as she found herself unable to breathe. Seawater drained from within her cavity in sheets.

Still she pressed forward.

Splayed on the dark concrete, her lead arms groped desperately ahead of her. There had to be water somewhere ahead. Her trailing arms were now leaving the ocean behind her. She felt the first impulse to stop. To turn back. A faintness began to overcome her. Her arms extended again. With immense effort, she lurched forward. Extended an arm as far as its length would reach.

Water.

She dragged her bulk toward it, along the hard ground, feeling many small tears erupting in her flesh. But now her arms were entering another pool of water. Immediately, their chemical receptors tasted the prey. The clicking sounds had come from here. But thoughts of feeding had left her mind. She felt herself losing consciousness, and desperately pulled her bulk toward the water. Toward safety.

She reached the edge. The pool of water dropped off steeply, providing a solid anchor from which to pull with her lead arms. She pulled again, and her flattened, wet body overhung the lip of concrete. A final lurch, and then she was rolling forward.

She sank heavily into the pool, sending a large wave across its surface.

CHAPTER 52

Ashley made her way through the casino, wishing for a more direct path. She needed to get home, to get a few hours of sleep before the helicopter arrived tomorrow morning. Her supervisor had insisted she be there.

The resort's designers had intentionally made it difficult to find a path through here, to increase the odds that gamblers might pause to drop a few more dollars into a slot machine or rest at a card table as they looked for a way out. Around her, the ceaseless beeps and dings of the machines rose into cool air scented with cigarette smoke.

She never gambled. Ever. She knew it was a losing proposition in the long run, and she wasn't comfortable with the risk involved. But she appreciated that many of the guests here *did* gamble, bringing in good revenue, although not as many on a Friday night like tonight. This was the final night for a large percentage of weeklong guests, so many had already lost their money and drunk more alcohol than they had intended—

"Hey, girl!"

Ashley turned her head. Two young men near the blackjack tables were leering at her. She remembered these men, and their fathers. The Russians. She smiled, but kept walking.

"You there. You work here, right?" He had a slight accent.

Her shift was over and she was ready to go home. But she retained the fake smile and approached the pair.

She remembered that they were staying with their families in upper-floor suites. They were the spoiled, entitled sons of two men she had pegged as criminals the moment she met them at check-in. Russian gangster types, who'd moved to America to continue the family crime syndicate. Who did bad things to get rich. And who, like normal families, apparently brought theirs to fancy resorts on vacation.

They were dressed well, in pressed shirts and nice slacks. But their eyes were bloodshot, their faces sunburned. Each held a mixed drink. The shorter one was weaving.

"Can I help you?" she said.

"Hey zare, Bahama Mama. How tall are you, girl?" It was the one with curly brown hair and stud earrings, who had called her over.

"Taller than you," she said, knowing she was only that way because of the heels she wore.

He laughed, but his eyes narrowed. "Funny. You may be tall, but I am very long."

His friend, shorter with a shaved head and large gold medallion, laughed as he looked her up and down.

She said, "That's nice. Where are your parents, boys?"

"Not here. Why you asking? You wanna be my mama . . . Bahama Mama?"

Curly Hair moved closer to her. His breath smelled like a still, and Ashley suddenly felt uncomfortable, despite all the people around.

"I'm Niki," he said.

"Is there anything I can help you with, Niki?"

"I can think of something." He reached out and traced a finger along her shoulder. "Want a drink, girl?"

"I'm afraid I can't. I'm working."

"Come on. Just one drink. We're harmless." The way he looked at her made her wonder what awful things he had done to other girls, girls who had had a drink with him.

"Really, I need to be somewhere now. I'm sorry. Good night, gentlemen."

Niki waved a hand at her dismissively. "Whatever. You don't know what you're missing."

The smile left her face and she turned and hurried away to the doors that led out of the casino.

In the warm, humid air outside, it was far more deserted than usual, even this late. People were afraid to go onto the resort grounds at night. After the woman at the beach had gone missing, guests had become scared that somebody might be kidnapping guests. Rumors were even spreading that she had been killed.

Ashley heard a noise behind her and glanced over her shoulder. Nobody was there.

She hurried down the serpentine path, lined by greenery and lit from below by carefully concealed floodlights. The only sounds were the distant roar of rushing water and her heels clicking on the smooth stone pavers. She continued toward the far end of the grounds, and the main entrance. It was still five minutes away. She looked over her shoulder again, and suddenly felt very alone. She wished she'd stayed inside the casino.

She rounded a bend and saw the flat, dark expanse that marked the Dolphin Playground. The attraction, fed by water piped in from the ocean, allowed guests to swim with the playful animals. She'd always felt sorry for them, cut off from the ocean, even if it was a large pen.

The roar of water grew louder as she neared the attraction. The stone pathway entered a narrow strip where it passed between the playground and the adjacent water-park. Opposite the darkened dolphin enclosure, the Neptune Pool was lit from within. The sound came from water surging into the otherwise calm pool at the base of the park's tallest waterslide. The man-made obelisk rose eighty feet above her into the night sky.

She wondered why tonight the water in the slide had been left running. Perhaps for some maintenance purpose. But she didn't like not being able to hear anything over the rushing water, and she moved faster. She glanced again over her shoulder, then at the dolphin enclosure. The water in it was now sloshing inexplicably, as though a small earthquake had rippled the surface. Maybe the dolphins at play? But they normally slept at night, and she couldn't see them anywhere.

She felt the hairs on her arms and neck stand on end. An overwhelming urge to get away overcame her.

She hurried down the path.

CHAPTER 53

Sergei had finally passed out facedown on the red felt of the blackjack table, forehead on a forearm. The bald, fat fuck could never hold his vodka. He was an embarrassment. Niki Melnikov shook his friend's shoulder again, but Sergei didn't move. The dealer, a young Asian woman, had stopped shuffling and looked at him with concern.

"Sir, I'm sorry, but if your friend doesn't get up I'll have to call security."

"Chill out, girl. He's just tired. Sergei!" Niki shook him again, and he groaned, and then buried his face deeper into his arms.

Niki hadn't stopped thinking about the front-desk girl who'd passed them a short time ago. Bitch had nerve, turning him down like that. Back home, on Long Island, the girls knew who he was. If *she* knew who he was back in New York, who his family was, she wouldn't be turning him down. Even if he was younger than her. She'd be *begging* him.

The dealer said, "Sir, I'm going to call someone. They can help escort—"

"Do you know who we are, skank?" This stupid bitch

wasn't going to embarrass them too, even if Sergei was a fool.

She took a step back, raised her hands off the table. "Please, calm down."

"Nobody needs to call security. You got it? I'll take care of this." He smacked Sergei on the head, hard. Sergei lifted his head and looked at Niki, bleary-eyed.

"Get up, asshole. You want your father to hear you passed out here?"

Sergei looked at him dumbly, his jaw hanging open, then shook his head. He fished in his pocket for a moment and produced another fifty-dollar chip. The idiot had probably blown a grand already. He started to lay it on the table and Niki snatched it up.

"Enough! Where do you keep getting those, fuckhole? No more blackjack. Let's go. I need a cigarette."

Niki dragged his friend out of the casino, in the direction the desk girl had gone. Maybe they could still find her. Teach her some respect.

"I think I'm gonna be sick, Niki."

Niki shook his head. "You sure you're Russian? You drink like a girl, fat ass."

He watched as his friend staggered to the greenery beside the path and bent over, hands on his knees. He shook his head.

He'd pulled Sergei along as they smoked their Marlboros, hoping to catch up to the tall Bahamian girl. Not sure what he would do if he found her. But they'd already crossed through much of the resort, and hadn't seen her. She was gone.

They'd only passed two other people. Everyone had gone to bed hours ago. This place was nothing like New York. It was fuckin' dead at night. Sergei stopped just before the pool with the big waterslide. The water roared down from above.

The water. It was still running.

"I'll be over there. You hear me, Sergei?" He shook Sergei's shoulder and pointed. "Over there! By the slide."

Sergei didn't respond, but Niki left him and continued down the path. Where it narrowed between the swimming pool and the darkened dolphin play area he'd visited yesterday, the cement was covered in water. He saw the reason why. The pool was overflowing. Its well-lit, baby-blue bottom looked odd in the darkness from this angle, as if curved and convoluted.

He thought he saw a small splash of water in the chlorine pool, accompanied by a faint plopping sound. He stared at the spot for a moment, but there was nothing there.

He shook his head to clear it. He was just drunk. Seeing things.

He stepped gingerly through the half-inch of water, cursing as he felt the water soak through his expensive leather shoes, and moved to where he could see the outlet of the slide better. Water rushed out of its mouth and into the empty pool. It had been off every other night, but maybe they'd accidentally left it on, and it was somehow overflowing the pool. He looked around, saw nobody. He suddenly had an idea, and grinned.

It was their last night here. Even if they caught him, what the hell could they do to him anyway? What was the worst that could happen?

He began stripping off his shirt.

In the new pool of water, her skin began to burn. This water was different.

She had left the safety of the salt water, to explore the

strange-tasting pool she had tested with her arms while still within the confines where she had found the dolphins. She had fed, but she was still hungry, and the impulse to hunt had not abated. From the edge of the saltwater pool, she had been able to reach the tips of her arms into this other body of water. It had tasted odd, and felt very shallow, but curiosity pushed her.

She had labored out into the air once again, dragging her tons of heavy flesh over the narrow spit of hard land before rolling into the new, smaller pool. Although her entire body did not submerge, this water tingled against her skin. Then it started to burn, to cause intense pain where it flowed past her gills, against her eyes. This water was not like the ocean. It was not safe for her.

Her huge bulk still curving slightly above the shallow water, she moved back toward the side where she had entered, to return to the other pool. The saltwater pool. But then she stopped.

Vibrations.

Something was coming.

She flattened herself down as low as she could, displacing even more water around her. *Conforming.* A moment later, she was entirely below the surface, compressed to the bottom. Instantly, her skin turned a lighter shade of blue, smoothed out to match the bottom surface of the pool. Dark, regular spots began to form on her skin, at regular intervals, as the chromatophores in her flesh patterned themselves after the dark tiles laid into the submerged surface.

She fought the burning in her gills, against her skin and eyes, and waited.

The pain quickly became unbearable. Her gills began to feel swollen. Just as she began to abandon her camouflage, she felt the vibrations again. Tasted something new. She slid an arm very slowly toward the incoming flow of water, into a large hole from which it flowed. Radial muscles contracted as longitudinal ones extended, and the arm stiffened, elongating as it moved upward into the pipe.

Within it, she tasted prey.

Niki had left his clothes in a pile, and in his underwear he jumped the heavy rope guardrail strung alongside the path. He knew there might be a guard positioned to watch the actual entrance to the tower stairs. He'd been on this slide several times already, but the rush of doing it now, at night, when it wasn't allowed, added novelty.

He found his way through the trees and other greenery planted between the path and the tower, the pain from small rocks jabbing into feet numbed by the alcohol, and soon found himself beside the stairway built into a man-made hill. He stepped over another heavy rope that bordered it and charged up the stairs, two and three at a time. He didn't care if he was caught, as long as he got to go down first.

He reached the top of the stairs and paused, looking out. From eight or nine stories above the resort, at night, the view was pretty cool. The artificially lit grounds spread out beneath him, and he could see the white line of the surf breaking on the dark beach nearby. He could see a handful of people moving between the casino and their own rooms. But he knew they could not see him. He stepped under the roof covering the top of the water-slide.

Whitewater surged loudly into the pipe from large jets on either side. The water disappeared a few feet later, where the steep pipe dropped almost vertically before curving near the bottom to slow guests before spitting them out into the pool. He stepped into the trough of shallow water just above the jets and sat down. The water felt cold.

The pipe shuddered. He paused. Was something really wrong with it, making the water run at night? For a moment, he considered heading back down the stairs. *No,* he told himself. *Stop being a bitch. The slide is fine.* Grasping the rim of the pipe, he crossed his legs and thrust himself into the darkness.

He screamed in delight as he went over the precipice, his stomach fluttering as the bottom dropped out from under him. He plummeted down, his eyes and mouth shut. In just a few seconds he would enter the water at the bottom—

He slammed into something in the pipe.

His knees buckled as he stopped suddenly, violently, his limbs crashing into the mass and the sides of the unyielding pipe. One knee slammed into his jaw, shattering it, and he felt something in his spine give at the sudden compression. He cried out in pain.

Crumpled inside the dark slide, disoriented, and no longer moving, he looked up and realized he hadn't reached the pool. He was stuck in a fetal position somewhere near the bottom of the steep part of the pipe, before it curved out horizontally. He was sitting on something.

The water from above was quickly filling the space, blocked by the obstruction below him. The water rose quickly, passing his shoulders as it filled the pipe around him. He tried to stand, to keep his head above the water, but his legs wouldn't work. He looked down toward his feet, but it was too dark to see anything. He reached a hand down through the water. The obstruction below him felt firm, textured, and yielded slightly to his touch. Like pressing down on an overinflated inner tube. Maybe one of the tubes from the waterpark—

Then the obstruction began to move. To change shape. It was not an inner tube. Under his fingers, it slid below him, harder discs protruding from its surface starting to latch on to his thigh.

It was alive.

Niki reached upward, trying to grasp anything in the smooth pipe, and screamed just before the rising water reached his mouth.

CHAPTER 54

In the predawn darkness, Ashley knelt by the dolphin enclosure, trying not to get water on her black skirt or turquoise shirt. She looked down at Ella. The female dolphin was not moving, pressed against one wall of the artificial lagoon.

"What happened, girl?" she whispered. "Where's Captain?"

Ella saw Ashley and swam over to her, poking her head out of the water when she recognized her. Ashley touched the animal's smooth nose. She quickly turned and dove under again, heading for the far side of the enclosure. She lunged out of the deeper water onto a shallow man-made shelf covered in eight inches of water. The dolphin faced away from her, uncharacteristically restless this early in the morning.

Normally, the dolphins only swam onto the shelf when they were doing a show and were coaxed up with frozen fish. It was located in front of a set of bleachers, and here the dolphins had been trained to interact with handlers as part of two daily shows. But there would be no shows today. Captain was gone, and the shows would be cancelled.

"That's where we found her this morning," Chris, one of the young dolphin handlers, said as he walked over to Ashley.

"Has that ever happened before?"

"No. Never."

"Where do you think Captain is?"

He shook his head. "We have no idea. But he's gone. I've gotta go get her breakfast ready." He patted her shoulder and walked away.

As soon as Ashley arrived at the desk at five a.m., after getting a few hours' sleep, she'd heard the news about Oceanus's male dolphin. He'd somehow escaped overnight. The only thing the aquarists could figure was that Captain had incredibly, almost impossibly, leapt out onto the narrow strip of land between the lagoon and ocean and then wriggled his way to freedom. Were any outdoor cameras trained on that part of the grounds last night? She'd have to go talk to Dennis Gladwin, one of the resort's security heads.

"You ginned it all up with your man too?" Ashley said to the dolphin. Maybe Captain was just trying to get away from his girl.

She thought about Eric. Despite her height, she was a magnet for most men—even the shorter ones. But Eric was different. Even though he obviously was attracted to her, he didn't fawn over her or seem desperate to get physical. He enjoyed just talking with her. Seemed to respect her. Why hadn't she called him back?

It was she, who never lost her temper, who had driven him away. Yes, he'd upset her with his negative comments about Oceanus, but she knew he only meant well. As she looked at the lone dolphin trapped in the lagoon, and thought of the other who had escaped, she knew he was right. This resort wasn't natural, or as eco-friendly as it pretended to be. But what choice did she have but to work here? If she ever had a resort of her own, it would be more natural, simply abutting the environment, rather than trying to recreate it, and any dolphins a guest might happen to see would be free. Living in the ocean. But for now, her loyalty was to Mr. Barbas, and his resort.

She knew she should probably return Eric's call, but something held her back: the simple fact that he was leaving. What was the point?

Ashley stood and said good-bye to Ella, then headed for the security room at the base of the resort's middle tower. There, Dennis would have footage from all the outdoor cameras. She stepped around two groundskeepers, hosing what looked like blue paint off the cement, and continued through the waterpark.

In the silent black-and-white video, the young Russian-American appeared from the side, wearing only his underwear. He leapt the thick rope guardrail onto the stairs leading up to the waterslide, glanced about for a moment, then turned away from the camera and hurried up the stairs. Dennis Gladwin, sitting beside Ashley in the dim room, paused the image. Dennis was the senior security and loss prevention specialist at Oceanus, and he and Ashley were friends. They had roots in the same island chain, and his family knew hers quite well. Now in his early sixties, but still relatively fit, Dennis had been like an uncle to her.

"Then young Mr. Melnikov appeared on camera fourteen . . . here." Dennis pushed a button on the remote control.

On a separate monitor, the young man appeared again. This image was darker, taken at night on top of the tower. He paused at the edge of the screen to look out over the side, perhaps enjoying the view, and then moved to the trough at the top of the slide. He sat down in the rushing water, crossed his legs to brace for the impact at the bottom, and disappeared inside the tube.

"And that's the last time anybody saw him," Dennis said, sipping his coffee from a Styrofoam cup. "His father just called us a few hours ago, when his friend came back and said he'd looked for hours, but couldn't find Melnikov. The friend claimed this guy left to go on the waterslide, and says they didn't meet up again. Obviously, the story checks out. We even found the kid's clothes and wallet hidden in the brush, right where he cut over to the slide."

Ashley was stunned to see that this was the same man who'd made advances on her last night. Not long before this footage was taken. And according to Dennis, who'd immediately shown her this footage when she walked in, apparently, he was now missing too.

"You don't have any cameras aimed at the bottom of the slide? At the Neptune Pool?" she said.

"No. Just camera twenty-one, aimed at the far edge of the pool, and at the poolside bar there. These cameras are intended to help us watch out for theft, or altercations between guests. Not to watch people enjoy the waterslide."

She nodded. "Right."

"But there *was* something odd in that camera," he said. "Hold on."

After a moment, he rolled the video. It was a wide-angle shot, also clearly taken at night, showing part of the Neptune Pool and the bar next to it. It was recorded from on high—clearly this camera was mounted somewhere on the waterslide tower. Nothing moved on the screen.

"I'll fast-forward to the part I showed Mr. Barbas earlier—"

"Barbas is already up?"

"You know him. Wants to make sure everything goes off all right today—here." He pointed at the screen. "Right about now, watch the left side of the screen. . . ."

Ashley stared at it for a moment, and then thought she saw part of the pool darken momentarily, as though a shadow had suddenly been cast over it.

"What was that, Dennis?"

"We don't know yet. Want to see it again?"

"Please."

He moved the slider bar back a minute and replayed the digital video. Again, Ashley saw the pool darken at the edge of the screen, just for a few seconds, before the shadow went away. She thought of the blue stains she had seen the men washing off the sidewalk.

"Was something dark poured into the water, maybe? Maybe from the top of the slide? I saw maintenance cleaning what looked like paint off the sidewalk by the pool. "

"I doubt it. We would have seen that kid doing it."

"What else could that shadow be?"

"I don't know. There aren't many lights overhead at night, and no bird could cast a shadow that big. It might just be a glitch. Either way, I'm stumped." He leaned back in his swivel chair. "So that's it."

"But there's nothing at all from the edge of the dolphin enclosure? That might show us how Captain got out?"

"Sorry, Ash. Already looked."

She sighed. "Thanks for showing me those, Dennis."

He looked over his shoulder, out a small window into the main room at security where a few others were talking at their desks. He lowered his voice. "There *is* one more video. But I really shouldn't show you."

"Then why are you telling me about it?"

"I don't know, Ash. You're a smart woman. And we can't figure out what the hell happened here. Not yet. Maybe you'll have an idea." He leaned toward her, raised his graying eyebrows. "But you can't say nothing."

"Of course not, Dennis."

He slid another thumb drive into the computer in front of him. "This is the footage from about four this morning, when I first interrogated that other Russian kid. Taped in the room next to us here. After Melnikov's parents raised hell. We're only gonna watch the end. The young man doesn't have much to say, and doesn't remember shit. He's still pretty drunk here."

Dennis skipped forward through several frozen frames, and then played the video. On it, the other Russian-American, the short one with the shaved head, was hunched over a small table, his face in his hands. He was sitting across from Dennis, whose arm appeared in the edge of the frame. She heard him clear his throat, then start talking. This time, there was audio:

"Come on, Sergei," Dennis said. *"You really expect me to believe you have no idea what happened?"*

"I already told you. I don't know where he is."

"What happened, man? You can tell me. Then you can go get some sleep. I promise. Did you get in a fight?"

The kid rubbed his temples. *"I don't know."*

"When was the last time you saw Niki?"

"I told you. I think he was going to the waterslide. But he never came back. So I went back to his parents' room. To tell Mr. Melnikov."

"After you looked for him?"

"Yes."

"But you didn't see him? Or anyone else?"

"No. All I saw was that one waterslide running, and the big waves on the pool."

"What waves, Sergei?"

"You know. The big waves in that pool."

"Where the water comes out of the slide?"

On the screen, Sergei shook his head. *"No. Big waves, all over the pool. Like waves at the beach."*

"Have you taken any drugs, sir?" Dennis asked him.

"What? No. I don't think so."

"Well, which pool are you referring to?"

"The one under the slide. And that's all I remember."

Dennis stopped the video. "That's all. His story is full of holes, but it's pretty consistent. What you think, Ash? Any ideas?"

Ashley frowned. They didn't have any artificial wave machines at Oceanus. Certainly not in the Neptune Pool. "Can you see the waves he was talking about?" she said.

"It's hard to tell on the footage, but not really. The water level in the pool did appear to be too high. It was overflowing onto the cement."

"Why?"

"We don't know that either."

Ashley had just walked past that pool. "But it isn't overflowing now."

He raised his eyebrows again. "I know." He stood to leave. "I gotta do my rounds real quick, before the show starts. See you there."

CHAPTER 55

Dennis Gladwin refilled his cup with steaming black coffee and made his way across the still-dark resort. At a little before six a.m., it was damp and comfortably cool, the air smelling sweet and earthy. This time of day was always quiet, even at Oceanus. It was normally Dennis's favorite time of day. But not today.

Mr. Barbas's call had woken him a few hours ago. He'd been in a foul mood, having himself been awakened from his slumber by night-shift security. The Russian kid was missing, and the main outflow pipe for the resort's network of aquariums had again become clogged, just as it had last week. Barbas had ordered him to hurry to his post. Dennis lived twenty minutes away from the resort, and had to hurry to get there by four.

Mr. Barbas had insisted that after poring over video footage and sending security personnel to look for Melnikov, Dennis was to pay particular attention to the water in Pirate's Cove—the tank from which the manta would be removed. If silted, cloudy water was backing up to where visitors might see it, he'd been instructed to take action to keep all eyes away from the aquarium viewing areas. They might even need to postpone the manta relocation.

He understood the problem. News cameras would be at Oceanus today, and many guests also would be up early to watch the rare event. Nobody wanted the reporters or anyone else to start asking questions about why the tanks suddenly looked filthy, or if the health of the animals was impacted. A PR opportunity could suddenly turn into a PR nightmare.

As he neared the main aquariums, the handheld two-way radio clipped to Dennis's chest harness crackled quietly as another guard sent a standard morning message to the security center. A shift change. Dennis adjusted the volume, turning it even lower. He passed a janitor on the lit path and said good morning to him, then turned off the main avenue onto a walkway that sloped downward. Underground, to the viewing tunnels. He'd start at Pirate's Cove.

He descended the ramp into the underground tunnel, alone, the echo of his footsteps bouncing off the hewn rock walls. He reached the start of the viewing area for the resort's largest tank. The first pane of glass was triangular in shape, starting in a point and then increasing in height to eight feet at the far end, where past a seam the next, taller viewing window began. A bit farther the thick panes of clear, shatter-resistant acrylic rose to many times his own height in the main viewing area. He sighed in relief. The water inside looked clear. Maybe the outflow pipe, which ran into the ocean, had cleared itself, or maybe maintenance had already somehow fixed the problem.

He waited there for a few minutes, sipping his coffee and watching schools of colorful fish move past. Soon, Spirit appeared at the edge of his field of view.

Dennis smiled and tapped the tank lightly as the huge ray neared, seeming to grow in size as he moved in front of Dennis. He was flat and diamond-shaped, with two hard, horn-shaped fins marking the sides of his gaping mouth. He swept slowly by, propelling himself with wing-like movements of his broad, triangular pectoral fins.

"Good morning, big fella. You ready to head back to sea?"

Ashley would be happy to see this ray go home. He remembered that when she'd been a little girl, back home in the Abacos, she'd always been interested in everything that swam in the ocean or crawled on the sand. And she always wanted to save everything, even the damn cats that kept killing off her neighbor's chickens. He'd always figured she might go off to some university, to become a biologist maybe. Or some kind of activist. Then again, nobody from Two Finger Cay had ever gone to college.

Instead, they both worked here.

He needed to fly back home soon, hop the ferry to the cay. He hadn't been back in a while, to see his grandkids. Too busy working. He rarely left Andros anymore.

He watched Spirit swim off, and then continued down the tunnel, past a darkened underground gift shop and a set of restrooms, toward the next big aquarium. He passed a trash bin and tossed in the empty foam coffee cup, then rounded a corner and spied the start of the exhibit.

Shark Alley also housed many of the aquarium's largest fish—nurse sharks, reef sharks, groupers and the like. Just not the mantas, or the more aggressive hammerheads or sawfish, which each had their own tanks. Looking into the exhibit, he stopped when he stepped in a shallow puddle.

He looked down. The cement floor was drenched, and there was standing water in a few shallow depressions. Unless someone had been working down here, there was probably some sort of plumbing problem. Or the tank was leaking from above, where there was a narrow gap between the rock ceiling and the acrylic panes more than twenty feet above his head. Mr. Barbas would not be happy.

But he was relieved to see that, at least at first glance, the water in this tank also looked clear. He moved farther down, inspecting the acrylic panes, but didn't see any cracks or leaks. It would take an incredible force to break the thick, shatterproof pane.

He paused as he reached the highest section of the wall. During the daytime, the gap above it allowed more light into the tunnels from the outside world, and offered ventilation. Here the thick imitation glass was streaked with dried salt water.

He could immediately see why. The tank was fuller than usual. Normally the waterline was a good foot below the upper rim of the clear acrylic, but now it was right at the top. Any small wave now would cause the water in the tank to splash over, to run down the outer face inside the underground viewing tunnel. It must have something to do with the clogged outflow pipe.

At least he knew now why the floor was all wet. He'd say something as soon as the aquarists arrived, which would be very soon since Spirit was departing this morning.

He looked into the tank, at the curved contours of artificial coral on the far wall, the structures rising in the center that mimicked features in a natural reef. The colors the fake corals added to the exhibit were hard to discern by the weak lights of the tank, without the sun overhead.

A few small fish passed by. The water *was* clear, but something was wrong—

"Dennis, you there?"

Dennis flinched, and then lowered the volume of his handheld radio, realizing he'd accidentally turned the dial the wrong way just before he'd headed down into the tunnels.

"Yeah, I'm here," he muttered. "Damn near gave me a heart attack, though."

He lifted the radio out of the harness and pressed the talk button. "Ronnie, I copy. What's going on?"

"Just talked to the boss man. Good news. Water's flowing again."

"Pipe's not clogged no more?"

"That's right, Pop."

Dennis thought, *Then why is the water level still so high?*

Clogged, unclogged, clogged. Wait a few hours and the damn pipe would probably be clogged again. He lifted the radio back to his mouth. "Tanks One and Two look good, but the water level in Two is high. Headed to Three now."

As he lowered the radio, a drip of water struck his forehead. He wiped it away. Now there'd be even more damn condensation down here. If they didn't disinfect these subterranean tunnels as often as they did, there'd be mold everywhere.

"Copy," Ronnie said. *"You coming back by the booth first? Freshen your coffee?"*

Dennis scrutinized the water inside the aquarium. "No. I'm gonna finish checking the other tank—"

He stopped. He realized what was bothering him about the tank.

They're all gone.

"Stand by, Ronnie."

Another drop of water struck the top of his head, but he ignored it, transfixed on the tank. He stepped toward the acrylic glass. The small fish were still in there, but this was the main shark tank. Those little fish were just in there for food.

But where were all the sharks? Where were *all* the bigger fish? The stingrays, and groupers?

He started to raise the radio to his mouth again. Paused. His memory wasn't what it used to be. Had he forgotten to read something? An e-mail? Maybe they'd moved these sharks as part of the manta ray's relocation today. Had someone already said something about that to him?

"Dennis, what's going on?"

He scanned the water. Maybe the sharks simply were concealed behind the artificial coral formations. His eyes settled on one part of the rock wall, off to the side. It was much larger than he remembered, bulging outward too far, almost closing off the space between it and the fake glass. As if it had . . . *grown*.

As he stared at the rock, it moved. Swelled out even farther, in front of his eyes. He blinked. It was pulsing.

He took a step backwards. A small wave of water splashed over the top of the acrylic wall and ran down the outside, streaking the clear pane. He looked up, thought he saw something red moving above him, and then closed his eyes as buckets of water suddenly rained down on him. Was the glass cracking?

He turned to run, but immediately slammed into something that knocked the wind out of him. Thick and wet, it wrapped around his midsection.

Squeezed.

His radio clattered to the ground. On it, he heard Ronnie calling for him again.

In pain and confusion, he began to pound his fists on the wet mass enclosing his body. He heard his ribs crack, and his mouth opened in a silent scream, but there was no air in his lungs. He felt his feet lifting off the ground, and realized he was spinning in slow spirals as the fleshy, reddish mass continued to coil around him.

CHAPTER 56

Val stared at her breakfast cereal, moving the granola around in the milk with her spoon. She'd hardly eaten anything. She was feeling sick again. Like she might throw up.

She stood and walked outside onto the back patio of the guesthouse, and closed her eyes, breathing in a gentle morning breeze off the water. After a moment, she felt better and opened her eyes. On the eastern horizon, where the sun would soon rise over the ocean, there was an angry dark orange over the water, backlighting the darkness of building clouds. A rare late-winter tropical storm had been forecast for today, and it would be cooler. She crossed her arms to ward off a sudden chill.

She tried to push away the worried thoughts, the mixed emotions, as she tried to enjoy the early morning light. She hadn't slept much. And she'd still said nothing to Will. Even though she was now becoming convinced.

But she couldn't really be pregnant. She wasn't ready now. *They* weren't ready. And she couldn't actually have a child. Could she?

She'd lost her first pregnancy, as a stupid teen, even before she and her mom had been able to decide what she should do, or what to tell her dad. Even though she'd felt some relief back then, knowing she wouldn't be a young mother trapped with a baby right after high school, she had cried. Had felt so sad that the baby that had started inside her was gone.

After that, the doctor had recommended a D&C, to rid her body of the "unnecessary tissue." But something went wrong. The trauma from all the scraping had left her uterus scarred. Permanently.

She was infertile. Or so she had thought, until she had unexpectedly gotten pregnant once again, last year. She and Will hadn't been practicing birth control, as she had thought there was no need. This time, she'd been planning to move forward despite her demanding career, and they had been so excited.

But she'd lost that child as well.

She took a deep breath. Closed her eyes and tried to enjoy the relative silence. She began to feel sick again. She wondered again if what she had felt in the ocean when she'd gone lobster diving—what Mack had thought was induced by the Navy's antipersonnel sonar—had simply caused some sort of lingering symptoms. Maybe that's all this was.

But that had been a week ago, and she hadn't felt sick anymore once she'd been out of the water a few hours. She thought of the Obeah woman. What she had said to her—

"Mornin', Val."

She jumped. Sturman had just walked out onto the patio, cowboy hat in hand. He'd slept on the couch last night.

"Good morning, Will. You guys leaving soon?"

"Yeah. Got to if we want to catch the show. Aren't you coming?"

"I don't think so," she said. "Is your Navy pal joining you?"

"Wits? No. I'll try to catch up with him tonight or tomorrow."

They'd all planned to head over to Oceanus. She, Sturman, and Eric would watch a captive manta ray get transported to the ocean by helicopter, and Mack had said he'd head over with them to gamble in the casino. He claimed you always had better luck early in the morning.

Sturman moved beside her and studied her face. She looked away, back at the ocean.

He said, "What's the matter. You doing all right?"

"Yeah. I'm okay."

He nodded back at the kitchen. "Well, I saw your uneaten cereal. And you look kinda green."

"I just feel a little nauseous. Maybe I ate something bad. You want to finish my breakfast?"

"No thanks. We'll just bring something with us. Besides, I don't wanna get what you have." He frowned. "You sure you're all right?"

She thought again of the Obeah woman. Her toothless grin. *You big up, ain't ya?*

She said, "I'll be okay. But I'm gonna stay here and rest. You guys have fun without me."

He nodded, and looked at the eastern horizon. "Hopefully, they get this done before that storm gets here."

Sturman hugged her and went back inside, yelling for Eric to hurry up. Val smiled. Will seemed genuinely excited. He'd really become fascinated with commercial aquariums.

She thought about the other things the Obeah woman had said. That this octopus, this *lusca*, if it did exist, might be feeding more than usual because it too was pregnant, or going to be. That it would have a den in which to raise its brood. But it just made no sense. If this was an undiscovered species, where were the others of its kind? Where were its young? People had to have seen them by now, right?

Why was she giving any weight at all to some old island sage? To some crazy old woman?

But she knew why.

Her hand went to her womb, and she felt another wave of nausea. What if the old woman was somehow right? What was she going to do? And what was she going to tell Will?

She heard the distant rumble of thunder.

CHAPTER 57

Ashley watched the huge manta ray glide past, revealing a pale underside vented with long gill slits. Despite his devilish appearance, with what looked like two horns jutting from his brow, Spirit was a harmless filter feeder. A favorite of the tourists. He'd been with Oceanus since the opening of the resort, already quite large when he'd been captured off the coast, and had grown quickly. He was now nearly fifteen feet across. The habitat in Pirate's Cove, despite its size, could no longer contain him, and Mr. Barbas was keeping his promise.

Today, Spirit would go home.

Ashley stood in the dappled light of the softly lit, below-ground viewing tunnel. Most of the light usually came in from the aquarium itself, where sunlight refracted down through the water from the outside world. But the sun wasn't up yet.

She smiled as the ray disappeared around a bend in the tank. She looked over at Barbas, who stood a short distance behind her, talking with a few of the aquarists. This was something she appreciated about the man. Even if he didn't really want to part with a main attraction, and might have kept the animal forever if he could, at least he had the decency to listen to his aquarists and accept when it was time to—

"Ashley?"

She turned. Striding down the rock-walled corridor, in his proud but uneven gait, was Valerie Martell's uncle. Beside him walked another rough-looking man she'd never seen before—much taller than Mack, younger, and wearing a cowboy hat.

"Mack! How are you, love?" She gave him a hug and kiss on the cheek.

"Same as always. How are you?"

"I'm all right, you know. What're you doing down here? I thought they'd already closed off this tunnel?"

"Apparently not where we came in." He thumbed at the younger man next to him. "Sturman here wanted to see the aquariums."

She recognized the name from a conversation with Val. She turned to him. He wore a plain white T-shirt and jeans. He was attractive, but not in a Hollywood way—more like an old leather jacket, with stubble along his jawline and wrinkles creasing his skin. She could tell he'd led a hard life.

She said, "I'm Ashley. I work here at Oceanus."

Sturman took his hat off and shook her hand. "Will Sturman. Val's told me a little about you. You *are* tall."

She smiled, looking down at her feet. "The heels add a few inches. Did you come down to see her?"

"I reckon so."

"Are you getting along again, then?"

He smiled. "We'd have to ask her."

"Indeed. So Val said you work at an aquarium back in California?"

"That's right. You done a pretty decent job here. How do you keep the pH, the salinity regulated in such big tanks? And how do you keep the water fresh?"

"Well, I'm no expert, but it has something to do with the high volume flowing in directly from the ocean. The water in here turns over pretty quickly."

"I'll be damned. So how you get a job at this place?"

"Well, you could start by asking Mr. Barbas." She pointed at him. "He's the owner."

Sturman nodded, fitting the straw cowboy hat back on his head. "I don't wanna interrupt him now. He looks busy."

"We're almost ready for the release. The helicopter will be coming in very soon."

"Amazing," Sturman said.

"I'm assuming you're both here to watch?"

Mack snorted. "Not me. Just Sturman and Watson. Seen enough helicopters and big fish in my life. I'm headed to the casino."

"Eric's here?"

Just then, he came around a corner in the tunnel.

"He had to visit the little boys' room," said Mack.

They locked eyes for a moment, and Ashley felt her face flush. This wasn't the time.

"Well, I'll make sure they allow you to stay down here, if you'd like. Now if you'll excuse me, gentlemen, I need to get back to work." She turned away.

When Ashley walked up, Barbas was pointing at the heavy security doors at the end of the elaborately formed hallway. He and the aquarists had been joined by a few guards. But where was Dennis? He was in charge of security today. Only a handful of VIPs would be allowed down here to watch the entire process, as divers maneuvered the huge ray into a broad hoop net suspended from the aircraft.

Nobody besides the VIPs would see anything but the helicopter arrive and leave with Spirit in the net. All the guests would be invited to watch the spectacle, but only from designated areas above ground. They just wouldn't be granted access down here, where outer doors would be locked and guards would be posted so that if something went wrong—or Spirit was hurt in the netting process—nobody would be able to film it on an iPhone.

She watched as the manta reappeared, swimming in slow circles around the enclosure. If only he knew that very soon he would have his freedom. Ashley just hoped everything went smoothly.

CHAPTER 58

Sturman stood with Eric beside the aquarium, as the sun's rays began to light it from above, marveling at the scene inside the huge tank. Mack, without speaking to Eric, had left them to blow some money at the tables.

The divers above them gently drove the massive manta toward a platform of shallower water at the edge of his vision. According to handouts they'd been given, the resort's plan was apparently to get the oversized critter to move above a net on the platform, where a number of hands would then lift the rigid edges to prevent his escape. When the helicopter arrived, dangling a long rope, they would clip the net harness to it and then off it would go, manta in tow, to a drop-off point in the ocean just past the reef.

"I'll be damned," Sturman said. "They're just wranglers."

Eric finished taking a picture and glanced at him. "What did you say?"

Sturman nodded at the divers. "They operate the same as ranch hands. They're driving that manta to where they can lasso him, like cowpokes corralling a steer."

A group of what looked like reporters, one of them carrying a large video camera and tripod, came down the tunnel and stopped by them. A few other distinguished-looking guests had also arrived.

"You really think this will work?" Eric said.

"I guess so. Your girlfriend there said it's been done before." Sturman looked at Eric. "She is your girlfriend, right?"

"Not really. We've been on a date. But she's not talking to me."

"Join the club."

Eric smiled weakly. "Too bad Val isn't here to see this."

"Yeah," Sturman said. "I guess. But she's never been big on aquariums. She likes to see animals in their own environment."

But Sturman knew Eric was right. She'd really enjoy the novelty of this operation. He was a little surprised she'd backed out, and a little worried. She didn't look good. And there was something else. Last night, and again this morning, she'd seemed like she'd been hiding something.

He looked over at Ashley and the others. She was talking to someone in a security uniform and to her boss. He was a good-looking older man, with a well-trimmed beard, and apparently the owner of the resort. They'd been joined by a mid-forties blonde in a skirt and jacket, who appeared to be his assistant.

Sturman could tell by their body language that the conversation was serious. Ashley turned away from them, a concerned expression on her face, and passed by the small group of reporters. They were visiting casually with a heavyset young woman who, like Ashley, wore a turquoise shirt with the resort's logo. He saw that Ashley flashed them all a brilliant white smile, but as she moved away from the reporters, the smile quickly left her face.

She saw him looking over at her and the forced smile returned. She headed back toward him and Eric. As Ashley drew closer, Sturman thought she looked worried. Ill, even. Almost as bad as Val had looked this morning.

She stopped a few feet in front of them, the well-practiced fake smile of a resort services employee still on her face. "It's almost time, gentlemen. Once they get Spirit netted, we'll make our way outside so you can watch the rest of the action from above. Hopefully, we can beat this storm, or we'll have to call it off."

"A hurricane?" Sturman said.

"No. But there's a tropical cyclone offshore, headed our way, and it's nasty looking. The wind and rain would make it too dangerous for this operation."

"I didn't think you got that kind of weather this early in the spring."

"We usually don't."

"Thanks again for allowin' us to be down here," Sturman said.

"It's no problem. No problem at all." Her gaze dropped, and the smile finally left her face.

Eric finally spoke. "Ashley, is everything all right?"

"Yes. I'm fine."

"Look. If it's me . . . if I'm making you uncomfortable being here . . ."

"It's not like that, Eric." She paused, glanced at Sturman, then back at Eric. She lowered her voice to a whisper. "I just found out there's a problem. In another tank . . . the fish, the sharks, they're all gone."

Eric said, "What? What do you mean they're gone?"

"They're not in the tank. Like somebody somehow came and took them. But that's impossible. A dolphin is also missing from our enclosure. And . . . I just heard that one of our security guards is missing. A friend. Someone found his radio by the shark tank."

"Jesus," Sturman said. "What the hell's going on?"

She shook her head. "I don't know. But something happened in that tank. And to Dennis. We can't let the media know."

She stared past them, a faraway look in her eyes, and Sturman felt sorry for her. She began to chew on her lower lip, and Sturman could tell she was fighting off tears. He considered excusing himself from the conversation, so she could talk to Eric, but he figured it might upset her even more.

He said, "Can't they just postpone this whole circus?"

"Mr. Barbas is insisting we continue—"

Sturman snorted. "Your boss? The fancy-looking fella with a beard?"

She nodded.

"What an asshole. Want me to talk to him?"

Eric shot him a look and subtly shook his head. He said, "Ashley, is that why those doors down the hall are now closed off? To keep everyone from going near the shark tank?"

She nodded. She glanced over her shoulder, where Barbas was gesturing for her to come back over, a broad smile on his face. She smoothed her skirt with both hands and took a deep breath. "He's calling for me again. Please, don't say anything."

She hurried off. Sturman looked at Eric and raised his eyebrows.

They stood and watched the operation unfold, as the

divers in the tank finished maneuvering the half-ton ray into the net, as the wealthy guests beside them oohed and aahed. Then Sturman heard something over the conversation.

The low, rhythmic thump of helicopter rotors.

She felt the deep vibrations. They were unfamiliar, but not unlike those she had felt recently in the depths. The vibrations from the objects on the sea floor, which since her birth had regularly pulsed through her body. But that now gave her tremendous pain.

Pressed against the unusual, almost tasteless corals in the small enclosure, her body swelled slightly in her agitation, a burst of red patterns briefly marbling her skin.

She was fully sated. Unable to feed any longer, and with nothing left to feed upon, she was desperate to return to her den. To protect her young. And to avoid the bright light of a sun that had recently risen. But she was trapped. She had been unable to locate a way out of this strange lagoon. There was only the way she had come in, from above, in the sunlight. In the air.

The rhythmic thrumming grew louder. Her body swelled with seawater and she finally revealed herself, filling much of the tank's volume with her own loose form, her great arms uncoiling, still seeking a means of escape. She saw something move on the other side of the glass, but ignored it, pushing her body toward the base of the exhibit. Her sudden movement lifted a wall of water up and sent a wave over the side of the tank, where it crashed down inside the vacant viewing passage below.

The noise, now overhead, throbbed into the water. Ached between her eyes.

Feeling below her, one of her arms met with a small hole. No. A series of holes. She felt water flowing into them.

There was some sort of obstruction blocking a larger hole. One that might accommodate her. She thrust the tip of one arm into the metal grate and tore it free with a muffled clang, casting it aside. Below the grate she felt a round opening. It might be large enough.

The tips of a few of her arms entered the hole first, and quickly met a ninety-degree bend, with narrow tunnels leading in opposite directions. Unthinking, the lead arms wriggled quickly in one direction, and began pulling her colossal form after them.

Overhead, the noise grew louder.

CHAPTER 59

By the sound of it, the bird was directly overhead. The loud, fast whumping generated by the rotor blades passed down the stairwell into the tunnel, through solid earth and cement walls, to reverberate throughout the passage.

Sturman waited in the dim underground tunnel, near the bottom of the exit stairwell. He could no longer see the netted manta ray, as the aquarium glass began a good hundred feet behind him. A small crowd of people milled on the staircase in front of him, waiting to head up to ground level where they could watch the helicopter bring the manta from the tank out to the ocean. But what the hell was the holdup?

When he had walked away from the glass, the crew in the tank had been standing on the shelf at the edge of the tank, in waist-deep water, to prevent the manta from leaving the net. They might at this moment be fastening the rig to the helicopter's sling. But still Sturman and the others were being held back.

Up on the stairs, he could see Barbas talking with a police officer. Clearly there was some sort of problem. The bearded owner finally nodded at the policeman, who then walked up the stairs and out of sight. Barbas came halfway back down toward the crowd. His blond, birdlike assistant remained at his side. He raised both hands, waved them in the air. A reporter for what was perhaps a Bahamas television station trained his camera on Barbas.

"Ladies and gentlemen. May I have your attention? Please." He shouted at them over the drumming rotors outside. His voice was inflected by some Old World accent.

"I apologize for the delay, but apparently the transport helicopter arrived from a different direction than we had anticipated. There is an approaching storm. The police have informed me that, due to the downdraft from the helicopter, it would be unsafe for us to head aboveground at the moment."

There were some groans from the VIPs standing near Sturman. He studied the lot of them, so unlike him in their expensive clothes and jewelry, and shook his head. Bunch of entitled pricks. It had to be a hell of a thing in itself to navigate a helicopter in here, near the resort's huge towers, to make the pickup. Any wind would make it that much harder. But they simply expected a show.

Barbas continued. "Please. If I can finish. Your safety is our top priority. We have two options now. You can move back to the tank, to watch the release from below. Or, if you are willing to wait with me here a bit longer, we may still have the chance to exit the tunnel to watch the helicopter if the captain gives us the green light. The choice is yours. Again, I am terribly sorry for the inconvenience."

A female reporter hurried up the stairs to speak with Barbas, parting the small crowd of people gathered below him, the cameraman at her heels.

Sturman turned to Eric. "Well?"

Eric shrugged. "I guess I'll wait here. Nothing to see back there now. You?"

Sturman looked back down the tunnel, weighing his options. "I seen plenty of helicopters, and I doubt we'll be allowed up there in time. I'm headin' back. Maybe I can find another way out."

"Don't get yourself in trouble."

"Me?" Sturman grinned and turned away from the stairs.

As he headed alone back into the tunnel, the heels of his Western work boots clopped hollowly on the cement. He reached the viewing area a few moments later and walked up to the glass, removing his cowboy hat. If he strained, he could see the helicopter overhead through the distortion of the glass, through the water's wind-washed surface four stories above him. But there was simply too much chop. No point in watching from here.

He heard a shout, punctuated by a loud slam, and he turned to look down the tunnel. Two younger security guards had burst through the heavy double doors closing off the end of the passageway. The ones that had been sealed off to the public. The ones that led to the shark tank.

A pool of water was spreading beneath their feet, pouring in from the passageway behind them. It was quickly flooding the floor.

The guards splashed toward him, running now. They look petrified, frantic, their white pant legs wet to a few inches above their shoes. Sturman tensed. They were shouting at him in thick Bahamian accents, and he could make out only one word:

Lusca.

One of the guards shoved at him, yelling, as the other man rushed to the recessed door nearby, which by the signs apparently led to a construction zone. He unlocked it and swung it open, flipping a switch inside. Maybe to turn on some industrial sump pump, to clear the water? Then he ran back out and shouted to the other guard beside Sturman, and both men hurried off toward the exit stairwell, leaving the door ajar. Sturman turned and watched the metal doors from which they had come. His instincts told him to leave, now, but he didn't want to turn his back on whatever they had seen farther down the tunnel.

"To hell with this," he said.

As the guards' shouting faded up the tunnel, he turned and began to run after them. Then came another sound: a loud creaking, as of twisting metal, coming from within the aquarium directly beside him.

Sturman stopped and turned to his right, toward the glass. An instant later, there was a loud clang from inside the tank as a round metal grate blew forcefully upward. In the cloud of silted water, an explosion of long, orange tendrils followed, erupting from the manhole-sized opening to wave madly through the water. Fish darted away from the wriggling snakes of flesh, which thickened and squirmed forth and displayed a palette of shifting colors—oranges and browns, mottled grays and streaks of incensed red—as they spewed into the water above the hole.

But they weren't snakes. They were all part of something else. Something even larger.

Yard after yard of the enormous appendages continued to emerge from the small hole, a living, wet eruption of flesh. The colossal arms spread in each direction, and the slender tip of one struck the thick glass near Sturman, causing him to flinch. The tapered arm clung to the clear surface briefly, using the tiny suckers at its tip before twirling back into the water. The fleshy eruption slowed, stalled. Sturman held his breath.

Then the beast emerged. A gigantic, pulpy sac of flesh that popped through the small hole as if by great force. It quickly ballooned outward to fill the tank.

An octopus.

It looked remarkably similar to the creatures he had spent so much time with. The beast before him had almost the same relative dimensions as a giant Pacific octopus, and was similar in color. It even moved the same. But it was impossibly larger, spanning the tank.

The beast's bulbous body was the size of a fifteen-passenger van, its writhing arms much, much longer. Sturman felt like Gulliver after he had left the tiny Lilliputians behind and arrived in the next land—where everything around him was greatly oversized. He was a mere mouse, looking out from a crack in the wall into a normal-sized aquarium, at the octopus inside it that barely fit.

He glanced up to where water sloshed madly against the glass above him. There was no gap between the glass and ceiling here. He figured the beast could not seize him, not yet, and although the primitive part of his brain demanded he run, he remained rooted in place. Unable to stop staring. Slowly, it turned toward him.

Above where the arms attached to the body twitched two basketball-size eyes. Golden eyes, seemingly turned sideways and bisected by black horizontal slits. The eyes of a cat. A hunter.

They were looking at him.

CHAPTER 60

She saw something looking back at her through the flat, clear surface. Like the surface in the other lagoon. It was another of the unusual, sinewy prey.

Her arms worked independently to assess the tank, quickly wriggling into every corner, every nook, sending information back to her complex brain. The taste of prey was strong here, and concentrated near a platform of very shallow water. One arm tip slid up onto the platform, met with something moving, which moved away from her touch. She had tasted it. *Flesh.*

But she was not hungry.

The great octopus had pressed herself through the pipe, seeking the deep ocean. Seeking to return to the darkness, the quiet of her den. Yet she had merely entered another small, shallow lagoon. Was still confined, with bright daylight upon her, blinding her. And now the noise from above was even louder. The threat nearer.

She ignored the tank's sea life, which darted away from her, and flattened her enormous body against the odd corals beside her, trying to mimic their colors and textures to conceal herself. But it was too bright here,

and there was not enough room. She was too agitated to
control her camouflage. The painful noise grew louder.

Whump. Whump. Whump. Whump.

The deep vibrations from above escalated, and the pain
became unbearable. One of her arms, the one she had
sent slithering up to taste the prey on the shallower flat
above her, felt something lifting, moving upward. Over
her.

She could not escape. She was in danger.

Her body expanded, filling with oxygenated seawater. Her skin blossomed in thick veins of red and
brown, and her muscles tensed.

The huge octopus was no longer looking at Sturman.
He watched in awe as the monstrosity pressed against
the far side of the aquarium, somehow changing a moment later into the rigid rock itself. Its flesh took on the
colors, the textures of the man-made reef. Despite his
fear, he was entranced.

The creature paused momentarily, as if to hide. But
then its body again began to change shape, bulging outward in places, caving in in others, and rapidly reverted
back into a fluid, moving mass, thinning out its flesh
into a great canopy that shadowed the lower portion of
the tank. Like a massive sheet billowing free of a
clothesline in the wind, the octopus's webbed body un-
dulated to the center of the tank, then stilled and sank. It
pressed its body against the bottom, looking up. Dis-
tancing itself from the surface.

The helicopter. It was frightened by the sound of the
helicopter.

Sturman remembered. The manta release, the helicopter. The capture team.

There were people in the tank, right now, gathered on the platform above the octopus, only their legs visible below the waterline. They probably had no idea what was moving right below them.

He pounded the glass with both palms, shouting. But they remained, only their legs visible, as the sound of the helicopter grew louder. Nobody ran. Of course, they wouldn't. They would be facing the net right now, heads above water and eyes focused on the manta ray, or on the sky, and would see nothing below. Hear nothing, especially over the drone of the helicopter.

A shout came from off to his left, where the long staircase came down into the tunnel. He turned and saw motion in the shadows of the high-ceilinged corridor. A group of people. Ashley, her boss, and a few others, a few hundred feet away were moving toward him, from the stairwell. Leading them was one of the guards he'd seen before.

"No! What are you doing?" he shouted, waving his arms at them. "Go back!"

They kept coming. Apparently, they couldn't hear him. Or they were ignoring him. And they clearly couldn't see what was in the tank beside him.

He started toward them. The sound of the helicopter's rotors thundered into the passageway now. He gestured madly, yelled, but still the small group approached the tank. They couldn't see inside the glass from so far away, from such a sharp angle. With Ashley, Barbas, and the guard were the blond assistant and the heavyset resort worker, and running after them was a young boy with curly brown hair, chased by an older woman who appeared to be his grandmother.

Through the glass next to Sturman, past the waves on the surface, the net began rising out of the water. Even through the chop, within the net's circular yellow outline, the diamond-shaped silhouette of the manta was visible as it passed through the waves. It disappeared as it rose into the air. The net moved out over the tank, directly over the octopus, the rotor wash of the roaring helicopter above it churning the water.

Suddenly, the octopus appeared to grow in size, swelling. It lifted off the bottom and moved toward the thick glass that separated them. Toward the others, now only thirty feet away.

"Run! Get out of here, goddammit!"

They ignored him again, but this time for a different reason. They had now seen it. First to scream was the heavyset woman in resort attire, followed by the grandmother.

Ashley's eyes widened, and she covered her mouth with her hand. "Oh, my Lord."

"What *is* that?" the boy said.

The tunnel grew darker, as when the sun disappears behind a cloud. Sturman turned and looked back toward the aquarium. The great octopus was up against the glass, covering the smooth, clear surface.

The obstruction on the opposite side of the glass became more defined in the dim overhead lights. Pale shapes emerged. Dimpled circles, of all sizes, that were pressed against the glass inside the tank.

Suckers.

Like some massive, fluid fresco, alternating between wavy lines of flesh and rows of hundreds of the suckers, some as large as car tires, the bizarre image slid along the glass, obstructing the light outside. Changing shape. A few people murmured in awe.

In the middle of the glass, where the rows appeared to converge in a single dark point, a large blob of brownish-black flesh pressed forward against the glass. Symmetrical lines traced outward from the dark point, in a star-like pattern. The point began to expand, a dark circle materializing in the pulpy body. The circle, like some great pupil, began to dilate. It grew outward until it was bigger than all but the largest suckers. The dark spot changed shape. A huge, parrot-like beak, dark as onyx, slid free from a sphincter of muscle. And struck the glass.

Tap.

Sturman turned and grabbed Ashley's arm. "Show's over. We need to get out of here. Now."

She looked at him, mouth agape. She appeared to be in shock.

"My God. Is anybody filming this?" Barbas asked. He laughed. "Amazing!"

His blond assistant obediently took out her smartphone and pointed it toward the octopus.

Tap-tap. The sound of the huge beak striking the glass was louder now.

"Don't worry," Barbas said. "This glass is shatterproof. It is unbreakable."

But Sturman knew it wasn't designed for this. He turned and spread his arms around the group, shoving them back from the glass, herding them back toward the distant exit. The grandmother clutched at her chest, dropped to her knee.

"Nana?" the boy said. "Nana, run!"

Sturman grabbed him by the arm. The boy fought as he dragged him away.

Tap. Harder now. The sound changed as the blows increased in force.

Rap-Rap–RAP.

Sturman heard a hissing sound. A stream of pressurized water spurted into the tunnel in front of them, through a narrow crack in the shatter-resistant glass.

As he struggled to drive the group toward the distant stairs, in unison they finally began to move of their own accord. But then another fire-hose stream of water erupted from the glass. It blasted across the tunnel, striking the blond woman and knocking her off her feet. Then another jet of water spilled out, near the others, shaped like a fan.

They weren't going to reach the exit. And the closed double-doors behind them, farther down the tunnel, only continued deeper underground.

There was nowhere to go.

Outside, the small crowd cheered as the helicopter tilted forward and picked up speed, heading out past the reef. The manta ray, suspended a hundred or so feet below it inside the circular net, looked as flat as a pancake. There was a distant rumble of thunder and Eric looked past the helicopter toward the east, where lightning flashed inside the dark clouds.

They had beaten the storm. It had gone well, and Eric was happy for the animal. In a minute, the pilot would lower it down into the waves and gently release it back into the wild.

Moments ago, right before the helicopter had started to rise with its cargo, the police officer had finally allowed Eric and the others waiting in the underground stairwell to exit the tunnel to watch the scene aboveground unfold. At that same moment, he'd heard shouting behind him and seen two guards rush up from below, looking upset—frightened, even—to find Barbas. As Eric had followed the larger group out of the tunnel, unable to stop as he was pushed along by those behind him, he'd glanced back in time to see Ashley turn and walk back down the stairs with Barbas and the guards.

"What *is* that?"

A round man next to Eric was tugging at his wife's

sleeve now, pointing down into the water inside the immense aquarium. The man's wife shrugged him off, still watching the helicopter depart like everyone else.

"You don't see that?" the man said to her. He turned to Eric. "Do *you*? Or am I seeing things?"

"See what?"

Eric looked where the man was pointing. He gazed down into the tank, past the small group of aquarists in wet suits on the ledge where they had held the manta in place. The exposed surface of the water was just below Eric, but the bottom was forty feet down, and the water was choppy from the helicopter, so it was like looking down at one of the island's coral reefs from a boat.

Still, something did look odd.

Through the subsiding waves sloshing at the capture team's midsections, in the much deeper water behind them, he saw a large shadow. A shape near the bottom, up against the high wall of glass that faced the underground tunnel. He couldn't make out what he was seeing, through the refracted light and the choppy surface, but it appeared as though . . .

There.

Yes. It *moved*. The shape, much, much larger than the departed manta ray, had moved. The huge shape underwater was pulsing.

"You do see it!" the man said.

Eric pushed a few gawkers aside and hurried around the waist-high rock wall for a better vantage point. He hurried off the path into some greenery. He stopped right at the edge of the pool, next to a wire barrier built onto the rock wall to keep tourists from jumping into the tank. He placed his hand on the wires.

And with each pulse of the shape below, he felt something in the taut wires. A vibration. A pounding, in cadence, like somebody swinging a sledgehammer into a wall.

Suddenly, the air was filled with a tremendous whooshing sound. The water level in the tank began to visibly drop, as though it was an enormous bathtub and some great plug had been pulled below.

There was a tremendous crack, and Eric jumped backwards. The force of the moving water had separated a forty-foot-tall section of the wall from its mountings. In seconds, millions of gallons of roaring water plunged to displace the air in the tunnel beneath the tank. The crowd began to run away, screaming.

The six-inch-thick glass panel leaned over and stopped, tilted at an angle over the tank as water rushed around it. The massive, dark shape in the water moved. It slid under the leaning wall, forced through by the water flooding the tunnels.

Quickly, the water level in what had been the tank dropped two full stories below its previous level, leaving the fake corals inside exposed. There was another cracking sound. He looked at the far side of the aquarium, toward the natural rock that separated it from a small lagoon. A breach had now occurred there as well. More water was now pouring back into the tank from the other side, refilling it.

Where moments ago an aquarium had been, there was now only an extension of the lagoon. And the viewing tunnels had disappeared entirely under the surface, hidden by swirling, silt-laden water.

Ashley. Sturman.

They were down there. Eric turned and ran toward the underground stairwell.

CHAPTER 61

Val found what she'd been looking for. She lifted the amulet out of the bathroom drawer and looked at it. A leather pouch, shaped like a block-headed sperm whale, hung from the thong. She smelled it and winced, jerking it away. It too was making her feel ill. The smell was sweet, almost fruity.

Then she knew.

Ambergris. It smelled like the waxy secretion produced in the digestive systems of whales and used to make perfume. The Obeah woman had probably gotten a chunk from a dead whale, or a globule washed up on the beach. That explained why the pouch was shaped as it was.

She stared at it a moment. She wasn't sure why, but something had compelled her to find it. She carried it back outside, to where she was working on her laptop and trying to catch up on e-mail. She dropped the amulet onto the table and sat down.

She thought about Sturman. Planning to go back home with Will made her anxious. What would happen when they got back to Monterey?

She heard a distant, high-pitched noise that might

have been sirens. She strained to hear more, but there was nothing over the mounting breeze in the palms.

The bank of heavy approaching clouds hid the sun, but she'd seen the black dot of the arriving helicopter appear miles away as it crossed over the broad Tongue of the Ocean from New Providence, from Nassau, and finally reached Andros, descending and disappearing behind the distant towers at Oceanus. Several minutes later, the distant drone of the helicopter had grown louder, and she saw the black dot moving back out to sea. Presumably with the manta ray dangling below it. The operation must have been a success.

She stood and moved to the edge of the patio, looked down the coast of the island. She could see the towers of Oceanus in the distance. Then she heard it again: high-pitched wailing. Yes, they were sirens.

Oceanus looked peaceful from here. Maybe there had been a car accident—

She jumped as her cell phone rang. She turned and picked it up, looking at the display. *Mack.* She answered.

"Mack, hi. What's going on? Did they release the—"

"Valerie, get down here. Now."

"What? Has something happened?"

"There's been some sort of accident. An aquarium tank collapsed. The big one. Flooded a tunnel, with people inside. I just left the casino a few minutes ago. I'm trying to get down there now."

"Is Will all right? Eric?"

"I don't know. I don't see them anywhere. But people are hurt."

"Oh, my God."

"Get down here, Val."

"How? I don't have a car?"

"Find a way."

"Mack, are *you* okay? Mack?"

But he'd hung up. She ran through the house, found her sandals, and burst out the front door. She paused, and rushed back to the patio. She grabbed the strange necklace and stuffed it into a pocket of her shorts. She found one of the rusty bicycles behind the house and jumped onto the torn seat. She pedaled furiously toward the highway.

CHAPTER 62

Eric stood, dripping water, beside a small crowd at the top of the flooded stairwell, looking helplessly into the dark water. He could only see five or six steps down, with the water stirred up and the lights in the submerged tunnel now shorted out. A woman's body had just floated to the surface. She was a resort worker, in a turquoise shirt. Like the one Ashley was wearing.

"Oh, no."

He moved toward her. But he quickly saw that it was not Ashley, and felt guilty at his relief. It was the heavier woman, and before he or anyone else could reach her body to fish it out he could tell by the massive head wounds that she was already gone.

When he'd first arrived at the stairwell, an old woman had miraculously popped up in the churning water, still alive but choking on water, wet strands of gray hair clinging to her ashen face. He had plunged down the steps with a few other tourists and helped pull her out. Once up the stairs, she began to cry, talking about a missing grandson. She had been whisked away to an ambulance, seemingly having heart trouble.

Moments later, another person had floated up into the opening between the stairwell and the angled ceiling. That one had been facedown. He appeared to be one of the young resort guards. Others had helped fish out the man.

Eric looked over to where he was now splayed on the wet concrete twenty feet away, one arm flopped grotesquely off to the side as a young woman still stubbornly administered CPR to revive him. Eric knew it was probably too late.

He helped two other men fish out the heavyset woman's body, and drag it irreverently up onto the cement by its arms, like some clubbed seal. Then he turned and looked at the pool. The underground tunnels appeared to be completely flooded. There was no way down there, where he was almost certain Ashley, Sturman, and many others had still been when the glass gave way. Even if there was a way down, something else was down there now.

The ruined tank had refilled, through the breach in the man-made wall that had previously separated the tank from a natural lagoon. These state-of-the-art aquariums had been built below sea level, utilizing the cay's natural submarine caverns to create the incredible display. Seawater must have always remained in this cavity throughout the construction process, unless they had pumped it out at some point to complete the project. Now, with the hydrostatic pressure in the tank suddenly gone, the lower cement wall on the opposite side from the tunnels also had collapsed. Where the broad fissure had opened up, the surrounding rock had also come free, and jagged boulders the size of small cars had crashed down into the water in the tank.

A security guard arrived and began relaying the information to the local emergency services over his radio.

He made Eric and the others move back from the stairwell as some semblance of order was established.

It didn't matter. It had been too long now for anyone to make it out by holding their breath alone. He had to check the other exits to the tunnels, to see if anyone had come up alive there. He took a deep breath to calm himself, feeling hot despite his clothes being wet up to his chest. There was still hope.

He hurried back toward the opaque pool where the aquarium had been. A number of tourists stood in groups around it, staring down in awe as security guards tried to herd them away. Something moved in the water.

He looked down into the clouds of suspended sediment in the tank, where the clear waters of the aquarium had been not ten minutes ago, squinting to see past the rippled surface. After a moment, he saw something move again, out of the corner of his eye.

There was a wave, on the far side of the pool, created from the upward movement of something below. Something big. Just below the surface, the dark shape was rising. He looked at a couple still near the water. He had to warn them.

Shouting, he ran down the broad, cobbled path toward them. He cut off into some landscaped perennials, racing along the edge of the pool. A groundskeeper listening to music through ear buds as he hacked at some brush with a machete jumped back as Eric hurtled past. Eric brought his forearms in front of his face as he crashed through the screen of vegetation at eye level.

The woman screamed.

Near the center of the pool, the elongated tip of a huge tentacle rose vertically out of the calm surface, ten feet or more, snaking skyward with the last foot or two dangling back down. Long rows of pale suckers, visible even from here, ran up one side all the way to the end.

Several other appendages followed, dripping water as they fanned out like reddish serpents. They extended rapidly in all directions. The two tourists turned to run.

Two of the arms danced across the water in seconds. One seized the man, coiling around his torso. The octopus silenced his cries of terror with a squeeze, the meaty coils thickening as they applied pressure. There was the sound of bones breaking before the tentacle flung his lifeless body through the air.

Before the body even landed in the water with a loud splash, the other arm caught the woman and crushed her. It tossed her body sideways, headfirst into the rocks. More arms rose, and moved toward a family trying to gather young children to flee.

The groundskeeper behind Eric muttered something, and he turned to see the man drop the machete and run.

CHAPTER 63

Mack hobbled down the ornately cobbled walkway, toward the sound of Eric's voice. The nub where his leg had once been throbbed painfully from running across the grounds on his prosthesis, and he gnawed on the ruined toothpick in his mouth to get his mind off it. He'd just arrived from the casino to find a group of resort staff gathered where the aquarium had collapsed. Then he'd heard Eric's desperate shouting and hustled toward it.

Mack could see him a stone's throw away, standing above the ruined aquarium tank, yelling. He was alone, his back to Mack as he shouted out over the water. He kept leaning down and thrashing the water with his arms, then standing to yell again.

Mack stopped, breathing hard, and listened.

"Come on, you son of a bitch! Over here!" Eric was shouting at a family on the other side of the pool.

Mack spit the toothpick out of his mouth. "Eric!"

Eric ignored him, still hollering and slapping at the water with something he held in his right fist. Mack saw a shortcut and dashed through some brush. He emerged and stumbled to the water's edge, fifteen feet behind the kid. Eric's clothes were drenched, and he was holding a machete.

Then Mack saw them.

Huge shapes, darting up through the water, directly at the family. *Tentacles*. And he could see another one, moving more slowly, in the opposite direction. One that Eric couldn't see from down at the water's edge.

"Don't move, Eric."

Eric turned when he heard Mack's voice. Twenty feet behind him, the tentacle rose quietly from the water, lengthening into a long, inverted hook of rigid flesh.

"What?" Eric said. He slowly turned his head back toward the water.

The tentacle continued to rise behind him. It was tapered, each visible foot of length thicker than the last, and reddish-brown in color, with two rows of round suckers.

It fell forward. Slapping the water, it rushed at Eric. He started toward Mack.

The arm tip swept sideways and just missed Eric's head as he flinched downward. He splashed through shin-deep water on a ledge in the pool and was almost on the shore when he stumbled and went down. Mack ran toward him, into the water, and saw why he had fallen. The slender tip of a second tentacle was corkscrewed around his ankle.

Eric reached for Mack. "Mack! Help me!"

Eric fell onto his belly, hard, as he was jerked backwards. He began to slide away in the knee-deep water, twisting as he was rolled onto his back. He tried to hack at the tentacle with the machete. As Mack scrambled after him, he continued to rotate clockwise, sputtering each time his face went under. He dropped the machete and reached both arms toward shore, clawing for a grip on the bottom.

As they twisted Eric's body, the coils around his legs had thickened, advancing up his frame in spirals as the thing easily turned him over again in the shallows. Like some deadly python, the arm was going to coil up his body and crush him to death.

Mack plunged his hand in the water and snatched the machete just as the other tentacle came back toward them, whistling past his head. He swung the machete after it, but he was late and missed. Eric was wrapped up to his hips now, grimacing in pain. He looked at Mack in agony.

Mack splashed toward him as the tentacle hauled him away, back to the deeper water. He was almost to the drop off. Mack raised the machete. The first tentacle came back at him again and he turned, swinging the curved blade as he ducked.

This time it struck home. The machete lodged into the tentacle a full twenty feet from the tip, where it was thicker than Mack's own body. He pulled on the handle, but the blade was imbedded six inches into the dense flesh.

The arm recoiled, twisting away and taking the machete with it. It wriggled in the air madly and the weapon finally came free as blue blood spurted into the air, spraying both men and the water around them. The wounded tentacle flopped down, splashing furiously, and then retreated into the pool.

Mack found the machete again and turned back to Eric. The coiling tentacle had lifted him up out of the water, and now slowly swung his body around, turning his head away from Mack. It seemed to be toying with him. Eric dug at the crushing flesh around his waist with both hands, his eyes shut in pain, and then his feet were thrust skyward and his head went under.

Mack lunged toward him, focused on the foot-thick

arm. The suckers slid past as the tentacle twisted higher up Eric's body. It was almost around his chest. Mack raised the machete over his head and took aim at the thickest part of the arm, just below the surface and six inches from Eric's torso, and brought the blade down.

He felt the machete strike home, passing clean through. There was a tremendous splash as Eric and the severed arm fell back down into the water.

The water clouded with blue blood, and Eric's head popped above the surface. He was turning purple and still struggling to breathe. A meaty stump spouting blue fluid popped out of the water next to him momentarily before twisting back under, rolling on the ledge and taking Eric under with it.

Mack tossed the machete aside and grabbed at the severed tentacle with both hands, trying to uncoil it and lift Eric's head to where he could breathe, but it was impossible. The meaty arm, despite being amputated, was still squeezing, and with Eric's weight it was like lifting two or more men.

Mack instead dug his fingers under Eric's armpits and lifted slightly, getting his head above water, then heaved backwards. He grunted as he slid Eric's body and the tentacle ensnaring it toward shore. They were almost there when Mack tripped on his prosthetic leg and splashed onto his rear.

He kept Eric's head above water, but the kid was losing consciousness and unable to speak. The detached arm coiled up as far as his ribcage, slowly crushing the life out of him.

CHAPTER 64

Total darkness.

Ashley held the boy against her breast, keeping his head above the water, both of them trembling. He was no more than six or seven years old. She pulled his face back against her wet blouse.

She could hear the others' heavy breathing in the small room. She had gotten a momentary look at the area behind the door before the water had shorted out the electrical system, causing the overhead lights to go out. She remembered seeing only a pile of construction tools to one side, a workbench with schematics on it, a rough tunnel running away into the rock. In the light, she'd seen the shocked expressions of the boy, of Barbas, and Roxanne. And the man wearing a cowboy hat was standing in the water, his back to them, bracing something against the door.

She now stood on something submerged in the water, maybe the workbench or another table of sorts. Her damp head was only inches from the hard ceiling, but still the water came to her shoulders. At least they could still breathe. And the water seemed to have stopped rising—for now.

In the tunnel outside, the rushing water had settled, calmed. She hadn't heard anything against the metal door, now totally submerged below them, for some time. She breathed slowly, and recited the Lord's Prayer in her head. She had managed to calm the child's cries enough that he now only sobbed quietly against her neck.

"Is everyone all right?" It was Sturman's deep voice, coming from the far corner of the room. She knew he was alone there, standing on some lower object, but with his height he was able to keep his head above the water.

"There's something wrong with my knee," Roxanne said, her voice quavering. She'd been in an utter panic until Barbas had shaken her and told her to control herself. From the sounds of their breathing, he now held her the way Ashley held the boy.

Sturman said, "Anyone else? Anything serious?"

Silence.

"Good. Does anyone have any sort of light?"

"I have a cell phone, but it's filled up with water," Ashley said.

"There may be a work lamp, somewhere farther up the tunnel," Barbas said.

"Battery-powered?" Sturman said.

"They use mostly plug-ins down here, but I'm sure we purchased some cordless lights as well."

Sturman said, "Is there any emergency phone down here? A radio? Any way to communicate with the resort?"

"No," Barbas said.

"All right then. Everyone stay put. I'll be back," Sturman said. Ashley heard him swim past her, farther into the tunnel.

* * *

Just before the tank gave, the guard—a young man Ashley barely knew named Arthur—had tried to run away, through the jets of water. The boy's grandmother had looked at them pleadingly from the ground as Sturman had roughly shoved the rest of them through the door into darkness.

Then the boom. The moving wall of water. Him slamming the metal door shut.

She remembered the screams. They punctuated the sounds of the water at first, rising in high-pitched terror above them. The old woman, and more people farther down the tunnel, wailing as they were washed away, just before they drowned. Or worse.

And Georgina . . . She felt tears rise and pushed away the thought. Not now.

She had thought the door's hinges would fail when she heard the wall of water burst through the glass and crash against it. The raging torrent had continued rumbling against the door in a deafening rush, pouring in underneath it, hissing through in pressurized jets along its sides and top, quickly filling the fluorescent-lit room with powerful, stinging streams as they groped for a way out. The lights went out then, but the hissing had continued as they stumbled in the darkness, seeking perches, finally fading only when the water had completely submerged the door. But the heavy metal door had held, probably in part because Sturman had anticipated the sudden pressure change and quickly braced a long board against it.

"Where does that construction tunnel go?" Ashley said, peering into the darkness where she could hear Sturman splashing through the water.

"Nowhere," Barbas said. "It ends in another seventy or eighty feet. There's no outlet."

"Is there any other way out of this room?"

"No." Barbas said irritably. "Just the way we came in."

After several minutes, Sturman shouted that he'd found something. Then, from a short distance away, a white light bounced along the tunnel walls as he swam back with it. When he rounded the bend, she saw that he was holding the light above him. It was protected by a metal frame and had a hook above it, like those used to hang under car hoods, but it was apparently battery-powered. Ashley could now see the heads and shoulders of the others poking out above the water.

In the harsh glow of the lamp, they quickly re-examined their underwater prison. A pocket of air remained in the last foot or so of space near the nine-foot ceiling, but silt-laden saltwater had flooded everything else, to a level just above the top of the door.

"That tunnel appears to slope upward," Sturman said.

"Yes," Barbas said. "It does. It will eventually head to the surface."

"We need to head that way. The water in here may keep rising."

The boy suddenly stiffened. "What's that?" he said.

"What's what?" Ashley said.

"That noise."

Everyone else remained silent. She held her breath, listening. Hoping she would hear nothing at all. But then she heard it too. Something sliding across the outside of the door, making a slight squeaking sound. Like a squeegee on a dirty window.

Roxanne said, "They're here. They're here for us!" She moved toward the door.

"Stop," Sturman said.

"But we need to let them in. Help is here!"

"No," he whispered. "Get back."

She moaned, but her voice was muffled an instant later as Barbas pressed his hand over her mouth. There was a rattle, and the doorknob jiggled.

"What's it doing?" Ashley whispered, looking at Sturman.

"It's trying to get in."

CHAPTER 65

The severed octopus arm was less animated now, but still writhed on the ground in front of Val. She kept her distance as she stared at it in wonder. It was enormous, the shape of an elephant trunk but longer, brownish-gray in color, the reds now fading to narrow streaks. It still moved on the wet concrete, like one of the headless vipers her father had killed when she was a child. It twisted, rolled over again, as if fighting to return to the water.

As if it had a mind of its own.

Biologically, an octopus arm wasn't much different than a snake's body. It contained a developed-enough nervous system to keep functioning to some degree, even after being separated from the animal's brain. In a way, it had a life of its own.

But on its severed end, the blue blood had nearly stopped seeping out. It would be unable to function soon. She wondered how much longer the arm had been before her uncle had lopped it off. How big this animal was.

A young policewoman stood nearby, to keep the tourists snapping images of the arm on their iPhones from going any closer. She had allowed Val to approach after she explained who she was.

Mack finished reattaching his limb on a nearby bench and stood. He walked up to the arm and kicked it, hard, with his prosthetic. "Hurts, doesn't it?" he yelled. He turned toward the water in the tank. "You only got seven-and-a-half now, you fuckin' squirter!"

Val said, "Mack, please. Move away from it. It could still hurt you."

"Fine." He moved over beside her, and nodded down at Eric. Resting on the ground near them, he was awake now, with a paramedic talking to him, but still grimacing in pain.

Mack told Val everything that had happened. He seemed overly happy when he talked about hurting the octopus. "So I guess now the kid here's a damn hero," he said. "Unlike me."

Eric glanced up at him for a moment, and then looked away. He was pale, and clearly in pain, but she knew that wasn't what hurt him the most.

When Val had first arrived, Eric had been semiconscious, attended by the paramedic inspecting the bruises forming on his hips and legs. Mack had been watching the lagoon anxiously. Will, Ashley, and several others were still missing. Apparently, they were all last seen headed into the underground aquarium tunnels, before they flooded.

"We need Eric's ROV," she said.

"What? Why?"

"To see if they're still down there. They could still be alive. Eric?"

He looked up at her. "Yeah?"

"We're going to run back and get some equipment. And DORA. You think you can run her?"

He nodded.

Mack said, "You got a plan?"

"Come on. We'll make one as we go."

They started to turn away when Eric spoke.

"Mack, I need to talk to you."

"Save it, kid. And you're welcome."

As they hurried toward the lobby, Val's thoughts returned again to her dad. He'd been a tall, rough man. A heavy drinker, with a temper. So flawed. But she'd always known that he loved her, and she'd loved him back for who he was. The way she loved Will.

Maybe there was still a chance for him. For *them*. If he was alive.

Pain.

Anger. Confusion.

The octopus clung to the bottom of the tank, beneath the listing, four-story section of submerged safety glass. She had eliminated every possible threat she had encountered. Except one. Something small and unseen, outside of the water, had cut off a third of one of her arms. Her instincts had forced her to retreat.

She had lost arms before, when she was younger, and they had always grown back. But now, at this phase in her life, her body would no longer devote resources to regeneration. And the wound was painful, diminishing her capabilities to defend. She needed to return to her den, and to remain there to protect her defenseless young. But she could not. There was nowhere to go.

Bleeding, she had coiled the wounded arm close to her body and slid silently back into the deepest part of the tank. Then the currents in it had shifted, and she could taste familiar odors. Taste her den. From somewhere in the tank, water from near her brood was somehow flowing back into the tank.

She sought the small opening from which she had come, the narrow pipe that might lead to some way out, perhaps to the ocean. But it was obscured in rubble now. The thundering wall of water had broken apart rocks and glass, and the structures along the bottom of the space had changed. The opening was no longer there. Still, she could taste the deeper ocean water seeping in from somewhere below. She had searched the confined area for any way out, but found nothing.

So she rested, concealed at the bottom as her brain processed her options. She forced her inquisitive arms to remain still, so as not to reveal her position. She could not risk further injury. She would not fight again unless threatened. But the steady noise from the wind whipping across the surface above, and the relatively shallow water churning so close to her sensory organs, disturbed her. She needed deeper, quieter water. Safer water. And she needed to protect her young.

She rose off the bottom again, and moved into the tunnels.

CHAPTER 66

The sounds against the door had stopped. It was quiet again, except for everyone's breathing.

"Maybe it left," Ashley finally whispered.

Sturman said, "Maybe. But we need to move. Follow me."

He turned and started swimming toward the construction tunnel, the light held above his head. Barbas tried to follow, towing Roxanne with him, but she was resisting in her panicked state. He stopped as he fought to calm her. Ashley lunged into the water directly behind Sturman, trying to keep her face above the water, the boy clinging to her shoulders.

Something slammed against the door. Something very heavy. The boy cried out.

"Oh, my God!" Roxanne shouted. "It's here again!"

Ashley heard a splash behind her and looked back. Barbas had released Roxanne and dived in after the others. The metal door groaned and then made a popping sound as it bulged inward. The long board Sturman had braced against it snapped, and it burst inward, sending up a wave.

A huge tentacle burst from the wave and slammed

into the low ceiling, then crashed back into the water. It found Roxanne. Winding around her, it thickened as it contracted, the coils swelling under the strain. Roxanne's screams turned to a gurgling sound as blood erupted from her mouth and nose, spraying the ceiling.

The terrified boy tried to climb onto Ashley's head and she went under. Water went up her nose. She opened her eyes underwater as she fought to loosen his grip on her hair. She saw Roxanne's body moving sideways in the dim light, moving away from her. The thing was trying to pull her back through the doorway, but it was only opened partway, and her body wouldn't fit. The arm jerked at Roxanne's body several times, slamming her into the doorjamb until her crushed body finally disappeared into the rectangular hole.

Ashley felt her bladder go. She turned and kicked madly for the surface, her lungs burning. Then the boy's grip in her hair was gone, and his weight left her.

She popped back up to the surface, gasping. She turned around to see what had happened to him. But the boy was still there. Sturman had swum back to them, and now held the sobbing child against one shoulder.

"Here." He thrust the light into her hand. "You lead. I got the kid."

She grabbed the light, and without looking back she kicked into the dark tunnel.

"What *is* that?" Ashley whispered.

Until now, the question had remained unspoken. Nobody seemed to want to accept what they'd seen inside the tank, the living thing pressing its enormous body against the tall glass, covering it. The thing that had shattered the tank, and killed Roxanne.

"An octopus," Sturman said. His cowboy hat was gone, floating somewhere in the darkness.

"What do you mean? It's too big. Nothing is that big."

They stood in waist-deep water now, at the back end of the tunnel. Ashley was up against some tools submerged near them, where they leaned against the rough stone wall: a jackhammer, a few pickaxes. The light cast an eerie glow on the walls and ceiling, but barely penetrated the surface.

"How do *you* know what it was? Are you a scientist?" Barbas said.

"I know."

Barbas said, "How did it get into my aquarium?"

"Good question."

"Do you think it's coming back?" Ashley said. "Can it get in here?"

"I don't know," Sturman said. "Probably."

"Where's my nana?" the boy said.

Sturman held him to his chest. He looked at Ashley, shook his head. She bit her lip and took a deep breath before answering.

"I don't know, child. We'll look for her later, okay?"

"I wanna go home."

"I know you do. I know. Soon."

She wondered if he knew she was lying.

CHAPTER 67

"**S**o it *is* an octopus?" Mack said.

"Maybe. A cephalopod, for sure, but it's definitely an undescribed species."

He sat beside Val in the backseat of Mars's taxi. They were barreling down the highway, passing oncoming cars dangerously as they headed back toward the resort. Piled behind them, in the back of the van, was DORA and their scuba gear.

"So how big is this thing?" Mars said, glancing at Val in the rearview mirror.

"Depends on how much of the arm we were looking at. I'd have to see more to be sure, but this animal has gotta be at least fifty or sixty feet across, arm tip to arm tip. Maybe much larger than that, based on what you described. That makes it far bigger than any known species of cephalopod."

"Even a giant squid?"

She swallowed. "A lot bigger than that. But we need to focus on how it got into that tank."

Mack said, "So you can figure out where it can leave?"

"Exactly."

He looked out the window, then back at her. There was a fire in his eyes. "Maybe we shouldn't let it leave," he said.

She looked at him. "What do you mean?"

"It's trapped. Right now. Now's our chance to kill it."

She shook her head. "No, Mack. This isn't about revenge."

"You're right. It's about stopping that fuck from killing anyone else. Stop being a biologist for a minute, will you?"

"I'm not having this conversation." She looked away from him. Mars glanced at them in the mirror.

Finally, Mack said, "So how *do* you think it got in there?"

"I don't know. But octopuses can fit through very small openings. And they're the smartest invertebrates on the planet."

As they wheeled their equipment through the resort on a luggage cart, a gurney rolled past, pushed by two EMTs, the motionless figure strapped to it hidden under a sheet. The police and other EMS were all on scene now, and together with resort staff and good Samaritans had retrieved another three bodies that had floated up from the flooded tunnels. Apparently, the US Navy had also been alerted.

The authorities were still trying to make sense of the stories they'd heard from the witnesses at the lagoon. Firefighters were working to get dive gear together to search for the missing. They were smart enough to know they couldn't go in now. Nobody else had seen anything in the tank, but it was probably still in there. Val convinced them to hold off longer, to wait for Eric to explore the space with his ROV.

After the gurney was gone, they continued rolling toward the tank. Mack turned to her.

"How did that thing get so big? And how could it remain hidden until now?"

"Obviously, it's a new species." She thought for a moment. "Ever heard of Humboldt squid?"

"No."

"Well, they don't live around here. Anyway, they're animals I've studied for years. They spend a lot of time in colder, low-oxygen waters to slow their rapid metabolisms and devote more energy to growth. Giant squid get big for similar reasons. Maybe the deepwater offshore environment, the anoxic blue holes running under these islands, have the same effect—they keep these octopuses alive longer and allow more calories to go into size, like any cold-blooded animal."

"What do you mean, 'these octopuses'?" Mack said. "You think there's more than one?"

"Hopefully not here, now, but there have to be others. Otherwise, they wouldn't be able to breed."

He frowned and spat on the ground.

When they arrived she left the cart by the flooded stairwell and walked over to where she could look down into the water of the ruined aquarium. A yellow line of police tape now ringed the water, and all entrances to the flooded tunnels. Security and police were keeping bystanders fifty or more feet away. But tourists were everywhere, and many others also lined the balconies of the hotel's towers, trying to film everything from a distance.

Looking down into the clearing water of what had been Pirate's Cove, she wondered where the massive octopus was now. Nobody had seen it since it went after Eric. She wondered if there was any hope, if there could be any survivors in the submerged tunnels, where Sturman and the others had been. They'd already been missing for almost an hour, and if they weren't somewhere safe, where they could breathe . . . She realized she had again touched her belly.

No. She pushed the thought from her mind.

"You hear about the Navy yet?" Mack said, limping over to her.

"What now?"

"Looks like a warship is headed this way."

"What for? They going to blow up the resort?"

"If they want to help, I say let 'em. They got more resources than anyone else on Andros. And their weapons could really come in handy right now."

"Is Will's friend coming?"

"I don't know. But they'll be here soon."

Val thought of the gift from the Obeah woman. She reached into her pocket and pulled out the whale-shaped talisman. The one that smelled like ambergris. She stared at it for a moment.

Valerie Martell was not a superstitious woman. But as the first heavy drops of rain hit her face and began to spatter the concrete, she fastened the leather thong around her neck.

CHAPTER 68

Sturman wondered if anyone else knew the water level was rising.

They were at a dead end. The surface was still far above them, and because the tunnel construction was occurring from below—Barbas said it was because he didn't want to disrupt the resort grounds until the tunnel was almost finished—there was no way out except past the octopus.

They were trapped, and nobody was coming for them. Not coming in time, anyway.

The water had risen from Sturman's hips to his abdomen, and he knew it was because the construction workers had previously drilled a few narrow, vertical holes down from above to permit fresh air to enter the shaft. A wise move, but one that might cost them now. If the holes hadn't been there, the water wouldn't be able to fill the tunnel completely, because there wouldn't be anywhere for the subterranean air to escape.

He'd first become aware of the holes when he heard rainwater dripping down through them, between the muted rumbles of thunder. Now, with the cordless light turned off to save the little remaining battery power, his eyes had adjusted and he could see the ventilation holes as tiny, brighter spots in the ceiling—one ten feet from him, the other one maybe thirty feet farther away. They cast weak cones of light into the darkness.

But the holes were only a few inches wide. They might provide air, even communication to the surface, but nothing more. Sturman and the others had shouted into them for ten minutes, but nobody had called back. Barbas was furious at his staff.

And there was another problem. Sturman was also starting to hear things, and struggling to concentrate. Oxygen deprivation, or else there was some noxious gas trapped down here. Because even though the holes in the ceiling were designed to allow air to flow in, it was only flowing out now, with the water rising up from below and pushing it out. The air they were breathing smelled a little like gasoline, or paint thinner.

"The Beast out of the Sea," he whispered.

"What?" Ashley said.

"From the Book of Revelation. I know you're a Christian. Saw the cross you wear around your neck earlier."

"Yes. My faith's important to me. Are you a believer?"

He shrugged. "I don't know. Maybe. Don't go to church anymore. When I was a kid, before my mom died, she made my brother and me read the Bible. I got into Noah's Ark, the leviathan . . . and the Beast out of the Sea. That one painted quite a mental picture."

After a pause, Ashley whispered: "'And I saw a beast coming out of the sea. It had ten horns and seven heads, with ten crowns on its horns, and on each head a blasphemous name.'"

"How can you remember all that?"

"As a child, I spent a lot of time in church."

"That's all nonsense," Barbas said from the far corner. "There is no God."

"Ignore him," Sturman said. "He may be rich, but he doesn't know shit."

In the near darkness, the boy was now either asleep or unconscious. Sturman grunted, the muscles in his arms burning. Holding the kid's deadweight was like supporting a sixty-pound bag of sand. At least the rising water had started to help support some of his weight.

He was becoming increasingly lightheaded. And he was getting a headache. They all were. The toxic air was affecting his ability to form focused thoughts. But he couldn't figure out why nobody had thought to try to contact possible survivors through the air holes.

"We can't wait any longer," Ashley said quietly, sounding tired. "We need to do something."

"What do you mean?" It was Barbas's deep voice.

"You know what I mean. There's something wrong with the air. And the water's rising."

"What can we possibly do?" Barbas said, panting. "We need to wait. Maybe they are making progress."

Sturman said, "No. She's right. We may be dead before they can get here. They need to know we're alive."

"And how do we tell them?" Barbas said.

"Someone needs to swim out."

"What?" Barbas laughed nervously. "Where? Where will we swim? That thing is still out there. Or else . . . or else help would be here now. And the tunnel entrance is hundreds of feet away."

"Maybe," Sturman said. But he knew that there was only one possible option. Only one way out.

"Well, I'm not going anywhere," Barbas said.

"I can't go," Ashley said. "I'm sorry. I'm a good swimmer, but not that good. It's much too far."

Sturman felt an overwhelming urge for a drink. He pushed the thought from his mind, hating himself, wishing he had thought only of Val, of his survival, as motivation for getting out—and not of alcohol.

"I'll go," Sturman said.

He waited for more protest, but the others were silent.

"Finally, Barbas, you don't argue with me," Sturman said, smiling.

Barbas said, "Why? It's a fool's errand. You'll barely make it back to the main tunnel."

"Maybe. But we're almost out of time. Someone take the boy."

"Give him to me," Ashley said.

In the near darkness, she waded toward Barbas first, though, and Sturman figured she was probably handing him the light. She then came toward Sturman. He moved to meet her and gently lifted the boy toward her. He felt her arms wrap around his inert form. He didn't struggle.

Maybe the boy was worse off than they were, taking in more of the toxic air, with a faster heartbeat and higher metabolism. Maybe by leaving now, regardless of what happened to him, Sturman would buy the others just enough time. He had to. He didn't really know these people, what they had done in their lives, but the boy, at least, deserved to live.

"If I don't come back, and nobody else does, keep shouting every few minutes," Sturman said.

Ashley said, "Good luck, Will."

Sturman moved away from the others, back toward the main tunnel. He realized his heavy Western boots were still on, making it harder to swim. Holding on to the wall, he removed them and let them sink to the bottom.

Soon the rising water's surface met the angled ceiling. He held his breath and dipped his head under, to gauge what he was in for, to see how dark it was under water. He could make out almost nothing in the darkness. But he heard a sound. A faint whirring.

He came up for air and shook his head to clear it. *Only your imagination.* He would probably pass out before he made it even back to the door.

Treading water, he said a silent prayer. What a fool he'd been. He'd actually had thoughts of suicide in his life, even recently. He'd made so many mistakes. Wasted so much of his time here. He took a few deep breaths, but his head felt the same.

So be it. He took three more deep breaths, exhaling loudly each time to clear the carbon dioxide from his body. To have any chance, he would need to stay down for a long time. He slid under again.

There was another sound underwater, a loud clang. He was not imagining it. It was very close, sounding like it came from the door. He felt movement in the water, a stirring. Something was coming toward him.

He spun and kicked away from it, back toward the others. Reaching the air pocket, he popped out of the water, gasping for breath. He swore.

"What is it?" Barbas said.

"It's coming back," he said. "Now."

He swam to where his feet met the sloping bottom and splashed back toward Ashley, toward the corner, and found the handle of one of the pickaxes. He hefted it. The tool felt so small, so useless as he pictured the beast, pressed against the aquarium glass, its immense form blocking out everything else. He braced his feet on the bottom.

"Barbas, when it gets here, turn the light on," he said.

The surface of the water rippled as it rose toward them.

CHAPTER 69

"I've found someone!" Eric shouted.

Val, who'd been standing a few feet away at the window, watching the storm, turned to join him and Mack at the computer. Eric sat with his laptop on the desk, connected to power cables that ran out the door and into the rain. It was now coming down in sheets.

They had moved into the hotel's security offices, not far from the flooded tunnel, into a small A/V room, where a panel of monitors used to survey the grounds dominated the small space. Outside the small room, police were gathered inside the offices, along with a small group of Navy personnel now on scene, all trying to come up with a strategy. They'd finally located a tunnel schematic, which apparently lacked the new construction areas, but nobody had any safe ideas for a rescue. So they'd allowed DORA to go down to lessen the risk of casualties—after Val had told them it would be sort of like using an underwater drone.

Eric had carefully placed the ROV into the water twenty minutes ago, in the flooded exit stairwell, and run her power cables back to the security offices a short distance away, at the base of a hotel tower. After firing her up and piloting her down the dark, nondescript passage for a little over a hundred feet, he'd encountered a pile of rubble, perhaps where the tunnel had caved in from the power of the rushing water. It had taken him several long minutes to find a way through. They were running low-light so as not to attract attention, using only a weak LED for illumination, with the camera set for maximum light sensitivity. The resulting effect on the screen was what looked like a film negative.

There had still been no sign of the octopus. Perhaps it had somehow left. They had seen a dead resort worker, though, whose body had been jammed between two chunks of rock or concrete from the force of the outrushing water.

Moments later, the ROV had come across a mutilated metal door against the tunnel wall, hanging from its hinges, where a maintenance man had said the new construction tunnel led off. Eric and Val exchanged a glance before he turned the ROV into the doorway. Then they'd seen movement on the screen.

What might have been jeans-clad, kicking legs now reappeared on the screen, and then what appeared to be a bare foot nearly struck the camera on the front of the ROV.

"Is that a leg?" Mack asked.

The door to the A/V room swung open. It was Will Sturman's Navy buddy, Tom Rabinowitz, wearing a drenched raincoat over his khaki uniform. He was a shorter man, with close-cut brown hair and a slight paunch. As part of the Navy contingent on site now, he'd met them upon their arrival and quickly persuaded his commanding officer to let him be the Navy's official observer of their ROV effort, since Sturman was his friend.

"What's going on?" he said.

Eric said, "I think the ROV just found someone. A survivor."

"Who?"

"I don't know. But look . . . this one is definitely moving. They're alive."

The screen went all-white.

"What's wrong now?" Mack growled.

"It's blinded," Rabinowitz said.

Eric nodded. "Right. I think someone turned on a bright light. We'll switch off high sensitivity, and use DORA's other lights."

The image on the screen regained clarity. DORA seemed to be pointed downward. Two sets of bare feet, standing on the bottom, were partially visible on the monitor. The camera suddenly started to turn sideways.

Eric said, "I'm not doing that. They must see us. . . ."

On the laptop monitor a man's squinting face, distorted in the fish-eye view, appeared as he trained DORA's camera on himself.

"Will!" Val said. She put a hand over her mouth.

"I'll be damned," Rabinowitz said, smiling. "Way to go, Sturman, you lucky bastard!"

Sturman looked pale, exhausted, and from the shaking camera he might have been shivering. But he didn't appear hurt. Val felt a huge weight lift off her chest. He was alive, but definitely not out of the woods.

He held his hand in front of his face and pointed first to himself, then held up three fingers. He then turned the camera on someone else in the tunnel: It was the resort's owner. Then, on a young boy, clinging to someone's shoulder, then . . .

"Ashley!" Eric yelled as her face filled the screen. She looked scared, but she was smiling. "All right, then!"

The camera went back to Sturman. "So it looks like there are four survivors in that air pocket," Mack said.

"Right," said Rabinowitz. "Wait . . . Sturman's doing something."

Sturman held the camera back from his face. He mimicked choking himself with one hand, drew his index finger across his throat. He paused, pointed downward with a finger and then lifted a hand, palm down. Then he pointed upward, jabbing with his finger, and held up two fingers in a V.

"What you make of that?" Eric said.

Val said, "He's trying to tell us they're out of air. Or almost out. And maybe that the water is rising. They're in trouble." She bit her lip. "But I don't know what the two fingers are for . . . Something that starts with a 'V'? Or two of something?"

Rabinowitz said, "I don't know. But I need to tell my CO we have survivors. Maybe we can get a dive team in there." He hurried out of the room.

Sturman turned the camera off himself and set it back in the water.

Eric said, "They aren't really going to send Navy divers in, are they? That thing's in there."

"I don't know," Val said. "Eric, just get DORA back out here to us. As fast as you can."

"All right." On the screen, the tunnel walls began to move past, more clear now that the headlights were on.

"You think your ROV can bring a scuba tank back to them?" she said.

He frowned. "Maybe. But it could easily get stuck."

She turned to her uncle. "Mack, let's get a tank ready anyway. Maybe we can rig something."

He grunted and left the room.

Val sat down by Eric. "Will kept pointing upward, at the tunnel ceiling, or the ground above. And held up two fingers. What do you think he meant by that?"

"Beats me."

"We need to figure out what's right above that part of the construction tunnel."

The octopus stirred.

She had been resting, gathering her strength before she resumed her own search for a way out. Before something had alerted her to its presence. She waited, wondering what she had sensed or tasted.

She sensed a whirring sound, and extending a tentacle toward it she felt a light movement in the water. It was close. Her eyes focused in the direction of the sound, and then she saw lights.

Another arm uncoiled. Slithered toward it.

As the arms moved to meet the object, her eyes focused on it. There was definitely something there, coming out of the side tunnel, something the size and shape of a large fish. But it didn't move like a fish. It drifted forward with no sweeps of its tail, no visible actions to propel it.

Her arms met it, wrapping around it tightly. Her suckers felt along the smooth, hard surface, sending information back to her brain, and then she twisted several more feet of a muscular arm around it. It hummed with activity within. But it was not alive.

She brought it back toward her, and regarded it only briefly with one eye before sliding it up underneath her body, where she could no longer see it. She forced it into her open beak.

There was a muffled pop, and a burst of bubbles.

Chapter 70

"**S**hit! DORA's offline," Eric shouted over the sheeting rain.

The doors to both the A/V room and to the storm outside were propped open now. Water was running in a small river over the concrete outside.

Beside Eric, Rabinowitz took off his hat and rubbed his head. "Can someone please tell me what we just saw?"

On the screen, briefly, had been rows of round suckers, then what looked like some huge eye, then a dark opening before the camera went black. Eric moved to the outer door, and began pulling the ROV's umbilical back in, hand over hand. Far too easily. He turned to Valerie.

"She's not even attached anymore. The son of a bitch crushed her, Val. She's gone." He tore his glasses off and began to clean them.

Rabinowitz said, "What crushed her? What *was* that?"

"What do you think it was?" Val said. "We just saw our giant octopus."

"No shit?"

Val said, "Never mind that. We need to find a way to get air to Will and the others. Right away."

Eric finally pulled the end of the severed cord across the concrete and held it up in front of them. Something had torn through it crudely, and cut copper wire was exposed. He dropped it and came back into the A/V room.

He said, "How are we gonna do that? DORA's ruined now. We can't just dive down there with it. You heard what Rabinowitz said. Even the Navy's smarter than that."

"Thanks," Rabinowitz said.

Mack burst through the outer doorway and hurried into the room. He was drenched, and panting from exertion, but grinning.

"Air holes," he said.

Mack soon left the room, followed by Eric and a few emergency services personnel. They were headed to deliver fresh air down to the survivors.

He'd located small ventilation holes, concealed under vegetation on the rocky ground, which were bored straight down to the tunnel where Sturman and the others were huddled. Mack's plan was to lower the air hoses from the resort's SNUBA underwater breathing apparatuses, sending them twenty-five feet below the surface.

When Mack had found the holes, he'd communicated with the others. Apparently, the rain had made it very difficult to understand them, but Mack thought Sturman had shouted up to him that rising water was reducing their airspace. And something about toxic fumes. They still needed to hurry and think of a way to get them all out. The SNUBA rigs would only buy them a little more time.

As Val stepped out the door to follow Mack and the others into the rain, Rabinowitz stopped her.

"Wait, Dr. Martell."

"What?"

"I think I need to share something with you," he said. He looked guilty. "But I could get in a lot of trouble for doing this."

She nodded. He led her back through the door into the small A/V room. He shut the door behind them.

"Well?" she said. "We need to hurry."

He glanced over his shoulder nervously. "I think I might know why that thing's here."

Val put her hands on her hips. "Go on."

"This is classified information, so you can't—"

"Spare me that bullshit. My boyfriend—your friend—is down there now. He could die. If you know anything, you need to tell us."

"Look. I'm heavily involved with our research team. Sonar and weapons testing, here off Andros, in TOTO—the Tongue of the Ocean. Anyway, the sonar we're testing now mimics the booming clicks produced by sperm whales."

"The loudest sounds in the animal kingdom," Val said. "Used to locate and subdue prey."

"Right—230 decibels. Generated right inside the whales' blocky, oil-filled heads. The idea is that if we can generate sonar similar enough to the sounds emitted by whales, not only will this technology not harm sea life, as some of our other sonar devices have, but it would be undetectable to the enemy."

"Go on."

"So if it works, all we need to do is add in recognizable patterns, something like Morse code, and then the whale sounds could be identified by the US Navy alone, even convey information. But I think it's having an . . . an unintended consequence."

Val mulled it over. "So you think this sonar drove the octopus up out of deeper water?"

He looked over his shoulder again, through a small window in the door. "Why not? It makes sense. Maybe whales eat giant octopuses, or whatever that is, just like they eat giant squid."

"Okay . . ."

"And I'm pretty sure this octopus or others like it have encountered our equipment on the seafloor before. I've never seen one until today, but we've found evidence. Things get destroyed."

"I think you may be on to something. But how does that help us now?"

"I don't know. I guess it doesn't."

"So let's say your testing scared it up to the shallower reefs. It headed into familiar, safe environments. The caverns under the island are dark, low in oxygen, protected. It found food. . . ." She paced around the room, thinking. "It's killed people. Probably for food. But it isn't eating anyone now. Maybe because it only wants to escape."

She thought of the bodies officials had recovered from in and near the ruined tank. She'd also learned of an older security guard's body they'd found, inexplicably crushed and floating in another aquarium. Octopuses near death, or females guarding their eggs, ceased to eat. But then why had the animal eaten all the life in the tank? It didn't matter. It was still aggressive. What mattered was how to stop it from killing people. To separate it from the survivors, so they could dive down and get them out. They couldn't get past it unless it was gone. Unless they got it to leave—

Of course. She's seen the schematics. A long outflow pipe ran beneath all the big tanks here, allowing water to circulate out to the ocean. It led to the reef. It might be big enough. But then why wasn't it leaving now? She thought of the images of rubble inside the tank, when DORA went in.

She looked at Rabinowitz. "I think I know how it may have gotten in here. And how we might get it to go back to the ocean."

CHAPTER 71

"**W**ait!" Val yelled, jumping and waving her arms in the rain near the edge of the ruined tank. The crane operator probably couldn't hear her, sitting inside the cab fifty yards away. Lightning flashed, followed seconds later by the crack of thunder.

"Rabinowitz, go tell him he's in the wrong place. We need to focus near the center of the tank. That's where the pipe opening would be."

Rabinowitz ran over to relay the message. He leaned in and spoke with the operator—an American contractor named Mark, who wore an orange hard hat and had a cigarette dangling from his lips. He reached forward and adjusted some levers. The long cab and steel lattice boom pivoted, and the massive clamshell bucket suspended from the cables swung slowly over the gap, ten feet above the water.

With the naval officer's help, Val had convinced the construction crew to bring the massive crane over. From up on the rock wall, she looked down into the deep water of the tank, but could see nothing. Where the hell was the octopus?

Despite the lightning, the rain had slowed some, at

least for the moment, increasing visibility. But rubble obscured the bottom of the tank, and the octopus was nowhere in sight.

The operator lowered the metal claw. A minute later, it returned to the surface, water pouring out between its teeth. Filled with tons of rock dredged from inside the aquarium, it pivoted and dropped the load onto the cement near the tank, backing up two policemen there to keep others away. He swung the arm back over the water and lowered the claw for another load.

He withdrew a boulder, and then dragged a long piece of Plexiglas off the bottom and out of the tank. He lowered the claw again, filling it with debris. He was raising it again when the octopus revealed itself.

Two enormous, reddish arms erupted out of the water beneath the clamshell. They slammed into the side of the boom, causing it to sway. A third arm darted up the claw, sliding over it and spiraling up the cables toward the head of the boom.

As a blob of flesh the size of a shed emerged out of the water beneath the arms, Rabinowitz scrambled behind the cab. He saw the policemen running away. He considered jumping from the crane, running after them. But he couldn't go without the operator. He started back around the crane platform.

The operator stepped outside the cab, to see why the load had stopped moving. Val yelled at him. When Rabinowitz joined in, the man finally saw the beast. He turned to jump from the machine. But just as his front foot left the tracks of a skid, one of the tentacles found him. It encircled his torso and lifted him lightly into the air. He screamed and struggled. Then his limbs whipped to one side as the tentacle cracked like a whip.

The monster slammed his limp body against the crane's metal framework, and there was a sharp report as his hardhat blew apart. His head was now bent impossibly far backwards, bouncing off his own spine, his mouth agape, as the tentacle shook him like a terrier worrying a rat.

Rabinowitz ducked behind the cab as the octopus pulverized the man's lifeless body, smashing it against the crane until his head came free. With a sudden flick, the tentacle tossed the headless corpse thirty feet into the air. Val jumped back as it thudded onto the rocky ground ten feet away.

The octopus was distracted. Without thinking, Rabinowitz hurried around the cab and moved inside the crane. He heard Val yelling at him.

But he had watched the operator, and thought he knew what to do. He fell into the torn black seat and seized the levers. A moment later, the claw began to move again. The crane groaned as it cleared the water.

A huge tentacle slithered up the wet cables above the claw, then another, each seeming to test the machine. The crane shuddered under the weight as more of the steel attachment rose into the rain. Two more of the octopus's arms slid above the waterline, stretching upward to grasp the lattice boom. Rabinowitz looked out the door, toward the safety a short distance away. But he knew why this thing was here. Why people were dead. He gritted his teeth.

The claw continued to rise. And the crane held.

The arms tugged at the steel frame, squirming like earthworms that had just felt the pierce of a barbed hook. If the tentacles slid Rabinowitz's way, they would easily reach the open cab.

He pivoted the arm away from the pool and over the wet concrete, the claw still rising toward the pulley at the tip of the towering boom. Suddenly, there was a huge flash of light, and searing pain behind his eyes.

And then everything went black.

Val was sitting on the ground. She was unable to see, and her flesh tingled. There was a high-pitched, steady ringing in her ears.

There had been a blinding flash, and a deafening boom. She realized a bolt of lightning had just struck the crane directly. Burned into her retinas was the momentary image of the jagged bolt descending from the clouds to course over the crane and the octopus's outstretched body, like molten fire.

Rabinowitz was in the crane. He might have gone into cardiac arrest. She had to get to him.

Her vision returned some. The octopus had disappeared back into the water. Val stood unsteadily and moved toward the crane, groping slowly around the pool. After stumbling into a railing and then moving a few steps along it, her vision fully returned. She hurried around the pool, until she could see Rabinowitz slumped inside the cab. A bolt of lightning could heat the adjacent air to 50,000 degrees, and carried hundreds of thousands of volts.

She wondered if he was still alive.

CHAPTER 72

She was hurt. Badly.

Her flesh, her skin and muscles, all burned with pain. She could not remember where she was, or how she had gotten here. But she needed to escape.

She moved across the bottom of the small water-filled cavity, still blind but feeling every surface with her tender suckers. She sensed a light current, pulling the water downward.

An arm tip followed it, and came across a small hole. Water flowed down into it. It might be wide enough. A large rock partially covered the hole, but she shoved it aside and began to force the tips of half her arms into the space. Inside it felt smooth, cylindrical. It ran sideways. She remembered. She had entered this way. But where did it go?

It might lead to the ocean. To her den.

She slid the slender tip of another arm into the narrow opening, then two more, elongating them into the pipe. Each raced forward, trying to surpass the others, causing the arms to shrink in size. To align against one another. They slid together along the smooth surface, worming forward in unison, through a series of rhythmic contractions. Each pull was anchored by hundreds of suckers pressing against the sides.

Soon the only solid, inflexible part of the great octopus's boneless body arrived at the opening. She eased herself forward, pushing with her trailing arms, pulling with those already inside. She squeezed her hard mouth-parts, and the rigid ring of tissue around them, into the pipe.

She fit.

She pressed her body forward. Soon she reached another opening to a pool above, and knew that she had entered here. But before she had gone the wrong way.

She moved with great difficulty down the long, narrow pipe. Each contraction of her muscles brought intense pain, but she continued, inching forward toward the open ocean. She stopped to rest, but realized in this constricted state that she was almost entirely unable to breathe. Not enough water could flow past her gills to deliver oxygen. If she lingered here, she would quickly die.

She reached her arms farther down the dark tunnel, gripped the sides with her suckers, and again pulled her body forward.

At last, when her arm tips stretched forward, instead of meeting the unvarying, curved walls of the pipe, they arrived at the end. She felt something blocking her exit, but could now taste familiar waters. She was near her den.

She slid a slender arm tip through an opening in the lattice and coiled it twice around a metal bar. There was a loud clang as the bolts burst from the rock wall and the circular grate came free in a single, powerful jerk. With the metal grate now gone, her arms began to emerge and eagerly fan out. When her head and mantle reached the end, with one final great heave she spilled free and rolled forward, melding with the rough, slanted cavern floor below her.

She felt cool, fresh seawater fill her mantle. She moved toward her den, her young.

She was home.

PART IV
THE DEN

CHAPTER 73

"**I** think the octopus is a she," Val said.

Sturman stared at her across a restaurant table puddled with water. The rain had stopped. Mack and Eric, sitting with them on the deserted patio near a large swimming pool, also stared, but with more puzzled expressions.

"What are you talking about? Why?" Eric said.

Val pointed at the policemen in yellow rain slickers a hundred yards away, struggling to remove the remains of the crane operator's body near the edge of the ruined tank.

She said, "It didn't consume any of the bodies. It hasn't actually eaten anyone it's attacked here."

Eric had been upset when she'd described what was left of DORA. Val and Mack had found the ROV when they joined a few Navy divers to rescue Sturman and the others. Nobody down there was seriously hurt, but the EMTs on site insisted that they all get checked out. Somehow the resort owner, Barbas, had talked his way out of it and, still soaking wet, had already gone to his office to try to quell the negative PR being fueled by social media.

Along with Ashley and a young boy who'd been trapped underwater, Rabinowitz also was still being attended to in one of the ambulances that had maneuvered to the rear of the resort. He was alert, and seemed remarkably well. The bolt of lightning had only run through one side of his body.

"Do octopuses ever kill prey indiscriminately?" Eric said.

"No," Val said. "Just to eat. Something has to describe the conflicting feeding behaviors we're seeing here. This animal's inconsistent urge to feed."

"Maybe it's full," Mack said. "It sure ate a lot of shit in the aquarium."

She said, "Maybe. It did eat almost all the sea life in the tank. But I'm confused, because it didn't eat any of *these* victims, and at its size it could probably eat a lot more if it wanted to. So there might be something else."

"Senescence?" Sturman said.

She nodded. "Maybe."

"What are you guys talking about?" Eric said.

Sturman said, "When octopuses stop eating, usually it's because they're old. Gonna die soon. But the males usually aren't aggressive."

"Right," Val said. "Senescent males are indifferent to their own survival, practically suicidal sometimes, and typically show little urge to hunt. This animal here has done some active hunting, though, and has been very aggressive. So let's say it's a mature female."

"Go on."

"It's possible she's pregnant. . . ." She paused, thinking of her own failed pregnancy. And what might happen this time. She took a deep breath.

"You all right, Val?" Sturman said. He found her hand under the table.

"Sorry. Just lost my train of thought."

Eric said, "You were saying this octopus could be pregnant. . . ."

"Yes. And starting to lose her appetite, but the urge to feed hasn't left her entirely. So she's getting in her last meal, before she makes a den."

"Makes sense," Sturman said.

"Great," Eric said. "We're dealing with a hungry, pregnant, giant female octopus."

Val said, "There's at least one other possibility. That she's already laid her eggs."

Sturman frowned. "But females don't feed again, and never leave their den after laying eggs. Right?"

"Usually."

Eric said, "What do you mean they never leave? You mean not until the eggs hatch?"

Val shook her head. "No, he means never. After one lays eggs, she usually stays put. Her body gradually consumes itself. Usually, she'll die when her eggs hatch."

"Well, if she never comes out again," Eric said, "then how can a new mother be another scenario?"

"Here's the thing. The females of some octopus species have been known to continue to eat after laying eggs . . . if the eggs were never fertilized. If they never actually mated, in other words. Or, if the eggs are simply inviable."

"You mean if she lost her babies?" Eric said.

Under the table, Sturman squeezed her hand.

"I don't know," she said.

"So this thing could already have a den? With babies growing in it?" Mack said. He leaned forward.

"Or more likely, inviable eggs. It would explain the conflicting urges. The intermittent hunger, the aggressive urge to protect her clutch in a nearby den. If our octopus laid eggs, but there's nothing actually growing inside them, her hormones might not have triggered all the usual postpartum events."

Mack said, "You said the den would be nearby. Where?" He placed two thick hands on the table.

"Possibly just offshore here. It would have to be very close, for her to be protective of it."

Eric said, "What do we do now, then?"

"If we can get another ROV down here, we can try and locate her den. But I think we already know where it is."

Mack looked at her and nodded.

That evening, they decided to order takeout. Mack volunteered to pick it up, and asked Sturman to join him.

The two men stood near the edge of a bar at the mostly outdoor restaurant, waiting for their burgers to come out of the kitchen. Sturman watched a couple of aging female tourists downing drinks at the bar.

"You're thinking about having one. Aren't you?" Mack said.

Sturman looked at him. "What? No."

"Bullshit. I know that hungry look. And it ain't from watching the tits on those old bags."

"Get off my back. I been clean."

"Maybe."

The men stared defiantly at one another for a few moments.

Sturman said, "Well, get to it. Why did you ask me to come? What do you want to tell me?"

"You know that Val's dad was a drunk?"

Sturman nodded. "I do." In the past, she had made a few angry comparisons between the two of them.

"She ever tell you what happened to him? Why you two never met?"

"No. She doesn't talk about him much."

He turned and spit into the bushes. "Well, as his drinking got worse, he started hitting her mom. *My sister*. I helped throw him out after that. The bum ended up writing Val off before he died of cirrhosis. All alone, living on the streets."

Sturman held up a hand. "I know where you're going. I got it. I know I got a problem. But it's not bad like that."

"Not yet."

"I'm sortin' it out, goddammit." Sturman clenched his jaw. This guy had a lot of nerve. "I'm workin' on it. It just . . . it's always helped numb the pain."

"She told me about that woman you were married to. Son . . . she's dead. Nothing you can do about it."

Sturman thought of Maria's face. She and Val were so similar. The dark hair and eyes, the intelligence, the feisty personality. Maria would never have put up with his drinking, either.

Mack said, "Don't be a quitter. Not on Val. And she won't quit on you."

"This is some pretty heavy talk. You sound like a shrink."

Mack slammed his hand down on a table, causing the women at the bar to look their way. "I'm not fuckin' around here. I mean it. We're talking about my niece. If you want to be with her, stay clean. Stop feeling sorry for yourself. You can't live in the past."

Sturman gestured at Mack's leg. "Neither should you."

The old Marine gritted his teeth. "Stay clean."

"I will." Sturman regarded him for a moment. "Why you telling me this now?"

Mack nodded past his shoulder. "Food's here."

CHAPTER 74

The den was snug, no more than two or three times the volume of her own body. The confined space was intentional, chosen to allow her to best care for and protect her brood. Here, she would remain for months tending the eggs until they hatched. And then she would die.

In the darkness, she did not sleep. She used the tips of her arms to caress each strand of eggs, to clean them, ensuring that no parasites or other threats settled on them. Perhaps all of her young would also be dead soon after her, killed by predators before they ever had the chance to descend toward the depths of the abyss. But she had made the journey from her own birthing den. She had survived. So might some of them.

She filled her body with seawater and from her siphons gently blew water over the strands, to keep them oxygenated. The sluggish current moving past would not be sufficient to aerate them.

For the rest of her days, she would remain here, motionless, except to clean and care for her eggs. Conserving her energy so she could persist, only utilizing enough to tend to her clutch while she waited for it to hatch one day. But if anything entered her lair, she would not seek to conserve energy. She would not conceal her form against the cavern walls, or attempt to flee.

She would defend.

In the beam of his headlamp, Mack finally found the horned rock. There was no trail to this spot, miles away from Oceanus, 212 paces southwest of the intersection of the highway and an old logging road. He'd had to bushwhack in the dark. But when his light struck the geological feature, he remembered it right away, even though he'd only seen it twice before, also at night, many years ago.

Mack had left the house after everyone was well asleep, and then called Mars on his cell. The taxi driver wasn't happy about being woken, but agreed to pick up Mack after he heard how much the crazy American would pay him. Mack only had one condition: Mars would need to keep his mouth shut.

Back before Mack's last tour, before he'd lost his leg, he and Breck had come to Andros for some cave diving. His friend had taken him on one special night dive as well. Brought him to help retrieve an object he'd discovered in a coral cleft almost 200 feet down. Under cover of darkness, they'd brought it up to the surface, back to their boat. Before daybreak, over a final beer, they'd hid it here in the bush, in a natural cavity below the low, distinctly shaped rocky rise, where they'd be able to find it again.

A week later, they'd retrieved it and had taken it to a remote inland blue hole to try it out. See how it worked. They knew they couldn't use it in the ocean, because it generated sound and the Navy's detection grid would sense it go off.

They'd only used it once. But Breck had always felt

bad about the damage they'd caused that day. The reason he'd taken it in the first place was that he was angry about the impacts the Navy's toys were having on the offshore environment, and for years had refused additional contract work from them. Afterward, they'd secretly brought it back here, and never gone near it again.

But now Mack had a use for it.

Sweating, he walked up to the head-high ridge of rock. A pair of foot-tall horns of pale rock jutted from it, like the twin humps of a Bactrian camel. He set down his shovel and machete and scanned the rocky, uneven ground below the ridge, which was now covered in thick leaves and other forest litter.

They'd agreed to tell nobody else about this, because they both knew they could get in a hell of a lot of trouble. But maybe it wasn't even here anymore. Maybe somebody had already found it.

Mack ignored the sand flies biting his exposed skin as he shrugged off his empty frame pack and knelt down. He scraped away at the branches and litter with his shovel. After a few minutes, he found a dark opening in the forest floor. That darkness betrayed a large, mostly hidden pock in the ancient coral rock that was concealed under a few exposed tree roots. It was farther to the left than he remembered, and the roots had grown in almost to the point of closing off the hole. He tossed the shovel aside.

He got on his hands and knees and poked his head into the hole. Inside he saw the same few large rocks he'd placed in here himself, resting on what was left of the folded canvas tarp. He reached the machete in and with its tip he cleared the rocks away, and pushed at the tarp.

Then he saw the gleam of metal.

CHAPTER 75

At dawn, Val woke to urgent knocking at the front door of the guesthouse. As she entered the living room she saw that Sturman had already risen from the couch and in only his boxer shorts had just opened the door. It was Clive. He looked anxious, out of breath. His bike lay on the ground, its rear tire still spinning.

"I'm here to see Miss Valerie," he said to Sturman. He looked over the taller man's shoulder and saw her, and sighed. "Goodness, dear. I'm so glad you here."

She said, "Why wouldn't I be?"

"You know how early it is?" Sturman said.

Val said, "It's okay, Will. Please, let him in." She hugged Clive. "I'm glad you're okay. We didn't see you anywhere yesterday. Here, let me get a pot of coffee started."

"No. Not yet. Is your young friend here too? And your uncle?"

"What?"

"Are dey here?"

"They're still sleeping. Why?" She glanced down the hall, and could see that at least Mack's door was shut.

"You sure?"

"I'm pretty sure. . . ."

"I'll go check," Sturman said. He headed down the hall.

"What's going on, Clive?" she said.

"I wasn't around yesterday, when everything happened. But I was at da beach real early this mornin', even before da sun broke. I seen your boat offshore, near dat big blue hole."

"*Our* boat? You mean the pontoon boat we've been using?"

He nodded. "It sure looked like. I'm hopin' now I was mistaken."

"You must have been. It has to be someone else's. We're through diving."

Before they'd left Oceanus the previous evening, Val had talked to the local authorities about what they were dealing with, and described the precautions they might need to take. One of those included sealing off the larger pipes running to or from aquariums out to the ocean. This meant shutting down the aquariums all together. They needed to cut off anything that linked the resort to the ocean in any way—until they could gather more data on the animal. Her ideas hadn't gone over well with Barbas.

Back at the guesthouse, she and Eric had talked about getting at least one replacement ROV down to Andros, to seek out the octopus den near the mouth of the resort's main aquarium outflow pipe. It would take a few days before the equipment arrived, but all of them, Mack included, agreed there would be no more diving.

Clive said, "Whoever's boat dat was, I couldn't see nobody on it. I watched it for a bit. When I left, it was driftin' out to sea. Toward dat big Navy ship offshore. I was worried something happened to ya."

Sturman walked into the room. "Mack's gone."

Val said, "What do you mean he's gone?"

"He went alone," Clive muttered, then his eyes widened. "Oh, my. He didn't even anchor da boat."

"He doesn't want anyone coming after him, or he doesn't . . ." Val stopped breathing when it hit her. "The weapon."

"What?" Sturman said.

"He told us about some strange Navy weapon he and Breck found here, a long time ago. He swore it was still hidden somewhere. I never thought he was serious—"

"He doesn't plan on coming back," Sturman said.

She looked at him and swallowed.

Eric ambled into the room, only half-awake. "Sturman, why did you wake me—Clive? What are you doing here?"

Val held up her hand. "Later, Eric. Clive, you said that boat was above the Bottomless Blue Hole?"

"Dat's right."

"We looked over the resort schematics last night. That's very close to where the main aquarium outflow pipe leads. The pipe the octopus left through."

"I know," Clive said.

"Hang on."

She rushed to grab the schematics off the kitchen table, but they were gone. She hurried back into the living room, her heart sinking. He was down there. She knew it. Down in the blue hole. Down where the octopus had gone. She knew how vengeful Mack was, and after Eric had shamed him, he might feel like he had something to prove.

She said, "Mack took the blueprints with him. We need to get out there, now. I don't know what Mack's doing, but he's mad about Breck. And he may have some sort of naval weapon. He's doing something very stupid."

Sturman said, "I'm gonna call Wits. Maybe he'll know how to operate it." His jaw tightened. "Or disarm it."

He dug through his bag, looking for his phone. He turned to Clive. "You have a boat?"

Clive said, "Not anymore. But I can get ya one."

"It doesn't matter," Val said. "Mack's the only one who drove us out there. He's the only one who knew exactly how to find that hole from the surface."

"I never told him I was sorry," Eric said, staring off into space.

"You can tell him later, Eric."

"Maybe we can eyeball it," Sturman said. "The blue hole."

She shook her head. "It's practically impossible to see from the surface. If Mack's boat drifted away, it will take too long to find the site, especially in this weak morning light. It's too deep. And he has the schematics. Goddammit! We don't even know exactly where that outflow pipe leads. If we had coordinates, or something—"

"Wait," Clive touched her arm. The old fisherman looked afraid. "I can get you dere."

A threat. She sensed a threat.

Many fathoms below the surface, she was maneuvering large pieces of rubble together, piling them protectively in front of her den to close it off further, when she felt the vibrations. Echoing dimly down the walls of the dark fissure.

An intrusion.

She paused, releasing on old cinder block on top of the mound. It settled at an angle between a huge, barnacle-encrusted section of pipe and a hunk of dead coral she had retrieved recently.

From past the mound of rubble, there was a bright light.

Her skin suddenly darkened to an angry purplish color, swirling with reds. She drew a quantity of warm seawater into her mantle, then expelled the spent water, creating powerful eddies of water that swirled against the sides of the den.

She saw movement. A small silhouette, in the dim shaft, was bearing a small, bright beam of light. She pulled her huge form against the walls. Concealed herself.

And watched the threat near.

CHAPTER 76

"**I** might know what Mack has," Rabinowitz said, shouting over the drone of the engine.

He sat beside Sturman on one of the bench seats in the pontoon boat, opposite Val and Eric. The vessel was almost identical to the one Mack had rented, but in much worse shape. It had been anchored in a shallow private lagoon. Clive had found the keys in a shed near the house onshore, and taken them without bothering to see if the "friend" who owned it was home. He was now at the helm.

"What do you mean?" Val said. She thought Rabinowitz was doing quite well for someone struck by lightning a day before, having only received minor burns and gone briefly unconscious. He'd come reluctantly when Sturman called him. Wits was another Navy guy, and a technology and weapons expert. He might know how to disarm a device, if Mack actually had one down there.

"Tell her, Wits," Sturman said. "All of it."

Rabinowitz rubbed his face. "Well, you said he might have found a Navy ROV twelve or thirteen years ago. Our testing facility supposedly lost one around that time. And its rumored payload was what we called a DCD. Short for 'Deployable Cavitation Device.'"

"What did it do?" Val said.

"I really shouldn't be telling you this."

"Please, Tom. We need to know."

He winced as ocean spray came over the side and wet his face. "It was supposed to be some bad-ass sort of sonic weapon. But I never worked with one, or even saw one used. I wasn't even sure it was real."

Eric said, "The Navy actually lost an ROV, and a weapon attached to it?"

"They were both experimental. The details are classified, but rumor has it the ROV's guidance system failed after it retrieved a DCD, during a test run near the Andros wall. Nobody knew where the submersible ended up. But it disappeared in relatively shallow water—just a few hundred feet. Since we never found it, some of the brass supposedly suspected it had been stolen."

"Cavitation," Val shouted. "Isn't that what happens when a boat propeller generates bubbles underwater?"

Wits nodded. "Water produces more friction than air, so drag creates vapor cavities on fast-moving objects underwater. Basically, lots of small bubbles. Supercavitation technology has actually been in use for years, to address this problem. It allows our torpedoes to travel hundreds of miles per hour, by producing streams of bubbles from their noses that surround them in a coating of air. Presto. No friction."

"But it can also be used as a weapon?" Eric said.

"The idea is to use sonar itself to destroy things. A cavitation weapon requires two or more devices, set a few hundred feet apart, which create acoustic beams. At their intersection, the beams generate an intense pressure bubble and incredible heat. With enough power, you can essentially use pure acoustic energy to destroy targets."

"Seriously?" Sturman shouted.

"Seriously. I won't say much more, other than that this technology is real. But the DCD was only a rumor. Because it supposedly could create a destructive cavitation field all by itself, without the need for another device. It supposedly somehow overcame that, with two closely joined emission devices that could merge their beams effectively, even from a narrow angle."

Clive slowed the motor. "We almost dere."

Mack moved deeper into the cavern. In the beam of his dive light, he could see that here it became a sideways fissure, a split in the ancient limestone that ran laterally off the main shaft.

Arming the weapon had been simple enough. Years ago, back when Breck had brought the deceptively heavy device ashore that night, they'd spent some time looking it over, their beers on the ground beside it. Breck said he'd help set one before, as a Navy freelancer, but had never seen it actually go off. It had a benign enough appearance, consisting of twin toaster-oven-sized cylinders of metal affixed to one another, side-by-side, the way double air tanks are mounted for diving. But Breck had explained it was a state-of-the-art deployable weapon.

When at the inland blue hole a week later, he'd showed Mack how it worked. It operated off a digital timer, and was intended to be set stationary, by an ROV or Navy divers, and directed at its target—in that case, the far side of the blue hole they'd brought it into. Fifty feet under, they'd placed it on a ledge and set the timer for fifteen minutes, and then quickly surfaced. For good reason. When it had gone off, sending a sonic pressure wave against the far wall, there had been no loud detonation. But a small tsunami rose from within the hole when a submarine slab of rock blasted free on the other side of the pool, displacing the water around it.

Apparently, the device was designed to destroy mines and bridge supports, or rupture ship hulls. All using sonic waves.

Mack needed to hurry. He'd already been down for almost an hour, and this time he'd set the timer at the surface—for ninety minutes—in case something happened to him before he could complete his mission. He'd figured it would give him time to get down here, to find the beast's lair. To position the device. But not so much time that others might have the chance to figure out what happened, follow him down here if he didn't come back.

He knew he might not have enough time to safely resurface. But that was okay, as long as he found the den first, and the device still had enough power to fire one last time.

He had some idea what an octopus's midden would look like, or the pile of debris it might create outside its lair. He'd seen what must have been older ones on DORA's recordings from deep in the bottom of this pit. He hoped the old whore hadn't laid her eggs deep down there, where he couldn't reach, since he still hadn't been able to locate the new den. If he couldn't find it before the timer ran out, he'd decided he'd just find a ledge, and aim the device down the center of the main shaft, then swim like hell for the boat.

The resort schematics had provided exact coordinates for the mouth of the outflow pipe, and using a GPS to estimate where it would be before he entered the water, he'd located it in a side tunnel branching off the Bottomless Blue Hole. One they hadn't been in before. The metal grate that had guarded its opening had been torn free and lay ten feet away, on the bottom of the cavern, now bent and twisted. He'd sucked in a breath of air, a single thought entering his mind then:

She's in here somewhere.

He'd started at the end of the pipe, and began to search carefully through the darkness. The light would betray him, but at least he was wearing a rebreather, to give him extra bottom time and not give off air bubbles that would reveal him too soon.

Now, after investigating two smaller tunnels that yielded nothing, he entered the broad horizontal fissure. He moved slowly, taking deep, measured breaths. He stopped.

Ahead of him was a barricade of rock, with a cinder block and some other rubbish resting on top. The objects were free of excessive barnacles or other growth, which could only mean they'd been added recently. He finned toward the rock pile, clutching the heavy device in both hands. Underwater, its weight was manageable. But it dragged at him, trying to pull him down deeper.

When he reached the berm-like heap, he set the device down and pulled himself over the rubble, staying low, on his belly, like a soldier peering out at the enemy from a foxhole. At the crest, he took a deep breath, preparing himself, and shined his light over the top, into the darkness.

He'd found it.

There was no octopus looking back at him in his beam of light, no great tentacles squirming inside the protected nook, but what he was seeing he'd never seen

before. Nobody had. He knew he was looking at the brood
of something enormous. Looking at her spawn.

He swept the light around the cavern, which was
about the size of a basement. He waited. Nothing happened. But he knew she might still be here.

He was as sure as he could be that she wasn't inside.
It was time. He steeled himself for the crush of her tentacles as he lifted the weapon off the bottom and dragged
it over the embankment. Moving to the edge of the nearest targets, he shoved the device into a recess in the rock,
where it would be less visible, and directed its business
end toward them.

Here's a little birthday present for the kids.

He checked the timer one last time. It was still counting down steadily:

31:46 . . . 31:45 . . . 31:44 . . .

He turned away from it and kicked for the shaft. He
cleared the barricade and covered another twenty feet,
forty, sixty. Swimming down the broad, flat-ceilinged
tunnel as fast as his crippled leg would allow. Nothing
grabbed him. Finally, he saw a bright light ahead. He
was nearing the main shaft.

He checked his air supply. He still had plenty to make
it back. He could even make a safety stop. He hadn't
even considered what he'd do if he made it out of here.
He'd have to run, because the US government would be
after him. Maybe he'd spend a few years in South America, or the Virgin Islands. He smiled at a thought: Maybe
he wouldn't be seeing Breck anytime soon, after all.

The thought quickly faded. Because he *wouldn't* be
seeing Breck again. Not ever. To see him again, there
would have to be a heaven. A God. After seeing what
had happened to his friends, even to his enemies, in the
war, how could he believe there was a God?

He heard something. Something artificial. A clanging, a ceaseless ringing, resonating down through the dim water.

Mack knew immediately what it was. A sound he'd heard so many times, one that carried well underwater, and that he'd often made himself to get the attention of other divers. Someone was here. In or above the shaft of the hole. They were trying to get his attention. And his niece likely was with them.

It was too late, though. The device was set to go off in less than thirty minutes. He didn't know how to stop it.

CHAPTER 77

"**Y**ou're sure this is it?" Val said.

Clive looked down through the waves with the experienced eyes of a fisherman. He nodded at her from the helm. "Dis is it."

She glanced over the bow of the small fishing boat. The boat was rocking slowly, deeply, from their exposure to large waves at the reef edge. She couldn't make out the mouth of the blue hole—only darker and lighter blotches below them. She hoped Clive was right. She was an experienced diver, but she had no idea how anyone could identify dive locations by peering down through the waves.

They were idling just above the edge of the darker water, where the turquoise colors reflected off the shallower sand flats and corals of the island shelf began to fall away into the sharp blue edge of the mile-deep trench. The visibility seemed good, for now. The rain had stopped the previous evening, but the new volume of freshwater on the island might find its way into this hole, to be expelled while they were down there.

"Is this really a good idea?" Eric said, pausing to rest.

He stood knee-deep on the swim ladder lowered off the starboard side, slamming a lead weight against a scuba tank hung underwater. He'd started as soon as they arrived, upon her instruction, as the others assembled the dive gear. She wanted Mack to know they were here. Maybe by some miracle he'd stop whatever he was doing and come up.

Val looked back at Eric, then at the others: Sturman, Clive, and Wits. Above the men a torn Bahamian flag stood sideways in the stiff breeze. She gently touched her belly, and then pulled her hand away. She took a deep breath.

"I don't expect anyone else to go, but that's my uncle down there. I don't have a choice."

Sturman said, "Neither do I."

But of course he would come. She knew that, in his own way, he loved her. Loved her more than anything, or anyone. The man had many faults, but cowardice and lack of loyalty were not among them. She couldn't say anything to him, not now, or he would never let her go down there.

Val guessed that her uncle had wanted to find the octopus by following it where it had left through the outflow pipe. That's what she would have done. But the tank at Oceanus had been blocked off, the pipe sealed. The entire area would have been guarded all night. He couldn't have gone that way. Mack did have schematics, though—schematics that showed right where the pipe led. So he'd taken the boat here instead.

Clive had assured them that the buried outflow pipe, which ran out from the edge of the island, emerged in a side cavern off the massive underwater hole beneath them now. He knew the men who had helped install it.

"I should come," Eric said, looking down. "Mack probably wouldn't even be doing this if it wasn't for me."

Val said, "Don't be ridiculous, Eric. You're not even a certified diver." She placed a hand on his shoulder. "It's okay."

He leaned down into the water and resumed clanging on the tank with the heavy weight.

"Wits will be coming too," Sturman said. "If that weapon's down there, and it's armed, he has the best shot of knowing how to stop it."

Val said, "But he's still hurt."

"Bullshit," Sturman said. "He's fine."

Wits glanced at the nearby naval vessel, ran his hand through his close-cropped brown hair. "Man, I don't know. I'm already putting myself in a very bad position. You know what will happen if my CO catches me messing around with stolen naval weapons? I shouldn't even be out here."

Mack's vessel now appeared to be tied off to the Navy warship, which still sat in deep water a half mile out. Rising from its deck was a soaring mast platform, stabilized by scaffolding and bristling with radar housings, antennae, and weather gauges. An American flag waved behind it. Clive had said Mack's boat had been adrift. Abandoned. Either Mack had been in a real hurry, or he'd never planned to come back.

Sturman stopped attaching a regulator to his tank. He would be using a standard A-clamp, not ideal for cave diving because of the risk it could dislodge, but since they had no other caving rigs he didn't have a choice. He looked at Wits. "You owe me," he said.

"But what if it's down there, that thing—"

"You're coming, goddammit."

"But—" He looked down at his feet, then shook his

head and took a deep breath. "Jesus. Then I'm bringing a bang stick. Who else wants one?" He reached into his gear bag and produced a short, dark rod.

"Are you kidding?" Sturman said. "You're more likely to hurt yourself or one of us. That will only piss off this thing."

Val had never used one, but knew what Rabinowitz held in his right hand. A twelve-gauge shotgun shell was loaded into the tip, and a pressure trigger on the front made it go off, point blank, into whatever it contacted underwater. A crude but effective weapon. Macho divers used to use them to kill sharks, back when the big fish had a bad reputation. She hadn't seen one in years.

She sat down to strap on her tank. "He's right. Leave it here. We need to focus on finding Mack."

"Screw you guys. I'm bringing it. There's one more if you want it."

Sturman, rigging a BC vest to another air tank, shook his head.

Clive said, "I'll go without."

"You're coming, Clive?" Val said. "You know you don't have to."

He looked afraid, but smiled. "Mr. Wits gonna need a buddy. Keep him from shootin' himself."

Val considered for a moment, rubbing at the talisman now tied around her neck. "I guess it makes sense for us to split up. Wits, you and Sturman can't go together, since you both have the best shot at deactivating a classified military weapon." She knew Sturman wouldn't let anyone else go down with her anyway.

"I'm sorry," Eric said, gasping for air. "I wish I could do something—"

"Really, it's okay, Eric," Val said. "We need someone to stay with the boat. Move it away from the top of this hole, maybe two hundred meters. Just in case. If anyone comes over here, you need to tell them we're down there. And keep banging on that tank as long as you can."

"Val, they see us," Sturman said. "They're coming."

She followed his gaze. Beside the Navy frigate, several sailors were boarding an armed rubber assault boat.

She said, "Everyone in the water. Now."

Chapter 78

The clanging from above was constant. Resonant, like the toll of a mission bell.

It had to be Valerie. Only she could have figured out he was here. He swore into his regulator, releasing a cloud of bubbles. He didn't know how much damage the device might cause, but he didn't want anyone near when it went off. He had to get to them.

Mack's own breathing was too loud, too fast as he struggled out of the cavern, toward the narrow shaft of light ahead. He was fighting to not float into the ceiling, since he wasn't wearing a weight belt. The device had provided more than enough negative buoyancy on the way in. He looked back over his shoulder, his light bouncing wildly over the cave walls as he continued kicking forward. He wondered how close the octopus was. Unless it had left to feed again, it was back there somewhere, in that gloom.

He felt a slight change in the still water, as though he had just encountered a light current. He looked forward again, shined his light along the cavern walls. Nothing.

Maybe the blue hole was about to blow—to expel cold water from underneath it. All the more reason he needed to make haste. He finned hard toward the shaft, searching the cavern. Then he realized something was wrong. He no longer saw the shaft of light.

He slowed, hovered, catching his breath. He couldn't possibly have gotten turned around, could he? He'd looked back a few times, but only for a few moments. He didn't have a safety line—

He felt it again. A movement of water. It rushed past him, ever so lightly, like a muffled shock wave. He wasn't sure which direction it had come from. Then it was gone. It was not a current.

It could only be one thing.

A pressure wave. Created by the movement of something very large, very close, as it displaced thousands of gallons of seawater.

He kicked harder, toward where he thought the exit should now be visible, angry at his weaker leg, where a fin was strapped to his modified prosthetic limb. He didn't look back. If the octopus was right behind him, he wouldn't be able to outswim it anyway.

He felt confused, in the same way as a person in the woods who has just realized he has taken the wrong path, a path that has petered out into brambles in a dark, strange part of the forest. But he could not turn back now.

Where the hell was he? This had to be the right way. . . .

There. Ahead, the dark tunnel suddenly grew lighter again. But it wasn't natural light, from above. It was just his own beam, reflected off an obstruction. Something lighter in color. He strained to see past the smooth outlines of stone, to find the outlet that would deliver him back to the main shaft, and to the surface. But something wasn't right. In the dim light, the rock wall here looked too even, too smooth.

He slowed, turned and looked at the wall directly beside him, a few arm lengths away.

In his light, it too had an odd appearance. It was striated with what looked a little like conglomerate—a crumbly matrix of sedimentary rock cementing together numerous fragments of rounded stones. A geological class that didn't belong here, in this limestone cavern. The rounded river rocks embedded into it were too circular, too even.

Ahead of him, he spied a darker spot in the wall. Probably just large enough for him to pass through. A way out? He kicked toward it, paused.

He could still hear the slow, steady clanging of the lead weight.

He stared at the dark spot in the wall. It was near the center of the tunnel. He fluttered his fins once more, toward the black, almost perfectly round anomaly. Then he knew. It was not an opening. It was not part of the tunnel.

The fleshy confines surrounding him quivered.

He looked again at what he had thought were rocks embedded in the wall. They began to bulge out of it, to take their usual form. That of discs. And in the dark circle ahead, he saw movement as the great beak within gnashed once. And he knew it was too late.

I'm so sorry, Valerie—

The web of skin around him collapsed, huge volumes of seawater tumbling his body as he was smothered inside the impossible profusion of living flesh. He felt rigid suckers the size of dinner plates press against him, immobilizing him. His light now gone, he could no longer see what was happening.

But even through the thick blanket of flesh, he could still hear the hollow, bell-like ringing from above.

CHAPTER 79

"You can't just take our boat," Eric said.

"We have our orders."

The armed Marine standing in front of him, a serious young man in digitized camouflage, had boarded from the contingent on the sixteen-foot rubber Zodiac boat. The soldier looked unsure of himself, and unsure of Eric's story. He probably wasn't used to taking over civilian watercraft.

"But there are divers down there!" Eric said. "In the blue hole, right over there. One is a Marine." He swallowed. "An Iraq War vet."

The armed soldier moved Eric to the stern of Clive's boat. Eric watched the other one onboard start the engine. They were drifting on the swells, a few hundred yards seaward from the blue hole located between them and the reef crest.

The Marine near Eric said, "Look, man, we're not taking your vessel from you. We're just bringing it back to the ship. We can talk there."

"Your ship is almost a mile away."

But Eric knew it was hopeless. He watched as the

other three soldiers who'd come over on the armed Zodiac, its .50-caliber trained on him as he watched them come, now turned it back toward the US Navy frigate. Their driver gunned the outboard.

The one at the helm of Mack's boat engaged its engine as well, and the pontoon boat began to turn to follow the Zodiac. Eric considered telling them what Mack may have brought down there, but decided against it. He looked back at the ocean surface above the hole. How long had everyone been under now? Fifteen minutes? And Mack had been under much longer. What if they—

"Wait!" Eric shouted, pointing back at the dive site. "Someone's surfacing!"

The young Marine followed Eric's gaze, to where something dark had just broken the surface. He turned to the driver. "Slow down, Brooks! We've got something."

Within the dark passageway, Rabinowitz felt unnerved by the hiss of compressed air entering his lungs, the immense pressure of water so deep. He knew he was churning through his air supply. He hadn't logged a dive in almost three years, and never before had he entered a submarine cave. He wondered if Clive, who also moved somewhat awkwardly next to him in full scuba gear, was struggling as much as he was.

They'd already separated from the others. Once they'd descended to a hundred and twenty feet—roughly forty feet into the maw of the marine blue hole—Clive had led them into a broad gap in the shaft. It led to the west, toward the island. Just inside it, they split up, where the tunnel quickly branched into two, maybe three dark fissures. They all knew the pipe outflow, and the beast's den, would be in one of them.

He followed Clive farther into the cave, past curves

of rock that all looked the same. The place was like a maze. They could easily get lost.

Then the tunnel opened up. Here it had a remarkably level ceiling and floor. He was careful to keep the tip of his bang stick away from himself, from the cavern walls. It wouldn't take much pressure to discharge the shell.

Their cones of light danced across the rougher walls as they searched, and he wondered how they would ever be able to see anything. Outside the beams, it was almost totally black.

There still had been no sign of Mack.

Clive slowed, then stopped. He turned back to Rabinowitz and pointed. Wits directed his own light deeper into the tunnel. Something else, something that rose from the floor in a great pile and also looked like it was built by the hands of men, appeared at the edge of the beam's reach. A rusty barrel squatted on top. They moved toward it, peered over the top.

They had found it.

A new taste in the water. Faint, but distinct.

Entering a passage that led back to her brood, she expelled the last chunk of the dismembered threat from her maw. She was not hungry. And the taste unnerved her.

Her one enemy was here, now. Near her den.

The great octopus had detected the scent coming from somewhere near, perhaps in the blue hole itself. Yet her enemy only resided deep in the open ocean and never ventured to the reefs. She should have been safe within these protective caverns. Her brood should be safe. But inexplicably the foul smell of her solitary foe had reached her, overwhelming her instincts. Somehow, the leviathan was here.

As she shrunk against the wall of the side cavern, a small squirt of ink involuntarily erupted from the saclike organs in her body to cloud the water. Ink that would allow her escape. But she needed to protect her brood. And there was nowhere for her to go.

She pulled herself against the rock and changed color to match it. She ceased moving. She could still taste the great whale, through her flesh, the suckers on her arms, but more faintly now.

She waited. But nothing entered. Nothing fell upon her. No powerful bursts of painful sonar, much like those that had permanently driven her here from the sea floor. No cold, bony jaw filled with huge teeth.

Her eyes mere slits, she watched the opening to the deeper shaft. Then she felt something. A droning, high-pitched vibration came from somewhere above the hole. Getting louder. It was not a sound emitted by her enemy.

The taste had come from something else. And the taste was gone. She had been fooled.

There was nothing here that could hurt her. But her young, soon to emerge, might still be at risk.

Fear was again replaced by the urge to protect. She moved off the wall, into the main shaft of the hole, and rose toward the surface.

CHAPTER 80

Eric grabbed onto the overhead rail to keep his balance as the boat slowed, trying to maintain focus on the dark spot a few football fields away. But he didn't see it anymore. A low swell now blocked his view. He ran to the bow. Had he actually seen someone's head, or was it just something floating? It was too hard to tell at this distance.

The sound of the motor on the parting rubber Zodiac boat changed. Apparently, the Marines in that small gunship had seen something too, because they'd turned from the frigate toward the blue hole. The Marine beside Eric brought his radio to his mouth and called up his commander.

The Zodiac lost speed as it neared the hole, the three men onboard all looking down at something floating on the surface. The two not driving raised their rifles. Then, a shout.

Eric saw the rounds spraying the water a split-second before he actually heard the shots. Where the bullets sent up showers of seawater, he began to see something rising beneath the surface. Then the rubber boat was jolted to one side, sending the Marines sprawling as the driver throttled the motor to escape. One gunner went over the side.

Several enormous tentacles burst from the water, dwarfing the boat, rising above the men on it, and began to curl down around them. One arm flinched as it appeared to contact the propeller, and the sound of the motor stopped. From where he had fallen, the remaining gunner rose to a knee and swung the barrel of the mounted .50-caliber machine gun. He fired, mowing bullets into the thick tentacles. The roar of rapid fire was accompanied by a spray of blue mist as hunks of flesh were ripped from the flinching appendages.

The monster released the boat, its arms disappearing back into the sea.

"Do something!" Eric said. It had all happened so fast, and the Marines on the pontoon with him were still glued to the scene, unable to turn away, like Romans watching a lion unleashed upon gladiators in the coliseum.

The Marine at the helm began to maneuver the pontoon toward the Zodiac, where its gunner now stood with his weapon pointed downward. The driver was trying to get the motor started. Three huge tentacles rocketed up out of the water and loomed over the rubber boat. As the gunner began to fire, they fell in unison.

There was a resounding slap when they struck the Zodiac and drove it under the surface. One of the Marines bobbed up.

"Come on!" Eric shouted. "Swim!"

The man's head disappeared below the surface.

Rabinowitz didn't know what he'd seen. Something resembling heavy, grapelike clusters dangling from the top of the cavern. But the water was murky. Not just from the lack of light, but from swirling clouds of sediment within it, like dark puffs churned up by feet at the bottom of a mucky pond.

Something in there, past this rampart of rubble, must have stirred it recently.

Kneeling on the outside of the heap, he looked at Clive. Shrugged. What the hell were they supposed to do now? He didn't know how to communicate. They must have found the lair—those huge clusters, which might have been eggs, were created by something very big. But he'd seen no sign of Mack, no sign of any deployable weapon. They were down here to find Val's uncle, not try to fight some gigantic octopus. They should get the hell out of here.

Clive scanned the water behind him, then looked back at Rabinowitz, a strange calm in his eyes. He appeared to be thinking. He gestured with his hand: *Follow me.* He kicked off the bottom, over the rocky embankment, and into the darkness of the den.

They reached the far side and moved across the floor. As they drew closer to the eggs, the natural light from behind them dimmed. As though something had created a large shadow.

Rabinowitz spun to face the entrance, but nothing was there. He looked at the crescent of bluish light over the embankment, the exit that would lead to the surface, and hesitated. The opening looked deceptively narrow now—as though the mouth of the cavern was closing behind them.

He felt a hint of panic. Sure, they'd all say he was a coward. But at least he'd be alive. Then he felt a tapping on his shoulder. Clive tugged at him. They locked eyes through their masks.

No. He couldn't leave this man alone. And he did owe Sturman.

He took a deep breath, exhaled. Followed Clive farther inside.

He scanned the dead-end tunnel for any sign of the creature. But it wasn't here. There was no room for something so large to hide. The chamber was maybe twice his height, and packed with the countless, thick strands dangling motionless from the ceiling. If they hurried, they could search the small space and get out before it came back.

They neared the first strand. He turned away from Clive and swept his light over a scattering of rocks below, searching. He looked back at the old man, wondering how long they needed to be here before they could leave. Clive was staring at something on the floor of the cavern. It looked like a pale log, with a—with a *foot*.

It was a man's leg.

Behind Clive, near the entrance to the den, something moved. Then the crescent of light disappeared entirely. The pale cavern ceiling suddenly changed colors in the beam of his dive light, from drab gray and tan into sunset hues—orange, red, pink—as if by some unseen chemical reaction.

The hard surface was somehow changing shape, from rigid rock into a fluid, moving thing, like a massive sheet billowing on a clothesline in the wind. It began to bulge outward in places, collapse in others. Parts of it broke away from the ceiling, separating, twisting eel-like as they darted toward the men.

The tentacles reached Clive first. One seized him violently, began to wrap around him. He dropped his light and beat at it with his fists.

Rabinowitz thrust his bang stick toward the tentacle. But before it made contact, the tentacle jerked sideways. There was a loud pop as the tip of the stick struck the old man's forearm. The tongue of fire flashing from the weapon momentarily blinded Rabinowitz, but even underwater he heard Clive's muffled scream. As his vision returned, he saw that the beast was no longer holding the old man. The lead shot must have struck its arm as well.

Clive's regulator had come free from his mouth. He fumbled backwards, away from the beast, clasping his ruined arm against his body. His own blood and bits of tissue swirled in the light. Rabinowitz dropped the bang stick and grabbed Clive's vest, trying to haul him toward safety. But the octopus was blocking their way out.

Rabinowitz felt his body slammed into the bottom. He was no longer holding on to Clive. Something incredibly heavy pinned him against the rocks. He looked down and saw huge coils of flesh encircling his body. Then he was being crushed. He heard the bones in his hips pop and screamed in agony.

Before he lost consciousness, he saw another arm darting after Clive.

Chapter 81

Eric stood on the upper deck of the frigate, watching the water for any movement. Several minutes had passed since the wounded octopus had disappeared below the waves. But none of the others had surfaced. There had been no sign of them at all.

He'd been forced aboard the warship by the Marines. The one driving Clive's boat had realized the situation was hopeless when the last of his buddies had gone under, and he'd gunned the boat away from the hole, back to the frigate. On the upper deck, Eric and the two soldiers had joined a small group standing at the side railing, watching for the octopus to reemerge. The vessel had been slowly closing in since the first shots were fired from the raft, and they were only a few hundred yards away now. Eric looked over at the armored gun turret trained on the area. He wondered if even this huge cannon would be enough to kill the beast.

Someone yelled, and Eric saw why. A person's head emerged at the surface.

"Wait! Don't shoot," he shouted.

The cannon fired. The deafening noise made Eric jump. The heavy round struck the water just past the diver.

But there were no follow-up shots. The gunner had realized what he was seeing.

It was Clive. He coughed and raised an arm over his head.

Eric's ears were ringing. He grabbed the arm of the Marine next to him. "We have to rescue him!"

The soldier shoved him away. "It's too dangerous. He's on his own."

Eric looked back at Clive. Even though the frigate was much closer to him now, the old man was still some distance away. He seemed to be dazed, or hurt. He was leaning back in the water now, floating. Where were the others?

"Goddammit! You need to save him. What's wrong with you people?"

The Marine clenched his jaw. "All right. I'll see what I can do." He headed toward the bridge.

A minute later, Eric heard a whine next to him and looked over. It was a winch, mounted to a boom. From the side of the vessel, an ROV was being lowered into the ocean. But not to help Clive. Eric recognized the vehicle, and the payload it was carrying. They were sending in an explosive.

"Where's your captain?" Eric said to another sailor standing at the gunwale. "I need to talk to him, right now. Before they send any weapons in. There are more people down there."

But it was too late. A moment later, the boom released the ROV and it disappeared under the surface.

Eric swore and looked at Clive. He appeared to be unconscious now, and a dark spot was clouding the water beside him. Probably blood.

Eric glanced aft at the lower deck, where just past a deserted helicopter pad the two dive boats were now both tied off to the stern. Nobody was guarding them.

He took a step back and watched for a reaction from the Marines beside him. But everybody on deck was against the railing, transfixed on Clive and the water around him. Eric took two more steps, toward a ladder running to the lower deck. Still no one noticed. He turned and ran.

He scrambled down the ladder and leapt quietly onto the metal deck, then dashed across the empty pad to Clive's boat. As he cast off the lines, he wondered if the keys were even still on it. But there was no time.

He jumped down into the open bow of the much smaller vessel, collapsing against the padded seats as he landed. He hurried to the helm. The keys were in the ignition. He heard a shout from the frigate.

He fired up the engine and slammed down the throttle.

From inside a dark side tunnel, Val and Sturman heard the muffled boom. She guessed it was probably Eric's bang stick.

They'd been looking at what was left of a metal grate now torn free from the end of the outflow pipe. At the noise, they turned around and kicked in the direction the other men had taken. But before they reached the point where they'd first split with the others, Sturman noticed a cutoff in the side of the labyrinthine tunnel. They passed into it to find themselves entering the flank of a broad, flattened passage. To their right was a mound of rock, weakly silhouetted by light from outside, and to their left—

Val stared in wonder into the den, at the multitude of grapelike clusters containing thousands of the whitish, pale, teardrop-shaped objects.

Eggs.

They were enormous for those of a cephalopod, each the size of a large pear, and strands of them had been woven by their mother into hanging braids, which concealed most of the den like the beaded curtain in an Asian restaurant. It was even more difficult to see anything past the nearest strands because the water in here was murkier, hazy with dark particles of something.

They huddled inside the small opening on the side of the cave, waiting to see if the octopus would return. As the water cleared some, Val saw the light. A dive light, still on, resting on the cavern floor.

Sturman tugged at her shoulder, and they began to move into the den. As he turned left and moved under the mucus-covered strands, searching, she headed right, toward the mouth of the cavern, and the flashlight. While he searched for the device, she would watch for its return. Warn him if it came back.

They would have to hurry. The octopus would be back soon. As Val finned closer to the motionless light, she still didn't see anyone near it. She realized why they hadn't noticed it at first. It was pointed in the other direction, its bulb up against the base of the embankment built to guard the brood.

Val stopped when she noticed something else resting on the bottom. Just past the light, sunken into the rocks.

Oh, please, no.

But it was. What was left of a person. A man's arm, still connected to part of a torso.

She began to kick toward it, and hesitated. These were the remains of someone she knew. Maybe her uncle. She felt revulsion, but she moved closer. She thought she saw a ring gleaming from the hand.

She took a deep breath and directed her dive light at the curled fingers.

CHAPTER 82

Eric had almost reached Clive. The pontoon boat had covered the short distance in under a minute, but behind Eric the Marines had already reboarded the rubber Zodiac to come after him.

It didn't matter now. He might be in a lot of trouble, but once he got Clive out of the water, the Navy would bring them both back to the frigate, and Clive could receive immediate medical attention. The old man was merely bobbing on the surface, the regulator no longer in his mouth. His eyes were shut.

As Eric neared, he maneuvered the boat alongside Clive and slowed, then reversed the engines to a stop. He looked for something to snag his body with, to bring him closer to the vessel, but saw nothing. The water around Clive was clouded with blood, and the boat was already moving away from him on the waves.

Eric took a deep breath. He kicked off his shoes and tossed his glasses onto the driver's seat, then dove out over the ladder.

He surfaced only a few feet from Clive. He swam behind him, wrapped an arm around his neck, and began to tow him back toward the pontoon. Then the Zodiac appeared around it, curving toward them, the Marines onboard leaning over the front. He turned toward them. It would be easiest to slide Clive up and into the lower boat.

One of the Marines began to shout. He pointed at the water near Eric, and raised his rifle.

Eric looked down into the water. Something dark and amorphous was rising directly below him. Fast. He kicked for the raft.

The thing struck his foot.

Val felt a disturbance in the water behind her just before a cloud of ink billowed into the den, diffusing through the confined space, making it impossible to see anything. Momentarily disoriented, she couldn't tell which way was up.

She felt along the bottom, trying to move back toward the recess where she had entered with Sturman. *My God, did he even know what was happening? That the octopus was already back? And how would she find him?*

It didn't matter now. There was nothing she could do. She had to get out. *They* had to. She had more than herself to think about.

She moved into the swirling blackness. She wanted to turn her light off, but knew if she did she would be blind. The clouds of ink parted, just for a moment. And then it was there.

It was impossible. But it was there.

Through the dark water, the curved brownish form of the huge octopus materialized in front of her. It flattened itself against the bottom, sending a wave of sediment toward her, and then its body ballooned back to its regular form.

Its mantle alone, crisscrossed with dark veins, was a hump the size of a circus elephant. She caught glimpses of its inquisitive arms, squirming slowly through the ink-clouded water around it. Their great length was impossible to gauge as they coiled back on themselves, but some sections appeared as thick as mature oak trees where they met the immense, mottled body. She noticed that they appeared damaged, dark fluid seeping out of jagged holes in the rough flesh. The octopus had been wounded—

She felt a touch on her leg. Before she could react, it seized her, drew her toward itself. As she was pulled to it, slowly, deliberately, air bursting from her mouthpiece, she twisted and reached for the bottom. Tried to grab anything to stop herself from moving closer to it.

The arm tip coiled around her leg was drawing her toward a lighter-colored irregularity on the pulsating mantle. The fleshy protuberance was hollow, the size and shape of a fifty-five-gallon drum. A siphon. It suddenly compressed, as the behemoth body from which it protruded pressed down like a massive bellows. Spent seawater spewed from its dark opening in a geyser. Val felt more of her body encircled by the arm and knew she would not be able to free herself.

Val pictured the many smaller octopuses she had encountered. She was upside down, but was able to orient herself on the landscape of living flesh. She knew where the arm was bringing her. Toward a spot directly above the siphon, a platter-sized irregularity that stood out on the mantle, hooded by ridges of tissue.

The stream of bubbles trickling out of Val's mouth stopped when she arrived. She found herself staring back into its eye.

CHAPTER 83

Sturman caught the glint of metal in his dive light. He finned over to it. It was almost exactly as Wits had described it—twin cylinders of gleaming metal, placed inside a shallow rock cleft underneath a cluster of eggs. He'd almost missed it.

He carefully lifted the heavy object out of the cleft and stood it on the bottom. He swept his light over it until he found a small control panel. He held the light up to it.

On it, a few buttons, and a clear display. A digital timer, counting down:

7:21 . . . 7:20 . . . 7:19 . . .

He examined the device further. There weren't any exposed wires, no obvious way to disarm it. There was no time. They needed to get out of here, fast. Right now.

He set the timer on his dive watch for seven minutes, and then left the device where it stood and turned to find Val. The beam of his light was met with a billowing cloud of darkness. It swirled quietly toward him, and a moment later he couldn't see anything at all.

He moved the beam all around, but he was blind. *What the hell was—*

Then he knew. He'd seen this before, with squid, with octopuses, usually when they were afraid. Ink.

She was here.

The golden orb, its black pupil shrunken into a mere slit in Val's bright light, turned in its socket to regard her. Despite her fear, Val felt a momentary sense of awe. In the eye she saw intelligence. The huge creature shuddered, as if wracked with pain. She wondered why it hadn't simply killed her yet.

She felt something gently touch her abdomen and looked down. The thick arm encircling her had parted to allow the delicate tip of another tentacle to inspect her navel. Tiny whitish suckers slid along her skin, perhaps tasting, and then moved up toward her chest.

The octopus's pupil suddenly dilated. Its body flared into a bright, angry red. The arm around her began to squeeze, and she winced as the air in her lungs was forced out in a burst of bubbles. Val felt herself moving through the water, pulled down and under the hood of translucent flesh that formed a webbing between the arms.

Toward the beak.

She pushed at the arm, felt her fingers entering holes torn into the wounded and weakened flesh. She tried to retain control of her final thoughts, and remembered Mack. Hoped that those had not been his remains, that somehow the octopus had not found him first. She thought about Will, and despite her lack of religious faith wondered if somehow she would ever see him again. Somewhere.

And she felt another pain in her chest, near her heart, as she realized she would never become a mother.

Somehow she still held on to her light. Above her she could make out long, paired rows of enormous, dimpled suckers running inward, toward some center point, demarcating the bottom of each arm, and she had a sudden childhood memory of being under a travelling circus tent.

Then the tent began to collapse.

As the darkness beneath the octopus's body closed around her, Val felt a tentacle tip still moving along her flesh, searching for something, and she was grateful in some small way that this animal's suckers were smooth, not lined with serrated teeth, as in many of its squid cousins. Grateful that her death might come quickly, without terrible pain preceding it.

The groping appendage slid up her torso, and pressed against the hollow of her neck. Against something hard resting on Val's skin.

The amulet.

The arm tip jerked away. Val felt the coils around her burst open, releasing her as the creature recoiled from the tiny necklace. The octopus exploded off the bottom, tumbling Val in the water beneath like a rag doll. Val's head and elbows struck the rocky bottom. As she tried to regain her bearings she realized she again couldn't see. The octopus had filled the water with more ink.

But it had been moving away from her. She kicked in the opposite direction. For a moment, at least, she was free.

She passed into what she thought was the side tunnel where they had entered the den, but she didn't see Sturman. She looked back. Through the dark fog of ink, a snakelike arm was wriggling after her. She spit out her regulator in terror as she tried to pull herself backwards into the narrow space. She spun in the water and found the mouthpiece again, shoving it between her teeth as she clawed her way back into the constrictive passage. Nothing looked familiar.

She realized she was heading deeper into the caverns.

Something seized Val's fin and she kicked at it, grabbing on to the cavern wall. As she struggled to escape, she realized another beam of light was illuminating her from behind. She turned and saw Sturman behind her. He moved next to her in the narrow passage, crawling almost on top of her, then grabbed at her, trying to pull her back in the other direction. Toward the octopus.

She pushed his hands away and shook her head. He pulled harder, and she dug her nails into his flesh. He released her.

He jabbed at the watch on his wrist, and then held up three fingers. Then two. One. Then he threw his hands out forcefully. He stopped and looked at her. Held up three fingers again.

A blast? He'd found something. Mack's sonic weapon. She held up three fingers. *Three minutes?* He nodded and pantomimed an explosion once more. He grabbed at her again.

No. They couldn't go back. It would be waiting for them. She would rather die in here. She fought him off.

He looked back over his shoulder, and glanced at his watch. He held up only two fingers. She shook her head, remembering the feel of the pulpy flesh against her skin. At last he conceded, and pushed at her while pointing the other way.

Go.

She did. She lost track of time as she led them farther away from the octopus, farther from the blast that he indicated was coming. She followed her light into the oppressive darkness, her tank clanging against the rock above them. She thought about their air. She didn't bother to check, but she knew it would run out soon. They were a long way from the surface. They might not be able to head back now.

Their only option was to keep heading down this passage, deeper into the network of tunnels. She could only hope they somehow led to some other exit. She thought about her child. Their child. She'd never told Will. At least there was that. He would never know.

The tunnel branched, and she paused to scan their options. *Hurry, Val.* One passage appeared to end almost immediately, so she went the other way. Ten yards later, she ran into a restriction. A very tight one. Maybe too tight. There was only one way to find out.

She glanced back and saw that Sturman was still behind her, partially obscured in the dense sediment they'd stirred up. But at least for the moment they were alone. She thought of the image of Breck's corpse, resting silently, hundreds of feet under the nearby island. He too had chosen to run from the octopus.

Now they were facing the same fate.

She first became aware of the object as she worked to seal off the mouth of her den. A shiny, nonthreatening thing resting on the bottom near the middle of the chamber. Something that hadn't been there before.

It was small, symmetrical. It did not move. It was silent. She sent an arm toward it, but then hesitated.

She was in great pain. Blue blood seeped into the water around her from the many wounds to her limbs, and agony seized her each time she lifted one to gather anything she could find to fully close off the entrance to further threats. None of her injuries were immediately fatal, but they were taxing her strength, her reserves of energy. And, possibly, her ability to survive long enough to protect her eggs to maturity.

After a moment, one of her arms snatched the heavy object from below several braided strands of her gathered young. She ran her suckers over it, gathering information. It tasted of metal, and somewhat like one of the beings she had recently destroyed.

She squeezed it, tried to compress it, but it did not yield. It did not protest. Did not move. It was not alive.

As she held the twin metal cylinders in a coil of flesh, she extended another supple arm tip to a long, pale strand of her eggs, and caressed them. Feeling for the life inside them. Like the inert object, she felt no movement within them. Not yet. But soon.

She moved the shiny object to the pile of debris blocking entry to her den, now almost touching the ceiling. She placed it carefully beside a crumpled metal barrel. The opening was almost completely sealed off now. She did not require egress again, though. She would not leave. Ever.

She would remain here, until the end. And with her, her brood, her young, would be safe. She would protect them. She slowly closed her great eyes. There was a faint, metallic *click*.

The powerful pressure wave glanced off the ceiling and passed through her. She recoiled from the intense burst of sound, more painful than any she had experienced before. The ceiling split and rocks rained down all around her. She tried to pull the nearest of her eggs beneath her, but it was too late.

With a final shudder, the cavern collapsed.

CHAPTER 84

Val didn't hear the blast. But she felt it.

The pressure wave smashed into them, through them, causing pain in her chest and head—the parts of her body with air in them. Although the blast didn't propel her against the side of the tunnel, as she might have expected, it instantly compressed the gasses inside her.

She felt momentarily disoriented, clutching at her chest as she began to spin in the water inside the dark, narrow tunnel. The beam of her dive light swept across the rock in a great arc. She realized that Sturman's light had vanished, its own rigid, air-filled housing probably ruptured by the sonic pulse.

She knew that underwater explosions sent deadly pressure waves over long distances, and didn't dissipate, because seawater didn't compress like air. This sonic blast was probably similar. Even though they had moved some distance from the den, perhaps a few hundred yards underwater, they would be dead right now if it wasn't for the many angles and varying widths inside the twisting passage, which must have somehow reflected or altered the shock wave. Weakened it.

But Mack, and the other men. How close were they

when it went? If any of them had still been alive some-where back there, hiding from the beast, she knew they probably weren't anymore.

Whatever device Sturman had found—the weapon Breck had stashed years ago, and her uncle had brought down here to avenge him—had just gone off. Had possibly killed the single specimen of a previously undiscovered, almost certainly very rare, species of octopus. And its young—

Her hands went to her own womb. No. What if . . .

There was no time to think about that. Or to think about Mack and the others.

Sturman's hand found her arm in the darkness, squeezed it. He brought her toward him, and she looked into his eyes in the dim light. She could see dark blood trickling out of his nose inside his dive mask. It was cracked, and filling with water.

But he held up a hand and made an okay symbol with thumb and forefinger. *Are you all right?*

One of her ears throbbed. One side of her ribcage ached. She could only hope that there was no significant damage to her lungs. But at least she didn't taste blood in her mouth, or feel it leaving her nose, as it was his. She nodded at him and returned the hand symbol: *I'm okay.*

Then she pointed at him. Repeated the symbol. He began pointing at his head, toward the blood, and then something moved behind him.

Val jerked at him instinctively, trying to pull him away from the thing rushing up behind him, but then it was upon him. It passed over them.

It was a dense cloud of sediment, trailing the blast. In an instant, the visibility went to zero.

Val felt panic rising in her. Her air supply had already been dwindling. She had less than 1,000 psi, but she didn't know how much—500? And how much did Sturman have? It would take some time for this sediment to clear. Too much time, to see again, so they could try to find a way out. If there was one.

She tried to calm herself, to control her breathing as she knelt blindly on the cold cavern floor. She considered whether they should attempt to head back, toward the den, the mouth of the blue hole. The octopus would no longer be a threat.

No. It was too far, and the cavern might be damaged or destroyed now. They would have to try to somehow press on.

A fear unlike any she had known seized her heart. Because she understood the situation. She knew. Sturman's hand found her own in the darkness, and she accepted it. At least they were together.

Then he released her hand and fumbled across her body. Found her other hand, and the light. It was slightly visible now, at least up close to their faces. He pulled it away from her, and then tugged at her, insistently.

And she knew he was right. It would be better to die trying. Together.

He pulled her through the darkness, their gear thudding against unseen walls and ceilings, the tips of their fins striking the bottom. She could detect the light, moving erratically in Sturman's hand ahead of her, but its beam was still obscured by the churned sediment. She held her hands out in front of her, to prevent her head from hitting anything, contemplating her fate. The end. What would happen next? Would there be a next?

They arrived at a constriction. Sturman released her hand and slammed his body through it. But when he did, the top of his tank struck the rock. Bubbles began to erupt from where the regulator had become partially dislodged from the tank.

He pulled her through, and they continued. Then the bubbles pouring out of his tank stopped. He turned to face her. His mask had filled with water. He handed her the light, then squeezed her arm once and pushed her past him, but remained where he was.

She turned back to him and shook her head. *No.* She found the backup air piece attached to her vest and thrust it in front of him, and after a moment he shoved it into his mouth. He cleared his mask, and then moved beside her. She led them forward.

Now sharing air, they had only a few minutes left before it ran out.

The sediment obscured the cavern walls, and she was unable to maintain neutral buoyancy. Her head, her knees kept striking the rocks.

Then she saw something—a bend up ahead.

The water was clearing. She tried not to let hope overtake her, because that would just make it worse. Their air supply would be gone any second. Then she'd try to breathe in, but nothing would come. They would drown.

They kept moving. She started to make out more of the passage in the settling water. Then the beam of light became fully visible again, and she could see the pale walls clearly. Everything looked so drab, so gray and muted, except—

Red.

A flash of bright red. Her eyes had detected it for only an instant. But she'd seen something. Sturman grabbed her shoulder, squeezed it. He'd seen it too. They stopped.

She directed the light to her right, toward where it

had been. She slowly swept the darkness with the beam, and then it was there.

A fish. A small, solitary red fish, with white stripes running down its body.

It was not a blind, cavern-dwelling fish, like the others she'd seen under the island. And it wasn't unfamiliar. It was a fish Val knew well. A squirrelfish. A *reef* fish. Which could mean only one thing.

The fish slowly turned and with a flick of its tail began to swim off. Val kept her light trained on their tiny companion. It paused, hovering a foot below the ceiling, looking at them. As if waiting for them. They moved toward it, and it continued away. With Sturman next to her, she followed. It led them into a side tunnel, one they hadn't seen before, one they had nearly passed.

With the fish leading them, they moved through the darkness. The fish's red coloration, its white stripes, it oversized dark eyes, reminded Val of someone she had met recently. Someone who had given her more than advice. Someone she now owed a great debt.

There was light up ahead. The water began to take on a blue hue where the passage widened.

Moments later, the cavern opened up into the side of an undersea wall. They kicked vigorously toward the sunlight filtering down through clear ocean waters above. She didn't see the fish anymore, and scanned the water all around her.

But it was no longer there.

EPILOGUE

The Obeah woman was gone.

Val had almost walked right past her settlement, without Clive to guide her and with no smoke rising into the forest to give away its location. The shack was still there in the small clearing, near the vegetable garden, and the rocks that ringed the fire pit were just as they had looked before. But the dwelling was empty, and the old woman was no longer there.

"You sure this is it?" Sturman said.

"Yes," Val said. "This is where she was last time. I'm sure of it."

She and Sturman had set out after breakfast, again riding in Mars's taxi for the trip deep into the big island. Then, on foot, they'd passed through the tidal creeks and deserted fruit-tree farm and into the fresh-smelling pine forest. As they'd hiked along the rough trails, hacking at overgrown vegetation, Val had tried to explain to Sturman how the sage, and the ambergris-scented amulet she had given her, had saved her.

The amulet had no longer been fastened around Val's neck when they'd surfaced from the blue hole. She had no idea when she'd lost it. Perhaps it had been torn free by the octopus. And now, like the necklace she'd given Val, the Obeah woman had simply disappeared.

Sturman again poked his head inside the dim shack. He removed his new baseball cap and rubbed his head. "You were really here just last week?" he said.

"Yes."

"This place looks like no one's been here in months. Years, even."

He was right. Vines Val didn't remember seeing before grew on the hut's walls, and weeds had sprouted on the dirt floor inside the place. It looked as though nobody had lived here in a very long time.

"I know," she said. "This all feels like some sort of strange dream." She sighed. "I have so many questions, but I feel like they'll never get answered."

She wondered what Clive would say when she told him the sage was gone. He was still in the hospital, where doctors had him under heavy sedation. They'd needed to amputate his mangled forearm yesterday, just below the elbow.

Sturman said, "Maybe when Eric comes back, you'll get a few more answers. You sure you don't want to join him down here?"

Eric had already returned to Monterey Bay, to finish building a few more next-generation ROVs—"DORitos," he'd called them with a smile—and to recruit a few capable grad students. It was one of the few smiles she'd seen on his face since their ordeal. She knew he was suffering from how he'd treated her uncle.

But Mack would have been proud of him. He'd put himself at risk to save Clive, diving in to pull the injured man to safety. He said he'd had a hell of a scare when the ruined remains of the Zodiac raft had risen up in the water beneath him. It might have been funny in other circumstances, but there was little to smile about. So many had died.

Eric had vowed to come back soon, for months of research. And Val had a feeling his decision wasn't based only on a desire to finish what they'd started. It might also have a little to do with Ashley.

She said, "I just want to go home. Maybe down the road I'll come back, if they find something. Other biologists are more suited to this. Squid are really my specialty, you know."

Funding a project here on Andros wouldn't be a problem for Eric, or for any other researcher. The giant octopus and its brood were gone, buried when the cavern had collapsed. But Eric was already getting calls and e-mails from donors wanting him to use his ROV to further explore the blue holes, the offshore trench, to find this sensational kraken. Before he left, he'd shown them several of the unbelievable posts on YouTube and other social media sites, taken by visitors after the aquarium tank broke. Even though the octopus videos and images were all taken from a distance, and were mostly grainy, you could tell in a few of them what you were seeing. And now the press had gotten clear images of the severed arm section, with people in those shots for scale. The multimedia had quickly gone viral, and tourists had left Oceanus en masse.

But as they departed, Val's colleagues from around the world, the other cephalopod experts at universities, aquariums, and research centers, would soon be descending on Andros from all over. Other experts would be headed to Seattle, where the arm was now being shipped to on ice. They would study and dissect it there. Despite its size, it closely resembled the arm of a giant Pacific octopus, so it made sense to send it to an aquarium where the world's foremost experts studied that species. This was the biggest discovery since that of the aptly named colossal squid, off Antarctica. Even bigger.

At least PLARG would be largely involved in whatever exploration occurred here under the island, and in the Tongue of the Ocean. Its scientists followed protocols, and were careful not to alter environments they ventured into. But Val wondered what sort of damage the extended exploration, the numerous visits that were sure to come, might have on the pristine conditions here. Perhaps the US Navy would be a good thing, because it would restrict entry into so many areas offshore.

She wondered if the military had already known about this octopus species. And what else they knew that they might not be telling the public.

Sturman said, "Well, I'm glad you aren't coming back. I don't wanna lose you too."

He hugged her and then stepped back, moving his hands up to her shoulders. He looked good. Clean. Although he was tired, and still reeling from the losses himself, his eyes were clear, without the bags under them she'd become so used to seeing before she'd left California weeks ago.

"How you doing?" he said. "Really?"

"I'm okay."

She'd cried in bed last night, and she knew that the emotions would come back. Even though she knew Mack was dead, that there was no way for him to be alive, it just didn't seem like he was really gone. His wake would be down the road, maybe in a few weeks or even longer, when she was able to help her mom arrange it. Probably a small service in Florida, or in the Abacos. There would be no need for a burial or cremation, because anything that might have been left of her uncle had been destroyed in the blast.

She thought of Rabinowitz, and looked up at Sturman. "How are you?"

"I'm all right."

But she saw the emotion behind his eyes.

He said, "I'm just glad you're okay."

Sturman had said Rabinowitz had owed him, but he'd paid dearly. Wits had left behind a family. She wondered what the debt to Sturman had been for, but she didn't ask. He had to be taking this as hard as her, having lost another friend. She studied his face.

She had no illusions. Would Will ever drink again? Probably. He would have setbacks. But he hadn't had one last night, which was a very good sign.

He wasn't perfect. He would almost certainly make more mistakes. But she would try to make it work. Who else in this world would sacrifice so much for her . . . or for his family?

"What now?" he said.

"I guess we head back to Monterey. Are you going to keep working at the aquarium?"

"About that . . ."

"Will, what did you do before you left, anyway?"

He grinned. "Look, I was thinking. We should move somewhere new. I'm thinkin' of buying another boat. Starting a dive business again."

"Really?"

"Really."

"Well, you better not name your boat after me."

"Maybe we could come down here, or move to Florida, near your mom."

"Now you're really talking crazy."

She wondered if running another business would make him even more prone to his bad habits. But maybe him getting "back on his horse," as he would say, would be the best thing. Maybe they needed a big change in their life. They both clearly didn't do well in sedentary, routine situations. They thrived on excitement. Then again, if things worked out this time, then eight months from now they would have all the excitement they could handle.

"What are you smiling about?" he said.

"What?"

"I know that look. What are you up to?"

She smiled. "Well, speaking of names . . . how do you like the name Alistair?"

"For my boat? You serious?"

She took his hands into her own. "Will, there's something I need to tell you."

Something didn't look right.

The large undersea feature was about the size of her family's two-room summer cabin back in Ontario, but upside down and shaped more like an inverted scoop of melting ice cream. Natalie hovered at the same depth, drawing air in through her regulator in slow, measured breaths, her body relaxed in a state of neutral buoyancy as she peered into the shadows under the overhang, at the odd coral knob. Like many of the other interesting coral features here, the prominence jutted Dr. Seuss-like from the reef wall, just above the darkness of deeper water below. But something about this one was different.

Natalie glanced back at her husband. Twenty feet away, Dan's nose was glued to the exposed reef wall above her as he continued to study a tiny neon blue goby. The problem with having Dan as a dive buddy was that he was what Natalie's other friends called a "lingerer." While she liked to focus on the larger topography of a reef and scan the distance for passing sharks and

rays, her husband was the sort of diver who was most interested in the smaller, more colorful life tucked into the
reef. This habit often made it difficult for them to keep
up with their dive master when with a larger group.
Thankfully, today it was just them and another couple
who had dived this area with them before.

She looked past Dan, where their friends weren't
quite visible around a bend in the reef. She couldn't see
them, but their twin streams of bubbles rose above them
toward the surface. Dan had been in the same spot for
the past few minutes, and the others were moving even
slower for some reason. Natalie was getting restless. She
looked back at the large coral prominence. It bulged
downward, toward the hollow depths beneath the overhang.

The foursome was diving a wall off the Florida Keys.
They'd arrived in the islands three days ago, part of a
week-long vacation to escape the pre-winter cold in
Canada. It was only October, but already snow had fallen
back in Toronto, providing them the excuse they needed
to find an incredible last-minute deal online. Since none
of them had kids, it wasn't hard to be spontaneous with
travel. Last year they'd all managed to take a six-night
trip to Costa Rica to raft and explore the jungle, also on
very short notice.

This being their first of two dives today, they had
gone deep—planning for a 110-foot max depth—to explore a mostly vertical wall that rose to within fifty feet
of the surface. The wall dive had offered some interesting channels and other coral features to explore, like the
large knob in front of her now. Besides being upside
down, this one almost looked like it had somehow
changed in shape since she last looked at it moments
ago. As if it had become smaller.

Dan was still thirty feet above and behind her, moving slowly in her direction. They would soon need to start heading into shallower water and back toward their rented boat. If she wanted a better look at the coral prominence, she'd better hurry. Dan would easily be able to find her, with the vis around eighty feet. She descended under the overhang, into the dark hollow.

As she drew closer to the knob, something moved on its surface. Maybe it was an eel hiding there, or a camouflaged reef fish. She finned harder, to see what had caught her attention. A body length away, she stopped.

The rough reef surface looked mostly the same as the rest of the wall. As she'd seen elsewhere, what appeared to be a huge, encrusted barrel sponge clung to the knob. But there *was* something different. For one thing, this feature lacked any substantial micro-structure—no deeper cracks, no crevasses for fish to hide in. And . . .

That was it. There were no fish here. The entire stretch of wall had lacked any larger sea life—grouper, sharks, reef crabs. But this coral formation was itself strangely devoid of any sea life at all.

None of the smaller organisms that normally moved in and out of the cracks in a reef were present here. No fans or brighter living corals, either—as though everything had died. Maybe the prominence took the brunt of the ocean currents, which could have sculpted away the more delicate features and prevented the establishment of reef organisms, but from her experience, sedentary reef organisms preferred to affix themselves in areas swept by a regular flow of water. What had she seen move on the knob, then?

The bottom surface of the prominence suddenly shifted upward. Ever so slightly. As if it were collapsing.

Impossible.

She stared at it for ten or fifteen seconds. Nothing. She blinked a few times. Her imagination was starting to take over. Too many beers with everyone last night in that Key West bar, and maybe too much of that kickass weed afterward. Maybe she should surface now. She looked at her air. She still had five more minutes at this depth, and she wouldn't be diving again for a long time after this trip.

She drifted closer. She was just beneath the knob, almost close enough to touch it.

There. Something moved again. She was certain. Something was definitely hiding here, on the downward face of the reef. Something that hid itself very well. Her heart began to pound. She might see something interesting on this dive after all.

She focused on a dark crack the size of her forearm. Was there something within that hole in the reef? She stared at the dark slit, and saw movement again. But it wasn't a fish, or anything else hiding inside. The crack itself had moved.

It wasn't part of the coral reef. It wasn't coral at all. It began to change color.

The line moved again.

It *blinked*.

ACKNOWLEDGMENTS

The author wants to thank the following individuals for making this book possible:

My wife, April, for holding down the fort; Matt, my brother and editor-in-arms; High Plains Scuba, for certifying me as an open-water diver two decades ago; Bahamas Divers, for providing my first introduction to the reefs of their beautiful island nation; KT and Sara Colorosa, for helping me get some necessary time off from work; Brian Woodward, for manning my desk while I was away; Mrs. Brant, who got me started on the path to a good education; Gary Goldstein, my dreadfully busy editor; Arthur Maisel, Lou Malcangi, Karen Auerbach, and the other professionals at Kensington; Jim Donovan, my agent and trusted advisor; and my father, for teaching me early on the values of personal motivation and self-reliance.

I also want to thank Dennis, Frederico, Tony, Patrick, Axel, Erin, Anastasia, Brian, and the other very special staff of a quiet (and intentionally unnamed) resort on Andros Island, who helped me learn about the area and the fundamentals of technical cave diving and made me feel more than at home. Thanks also to fellow divers Drew and Chrissy Kinsman, for sharing their underwater images (and Led Zeppelin–inspired videos), and to the other friends I met in the Bahamas, especially globetrotters Andrew and Lydia.

Finally, a special thanks goes out to those who helped support me in achieving success with my first novel, *Below*: Tony Morelli (and TONMO!), Craig McClain (aka Dr. M), Danna Staaf and her Squid A Day blog, Jake Gengler at B&N, Web designers Wally Thompson and Dave Holmstrom, KT, Gwen (my other mother), the Arkwoods, the Alabama clan, superfan Sara Heideman, bulk book buyers Chinn, Beck, Kala, Norv, and Curtis, Mom (as always), and all my wonderful friends and fans—your support has been invaluable, especially at those times when I felt like I couldn't write another word.